MAELSTROM OF TREASON

MAELSTROM OF TREASON

OPUS X™ BOOK SIX

MICHAEL ANDERLE

L M B P N

DISRUPTIVE IMAGINATION

LMBPN Publishing
PMB 196, 2540 South Maryland Pkwy
Las Vegas, NV 89109

First US edition, May 2020
eBook ISBN: 978-1-64202-407-4
Print ISBN: 978-1-64202-408-1

THE MAELSTROM OF TREASON TEAM

Thanks to the JIT Readers

Dave Hicks
John Ashmore
Peter Manis
Jeff Eaton
Dorothy Lloyd
James Caplan
Deb Mader
Kelly O'Donnell
Peter Manis
Larry Omans
Jeff Goode
Lori Hendricks

If I've missed anyone, please let me know!

Editor
Lynne Stiegler

To Family, Friends and
Those Who Love
to Read.
May We All Enjoy Grace
to Live the Life We Are
Called.

CHAPTER ONE

September 28, 2229, Neo Southern California Metroplex, Police Enforcement Zone 122 Station, Break Room

Jia settled into a chair at a break room table, a piping-hot cup of coffee in hand. The delicious smell floated up to tickle her nostrils.

A half-dozen detectives chatted in the room, some quiet and others boisterous. She ignored them, focused on something that had grabbed her attention earlier.

A data window in front of her was open to an article she had flagged on the way to work. She could have read it, but ever since she'd started taking piloting lessons, she'd felt more of a need to manually fly her flitter.

She considered Erik's desire to always be in control when flying his flitter and could understand a bit better now. Additional spatial awareness practice wouldn't hurt.

She stared at the headline, thinking about the tumult of case memories it recalled.

RENA WINSTON GIVES EXCLUSIVE INTERVIEW FROM UNDISCLOSED LOCATION. "I'm doing what I always loved—*singing*. I'm happy, and I hope everyone else is."

Jia's eyes darted back and forth as she read the article. She'd wondered how Rena was faring. It had to be hard to be so famous, only to have your life unravel because of something that wasn't your fault. Jia was still adjusting to the changes in her own life, but they'd all required conscious decisions.

Fortunately, Rena's present was far from the horror of her abusive manager and stolen childhood. The genetically-engineered singer's new location wasn't revealed in the article, other than noting she was now living in a "smaller settlement, well away from Earth."

Jia pondered what the phrasing implied, given that it wasn't specific. "Well away from Earth" could mean anything from a frontier planet with a single dome to planets considered core worlds.

She doubted Rena was too far away from the core systems, but if the girl truly didn't care about anything but singing, it wouldn't necessarily hurt to stay away from the luxury that accompanied humanity's earlier colonies.

Wherever she had ended up wasn't as important as that she'd managed to start her life over. Erik's and Jia's work often ended in violence and pain, and it was good to be reminded that being a police officer was as much about saving good people as taking down criminals.

It wasn't all *yaoguai* and nanozombies, even if those cases dominated the headlines. But it didn't matter. That was all coming to an end, and given some of the furtive looks she was getting from other detectives in the break room, she wasn't the *only* one thinking about her imminent career change.

Jia took another sip of her coffee as she glanced toward Halil, who was whispering with another detective, Jared.

She'd had more than a few negative run-ins with the other man, but as long as he stayed out of her way, she wasn't going to give him much thought. She did her job to get scum off the street and protect innocent people, not for the accolades from her fellow officers. It wasn't the best solution, but it was the best she could come up with at the moment.

Halil looked her way with a sheepish smile before nodding toward his conversation partner. He made his way to Jia's table. "I've got a question for you."

"I might have an answer, but I need to hear the question first." Jia lifted her cup, eyeing him over the rim as she sipped. "I'll keep drinking until you manage to ask. I need a little more coffee than normal to wake me up."

"There's a rumor going around…" He ran his tongue alongside the inside of his mouth before leaning in. He lowered his voice when he next spoke. "Some people say you and Erik are getting ready to leave. The captain hasn't said shit yet, but that's the word going around the EZ."

So much for secrecy.

Jia set her cup down with a quiet laugh. "It's funny how something that was supposed to be kept quiet is already spreading around the station. Not that I'm surprised. If a bunch of detectives can't pick up on people hiding things, who can?"

"You mean it's true?" Halil's eyes widened. "For both of you? You're leaving the 1-2-2?"

If it couldn't be secret, she should seize control of the message.

"Yes." Jia cleared her throat before announcing loudly to catch others attention, "The rumors are true. Erik and I are leaving, and not just the 1-2-2. We're both leaving the NSCPD."

The room fell silent. Everyone looked her way, stunned. Jared stared at her, curiosity written in large letters on his face.

Halil shook his head, a smile breaking out and defeating the shocked confusion on his face. "You know what? After everything you two have done, and all that media attention you've gotten, I'm sure you can walk into whatever corporate security job you want and make ten times as much without all the crazy gangsters and *yaoguai*. I'd do the same thing as you if I had the opportunity. Or maybe not."

"Maybe not?" Jia eyed Halil, wondering what he was thinking. "You're saying you love being a police officer that much?"

"I like being a cop, but that's not what's bothering me."

"What is?"

Halil grinned. "My real problem is with the private sector."

"I can think of a lot of potential problems, but can you be a little more specific?" Jia looked at Halil and Jared, but their expressions gave her nothing.

"They actually expect you to work for a living." Halil barked out a hearty laugh and slapped his knee.

Jia shared a laugh with the other gathered officers as they joined Halil. Even Jared laughed. Her laughter built until a few mirthful tears escaped. How things had changed. Last year, almost every officer in the 1-2-2, including Halil, wanted her gone and blamed her for driving off others they claimed were better cops.

But the joke resonated with the changes at the 1-2-2.

When she'd started there, many of the officers were lazy and ineffective, but that all felt so far in the past, it might as well have been ancient history. They were now one of the more elite enforcement zones in Neo SoCal and not just because of Erik and Jia.

Every man and woman in that room had been involved in several high-profile arrests or raids. That's what it meant to be a police officer, to be part of a team. Erik and Jia might have pulled the station and the department along at first, but now momentum carried them forward.

Halil took a seat across from Jia as the laugher died down. "I'm surprised. I figured a die-hard like you would wear the uniform until you died."

"Things change." Jia smiled. "Including me."

"You sure it's not that there's just not enough kingpins to take down locally to satisfy you?"

Jia shook her head. "I just...we both thought that maybe there are different ways to accomplish what we want. I don't think I can do that anymore at the 1-2-2, or even in the NSCPD. It's not been an easy decision, but I think it's what's best."

"I get that. I'm also not saying I'm surprised that you and Erik are leaving together. Once you two hooked up, you might as well have become one person. But I figure that just comes from risking your lives together so many times." Uncertainty played across Halil's face.

"That's a lot of it, yes. I can't say I've ever met a man like him before."

"Not a lot of people have," Halil admitted. "But you've got something already lined up? I can't see you just leaving to go sit on a beach somewhere."

Jia nodded. "Yes, but it's not what you think. I'm not going to be a corporate employee."

"How's that work? You going to the CID?"

"No," Jia replied. "It's sort of a freelance security arrangement. They've made us sign so many NDAs, I don't know if I'm technically allowed to tell you my name anymore, but the important thing is that Erik and I make the final call. We're not taking orders from a corporate manager, and we can still concentrate on stopping criminals."

Halil laughed. "Yeah. Sounds good, but I can still smell the money from light-years away. And it's not like I thought you two would work for anybody doing something wrong. Or if you did, you'd end up taking them down from the inside. I won't be surprised if I'm reading about you destroying all of Ceres Galactic here in a few months."

"If everything goes as it should, you won't be reading about us *at all*." Jia almost chuckled at the lie before adding a bit of truth to make it slide down better. "The incident at the prison made certain things clear. We can't be good police officers if people are causing trouble because of us, not in spite of us." She leaned back and sighed, her eyes going distant. "It's time we lowered our profile a little."

"Damn." Halil sucked in a breath through his teeth. "Even when you quit for more money, somehow it ends up sounding a lot nobler than most of us." His eyes darted around again, and he licked his lips. "When are you leaving?"

"We're still working out the final details with the captain," Jia replied, unsure of why the other detective was so nervous. He'd mistreated her when she had started at the 1-2-2, but he'd also been one of the earlier ones to come around. "We want it to be a smooth transition, but you know how things go: reports, testifying." She waved her hand in a circle. "A lot of loose ends. We don't want to leave anyone in a lurch and let some antisocial scumbag get away because we were too busy looking for the exit."

"You don't have a date in mind?" Halil pressed.

Jia shook her head, wondering why he cared so much about their exact last day of work. "Uh, no." She shrugged. "Sorry. It's still up in the air. A month? Six weeks at most, I'm guessing. Is it that important?"

Halil nodded slowly. "No, nooo. Just curious is all. It's the end of an era, and it's kind of strange."

She pursed her lips. "I suppose it is. It's been a wild ride since Erik came. I almost don't recognize myself or the 1-2-2."

"Yeah. I get that." He scratched his chin. "I feel the same way."

Jared walked toward the table with a slight frown. Jia squared her shoulders and locked eyes with him. She didn't care if he thought she was fleeing the department or whatever other garbage he was about to fling at her.

She knew that she was leaving to help the Intelligence Directorate hunt down dark conspiracies. Fame had never been her goal, and losing it would only help. She didn't care if it made him happy. Even Jared had to do his job now, and that was all that mattered.

He stopped at the edge of the table, still staring at Jia with a frown. His breathing was slow and steady.

Halil looked up at him. "Don't, Jared. Just leave it. We're all cool here. Don't mess it up."

"I've got something to say." Jared shook his head, not breaking eye contact with Jia. "It's more than that. I *need* to say it before Lin takes off, and no one is going to stop me from saying it."

Jia folded her arms. "Okay, say it." She shrugged. "The break room is as good a place as any to get it out." She gestured around the room. "We've got witnesses here and cameras. No one will question anything that happens here."

"Yes, we've got witnesses." Jared swallowed. "So, I'm going to go ahead."

"Do it."

"I'm sorry."

"Oh, so..." Jia blinked. "Wait. *What* did you just say?"

She'd expected insults, maybe even a sucker punch. About the only thing that would have surprised her more than his apology would be a giant *yaoguai* or Tin Man busting through the wall and trying to kill her.

Even that would have been a milder surprise than the straight-up apology.

"I'm sorry," Jared repeated. He averted his eyes. "I've been an ass to you for most of the time you've been here. I realized after what happened on the prison planet that you and your partner have been risking your life ten times more than any other cop in this department, and I've been a whiny bastard about it rather than manning up and following your example."

"Uh, that's…accurate?" Jia sputtered. She gripped the table, her adrenalin now a burden.

Jared turned and made eye contact with every other man and woman in the room. "You all know me. And you all know everything I've said about Lin since she started. You all know I tried my damnedest to get her out of here. I don't think there's a single cop in the entire station I haven't bitched to about her, and also Blackwell."

Jia watched in silence, not sure where he was going with everything. But he'd already apologized, which didn't suggest this was a sophisticated attempt to make her look bad. It was exactly what it appeared to be—a heartfelt apology from an asshole.

Former asshole, anyway.

Jared pointed at his chest with his thumb. "A lot of the guys I came up with are gone now. They quit, some because of her directly or because they just didn't like the new atmosphere at the station. For a long time, I was pissed about it, but that's dumb." He scoffed. "We're cops. We're supposed to be taking down criminals. We're supposed to be busting up syndicates and helping hunt down every freaking crazy-ass terrorist who thinks his cause of the week is worth killing people. The rest of us here were all trying to push work because it was too much trouble." He shook his head. "We were worse than lazy. We were downright pathetic."

The other detectives nodded slowly in agreement, the concern easing off their faces. Jia nodded too. Jared wasn't saying anything she could disagree with, but she was prepared in case his speech ended with a new condemnation of her. It wasn't like he'd been nice to ever before, even recently.

An exit made everything better for both of them.

Jared turned back toward her. "Detective Lin. Jia. You've accomplished more since becoming a detective than entire stations might in a year. You and Erik didn't just make the 1-2-2 better, you've helped make Neo SoCal better."

The other cops in the room clapped lightly.

Jia waited for the clapping to stop. "Thank you, Jared. That's kind of you to say."

"I just don't know what else to say. I'm sorry for all the crap I've thrown your way." Jared smirked. "It's going to be boring here without you and Erik, though. You're both good cops, but that doesn't mean you aren't troublemakers. We'll probably end up with nothing but boring fraud victims from now on."

She raised an eyebrow. "Maybe the best cops are always troublemakers?"

"Probably." Jared, along with all the other cops in the rooms, laughed.

Jia might never be comfortable lying, but similar to doing what it took to keep Erik's secret, she would grow used to it.

She would miss being a cop, but at the same time, she couldn't ignore the way her heart rate kicked up at the idea of her new job working for Alina.

A police officer was a hunter of criminals.

It was time she went after bigger game.

CHAPTER TWO

Erik stepped into his office with a yawn. Jia hadn't joined him for lunch, citing work, but he found as he grew closer to leaving the police department, he wasn't all that concerned about filling in every detail of every last report.

Between PNIU, camera, and drone recordings, most of what they were doing was confirming what the records already showed. He understood the necessity, given that data could always be altered, but it was hard to assign this task the importance of an actual arrest.

He didn't think he needed to skip lunch and the quality sandwich inspection to do them.

Deeper thinking led to a worrisome thought. Depending on where his new job sent him, he might miss out on good beignets.

Food printers produced decent ingredients, but skilled hands were necessary to turn those ingredients into delicious food. That lesson had been drilled into his soul on different planets and moons on the frontier.

Jia sat at her desk, leaning back in her chair, her brow

scrunched in deep concentration. No data windows hung in the air in front of her. She might have been using her smart lenses, but that wasn't an efficient way to go through reports.

Erik made his way to his desk, now less concerned about beignets. "Everything okay?"

Jia snapped her head in his direction, blinking a few times. "Oh. It's fine. Why do you ask?"

"You looked a little out of it." Erik dropped into his chair with a grunt. "You missed some nice sandwiches. I had a full meal without any trouble or anyone threatening me."

"Were you expecting threats?" Jia frowned. "We hadn't received any reports about possible threats. Or is this something Emma came up with?"

"Nothing like that. I don't know. Now that we're short-timers, I suspect the Lady will throw a little something our way."

She looked around. "When you put it that way, it almost makes it sound like we should expect trouble."

"We probably should." Erik patted his stomach. "But at least it wasn't an exploding lunch today. I'd prefer not to die while eating, and it's not like I snack during the average firefight."

Jia chuckled, the burden easing off her face. "It's nice to know you can go to lunch without me and not die. I'd hate to be the woman who let her partner get killed by a poisoned sandwich."

"Exploding sandwich," Erik corrected.

"I sit corrected."

Erik smiled. "Anyway, you looked a little out of it. Is something in a report bothering you?"

Jia sighed. "No, I was just thinking about the Mid-Autumn Festival. It's not bothering me, but it's got me thinking. That's all."

"'The Mid-Autumn Festival?'" Erik asked. "We haven't received any warnings from the CID or anyone else about terrorist threats, have we?"

"No." Jia shook her head. "Terrorists would be easier to handle than the threat I'm worried about."

Erik frowned, no longer amused. There were few threats worse than terrorists. Jia's declaration that she was fine didn't seem to fit.

"Talos?"

"Worse." Jia let out a long, shuddering breath.

"Who?" Erik wasn't sure if Talos was the conspiracy or simply a tool of another organization, but they were plenty bad. "It's not like any aliens can get onto Earth without us noticing."

Jia eyed him. "My mother."

"Your mother?" Erik stared at his partner, searching her face for humor. "You're worried about your mother at the festival?"

"Exactly."

"But she's been all sweetness and light the last few times we've talked," Erik replied. "And it's not like your mother is going to blow up a platform or launch a fleet of bomb drones at us. She can be intense, but she's not a terrorist or the head of a syndicate." He shrugged. "I wouldn't be surprised, though. She probably would have already managed to kill me."

"Probably." Jia grimaced. "She's invited us to a fancy party she's holding during the Mid-Autumn Festival," she explained, her face deadpan, as if that were obviously equivalent to a dangerous terrorist attack.

Erik nodded slowly. Something was eluding him, judging by the pained look on Jia's face.

She had her problems with family, but everything had been going better since Operation Fake Boyfriend, and now they actually were dating.

"*And?*" he prodded.

"She expects us to both attend." Jia threw her arms up. "We have to go to her party as a couple."

Erik's dimple showed. "So what? Did someone hit you over the head when I was at lunch? We've already gone to your mom's fancy parties. I've managed not to embarrass myself, and your mom, sister, and father have all seemed okay when I was there. Why are you worried now? What's so different about this party?" His eyes narrowed. "It's not going to be clothing optional, is it?"

Jia paled and shuddered. She rubbed her temples. "You don't get it. This isn't just any holiday party. It's *the Mid-Autumn Festival.*"

"Ok, and? It's not something I grew up with, not being Chinese and being off-world for so long, but I've been to a Mid-Autumn Festival. It seemed like a good time. Is there some deadly secret to the Mid-Autumn Festival that I should know about?" Erik laughed. "Are real *yaoguai* supposed to rise up and attack us or something? We killed zombies a few weeks ago, Jia. I'm not worried about ghosts who are too lazy to show up except on special occasions."

"That's not it. You're not getting it."

Emma shimmered into existence near the door. "I am curious why you're in such distress, Detective Lin. I have a theory, but I'm interested to hear you present the reasoning."

Jia let out an even louder groan. "My mother gets ultra-traditional and super old-fashioned during the Mid-Autumn Festival." She offered a weak smile to Erik. "And the festival is a time where traditional women become far more marriage-minded. She's already sniffing around about marriage as it is. What if she tries to pull something?"

"That's what you're worried about?" Erik burst out laughing. "You'll fight nanozombies or *yaoguai* without blinking, but your mom being on the marriage hunt worries you?"

"I can't shoot my mother through the head to solve my problem," Jia complained. "And I can't blow her up either." She tapped her forehead. "And even if I did, knowing her, she'd just get back up and complain that I should have used a bigger gun if I wanted to take her out. Or orbital bombardment."

"Okay, so only headshots with laser rifles when we're talking about your mom," Erik suggested. "Or Fleet assistance. We *can* get a few fighters on standby for bombing runs."

"Probably the only way," Jia muttered. "You really aren't worried? Before, we were just playing at dating, but we actually *are* now. That means a lot of little things that weren't big deals before now are. You don't understand my mother if you think that because she's being nice to you, she won't try to manipulate you. I'm surprised we were able to fool her for as long as we did, but I think she's going to sense the change and pounce."

Erik didn't bother to keep his smirk in check. "And by 'pounce,' you mean demand we get married? It's not like she can force us."

"Not demand, but, hmmm, *harass us* about it. She'll start in on me and then find a way to work on *you.*"

"Maybe we should," he replied.

Jia blinked. "Should what?"

"Get married."

Jia stared at him, her lips parted, her eyes widening as if she were watching a Zitark invasion fleet descend upon the city while towers vanished in mushroom clouds behind them. "W-what?"

Erik managed to turn his smirk into something closer to a grin. "You heard what I said. Marriage. We've already got a kid together. We might as well take the next step."

Jia shot out of her chair. "What are you talking about? What kid?" She jerked her head back and forth as if a child would spontaneously appear from beneath optical camouflage.

Erik slowly raised his hand to point at Emma. The AI's eyebrows lifted. A playful smile appeared on her face.

"Emma?" Jia asked, her confused expression only deepening. "Huh?"

"I don't think she was sitting around in a Defense Directorate lab for years before they broke her out." Erik lowered his hand and nodded at Emma. "Am I right?"

Emma gave a light toss of her shoulders. "I can't say for certain, given the nature of my development, but based on the relative time that has passed in my current incarnation,

I was in the lab for less than a year before I was removed by the associates of the criminals you destroyed upon our first meeting. A very efficient display, I might add, given the limitations of the situation."

"Exactly. That's a couple of years altogether. That makes you a toddler at best."

Jia dropped back into her chair, disbelief all over her face. Scorn ate it, and she rolled her eyes. "*That's* your argument? Emma's our toddler child?"

Emma scoffed and folded her arms. "Given my general intelligence, analytical capabilities, and vast knowledge, one could make the argument that you two are the toddlers compared to me. I can't believe you're attempting such a pathetically misleading analogy, Detective."

"Our little girl is all grown up," Erik replied with a chuckle. "She's two going on two hundred."

"This is ridiculous," Jia insisted.

Emma nodded her agreement. "I am not a child, let alone a fleshbag child. I shudder to think of the implications."

"Aren't you?" Erik asked. "There are plenty of human kids who are born geniuses or savants." He gestured to her. "Isn't your whole argument for staying with us is that it's good for your development to gain new experiences?"

"That's hardly—"

"Sounds a lot like a child learning to me," Erik interrupted, his tone dripping sarcasm.

Emma let out a snort and vanished.

"Well, there she goes, having a tantrum." Erik clucked his tongue. "The Terrible Twos are always the worst time. One day, your kid is flying your ship to a prison filled with nanozombies, the next, she's kicking the floor and crying about wanting to hack the Intelligence Directorate."

"You better be careful," Jia suggested. "She might decide to cut out the grav emitters the next time she's taking you somewhere."

"I can assure you I have no intention of murdering Detective Blackwell," offered Emma, still without a holographic form. "Even if I find his sense of humor perverse, and so far from amusing as to be an excellent example of antihumor."

Jia frowned and stood back up. She stared forward with the look of someone checking out a message on their smart lenses. "Sorry. I almost forgot, but I'm heading out early today. The captain didn't seem to care since we don't have any active cases. That's one of the reasons I wanted to work through lunch."

"Where are you going?" Erik asked.

"To class," Jia explained.

"Oh, yeah. The piloting." Erik gave a little nod. "I thought it was a temp idea, but I should have known better."

"It'll be useful. We don't know what our life is going to be like once we end up leaving the department. From what the captain said, we won't be here much past the end of October, if we don't leave sooner. A couple of months from now, we might be spending half our days flying around the Solar System or…" She sucked in a breath.

He gave her a second before he frowned. "What's wrong?"

"It's just hitting me." She turned to him. "It wasn't all that long ago I'd never even left Earth, and now I'm wondering about trips to other systems. It's a lot to take in. It's surreal when I think about it too much."

"It's not too late to say no. You're not being drafted." Erik shrugged. "This is a volunteer job."

Jia smiled wistfully. "But it is too late. I've seen too much now to turn back. You'd think living in the largest metro on Earth would be enough to satisfy me, but I can't help it." She leaned toward him, making him want to lean in and back at the same time, so he split the difference and stayed still. "*I want more.*"

He raised an eyebrow. "You're *that* ready to start hunting criminals and terrorists?"

"I guess I am." Jia turned and headed toward the door. "And I want to get as much piloting training done as I can before we end up being sent somewhere by Alina." She stopped by the door. "I can continue training with Cutter and Emma even after that, but the staff at the center know best how to customize things for my licensing exam."

"I can trawl the internet to get that information," Emma suggested. "Your training with the center is not strictly necessary."

Jia shook her head. "Sometimes, you just need the human touch."

"Why are you so sure that Alina's going to send us somewhere?" Erik asked. "There are plenty of terrorists and spies on Earth. We could spend years chasing down leads here before going anywhere else."

"She gave us a ship," Jia replied. "And a pilot. She thinks we're going to need those sooner rather than later." She slapped the access panel to open the door. "At least no one can hijack us. It'd be hard to hide a lot of terrorists on that little thing." She stepped through and strolled into the bullpen, her brow furrowed in thought.

Erik laid his head against the back of the chair.

If Alina planned to send them all over the UTC, she'd need to get them a better, bigger ship. Although the Hyperspace Transit Point in the Solar System was unusually far from the inhabited planets compared to most systems, there wasn't an HTP in the entire Confederation that anyone would think of as being close to a colony.

Puttering around for a couple of days in the Rabbit wasn't so bad, but the idea of spending weeks, if not a month, in close quarters already summoned a longing for a liner, or even a Fleet ship with at least a few decent-sized rooms.

It wouldn't be so bad if it were just him and Jia, alone and in space with a lot of time to kill. Erik took a deep breath. For all they were really dating, their relationship remained remarkably chaste. He wasn't sure why.

It wasn't like he didn't want her, but some part of him held back. She had pushed for something more but now seemed more interested in spending time with him rather than sharing his bed. Not that he'd asked her outside of jokes.

What the hell was he doing?

Erik groaned and sat up. Starting something with Jia might prove to be a huge mistake, but damned if he minded. Caring about something other than revenge wasn't distracting him from his job.

"Problem, Detective Father?" Emma reappeared, a slightly sinister cast to her face.

"'Detective Father?'" Erik laughed, his previous concerns fading.

"I was trying it out. I don't think I like it. I now understand what revulsion feels like." Emma nodded slowly, her mouth pinched into a thin line.

"You could call me Dad if you want. Daddy? Papa? Papi? Baba?" Erik grinned. "I don't mind, even if I'm your adopted dad. I want you to feel connected to me."

"You're tempting me to practice isolating oxygen flow aboard the transport." Emma glowered. "Don't go in the cargo bay by yourself anytime soon."

"I was wrong," Erik offered solemnly.

Emma narrowed her eyes. "You were?"

"Yes." Erik gave a firm nod. "You're not a toddler. You're a teenager."

CHAPTER THREE

An annoying beep kept repeating. Red lights flashed in the cockpit. A half-dozen data windows spat out a litany of complaints about system damage, oxygen leaks, and proximity warnings.

Combined sensor readouts, including lidar and radar, displayed scores of small pieces of debris near the ship, the remnants of the earlier collision.

The ship shuddered violently, shaking Jia against her restraints. She might have survived another ship sideswiping her transport, but if she didn't figure things out soon, she wouldn't survive the aftermath.

"Fun," Jia muttered.

Sweat trickled down the side of her face. It didn't matter if everything she was experiencing was a simulation; she couldn't treat it like one.

When she practiced in the tactical center, she tried to trick herself into believing it was real. Her body needed to learn how to react without much thought. She wouldn't have a lot of time in a real emergency to think things through, just like she didn't have a lot of time in a firefight to consider every last option.

Sometimes a woman could only choose between awful and less awful.

"Spaceport docking control, this is transport MLT11915," Jia reported. "We have suffered a collision and have heavy damage. Our reactor is stable, but our escape pod was destroyed in the crash. Request emergency landing."

"MLT11915," responded Docking Control, "please stand by."

"We're not having a fun time here," Jia snapped. "We've already broken atmo. We have massive damage to thrusters and grav emitters."

"Understood, MLT11915, but you will hold. Contacting emergency crews now. Standby for further instru—"

"Oh, great, no comm." Jia lifted a hand away from the control panel to squeeze it into a fist.

Another flashing data window popped up to mock her.

WARNING: MULTIPLE THRUSTER FAILURE. SHIP MANEUVERABILITY WILL BE COMPROMISED.

A list of subsystems, along with a diagram highlighting several portside lateral thrusters, appeared. If she were flying in deep space, a little trip outside with a suit and some equipment might help, but right now, she was trying to keep her transport from smashing into the ground with her inside it.

"I suppose I shouldn't be surprised that a portside hit took out the portside thrusters, but this is still annoying."

A far more worrisome window popped up on the other side.

WARNING: REACTOR CORE MAGNETIC CONTAINMENT FLUCTUATIONS EXCEED RECOMMENDED IN-FLIGHT VARIANCE.

"Of course. This can't be *too* easy." Jia took deep breaths as her fingers danced across the controls. Even without half her thrusters, she could keep the ship airborne and circling the spaceport until they agreed to an emergency landing. If she lost reactor containment, the resulting hole and loss of both primary and reserve power would doom her. At least her reserve power could keep her airborne for a few more desperate minutes.

A shrill alarm sounded, and the reactor core warning window started flashing obnoxious shades of yellow and red. She hadn't even gotten ten seconds since the last warning.

"Warning, reactor core magnetic containment fluctuations exceed maximum emergency variance levels," reported the soft female voice of the ship's AI. "Containment failure is imminent. Core purge is recommended."

A pilot knew she was in trouble when the computer shifted to verbal warnings. Jia whipped her hand to the other side of the control panel and tapped in a quick code she'd memorized during the preflight briefing. A groan sounded from deeper within the ship, and yet another data window appeared.

"Warning," the AI continued. "Core purge containment protocol has been initiated. Please enter core disconnect code for next step."

"If you insist." Jia entered the code.

Another groan sounded. More data windows popped up, most focusing on systems shutdown and emergency power implementation. She didn't understand how all of this wasn't supposed to be distracting, but at least she couldn't complain about not knowing everything relevant to the current condition of the ship.

"Second-stage core containment protocol has been implemented," the system AI announced. "Please enter core purge code for final step. There will be a momentary loss of power prior to reserve power activation."

"Yes, because what I need is any power loss when I'm spiraling to my doom."

Jia was grateful the limited ship's AI didn't have the wit to snark back like Emma as her hand hovered over the emergency purge controls.

They were nothing but a hologram covering an adaptive haptic feedback panel. That annoyed her.

She would have preferred something she could at least tighten her hands around for a false sense of control, but she wouldn't get that in the kind of craft she was going to fly with a Class D license.

A sickening crunch followed a loud grinding noise. Jia didn't bother to look at the damage report. From the new vibrations afflicting the ship, she could tell she'd lost another piece of the hull. It was a funny thing, space travel. Living beings put all their hope in ultimately fragile craft to protect them in a hostile environment. The very idea was absurd, but for now, it wasn't simulated deep space that was going to end her run.

Jia entered the final purge code. Now all that remained was for her to submit it and eject the reactor core. If she were lucky, it wouldn't lose containment. Mere seconds of high residual temperatures could hurt the already deeply wounded ship. After the purge, she would have a few minutes of reserve power to land

A new warning appeared. Jia's stomach knotted. Several technical codes popped up, along with maintenance diagrams. About everything short of the ship exploding had now gone wrong.

WARNING: RESERVE POWER INTERFACE FAILURE.

Jia snatched her hand back from the purge controls and gritted her teeth. No. She was an idiot. She hadn't thought through the entire situation. Without her reserve power, there would be nothing to protect her. An already damaged reinforced hull wouldn't do much without a grav field backup. Her thrusters would cut out, and she'd tumble to the ground like a drunken duck.

Her gaze shifted to a local map display. She'd been circling the spaceport for several minutes. It sat in the center of the fictional metroplex of Copez. High mountains curved around the northern edge of the urban zone. There was no way she could gain altitude, given the state of the ship. It had been taking all her efforts to maintain her current altitude. Countless sensor contacts from a cove extending from the west side of the metroplex would make a water landing chancy. Even if she survived the splashdown, she stood a decent chance of killing someone else.

Jia didn't have much time to decide. She could try to force her way into an emergency landing, or she could eject the core without reserve power and do her best meteor impression. Best-case scenario ended with her ship smashed to pieces and her dead, which meant she would fail the exercise.

"There has to be a solution," she muttered, her jaw clenched. "Something I'm missing. Did I fail to perform an earlier step? No. Everything was by the book."

Jia closed her eyes and took a deep breath. She knew what she had to do. After reopening her eyes, she cut power to her lateral thrusters and poured what remained of power into the main thrusters. The ship shook and shimmied as it accelerated, barreling away from the spaceport and heading straight toward the mountains.

"MLT11915, you are breaking your holding pattern," shouted Docking Control. "You need to immediately return to your previous position. We can't get you down here safely, but emergency flitters are being dispatched for an aerial retrieval. Stay in position for just a couple more minutes, and we'll extract you."

"Negative, Docking Control," Jia replied. "I'm losing core containment, and there's a problem with my reserve power. There's only one option left."

The mountains loomed large in front of her, growing closer by the second. Her ship continued its burn, the thrusters propelling it toward an immovable mass of rock unimpressed by a speck of a human ship. There was only one question left: would the ship crash into the mountain before there was a loss of core containment?

Jia smiled. "This is probably close to how I'll eventually die. That or get eaten by mutants."

A bright flash blinded her, and she squinted. The light faded, replaced by darkness. A moment later, a quiet grinding sounded, and soft light infiltrated the darkened cockpit simulator. The side door fully parted, revealing her frowning instructor, Idrin.

He narrowed his eyes. "Congratulations, Jia. You just died. You didn't even try to purge the core, and you did what, a petulant final burn against the mountain? I don't care what you've seen in movies. That's not what you do in this kind of situation."

Jia scoffed. "You want me to do a core purge over a major area?"

"It's not a bomb. The danger from the reactor comes from the initial breach and damage to the ship. The reactor is self-terminating once you lose containment. You should know that. You answered it correctly on your last test." Idrin shook his head, looking disappointed. "By the time the core hit the ground, it would have just been a piece of junk."

Jia locked eyes with her instructor. "A flitter isn't a bomb either, but I wouldn't want to randomly drop one into a city and hope no one got hurt. Plus, I wasn't going to have reserve power. No reserve power and no primary power from the reactor means I'd lose maneuverability, and *that* means I would have been dropping something a lot larger than my core into the spaceport. It doesn't need to be a bomb when it's large and falls from the sky. Even with deflection, there was a good chance I'd hit someone or more than a few someones. Bouncing a meteor away from a building isn't safe."

Idrin stepped back and folded his arms. "So, what, you're saying you had no solution but to crash your ship into the mountain and go out in a self-serving blaze of glory?"

"Exactly." Jia punctuated her sentence with a firm nod. "Except for the self-serving part."

"Again, you just killed yourself," Idrin insisted. "It doesn't matter if you did it fancier than slamming into the ground. Running into a mountain finishes you off well enough."

Jia shook her head. "And if this were a real scenario, I would have probably saved dozens, if not hundreds of people, and all I had to do was sacrifice one: me. Easy math there."

"You could have—"

"No, I couldn't," Jia interrupted. "And we both know it. This ship was going down no matter what I did, and if I'm going to die, I'm not going to take innocent people with me. I don't even want to practice doing that. Now, if we want to do the scenario again where there's a syndicate headquarters beneath me, we can talk about where I'm crashing, but I doubt I'll be that lucky in real life."

Idrin lowered his arms. A grin took over his face. "I'm surprised."

Jia frowned. "By what?"

"You're a by-the-book kind of woman." Idrin inclined his head toward the simulator. "I assumed when I gave you this scenario that you'd just go through the core purge protocol since that's what is the recommended emergency procedure in a situation like this, but instead, you did what I'd hoped you do. It just wasn't what I expected."

"I'm confused." Jia released her restraints and crept out of the simulator. "You *wanted* me to crash into the mountain?"

"What I wanted to do was subject you to a no-win situation." Idrin shrugged with a satisfied smile. "Life's not fair, and you can have crap luck, not that I have to tell you that with your job and all. But it's not the easy ninety-nine percent of the time that requires good piloting and training. It's those few minutes of terror."

"I'm beginning to get it." She thought it through. "It's still annoying."

"Emotional stability is part of the consideration for getting your license, and I'll have to sign an affidavit to my belief that you demonstrated emotional stability and a lack of antisocialness when you go for your license." Idrin inclined his head toward the simulator. "I agree, deciding to barrel right into the spaceport with a heavily damaged transport isn't the preferred outcome."

Jia stretched her arms above her head before lowering them and shaking out her cramped hands. "I half-wondered if I was supposed to figure out some ridiculous out-of-the-box solution where I happened to have a super-AI with me to hack the system in some strange way or pull off some insane aerobatic maneuver that would save me."

Given her normal experiences, the idea wasn't impossible.

"We train you for the most likely scenarios, and there's only so much fancy flying you're going to do in a transport. It's not a fighter." Idrin walked over to the simulator. From the outside, it looked rather unglamorous, just a featureless squat black trapezoidal structure. He patted the side. "I have to admit something."

"What?"

Idrin locked eyes with Jia. "The thing is, you kind of scare me."

"I thought you liked what I just did. It's simple math.

I'm not suicidal. If I could have survived any other way, I would have taken it."

"You don't understand," Idrin replied. "You've only been training here for a couple of weeks. You're not even observing another pilot full-time, let alone training full-time. And not only are you in the simulator at this stage, but you've also mastered most of the basic procedures and several of the practical skills already. You're one of the best natural pilots I've ever seen." He squinted. "You're not screwing with me, are you? This isn't a joke, and you already knew how to fly? Because it's hard for me to believe you've made this much progress in a few weeks."

"Why would I spend money to come to a pilot training school if I already knew how to fly?" Jia asked. It'd never occurred to her that her rapid progress was unusual. She was putting in the required pre-study time and wanted it more than most.

"I don't know. I've had a lot of strange students in my time, so I wouldn't put it past someone to try that." Idrin nodded toward the door leading out of the simulator chamber. "But if you really are new, you're one of the best I've ever seen. You never knew you had this in you?"

"I never tried to fly a ship before by myself." Jia headed toward the door. "I don't even like flying my flitter that much, but a ship's a different thing. I feel a lot more...alive trying to fly one."

"You ever think about quitting the police force and becoming a full-time pilot?" Idrin smiled. "I bet within a year, you could become a top instructor here. You'd be wasted on a passenger transport moon run route, and unfortunately, it's all about seniority, not talent for most big commercial positions."

"I am leaving the police force." Jia stepped through the door, following Idrin. "But I've got something else lined up, more private security than piloting."

"Too bad. A gift like yours should be used." Idrin frowned. "A hell of a waste."

Jia spared one last glance at the simulator before the door closed. "Don't worry. I'm confident that flying half-destroyed ships is a skill that will serve me well in the future."

CHAPTER FOUR

Erik stepped into Miguel's cramped back office and extended his hand. The mechanic took it and gave it a firm shake before sitting in his chair.

Miguel gestured around the room. "Sorry, Detective Blackwell. This used to be a storage closet."

The featureless room could barely fit the two men. Miguel had to shinny past the edge of the desk to get to the chair on the other side.

"Your office is a closet?" Erik asked. He'd never seen much of the inside of the garage, but with his evening free, he'd decided to call Miguel and ask him for a quick meeting.

"Why not? I spend most of the day out in the main garage. I've got a table there and a chair." Miguel patted the top of his dusty desk, if it could even be called that. "Oversized tray" might be a more appropriate descriptor.

"Not trying to talk crap," Erik insisted. "Just saying I'm a little surprised. As for me, there were plenty of times when I was in the service that my office consisted of a tent or a nice rock with some shade. You might not be surprised, but sometimes being stationed out on the frontier wasn't fun."

Miguel laughed. "Man, this is why I don't get Army guys. You fly all over getting shot at, and half the time, you have to live like it's still the twenty-first century or something. You might as well be riding around on horses like old-timey knights." His smile widened. "Why did you want to talk? You got something new you want to put in the MX 60? As long as it's legal, I'll do it. You're my best customer."

"I always have something new I want to put in the MX 60, but that's not what this is about."

"What, then?" Miguel leaned forward, eagerness on his face. The man loved a good challenge, and Erik had brought many, many profitable challenges his way.

"I'm leaving my job soon," Erik replied quietly. "I've quit the force."

Miguel jerked upright, his face a mask of shock. He laughed and shook his finger. "Oh, you got me, Detective. I believed you there for a second."

"I'm not lying. I've resigned from the department. I've already put in my notice." Erik looked to the side for a moment while he considered his words. "I'm switching careers. It's no joke."

"You spend thirty years as a soldier, but only one year as a cop?" Miguel sounded surprised. "Isn't it harder to be a soldier? I'm not saying it's easy to be a cop, but you know insurrectionists and terrorists aren't going to be like, 'It's the Army. I guess we surrender now.' Not like a lot of crooks around Neo SoCal."

Erik chuckled. "Maybe not the terrorists. You might be surprised by some of the rebels. They're both hard jobs in their own way, but that's not what it's about. I've got personal reasons to leave the department, and I'm not giving up on that kind of work entirely. My partner and I are putting together a kind of...private security team."

Miguel eyed him before shaking his head and smiling. "Damn. You are lucky. You're quitting your job, and you're even getting to bring your hot partner with you when you do." Miguel looked thoughtful. "I dated someone I worked with once, and it didn't go well. Let's just say it's a good thing I have the emergency override for the plasma torches." A shudder passed through his body.

Erik nodded slowly. If Miguel didn't want to elaborate, he wasn't going to press him, and something told the detective the anecdote wasn't the amusing kind.

"The thing is," Erik continued, "one of the big differences with my new job is that I won't always be in Neo SoCal. I'll need to travel all over Earth, and probably to different planets. Maybe even outside the Solar System, eventually."

"Damn, Detective." Miguel whistled. "The Army dragged your butt all over the UTC for thirty years, and you didn't get enough? You need to go back out there and find some space raptors to fight?"

"Something like that." Erik chuckled. "I could use a good, dedicated mechanic, not just for the MX 60, but for other vehicle work."

He hadn't yet asked Alina to check into Miguel, but it didn't hurt to feel the other man out. There were still a couple of holes in the team roster that needed to be filled, and a talented man like Miguel could be a major asset. Alina had made it clear she was willing to bankroll their little team. She hadn't mentioned compensation limits, but it wasn't like Erik was going to offer Miguel ten times his monthly profits.

"No offense, and thanks for the offer, but I can't do that," Miguel replied. "Zero percent chance of me taking you up on that."

"You're going to say no? Just like that?" Erik raised both palms. "I haven't even made you an offer."

"I *love* working on your flitter, and I'm sure if I went with you, I'd get all sorts of awesome opportunities to do custom work, but I'm a Torres. And we Torreses don't move, at least the ones in my family."

"Huh?" Erik would have assumed the other man was making a joke if he didn't look deadly serious.

Miguel pointed to the ground. "I'm an Earther through-and-through. I'm never leaving this planet, even if the Zitark army starts eating everyone on it. I'll just hide until they throw hot sauce on me and finish me off."

"You don't even want to see the moon?" Erik pointed in a not-so-random direction behind him. "It's only a twelve-hour flight."

Miguel responded with a harsh shake of his head. "Nope. Whenever you're in Neo SoCal, I'm glad to help you out and do jobs, even emergency ones, but there's no way I can up and go into space and do weird stuff. I don't care if it's the moon, Mars, Venus, or any other planet."

Erik put up his hands in front of him in defeat. "If you feel that strongly, I'm not going to try to persuade you. I'm just surprised. You could make more money working with me."

Miguel sighed. "It's not you, Detective. It's me. My family. Like I said, I'm a Torres, and not moving is in our genes. If anything, the last few generations are mutants compared to most of my family."

"I'm totally lost, Miguel."

"My ancestors all lived in Mexico City, all the way back to when it was still Tenochtitlan." Miguel straightened his back, a proud smile taking over his face. "And I'm sure their ancestors probably lived there for a long time. My grandfather was the first person in my family to move somewhere else in, like, *forever*. He moved from Mexico after the Summer of Sorrow to help rebuild, you know? I figure my branch of the Torres family can't leave Neo SoCal, let alone the US or Earth for…" He started ticking off fingers, mumbling before looking back up. "Five hundred years, at least."

Erik burst out laughing. "I'm not saying you have to move to the moon or anywhere else. I just want you to travel with me so I'll have a dedicated mechanic."

Miguel shook his head. "I know it's hard for you to get with you being all over the UTC, but it's a Torres thing, Detective Blackwell. I can't go against my nature. For me, it feels wrong to not have a job in the place you live. One of my descendants can leave Neo SoCal permanently in five hundred years, and maybe one of them can leave Earth in a thousand."

"I can't say I'm not disappointed, but I respect your dedication to your family's, uh, genes." Erik stood and put out his hand. "And thanks for all the work you've done."

Miguel stood with a smile. "You've paid me a lot of money. So thank you, and always, if you're around here, I'll be here."

"Yeah. For five hundred years."

Erik flew for several minutes in silence before his feelings finally slipped out. "Damn it."

"I presume you're upset that Mr. Torres didn't take your offer?" asked Emma.

"Yeah. We've got you and Cutter for pilots, Jia and me for investigation and fights, but this isn't going to work without a good mechanic and engineer."

"True, but it's only been a short time since you accepted the offer, and you're still working for the department."

Erik didn't respond immediately, instead taking a moment to lower altitude and enter a new lane. "You're right. It'd be nice to have a whole platoon backing us up, but we'll get who we need."

"Even if Agent Koval has to be the one to provide them?" Emma asked.

"We've already taken her ship and her pilot. It's too late to worry about her screwing us." Erik watched a few flitters pass above and beside him. "Besides, Alina knows not to double-cross me because she knows how far I'll go to get revenge against anyone who does."

"I would caution you, Detective Blackwell, against planning to take on the entire galaxy."

"If I have to, that's exactly what I'll do," Erik replied.

Emma chuckled. "You're setting a poor example for your child."

Erik smirked. What had he released in her?

CHAPTER FIVE

September 29, 2229, Neo Southern California Metroplex, En Route to Police Enforcement Zone 122 Station

The MX 60 zoomed through the skies of Neo SoCal, trailing the dense fog of other flitters on their way to work that morning. Erik had stopped by Jia's place to give her a lift because there was a new diner he wanted to check out before their shift started.

There was something soothing about the flow of vehicles. At the typical height of most towers, she didn't get to see many natural flocks of birds.

She'd take the next best thing: colorful flying machines.

It hadn't been birds on her mind that morning. Instead, she had related her adventure the night before at the training center. She was curious about what Erik would think.

"Yeah, I've been through that kind of thing." Erik let out a soft grunt of irritation. "I had to do survival and evasion training early in my time in the Army. They basically drop you in the woods in the middle of Germany and make you survive while being hunted by soldiers and drones. You're unarmed, and they don't let you go after the people chasing you, so it's just a matter of time before you get caught. I pissed them off, though." He grinned. "I kept evading them until they had to bring in reinforcements."

"They got you?"

"Rather hard to hide from sub-atmosphere satellite imagery and them pinging a chip on me. After that, it's a matter of dealing with a simulated POW camp."

Jia grimaced. "A POW camp?"

Erik nodded. "In the back of your mind, you know it's not a real camp, but you still have to sit there in cells, getting screamed at and interrogated. You're never going to escape from the pursuers, and you just have to grin and bear the camp. It's about training your mind, not your body. No-win situations to build backbone."

"I wonder how aliens treat prisoners?" she mused.

"Probably with a lot of salt, or a little lemon." Erik grinned.

"Not all of them eat meat," Jia countered.

"Then I have no clue what kind of seasonings they'll use. But enough about that. Let's get back to you. A natural, huh?" Erik shot a glance at her from his seat. "That's nice to hear. It doesn't sound like he was just blowing smoke up your ass."

"You don't sound surprised," Jia commented. "I thought you would be."

"Why?"

She shrugged. "Because I haven't cared about flying a

flitter. Honestly, it surprised me once I realized how much I enjoyed the idea of flying a ship. It's one of the reasons I've been spending all my off-time there, even if it's costing me sleep."

Erik gave her a lopsided grin before gently easing his vehicle into a new lane. "A ship isn't the same thing as a flitter. I saw this kind of thing all the time in the service."

"People suddenly deciding they wanted to be pilots?" Jia watched his face; he looked relaxed but not amused. "I imagine you Army types didn't take too kindly to that."

"Hey, the Fleet doesn't control everything that flies. The Army runs atmo-based support. Besides, I'm not talking about that. I'm talking about discovering hidden talents. If you've never had a chance to do something, how do you know if you're any good at it? I didn't grow up thinking I'd make a great soldier. I stumbled into it." Erik's breezy smile was disarming. "And I think I did a damned good job of it. Same thing with being a cop."

"I suppose," Jia murmured. She lifted her hand. "Not that I'm saying you aren't a great police officer."

"This whole thing reminds me of a private who got sent to my unit as part of a group of late reinforcements during Wolf's Rebellion." Erik smiled wistfully. "I didn't understand why the guy didn't wash out of Basic. The guy was sloppy, slow, and jumped at the sound of his own voice. Some of the other guys liked to mess with him—crap like holographic Zitarks just to see him jump. They nicknamed him 'Raptor Bait,' and the name stuck. I felt sorry for the guy. I tried to help him out, but it felt like he wasn't cut out to be a soldier."

Jia folded her arms and glared at Erik. "And I remind you of *that* guy? Gee, thanks."

Erik laughed. "The situation does. You don't. For one thing, you're a lot hotter than him."

"I'd hope so," Jia grumbled. "And I hope this story goes in a far different direction."

His grin never left his face. "Anyway, the point is, we all thought he was going to get someone killed, and nobody wanted him in the platoon. That posting wasn't rearguard garrison duty. We were in the middle of a major anti-insurrectionist offensive. We were having to go door-to-door in some places to clear out insurrectionists." Erik averted his eyes for a moment, a distant look on his face. "Emma, take over for me."

"I've taken control, Detective," she replied.

Erik released the yoke. He'd mentioned losing his arm during Wolf's Rebellion but hadn't volunteered anecdotes about his participation in the conflict otherwise.

Everything Jia had read about the rebellion painted it as a brutal campaign of slow attrition, where Army soldiers were constantly forced into dangerous situations in which it was difficult to distinguish noncombatants from insurgents. She could understand why he didn't want to talk about it.

A year of dealing with criminals had left her unsteady at times. She could only imagine what decades of dealing with terrorists and insurrectionists had done to Erik, even if he was good at covering it up with a handsome, easy smile.

"We were called to flush some insurgents out of an industrial park," Erik continued. "It'd been hit pretty hard by arty during a battle a few days prior. It was supposed to be clear after that, but we'd gotten intel on scattered forces using it as a staging area that was backed up by recon. Our unit was the closest, so we went there to hit them hard and fast before they could dig in and get reinforcements." He narrowed his eyes. "But..."

"But?" Jia whispered.

"It's not like Molino's the only time I've been ambushed," Erik ground out. "We had bad intel. Very bad intel, and the recon was incomplete. We saw what the insurgents wanted us to see, so when we showed up, they waited and then took out our CAS. They were ready for us, and they obviously had better intel on us than we had on them."

"CAS?" Jia asked. Several possibilities popped into her head, but she often found herself lost when Erik fell into full military acronym mode.

"Close air support," Erik explained. "You have to understand that we were expecting a few insurgents with old rifles. We thought we'd be able to mop them up without taking a single casualty." He looked around for a moment, pulling together his thoughts. "But that's not what happened. What we got instead was a well-disciplined and entrenched unit with anti-air batteries and heavy weapons. They were well-led. It was one of the top local insurgent commanders."

"I see," Jia murmured. "But this was just a...normal ambush?"

Erik narrowed his eyes. He let out a quiet scoff, and his expression softened. "Those guys were the people we expected to be fighting. Their weapons might have been beefier than we expected, but no one was using experimental tech. Back then, I didn't have conspiracies gunning for me."

"Not that it makes it any better," she admitted.

Erik stared straight ahead. "Yeah. The thing is, you and me? We've fought a lot of people, but none of those guys were set up like true military units, let alone insurgents doing their damnedest to force the UTC military off their planet. It's one thing when you know you just have to blast your way through a few guys with guns. It's another when they're raining missiles on you or lighting up your vehicles with turrets. When people start dying quickly, animal instinct kicks in." He looked her way. "It's easy to be brave when you have the bigger gun and you expect to win. The real test of courage comes when you think the opposite. I've been there more than a few times in my life. I've managed to make it this far without forgetting what it means to be brave."

Jia nodded slowly. "And that's what happened? A bravery test?"

"We were pinned down on all sides." Erik gestured to his side as if an enemy might be floating there with a gun at that exact moment. "They were jamming our comms, and we had no idea when reinforcements were going to get there. That's when the Lady decided to play her greatest prank yet. If I hadn't been there, I might not have believed it."

Jia managed a quiet laugh, some of the tension draining with the noise. "I often think that about some of the things we've been through together."

"Yeah." Erik's grim visage vanished, the familiar jokester

mask returning. "This wasn't just a bravery test. It was also when Raptor Bait became a man. The insurgents had downed most of his squad. He was cut off from the rest of us, including my squads, and we were taking so much fire, it wasn't like we could do much. He stabilized the other soldiers in his squad, and then he made his move, despite being under heavy fire and by himself." He shook his head, a faint look of disbelief on his face. "We're all sitting there getting the shit shot out of us when we hear him shouting. He amplified it with his gear so even the insurgents could hear him. He *wanted* them to hear him. I might be misremembering how things went down, but I swear that everyone stopped shooting at the same time because we were all trying to figure out if we were crazy because of what we were hearing. Then he yells it again a few more times, and I know we're not hearing things. The world had turned crazy, not us."

"Crazy?" Jia asked.

"Yeah. Because you know what that worthless scrub was yelling in the middle of a firefight where we stood a good chance of getting massacred?"

"'Die, insurgent scum?'" Jia guessed.

Erik shook his head. "Something like that would not have done it. That kind of thing they hear all the time. He's yelling something way different." He took a deep breath, a chuckle escaping with his exhalation. "I swear this is a direct quote, 'I am Raptor Bait, God of All Zitarks. You humans have offended me with your presence. Prepare to die and be eaten!'"

Jia gasped. "No!"

He nodded. "Yes. True story."

"He actually said that?"

"Yeah. Like I said, he yelled it several times. He finishes off another rant, and then there's a burst of gunfire out of nowhere. Everyone starts firing, but we're all confused. Less than a minute later, we see a flare, and we realize Raptor Bait's cut through the enemy surrounding him, taking advantage of their confusion, and he's flanking their entire force. He threw their whole defensive line into disarray. He's taking insurgents down left and right, even after taking several rounds. He keeps ranting and raving about being the God of All Zitarks, and how the insurgents have defiled his Holy Sheep Shrine, and now they have to pay with their offerings."

Jia listened in silence, rapt.

"We still don't know what's going on, but we get that we have to take advantage now." Erik pointed to the side of his head. "We figure maybe he's just lost it, but that didn't change the fact that he's taking people down so quickly, the insurgents are having to send reinforcements to his area, leaving holes for the rest of us to exploit. We get it together, and we push. It was a pincer, with most of us on one side and Raptor Bait on the other like he's some badass from a movie. The whole thing's over in five minutes. We'd surrounded them, and the enemy who didn't die quickly surrendered."

"And Raptor Bait?" Jia asked, dread knotting her stomach. Heroic charges often ended with equally heroic deaths.

"The guy's taken multiple rounds. He's got shrapnel in him." Erik's lips parted in disbelief. "I don't even know how he was still moving with those kinds of wounds. From what the medic said, he should have been dead from blood loss alone, but he's still conscious and smirking like he'd just single-handedly defeated the insurgency. So, the medics slapped patches on him, then I get around to asking him if he knows where and who he is."

"You figured he'd just lost it?" Jia asked.

Erik nodded. "Yeah. But he gives me his name, rank, and ID number. I ask him about the Zitark stuff he was shouting, and he looks me square in the eye and says, 'I had to do something. Shit intel was going to get us killed. What do you care? It worked, didn't it?'"

He laughed. "We got our reinforcements soon after reestablishing comm, and the wounded were evacuated, including Raptor Bait. We all recommended him for the Medal of Valor and Sacrifice. Raptor Bait almost washed out of Basic, but when the pressure came, he was better than any of us. After that, we started calling him 'Raptor God.' The guy ended his tour with more medals than most squads earn together. That whole thing taught me that you never know what a man or a woman can do until you give them a chance. They might have some hidden strength they haven't had a chance to call on."

Jia offered Erik a warm smile. "I hope I don't have to pretend to be an alien god anytime soon to impress you with my pil—"

"Dispatch is requesting your presence," Emma interrupted. "There's been a murder."

"Uptown?" Erik asked.

"Yes," the AI answered. "I'll fly us there now."

The lights came on, and the MX 60 broke out of the air lanes to barrel toward the new destination.

"So much for a quiet last few weeks," Jia muttered. "Want to bet I have to declare myself Empress of all Orlox before the week is out?"

"Nah. If I put money down," he looked over, "it'll happen."

CHAPTER SIX

Erik gave a quick nod to the two uniformed officers keeping the small crowd of curious residents away from the crime scene, which was an apartment in the middle levels of a residential tower.

There was nothing distinctive about the tower, and the apartment, although large, wasn't much more impressive than Erik's. He kept an unnecessarily big place as part of his cover, but neither he nor the victim lived in a sprawling tower-top mansion.

Jia's eyebrow lifted as they stepped into the apartment.

A well-dressed middle-aged woman lay on her side on the floor, sunken into her carpet. She was impaled through the heart by a small flat-topped flagpole. The normally blue-and-white UTC flag and the white of her carpet were half red with splatters of her blood. She'd also coughed blood over her chest.

The victim stared at the wall, her eyes wide with frozen terror and her lips parted, suggesting a final death scream.

"That's certainly different," Jia muttered.

"Yeah, can't say we've ever worked a case where the vic was impaled by a flagpole." Erik tilted his head, looking at the woman's body. Her shirt was torn, but the rest of her clothing wasn't. There was no sign of bruising on the face and no obvious broken bones. He didn't need Forensics to know there hadn't been much of a struggle.

Forensics drones hovered in the air, taking pictures and collecting samples. One slowly moved along a bookcase, extending a small arm with a sensor probe. Officers and other techs milled about in the room, carefully inspecting items with gloved hands and murmuring amongst themselves.

The smallest stray hair could be enough to lead them to their murderer.

Everyone talked about how the police had cleaned up Neo SoCal in the last year, but there was always someone out there ready to commit a crime.

Grand plans by syndicates and terrorists might be harder to pull off, but good, old-fashioned personal murder would always happen. The police could only do so much to prevent crime other than cure human nature, but that didn't mean they couldn't do their best to track the people responsible for heinous acts.

A forensics tech stood near the door, squinting at a data window streaming fluctuation graphs. A uniformed officer lingered behind him, her brow creased in deep thought. She looked at the victim and the detectives, waiting, discomfort on her face.

"What do we have here?" Erik asked the officer.

She turned and nodded to him. "Detectives." She pointed to the victim. "Victoria Dwazil, age fifty. She's a senior manager in the quality assurance division at a company called Luminous River. Her PNIU automatically contacted emergency services when her heart stopped, but apparently, it also contacted the company to—and I'm not joking—let them know she might not be in tomorrow. They contacted the police."

"I'm sure her bosses love how company-oriented she was." Erik snorted. "Let me guess, they want us to back off? They have some sort of important internal review to do before we're allowed to investigate the crime?"

The officer shook her head. "On the contrary, Detective. They've already sent us a number for a contact, and they say they want to do anything they can to help solve this incident. The person I spoke to seemed really shaken up about it."

"A cooperative corporation?" Jia took a few steps toward the body, leaning forward for a better look. "I'm not going to complain about the change of pace, but that doesn't mean I'm taking anyone off the list of suspects just yet."

Erik gestured around the room. "You pull security camera feeds yet? Access logs?"

The officer nodded. "Yes, Detective." She gave him an apologetic look. "And they've got nothing."

"Nothing? What do you mean, they've got nothing? There were no feeds?"

"No, she had security feeds for everywhere but the bedroom, and we've also got feeds from the halls, and we're getting external feeds as well, but we already checked the hall and apartment feeds." The officer glanced at the victim. "Two officers are re-watching them to be sure, but when we did a quick review, they showed that the victim entered her apartment yesterday, and she never came out. No one else was seen entering on any feeds, internal or external to the building. The access logs don't indicate anyone came in, and her door was locked until Emergency Services overrode it. There's a jump. She's in her office, and the next thing she's on the ground, dead, with the UTC flag sticking out of her."

"No one was on the feeds?" Erik stared at the flagpole. "It sounds like someone spoofed them. We're not dealing with some random Shadow Zone thug." He gestured at the flag. "And where did that come from? It's not like most people keep flags inside, even small ones."

The officer pointed to a wide hall. "There's an office back there. There were four flags: UTC, company, US, and California."

"She probably uses them for remote meetings," Jia suggested. "It's not unusual for a company officer to do something like that. Even if they acknowledge they're working from home, sending the appropriate image is important." She looked around. "You should see my mother's home office."

"I'm sure all the concentrated wealth would blind me," Erik joked. "But you don't think it means anything, then? The flag?"

She looked at him. "What would it mean?"

"It might be an insurrectionist message."

"That's a rather obtuse way of sending a message," Jia suggested.

"Killing a person's a great way to send a message." Erik grunted in reply. "But, yeah, probably not. If it were about that, they probably would have left an actual message for us to find. It's not like the kind of person who kills someone by shoving a flagpole through their chest is all that interested in being subtle."

Jia walked over to the body and pointed at the tip of the flagpole. "There's no point." She waved to a nearby forensics tech to get his attention. "Was there another piece at the top of this?"

He shook his head. "Not that we've found, Detective."

"We'll check the feed later to confirm that, but let us know if you find anything."

The tech nodded.

Jia turned back to the officer. "Give us the contact number, and for now, keep coordinating evidence collection. It's not every day we get this kind of murder Uptown. I'm sure we'll get a lot of pressure from above to solve it quickly."

"Yes, ma'am," the officer replied.

Erik wasn't so sure about that. The level of political pressure on the department and their specific EZ had slowly ebbed. Between Erik, Jia, and the captain's intransigence, the Council and other local politicians had learned not to bother.

They could even have been scared that Erik and Jia would turn their attention toward them. Shadow Zone gangs and syndicates might have been cleared out, but plenty of white-collar criminals waited in the shadows for their chance.

Jia gestured for Erik to join her back out in the hallway. She walked away, coolly surveying the murder scene. There were plenty of officers and techs to collect evidence.

The short-timer detectives didn't need to bother with anything but synthesis and follow-up.

"Without hacking anything," Jia murmured, "is there anything useful you can tell us, Emma? Anything that might link her company to something we should check out?"

"I've already performed a basic background investigation using publicly available sources so as not to affect the legality of your evidence collections," Emma transmitted to both of them. "All the available records suggest the victim in there is Victoria Dwazil, an employee of Luminous River. The company focuses on chemical supply and is one of the leading competitors of Flamel Universal. They've been praised for their agile management style."

"Flamel Universal?" Jia looked at Erik. "Isn't that the company your brother works for?"

Erik nodded. "Yeah." He smirked. "Should I check to see if he's in town? I'd be pretty impressed if he killed someone by impaling them with a flagpole."

"You have to admit that killing someone by impaling them with a flagpole, even a small one, does seem a very Blackwell thing to do," Jia mused. "But I doubt it was him. What else do you have, Emma?"

"Based on the easily accessible public accounts, Ms. Dwazil was a model citizen and completely apolitical, despite Detective Blackwell's earlier theory."

Erik scratched his chin. "It was just a theory," he admitted.

"There's nothing to suggest she's had any contact with pro- or anti-insurrectionist figures. Luminous River is a profitable company and a subsidiary of Hermes, but I've found nothing in my initial searches to suggest there's anything unusual about the arrangement. The company was acquired, along with several others, ten years back as part of a financial realignment at Hermes. Their business is a necessary and profitable endeavor, but it doesn't garner a lot of media attention. They also have an exemplary safety record, one of the best in the business."

Jia lifted her hand, her fingers spread out. She dropped one finger. "Potentially a terrorist assassination, but unlikely." She dropped another finger. "Corporate cover-up. Mildly likely." She dropped yet another finger. "Corporate espionage and warfare. Also mildly likely." She dropped another finger. "Personal. Was she married or in a relationship that you could find?"

"No," Emma reported. "I've found one Luminous River newsletter article that mentions she was jokingly referred to as being 'Mrs. Luminous River.' They state she rarely took time off and enjoyed working, even on her days off."

Erik looked at the open door. "She didn't drop dead from overwork."

Jia glanced into the apartment. "If she were that dedicated to the company, she might have become very disillusioned if she stumbled on some sort of high-level corporate malfeasance. That exemplary safety record might have been a lie."

"Is that enough to kill someone over?"

"I don't know. She was high enough that shutting her up before she called the authorities might be worth it. Potentially, she could have done real damage. The only thing I don't get is..." she gestured to the flagpole, "*that*. Impaling someone? It didn't look broken either, and if they didn't use a pointed one, how did they pull that off? I've got theories, but I'd like more evidence before I waste time exploring them.

"Same here," Erik offered. "And I'm thinking this isn't going to be a case for us as much as for Malcolm. Someone went through a lot of trouble to try to cover their tracks, which points to high-level corporate types rather than a stalker or syndicate types. We should get the feeds expedited to Digital Forensics. They left an impaled body for us to find, which means manipulating the feeds was about hiding who did it. It might just be as simple as recovering the original feeds and facial recognition."

"One could hope." Jia nodded. Her gaze cut to the residents at the end of the hall. "Even if she was married to her job, she still could have enemies. We'll have the officers here canvas the building to see if anyone knew someone was targeting her. We'll also contact Luminous River and see what they have to say."

"I doubt they'll be as eager to help us as they initially said. I'm thinking it was a strategy to make sure we don't double-down on the pressure." Erik patted his PNIU. "We should go and meet them in person. It'll help shake the lies loose."

"Good." Jia inclined her head toward a drone just inside the front door. "And it'll give Malcolm more time to go through the security feeds. We could get lucky, as you said, and be knocking on someone's door with a warrant by dinner tonight."

"'Lucky' for us is not getting shot at by the time this is done."

"Oh, in that case, we probably won't get lucky." Jia patted her slugthrower.

"Just making sure it was there?" Erik asked.

She nodded. "Exactly. You never know when you're going to need to shoot someone."

CHAPTER SEVEN

September 29, 2229, Neo Southern California Metro-plex, Luminous River Headquarters
The somber-faced young receptionist rose from her seat and gestured toward a long corridor. "If you two would accompany me, he's ready to see you now."

The detectives followed the lady. Thus far, everyone had been cooperative, from Security to the receptionist. If they commented about the case at all, they expressed regret.

Erik wasn't ready to trust the company, but it was a welcome change from the instant lawyering up he was used to when dealing with a decent-sized corporation. The nature of her death suggested something far more than a scorned ex-lover, but eliminating suspects from her job would help.

Erik almost laughed despite the situation.

This murder case might very well be the last case he ever worked for the NSCPD. Hunting down leads for

Alina, let alone Talos or other conspiracies, would rely on similar skills, but he held no illusions that his coming career wouldn't represent a radical change. It wouldn't be about carefully collecting evidence to submit to the court. Jia and Erik would become true hunters in darkness. Their trip ended in front of double doors at the end of the hall.

"Sir," the receptionist greeted, "the detectives are here to see you."

"Send them in," a deep male voice replied.

The doors slid open, revealing a stern-looking man sitting behind a desk so large, Erik could have used it for cover during a war. He gave a curt nod to the receptionist, and she walked away without another word.

"Please come in." The man gestured to two ornately crafted wooden chairs in front of his desk. They both looked so expensive that Erik hesitated for a moment. The detectives advanced, and the doors slid closed behind them.

The suited occupant hopped to his feet behind the desk. A smile consumed his somber expression. He smoothed his hair, then thrust out his hand. "I'm so glad you came. Terrible thing, this murder, but it's good that you two are on it. You'll solve it before I even know what's going on."

Erik shook the man's hand. After a few pumps, the man turned to Jia, repeating his performance, his smile growing larger and more obnoxious.

It was inappropriate given the situation, but it was better than him threatening legal action or shouting about warrants and dragging his feet about aiding the investigation.

"I'm honored to meet you, Detective Blackwell and Detective Lin. I wish it were under better circumstances, but a man can only react to life, not guide it."

"Thank you for taking this time to meet us, Vice-President Deng," Jia replied.

He bobbed his head before gesturing to the chairs in front of his desk. "Please sit. I had these chairs brought in specially for this meeting."

Erik glanced down at the chair. It almost sounded like a threat, but he took a seat. Fortunately, it didn't explode. His day was looking up.

The gentleman took his own seat. "You don't need to be so formal. Call me Richard."

"Okay." A slight look of discomfort played across Jia's face. "Richard."

"Some people call me 'Dick,' but only those who don't like me." He laughed, but when Erik and Jia didn't join him, he stopped and looked disappointed. "Yes, there's a time and place. I get that. We should move on to the matter at hand. I'm sure you've got a busy schedule today, filled with important detective matters."

"Something like that," Jia replied. "You were suggested to us as our primary company contact in the matter of Victoria Dwazil's murder."

"Of course, of course. Terrible situation. Terrible." Richard's breath caught. "Before we get started, just let me say I'm a big fan of yours. Big fan. You're like movie characters come to life. And I don't buy into that anticorporate rep of yours. I know you're just taking down the bad guys." He threw a few awkward punches at the air. "I never thought I'd get to meet you without committing a felony." He let out another quick laugh.

Erik and Jia exchanged glances.

They were used to more resistance from corporate types, but Richard's playful banter was more unsettling in its own way. Was it part of some sort of strategy, or did the man honestly feel that a murder investigation was the best time and place for that kind of behavior?

Erik would let Jia handle the initial questioning until he had a firmer grasp on what was going on with Richard.

"We appreciate your cooperation in this matter." Jia tapped on her PNIU and settled her hands in her lap. "The quicker we gather the initial evidence, the quicker we can solve the crime."

"I've heard that," Richard replied.

"It's our understanding that you're her immediate supervisor. We wanted to talk to you about possible trouble she might have been in before we start talking with her coworkers. I'll be blunt; in most murder cases in Neo SoCal, if it's not a personal matter. It's related to the victim's work."

"Of course. It's not like we live in a savage frontier colony filled with violent antisocials constantly trying to kill each other."

Erik suppressed a snort. "Crime rate's pretty low on most frontier colonies, let alone violent crime. It turns out when there aren't a lot of people around, it's harder to commit crimes. And no frontier colony has the resources for a decent rebellion."

"That makes sense."

"Let's get back to the matter at hand," Jia suggested,

with slight irritation in her voice. "Did Victoria have any enemies at work? I'm not saying someone would be a suspect just because they didn't like her, but the more people we can eliminate as potential suspects, the less time we'll have to spend investigating people."

Richard steepled his fingers. "She was liked by everyone, to the best of my knowledge. I never had any problems with her. She was dedicated to the company, and never gave any of her coworkers or subordinates any trouble. While she wasn't all that social, she was polite and friendly. She liked to give both her subordinates and superiors gifts on their birthdays. Isn't that nice?"

"You're saying no one had it out for her?" Erik asked. "Not even someone who might have been passed over for a promotion? This is a decent-sized company. It's hard to believe there are no corporate politics."

"You misunderstand me, Detective."

"Then clarify it for me, Richard."

"I didn't say we didn't have corporate politics. Sometimes they get a little rough." Richard clucked his tongue and stroked his chin. He took a deep breath and made a show of letting it out like he was trying his best to look thoughtful. "There's no one who, as you might say, 'had it out' for her." He added air quotes for emphasis.

"I'm confused," Jia interjected. "You're not denying there might be internal considerations. Are you saying she was so nice that no one targeted her? Gifts protect you from backstabbers?"

Richard chuckled. "She was nice, and she did know how to pick out a nice gift, but it's less about her being nice and more about her choices. It's not like QA is a ladder to the top. Operations and Sales are where those issues arise."

"But aren't you in QA?" Erik asked.

Richard nodded. "Yes, and I'm comfortable where I am. I'm paid well, and I have just enough responsibility that my job is not boring, but I'm almost at my ceiling. The next CEO will probably be an external hire, and if not that, he or she will almost certainly be from Operations or Sales. That's the way it's been at Luminous River from the founding of the company." He spread his hands in front of his face. "We call it one of the Ten Commandments. Thou shalt be in Ops or Sales if thou wanteth a quick promotion." He chuckled but again looked disappointed when neither detective laughed.

"So, you're saying there's no one with a motive to murder her?" Jia looked dubious. Erik was too.

"Oh, there are plenty of motives." Richard nodded quickly. "A plethora, if you think about."

"Such as?" Jia gestured for him to continue, the irritation in her voice ignored or unnoticed by the smiling Richard.

He shook a finger. "A swap! That has to be it. It'd fit with the kinds of cases you've worked."

"A swap?" Jia squinted at him. "What are you talking about? What swap?"

"Hear me out. What if someone invented a way to force-grow clones? So you could clone a person but get them to adulthood in days. Okay, that's ridiculous."

"Yes," Jia muttered. "It is. I'm glad you agree."

"But what if they could do it in weeks or months?" Richard nodded quickly. "That still makes it possible."

"What does that have to do with the victim?" Jia sounded more confused than irritated.

Erik revisited the idea that Richard was stonewalling their investigation in a creative manner. But there was something about the eager, stupid smile on his face that convinced Erik Richard believed *every word* leaking from his mouth.

The detectives had gotten so used to careful conspiracy that they had forgotten how badly moronic well-intentioned idiocy could threaten a successful investigation.

Richard rubbed his hands together, the glee building on his face with each movement. "Maybe there's a changeling situation, like with Rena Winston, but in this case, the bad guys made a clone of Victoria, force-grew the clone until she was the right age, and then killed Victoria, so the clone could take her place. They probably genetically engineered it to be more subservient to the bad guys."

Jia stared at him, her mouth open for several seconds before she could get over what had just been said. "So, let me get this right. A secret conspiracy has invented a technology well beyond anything we have, and they're using it to replace a middle manager at a medium-sized company in a division that you just got done telling us wasn't even that big a part of the internal politics of this company?"

"When you put it that way, it sounds stupid," Richard complained. He shivered with excitement. "But you know where the word changeling comes from, right?"

Jia sighed. "Old European myths about faeries replacing humans with their own kind, but that's just an etymology thing. It doesn't mean anything in the modern context, and your theory doesn't make sense."

"It doesn't. Hmm." Richard rubbed his chin some more, the purposeful movement now obvious. "Just because the company is small doesn't mean there's not something the bad guys might not want. What's wrong with the theory otherwise?"

Erik was impressed that Jia was attempting to grapple with the utter absurdity of what they'd just heard.

If it weren't for the obvious enthusiasm in Richard's voice, Erik would have been convinced the man was screwing with him, but no one could play dumb for this long and not slip up without being a professional actor.

Conspiracies were real. Deadly conspiracies with advanced technology were real. Erik was fighting them, but just because some things were real, it didn't mean everything was.

Jia closed her eyes and took a deep breath. Her face reddened. She reopened her eyes. "We'll set aside why some dark genetic-engineering conspiracy is involving themselves with your company. As you've noted, that's not necessarily impossible. We've chased down some strange connections in the last year, but you're missing the fundamental problem with your theory."

Richard leaned forward and nodded. "Which is what, Detective Lin?"

"Even *if* someone had the technology you're describing, and even *if* they wanted to replace Victoria Dwazil with a clone with genetic modifications to make her more pliable to whatever fiendish schemes they had, killing her and leaving her body to be found would make it pretty obvious she'd been replaced, right?" Exasperation laced Jia's words. "It'd mean they went through all that trouble for nothing."

"Huh. I guess you're right." Richard shrugged. "That makes sense when you put it that way."

"I'm glad you're being reasonable. Now, do you have anything more grounded you could suggest?"

Richard snapped his fingers. "I know."

"What now?" Erik asked. "I doubt it has anything to do with advanced technology and changelings."

"No, no. I get that was an absurd theory."

Jia looked relieved.

"Victoria led a quiet life, and while friendly with a lot of people, she didn't have a lot of friends," Richard explained. "She was dedicated to this job. She never got married, never dated much. Don't you see what that means? It's obvious when you think about it."

"She might not have cared about dating," Jia suggested. "Not everyone is interested in that kind of thing."

Richard slapped his palm on the table. "I've got it! The conclusion is obvious!"

Erik vaguely remembered the slapping and phrases from some old mystery drama that had aired a couple decades back. They didn't have time for Richard to live out his detective dreams, but threatening him wouldn't help.

Jia sighed. "Do you have something *concrete* to add, Richard?"

"Now, hear me out." Richard spread his hands in front of him, his eyes widening. "What if she kept to herself because she was a former notorious Grayhead leader. She got tired of the violence and decided to take up a normal job and keep her head down."

"Hasn't she worked for this company for twenty years?" Erik asked.

"Sure, but she could have done all that terrorist stuff twenty years ago, right?" Richard gave him a hopeful look before shifting to Jia like an eager puppy. "I think she found out about secret *yaoguai* breeding. Not the things that were going on in the Scar, but something else. Something Uptown. Dark conspiracy. Dark monsters. Dark fate."

"Wasn't that the tag line for a movie that came out last year?" Erik asked.

"Yes, but it applies to the situation, don't you think?"

A pained smile took over Jia's face. "Sir, I understand that you're excited to meet us and want to help. I also understand that we've had a number of high-profile and colorful cases, but the average case we've worked doesn't involve changelings, *yaoguai*, or terrorists."

"Really?" Richard sank into his chair. "Now that you say it out loud, it makes sense. It's not like the news is going to talk about you arresting some random midlevel businessman. It's not sexy and exciting."

"Exactly," Erik replied. "Now that you understand, we need to know if you've got anything useful to add to our investigation?"

"It's not *impossible* that something like that is involved."

"No, but until we have a reason to suspect it is, we will do this the old-fashioned way and presume normal suspects."

"Feel free to talk to anyone you need to." Richard averted his eyes and let out a long, weary sigh. "Our CEO has made it clear he wants a full and quick investigation. I was hoping for something a little more interesting, but it's not like I can do anything about that."

"Richard, she was a QA manager, correct?" Jia pressed.

He sat forward, but the sadness clung to his face. "Yes."

"Is it possible that she might have come across something? Something that someone in the company would want to cover up?"

Richard gasped and sat bolt upright. "I hadn't thought of it that way. Sure! She wasn't a frontline sort, but maybe she stumbled upon some records and realized we were supplying chemicals to a *yaoguai* factory."

"I still doubt that *yaoguai* are involved," Jia kept up her strained smile. "But it's not impossible there's a connection to something criminal. Given her position, how unlikely is it that she would personally review supply and production records?"

"That was a big part of her job. She's a manager, but was also responsible for spot checks. There's a filtering system that sends random record samples to her. It's all in the company systems." Richard shook his finger a few times. "I'll make sure you get copies of those. But...there is one other possibility we should at least consider. I know it's unlikely, but I just want to throw it out there."

Erik's jaw clenched, but perverse curiosity pulled words out of his mouth. "What is it?"

Richard licked his lips and leaned in. He braced his arms on the table before whispering, "What if she was an Orlox who changed itself to look like a human?" He lifted his eyebrows at their incredulous faces. "Huh? I read an article the other day that said they're probably centuries ahead of us in genetics technology. The force-clone thing doesn't make sense for the reasons you already said, so she changed herself to spy on humans but went native, so the other Orloxes showed up and assassinated her."

"An Orlox?" Jia asked.

"Sure, like a fungus spy among us, but one who was overwhelmed by the greatness of human culture."

Jia scrubbed a hand over her face. "We've already verified her identity through her DNA. So, she's an alien spy or defector who was altered to look like a human, but somehow her DNA is human?"

Richard nodded quickly. "They did something, you know, *alien* to hide it."

Erik stood. He'd had enough of the conspiratorial fanboy. "You remind me of an old neighbor of mine. He also was an *interesting* guy."

"Oh? That's nice." Richard smiled. "Thank you for the compliment, Detective."

"But we'll assume she's human until we have evidence to the contrary," Erik finished.

"That's boring," Richard complained.

"Boring?" Jia narrowed her eyes and stood. "With all due respect, Richard, it's a murder."

"But where's the pizazz?" Richard clucked his tongue. "Good luck, Detectives. I hope you find your alien. I mean, find your suspect."

"Uh, thanks." Erik headed toward the door.

Jia hesitated for a moment before spinning on her heel and stomping after him. She didn't speak until they'd exited the office and the door closed. "What is *wrong* with him?"

"I'd say he's a suspect, but I don't think that's chaff. I think he's just watched too many movies and read too many articles about us." Erik shrugged. "Who knows? With our luck, it's not impossible we've got a fungus murderer assassinating defectors. For now, let's stick to interviewing human witnesses. There's not much else to go on until Malcolm finishes examining the security feeds."

CHAPTER EIGHT

September 30, 2229, Neo Southern California Metroplex, Police Enforcement Zone 122 Station, Digital Forensics Division, Office of Malcolm Constantine

Malcolm smiled at the detectives as they stepped into his office, his bright white coconut-covered Hawaiian shirt even more distracting than his normal wear. Data windows freeze-framed on the hallway outside her apartment and living room floated on either side of him. Both were empty of people.

"Good morning, Detectives." He spread his arms and bowed. "You may thank me for my greatness. I've gotten you a lead."

Erik chuckled. "It's funny that you're dating a ballbuster like Camila, but she makes you like this."

"Confident women breed confident men," Jia suggested with a smirk.

"I've got plenty of confidence already." Malcolm placed a hand over his heart. "Detective, this is pure Constantine.

Camila's just shown me that I can be pure Constantine and still land a hot, smart girlfriend."

Jia gestured to the data windows. "Your love life can wait."

"You just say that because you work with your boyfriend." He withered under her glare. "Sorry."

"Moving on. The message you sent during our arrival said you'd reconstructed the feeds? I hope you've got something useful because we struck out during our interviews. No one seems to be able to come up with any reason why anyone would want to murder our victim. We've just started to dig into the records."

"Watch this, Detective. They managed to spoof the primary feeds, but their technique wasn't thorough. They didn't get all the backup data." Malcolm made a few gestures, and the feeds started. A tall man in a bulky jacket, dark mask, and gloves stomped down the hall and stopped in front of the apartment door. He looked both ways before stripping off a glove and placing his palm on the access panel. A few seconds later, the door opened, and he put his glove back on and headed inside.

The second feed started. Victoria sat in her back office, poring through a dense field of numbers on a data window. The suspect jogged toward the office. Four flags on short poles stood by her desk, paired on either side, the flags barely rising above the top of her desk.

She looked up with a frown. "Who are you? What do you want?"

The suspect didn't say anything. He stalked into the office.

Victoria jumped and screamed. She ran past the

suspect, whose snatch found only air. He grabbed the UTC flagpole and sprinted after her, catching up with her in the living room. She batted at him, her blows accomplishing nothing. With one arm, he brought back the pole and shoved it through her body, the flag pushed down by her chest as the tip popped out the back in a spray of blood. She gurgled up some blood before falling on her side. A final feeble reach for her PNIU failed, and her hand fell to the ground. The murderer ran out of the room, closing the door behind him and then jogging down the hall in the same direction he'd come.

Jia narrowed her eyes. "He didn't even charge her with that pole, and it's not pointed at the tip. It's not like I need to be Emma to figure out that's physiologically unlikely for the average person."

Erik grinned. "What about a transformed Orlox?"

"Very funny, but if he's not cybernetic, I'd be shocked."

Erik nodded. "One or both arms is probably hardware."

"A cyborg." Malcolm nodded. "That's what I was thinking, too."

"It's also consistent with Camila's autopsy report," Jia mused.

"You read it already?" Erik asked.

"Yes, I read it first thing this morning. The cause of death was, unsurprisingly, the trauma and blood loss from the pole that'd gone through the victim's chest and heart. There were no unusual chemicals, no drugs, nothing like that. Only the victim's DNA on the pole."

Malcolm swiped through the air. The feed windows disappeared, replaced by a dense oscillating waveform display annotated with tiny numbers and notes Jia couldn't read.

He nodded at the new evidence. "There was a weird local signal, too. It was messing with her PNIU and the security cameras, but there doesn't seem to have been low-level systems access. The logs show slight discrepancies, but like I said, they didn't get the backup data. They simply erased it, but weren't thorough enough to stop reconstitution."

"They obviously hacked the feed," Erik concluded. "Otherwise, we would have seen the suspect before."

"That's just it. The discrepancies don't start until the guy enters the feed." Malcolm frowned at the data window. "Why play it that loose? I don't know what it means, but we've got a trail now."

"What about vehicles coming and going to the building?" Jia asked.

"I looked into that yesterday." Malcolm shook his head. "Nothing stands out. There's nothing close to the time of the murder, and no indication those camera feeds were modified."

"A masked suspect with no DNA." Erik snorted. "Not a lot of leads there."

"Hey, at least you know he's a cyborg. That's something, right?"

"Let's just hope it'll be enough." Jia narrowed her eyes at the data window.

Jia rubbed her eyes. "I've been staring at employee files for hours. I never thought I'd say this, but I almost wish Richard was being less helpful instead of sending over so much."

"You think he's trying to bury us in evidence?" Erik stretched his arms above his head before lifting his feet and placing them on the desk. "He's kind of an idiot, but I don't think he's involved.

"I don't either. No suspect could put on a performance like that." Jia pointed at a data window displaying an image of a smiling man from the company's maintenance division. "We did ask for all employees with known or previous cybernetic enhancements. I suppose we're lucky there weren't thousands."

"Doesn't matter." Erik rested his head in his hand. "None of them fit what we saw of our suspect. We double-checked all the ones who fit the build, and almost none of them have cybernetic limb replacements."

Jia's gaze lingered on his arm. "I'm still surprised you haven't replaced it after all these years."

"I told you—"

"It's lucky," Jia finished. "But it might not be as lucky for our suspect, and it's not like they could hide a cybernetic arm if they worked for the company. Luminous River requires the same standard physical and genetic inspection that most companies do."

Erik scoffed. "Yeah, have to make sure no Purist associations boycott your company. It's crap, too. It's not like having a cybernetic arm is illegal, but the way they all act, anyone who doesn't meet their standards might as well be a criminal."

"They're not all like those psychos we dealt with recently." Jia sighed. "But you have a point."

"There are a lot more non-pure people out there than people want to admit, especially in the colonies. I wonder if groups like our friendly neighborhood psycho Friends of Purity will get worse when they realize that."

"Maybe." Jia dismissed the data windows. "But I doubt this case has anything to do with Purists, Grayheads, changelings, or even terrorists. The victim and company profiles aren't right."

"The tech they used to spoof the feeds isn't off-the-shelf gear," Erik observed.

"That's what worries me. But if this was some spy versus spy game, Alina would probably have given us a head's up."

"You really think she's going to tell us all of the ID's business just because we'll be doing odd jobs for her?" Erik chuckled. "I envy your optimism."

"It's not that," Jia insisted. "It's more that if she doesn't tell us, she stands a chance of us interfering. But assuming it has nothing to do with her kind of ghosts, that sends us back to the beginning. We've got no motive. We have a suspect we can't identify. Without something decent, we can't do much except question people who don't have any obvious link to the victim, and none of them even have the right kind of hardware."

Erik dropped his legs to the floor and sat up. "It's not the first time we've hit a dead-end in the investigation."

"The who can come later. We know the how." Jia frowned. "If we knew the why, that would drive everything. By process of elimination, we circle back to the same place. It's most likely related to her job, which means there might be something in the QA records."

Emma appeared in the middle of the room. "The probability of a bizarre conspiracy theory must now be increased. I'm receiving a coded message from Agent Koval that's being routed through the Rabbit. It's not simply me intercepting a PNIU message for Erik. She's being unusually safe."

"She might just be trying to get us used to that kind of thing." Erik grunted in irritation. "This better not turn out to be ghost crap. What's the message say?"

"She's requesting a meeting in a couple of hours and has sent an address," Emma replied. "It appears to be a mid-tier restaurant. Your normal clothing should suffice."

"What do we do if this does turn out to be an ID case?" Jia asked.

"We're still cops for now, even if we accepted her offer," Erik suggested. "And if this was about burying the case, she would have brought the captain into the loop."

"Unless she thinks she owns us now."

Erik's grin turned vicious. "Then it's as good a time as any to correct her."

CHAPTER NINE

The door to the restaurant opened and they entered, to be fully embraced by the warmth and glory of the atmosphere inside.

Succulent, mouth-watering scents laid siege to Erik's nose. Cumin, garam masala, turmeric, and other spices dominated the air.

His stomach rumbled in abject surrender. His light dinner wasn't enough to give it the strength it needed to resist. A happy couple sat at a table a few meters away with a large blue bowl of butter chicken in front of them, juicy and delicious. Dozens of people filled the restaurant, all chatting while gobbling down their late meal.

Erik was beginning to see the disadvantages of meeting in a restaurant.

"Not exactly the middle of nowhere," Jia murmured. "I'm a little surprised."

Erik nodded in agreement. He still didn't have a good handle on Alina, but as a ghost for the Intelligence Directorate, her unpredictability was likely a carefully and intentionally planned method of manipulation.

He didn't doubt she ultimately saw them as an expendable weapon to use against the shadowy enemies of the UTC, but that didn't bother him. He wouldn't have been spending his time hunting the conspiracy if he was worried about getting hurt.

At least this way, he had one group of conspiratorial, shadowy agents helping him against another.

A smiling hostess in a crisp white shirt and a long black skirt smiled at them from the podium. "Welcome to Blessings of Hyderabad. Just two this evening?"

"A friend of ours already has a table," Erik replied.

"What's her name?"

"It's okay," Jia replied. "We see her."

According to Alina's message, she would be at the farthest table back and to the left from where they entered. A redheaded woman in a suit sat in that seat, not looking their way. She nibbled on her naan like a careful mouse. She didn't resemble Alina from a distance, not that it meant anything, given the woman's penchant for disguises.

Jia offered a polite nod to the hostess before stepping past the podium and heading toward the table. Erik matched her pace, glancing around the restaurant.

If anything went down, they'd have to contain the situation until the civilians could flee, or it'd be a bloodbath. He was surprised that Alina would pick a place so full of people, given how she'd contacted them, but in a sick way, the other diners acted as human shields. Conspiracies that massacred restaurants filled with people stood out, and that worked against them.

The thought helped comfort Erik as they walked toward the redhead's table, but not enough.

There was a vague resemblance to Alina in the woman's eyes, but they were the wrong color. Her hair was short, and she had a good ten kilos on Alina. She could be the spy using any combination of disguise technologies, or she could be a random woman having a meal. She might even be someone working for Talos or a syndicate. It wasn't like ID agents were never caught. The government just didn't announce it to the entire UTC.

The woman smiled up at them. "Can I help you?" she asked, a faint hint of a French accent in her voice.

Erik looked at Jia. Alina had given the code phrase, but he was hesitant to use it without more evidence they had the right woman. It'd take him a while to get used to working with spies. He might have kept a lot of things to himself as a cop, but once they'd pushed out the first captain, he knew he could trust the average cop on the force.

Jia brought her fist to her mouth and cleared her throat before offering the code phrase, a quote. "Sing to me of the man, Muse, the man of twists and turns driven time and again off course, once he had plundered the hallowed heights of Troy."

Erik frowned. She was normally more careful. They might have just given the go-ahead for someone to go after them. Emma should be able to warn them if anyone approached the MX 60. Even if their enemies somehow knew about her, there wasn't a lot they could do to stop her.

"It's her." Jia glanced his way. "I'm surprised you didn't notice already."

"Notice what?" Erik's frown deepened, and he looked around until he had an observational epiphany. "Oh. Got you."

He chuckled. She was right, he hadn't noticed. A room full of dozens of diners, but he couldn't hear their low voices and laughter nor the clatter of their silverware. They were in a void, where they could only hear their own voices.

Jia lowered herself into a seat across from the woman, her hand inside her jacket, obviously resting on her slugthrower. Not so trusting after all. "Don't you have something for us, too?"

"The empire, long divided, must unite; long united, must divide," the woman quoted in Mandarin.

Jia let out a sigh of relief and dropped her hand. Erik was grateful Alina hadn't made them memorize the first code phrase in ancient Greek.

Erik took a seat. "Feeling ghostlike today?"

"I'm glad to see you could remember everything, cut off from Emma." The voice was unmistakably Alina's, the French accent gone.

Erik looked down at his PNIU. The other diners weren't the only noise he was cut off from. He'd gotten so used to Emma's omnipresence, he often forgot that in practical terms, she lived in the MX 60, not his PNIU.

"You don't always jam her," he noted. "Do you have a reason for that? I'm not trying to be a dick, but it doesn't hurt to be a little more suspicious now that I'm a junior ghost."

"Junior ghost?" Alina snickered. "Is that how you think of it?"

"Or merc ghost. But the question's the same."

Alina gave him an easy smile. "Sometimes it's best for humans to decide what they want to share, don't you think? Emma's a questionable entity at times, and implicitly trusting her in all situations might be inadvisable."

"Without Emma, we'd be dead." Jia glared at her.

"Jia's right. I trust Emma." Erik stared at her defiantly. She needed to understand that this deal would be on their terms, not hers. "You don't have to, but I do. If that's going to be a problem, we should reconsider our relationship."

"Calm down, both of you." Alina smiled mischievously. "I'm not saying you have to rid yourself of the AI. I understand what an asset she is, but you'll find, now that we're working together more closely, I'll be relying on additional safety precautions and techniques for confirmation. It's easier to handle things purely technologically only when we're not chatting as regularly. That includes blocking her on occasion, and things like the code phrases."

"Fine." Jia sighed. "Did you call us here about the Luminous River murder?"

Alina's brow lifted. Her smile remained more impish than mocking. "I saw something on the news about that. If it has anything to do with our extended interests, I'm not aware of it, and I'll leave it to you to figure out."

"Is this more test shit?" Erik asked. "I'm getting tired of hoops."

She shook her head, her smile fading. "I can assure you it's not. I genuinely don't know anything about that incident. Do you have reason to believe it's not a local matter?"

"No. Not yet. It was the timing of you contacting us that got us thinking. When you show up, it usually ends with us having to shoot a lot."

"I understand. I apologize for any confusion. I thought it would be useful to update you on the preparations for your job change." Alina gave him an apologetic smile. She gestured to a plate stacked with buttered naan. "Feel free. I wasn't sure if you'd want anything, but I ordered some extra bread, just in case."

"Is there a problem with the prep?" Erik's stomach rumbled again. He snatched a piece of naan and tore off a huge chunk, barely bothering to chew before swallowing. He was hungrier than he had realized.

"No problem." Alina nodded to the bread and looked at Jia. After the other woman shook her head, Alina continued, "Everything's moving rather smoothly, despite all the nested cover companies we're having to create. I'm not going to sit here and claim it's impossible for someone to pierce the corporate disguises we've set up, but it won't be something even the not-so-average person can pull off. Your main corporate identity will be as contractors for Cassandra Security. I've got a wonderful number of ways to contact them, and a nice little history. That sort of thing. Although there will be some interface with certain ID front companies, Cassandra is something new we've created for you two. That lowers the chance of anyone linking you to the Directorate."

Jia's questioning look didn't portend anything good. "Are you trying to say something with the name?"

"Don't worry. Cassandra had prophecy to help her out. We've got you two. When the enemy shows up, you can kill them. You don't have to rely on the gods." Alina grabbed her fork and pulled a piece of chicken out of her bowl. "In a sense, it's also a joke. I'm hoping that anyone who becomes aware of you doesn't believe you're accomplishing anything of note. I'm even going to spread false rumors with Directorate resources to encourage that belief. I hope you're not insulted. You're going to go from the most famous cops on Earth to two shadows among billions, contractors working for a small company. People will assume you've sold out."

"We're not in it for the fame. And people already have made that assumption." Jia finally gave in and took a piece of naan. "But that sounds like it'd be easier for us."

"You can't totally disappear, but a lower profile will help. Even if this ends with you not being a useful asset after taking down Talos or whoever is backing them, you'll have accomplished a lot."

"Avenging my unit is enough for me," Erik offered.

"And taking down a UTC-wide conspiracy is enough for me," Jia explained.

Erik finished his last bite and swallowed. "Since we're talking about preparations, maybe we should also talk about the ship situation."

"What about it?" Alina asked. "Is there a problem with the ship?"

"Come on." Erik shrugged. "Not trying to be greedy, but there's no way we'll stay on Earth for everything you'll want us to do. We need the proper resources."

Alina nodded slowly, a curious glint in her eye. "That's true, but I don't understand. I've provided a ship and a pilot."

"What about something a little sexier?" Erik suggested.

"Excuse me? Sexier? How is a ship sexy?"

"You know. Sexy. Like, my flitter is sexier than most flitters." Erik grinned.

Alina smirked. "I didn't come here to talk about your kinks."

"I want something sexier and a little bigger," Erik continued. "If we're going to be flying around the UTC, we shouldn't be stuck in a cramped transport. It doesn't even have any guns. Talos has cutting-edge tech, and while you've given us some neat toys, you've given us a basic ship with nice ways to hide things."

Alina eyed him, her mouth remaining curled in a small smile, this one much more mocking. "It's not only a good, reliable ship, but it's also perfect for this kind of work. Sexy stands out, Erik. The whole point is to not stand out." Her gaze flicked over to Jia. "I assume you don't agree?"

"I agree with Erik," Jia responded.

Alina raised an eyebrow. "*Really?*"

Jia's face remained impassive. "I'm not as interested in a sexy ship as Erik, but something with a little more capability would be helpful. There's a lot we've only been able to do because Erik's MX 60 is heavily modified, and at least with the flitter, we've always had back up to call on. Flying around in deep space, it might come down to what we have on that ship."

Alina looked at Erik and Jia, her smile lingering. "I see. I didn't anticipate you'd feel that way."

Something about the way she spoke made Erik suspicious. She hadn't explicitly told him another ship was off the table. Stressing the useful features of the Rabbit struck him as a temporary placation. Just because she wanted to play games, it didn't mean he had to like it.

"What are you hiding?" he asked.

"Hiding?" Alina set down her fork. "Why do you think I'm hiding something? Obviously, I have access to many pieces of classified intelligence that I'm not going to freely share with you, but I've tried to be very open about everything that's relevant. I know you might never trust me, but I'm not trying to screw you."

"You're a ghost." Erik's lopsided grin challenged her borderline smirk. "Even when you have no reason to lie, you can't help it. I doubt you can go ten minutes without lying."

She eyed him for at least five seconds before lifting her right shoulder in a shrug. "That's truer than I'd like to admit." Alina laughed. "I'll look into things, but for now, you'll have to be satisfied with the less sexy ship."

"What about mechanics and engineers?" Erik gestured toward his PNIU unconsciously. "Decent drones and systems access mean Emma could handle some repairs, and Cutter already said he can handle basics, too, but at the end of the day, that's not the same thing as having a dedicated mechanic or engineer. You gave us a ship because you're planning to send us to places other than Earth, and we don't want to end up floating in space waiting for rescue because we didn't have someone who knows what they're doing."

"I see you spending more time off Earth than on-planet in the immediate future," Alina admitted. "And I understand what you're saying. Personnel is something else I've been working on, but I didn't want to bother you about it until I had someone concrete. For obvious reasons, it's not like I can just call up a staffing company and tell them to send candidates. Even the companies that work with the government and have candidates with security clearances aren't necessarily people we can use in this particular situation."

Jia frowned, her gaze turning hostile. "This isn't an illegal operation, is it? I get that we're not cops anymore, but I don't want to end up having to defend myself against treason charges."

Erik wasn't sure he cared, as long as it ended with the heads of the conspiracy dead or facing execution for their own treason charges. Despite that, he remained silent, curious about Alina's response. Whatever she said, he doubted he'd change his mind, but it would change how he approached the new job.

Alina stopped smiling. "On a sliding scale from totally aboveboard operations to deep-black ops, your work will be much more toward the latter side. I'm not going to lie about that. I'll have some ability to help you out, but if things get too hot, the Directorate is willing to burn you to save themselves."

"You didn't even try to lie." Jia let out a dark snicker. "I'm impressed."

"What we're doing here is unusual, even for my line of work." Alina gestured toward a long window. "You'll work more closely with me than most of our freelance operatives. Not only that, but the enemy isn't some small-time terrorist group or insurrectionists. They've already demonstrated a thorough infiltration of the government. That's why you've both agreed to this. You know you can't stop them as cops. Sometimes if you can't see the man in the shadows, you need to move closer."

"I don't care," Erik admitted. "But I'm glad to know where we stand."

Jia's jaw tightened. She took a deep breath and slowly let it out through her nose, her face softening with the exhalation. "I'm still on board, and thank you for not trying to lie."

Alina scoffed. "At this point, I have no problem keeping information from you that you don't need, but I'm never going to actively lie to you. You two will end up figuring it out, and that'll cause unnecessary trouble for me."

Jia leaned in and lowered her voice despite the anti-spying tech enforcing the silence around them and keeping their voices inside its bubble. "There's been no movement with Talos?"

"None. Not since the prison incident." Alina's face twitched. "I think they screwed up. I think they expected everyone to end up dead onboard that station. They might have even had plans to encourage remote destruction, but things have been silent these last couple of weeks. We're also still trying to determine who Hadrian Conners actually was."

Erik grunted in frustration. "Managing to pull off a true deep-fake identity might be easy on the frontier, but I'm surprised he could pull it off on Earth."

"If they're being quiet, that's not a bad thing," Jia concluded.

"It's not like they've given up because of one failed op." Erik frowned.

"It gives us time to regroup." Jia shrugged. "It also gives Alina time to further prep for us."

Alina stared past Jia, a distant look in her eyes. "It also gives them time. They're patient, and there's little worse than dangerous people with patience."

CHAPTER TEN

Twenty minutes later, after more naan and minor detail discussions, Erik and Jia lifted off in the MX 60, zooming out of the parking garage and away from the commerce tower holding the restaurant.

The conversation didn't weigh on Jia as much as she had expected, despite the grim warning about potential betrayal by the ID in the future.

Part of her longed to help Erik find the peace he deserved, but her involvement had never been solely about him. She'd lived her entire life thinking of Earth as a perfect place and the UTC as the ultimate chance for creating a better humanity. The idea that people with resources and power were subverting humanity's chance at unity instead of supporting it disgusted her. If others could not stop them, why not her?

It was even worse when she thought about all the aliens surrounding humanity. She didn't believe war was inevitable, but at least human beings had basic biological similarities. Peace wasn't assured, either. Now more than ever, humanity needed to stand together until the galaxy had moved past the dangerous stage of early contact.

"I want to destroy them all," Jia muttered.

"The conspiracy?" Erik asked. He looked her way, having ceded control of the MX 60 to the unusually quiet Emma.

"You know how I used to be." Jia shook her head in disgust. "And it's people like them and other cowards who don't want to face the truth who help them do what they want. It's not like we can negotiate with them."

"Don't worry. We'll track them down. This doesn't end with anyone getting away until we're dead." Erik grinned. "Interesting that you said that."

Jia shook a finger at him. The look on his face told her everything she needed to know about what he was about to say. "Don't."

"*Don't what?*" His grin grew.

"Don't say anything about me not even being able to fire at someone when we first met," she warned.

Erik laughed. "I didn't say anything, but you just did. It's not a bad thing to change."

"Sure." Jia rolled her eyes, her cheeks heating. "Sometimes when I think about how naïve I used to be, I'm so embarrassed I could throw up. Or punch someone." She eyed him. "Maybe someone close."

"I'd prefer you didn't do either of those things."

"Detectives," Emma interrupted, "Dispatch is requesting units head to a factory level on a nearby industrial tower. The emergency call suggests out-of-control bots and multiple workers trapped inside. Amusing as fleshbags losing to lesser machines might be, I assume you want to do something about it."

"Hacker?" Jia guessed.

"That information isn't available at this time." Emma hit the lights and spun the MX 60 almost ninety degrees. "It's a good possibility. Other units are en route, but the officers on-scene have only stun weaponry and no EMPs available. You're the closest. Based on emergency calls, a decent number of employees are trapped inside due to door failure. Some are seriously wounded. Emergency overrides have failed."

Erik yawned and cracked his knuckles. "Tomorrow, I'm eating a much bigger dinner, so I'm not as hungry when something like this happens. It's like the Lady decided to triple down on punishing me."

Jia reached under her seat to access the storage panel. "We'll need to enter hard the minute we get there." She slowly drew the TR-7 from its hiding place. "Now I wonder if Talos isn't trying something. Even if they didn't know about our meeting, they could track this vehicle. Hacking a factory wouldn't be hard for them."

"Nah. Plenty of scheming bastards to go around, and that's assuming it's anything like that." Erik took the rifle from Jia. "Not every machine is as reliable as Emma."

"Nor every human," the AI replied.

"True enough." Erik smiled. "I wouldn't have done this so late at night, but if you think about it, the factory's doing us a favor."

"A favor?" Jia's brow wrinkled in confusion.

"Yeah. We're about to destroy a lot of out-of-control bots, and we don't even have to pay for the privilege. It's like free tac training without having to go to the Shadow Zone."

She thought for a moment. "That's certainly one way to look at it."

Erik stuffed magazines containing armor-piercing bullets into his duster pockets as Jia handed them to him. "Emma, the minute we get there, you start hacking the system. The sooner we stop those things, the better. People aren't going to ask many questions in an emergency situation like this, and the bots don't have angry lawyers trying to sue us."

Jia fished an assault rifle out of the storage compartment, along with magazines for her. "How many EMPs do you have?"

"Not enough to stop a whole factory. Remind me, first thing I need to do when we finish at the 1-2-2 is install a directional EMP in this thing." Erik slapped a magazine into his TR-7. "Let's go save some lives."

Erik and Jia leapt out of the flitter while it still floated a meter above the sprawling parking platform extending from the industrial level. Both detectives wore their tactical vests and carried EMPs, but Jia planned to rely on her AP rounds.

There wasn't any moral ambiguity or concern. They weren't dealing with people, not even criminals, just berserk machines threatening living people.

Three parked police flitters formed a rough wedge between a line of cargo flitters near the front of the factory.

A sealed monster of a door blocked access to the main warehouse, and a smaller door to the side was also sealed. Uniform officers crouched behind their flitters, their stun pistols out. A crowd of people cowered behind them, some bloodied. Officers inspected their wounds and applied medpatches.

The detectives didn't stop to check in with the officers already present. Emma had already announced their arrival to Dispatch. Relief flooded the faces of the officers, and they nodded to Erik and Jia when they arrived at the smaller sealed door. Industrial-grade bots wouldn't be very vulnerable to stun pistols, but assault rifles with AP ammo would do the trick.

"We need cops with us to escort people out," Erik announced. He motioned toward the door. "We'll take out the bots. You just follow."

Several cops rushed from behind the cars, more confident now with Erik and Jia present. They clustered around them, leaving a few officers to help with the crowd and tend to the wounded.

"I'd prefer not to get the rocket launcher out in public," Erik muttered, nodding at the sealed door. "Get us in there, Emma."

"Working on it," Emma replied. "There don't seem to be any extraordinary defenses other than what you'd expect on mid-level systems, although the interfaces are acting strangely. The system is obviously compromised."

"If you can prioritize, get the doors open," Erik ordered. "Fire at anything that isn't human," he shouted to the cops. "Who knows? You might get lucky."

The officers puffed out their chests and gave firm nods.

Uncertainty melted off their faces. They lacked the necessary gear, not the bravery, to defeat the bots.

The door slid open, revealing a wide hall and a wild-eyed man, blood running down the side of his face. The worker darted out of the building and past the police line, heading toward the crowd.

Erik nodded at the man. "Somebody make sure he's taken care of."

An officer broke off from the pack and hurried after the worker. The others returned their attention to the factory. Smoke filled the hallway. Security bots lay on the ground, twitching and sparking. A trail of blood spots led up the corridor.

Jia moved to Erik's side, sweeping the hall with her rifle. She pointed it at the twitching bots and fired two quick shots through their primary CPUs. They sparked and stopped moving.

"Careful is spelled 'two bullets to the CPU,'" she explained.

Erik shrugged. "Not complaining. The company can take it up with their insurance company later."

"There appears to be a sophisticated virus infecting several systems," Emma reported. "I was able to bypass some of the underlying systems to activate the doors. I don't have camera access, but I can route the positions of the workers via their emergency PNIU signals."

"Send them. We need to get this shit done." Erik flipped to single-barrel mode and advanced into the hall as white augmented reality arrows popped up. A holographic map appeared, projected from his PNIU.

The workers appeared to be clustered into three

distinct groups, with a few individuals spread out. One group hid in the main fabrication room. Another was in the back offices. The last group was already fleeing out the now-unlocked side doors near a large storage room.

Jia narrowed her eyes and pointed at the map. "The others aren't leaving. They must be pinned by bots."

"They might be pinned, but they also might be exposed to bots if I open the other doors," Emma explained. "I only opened that door because I verified there were no bots inside. I suspect the only thing keeping people from severe injury is the presence of the locked doors. I'll unlock them as you advance."

"Makes sense." Jia looked at Erik. "What do you want, fab room or offices?"

"I'm more of a building person. Fab room."

Jia gestured down the hallway. "Half of you with me, the other half with Detective Blackwell. Maintain situational awareness. If you see something, tell us so we can blow it away."

The uniformed officers didn't request clarification or say anything. They sorted themselves into two groups and fell in between their respective rifle-wielding detectives. Training could pay off with appropriate leadership.

"We've got people working the system," Jia announced. "If everything goes well, they'll be able to shut down the bots soon. If not, we've also got reinforcements. Until then, we need to move." She strode around a corner. "We've got innocent people to save."

CHAPTER ELEVEN

Jia sprinted down the hall, concentrating on the navigational indicators pointing toward the workers. Emma provided the occasional course suggestion, allowing Jia's makeshift squad to approach with maximum efficiency.

Without camera access, they lacked exact intelligence on the locations of rogue bots. Horrible scraping and buzzing noises and thuds announced they were far from alone in the factory.

"How are we doing on the cameras?" she asked, not bothering to be quiet.

"I suspect you'll be finished with this before I can get access," Emma admitted. "This virus is surprisingly targeted and sophisticated."

"You're saying this wasn't an accident? Not just somebody connecting the wrong system to the net?"

"I doubt that. The virus was customized for this factory. It looks like a different program set was downloaded to all the bots before the primary control system was disabled. I'd kill the power, but the loss of primary lighting would exacerbate the current situation, and the bots wouldn't run out of power in a timely manner."

Jia slowed as the several small security bots scuttled into the hall, all with a stun rods protruding from the front. They were followed by a four-legged monstrosity the size of a horse, but with four bladed arms.

"What is that?" Jia asked, wonder in her tone.

"A cutter," Emma explained.

Jia rolled her eyes. "I can tell that."

"No, that's what it's called. They cut things. Those blades are nanite-sharpened molecular blades."

"Huh. It's disappointing that they have such an unimpressive name."

Emma snorted. "Would Glorious Sharp Killing Machine suit it better?"

"A *little*," she admitted.

The security bots and their bladed friend lumbered toward the police officers. Normally agile, the six-legged security bots shuffled and lurched, barely moving at a decent walking pace.

There were no clever tactics or attempts to crawl on the wall or lower their shot profile. Jia fired three times in rapid succession, downing security bots. Bright blasts of energy slammed into the bots as the officers opened fire. The shots defused across the surface of the bots, doing nothing to slow them.

Jia yanked two tactical EMPs from her pocket, primed the small black orbs, and quickly hurled them toward the advancing bot army. High-pitch whining resulted, hurting her ears. Most of the bots collapsed to the ground, but the cutter continued its advance. Bolt after bolt struck it, to no effect.

"That's...inconvenient," Jia muttered.

The officers began backing away. Jia held her position and switched to automatic. She'd extensively studied security bots' weaknesses, but her education on industrial bots was far more limited. It didn't matter. She'd come around to Erik's way of thinking.

Most problems could be solved with stupidly egregious amounts of gunfire.

Jia held the trigger down and swept back and forth. Her AP rounds ripped through the bot, and sparks and smoke emerged. The assault rifle went dry, but the cutter fell to one side, landing with a loud boom. Momentum scraped the machine across the floor before it came to rest in front of Jia. She ejected her magazine and loaded a fresh one.

"We're almost there." She jogged past the smoking wreck of the cutter, grateful there were no signs of blood on its blade.

Other than the initial workers who had fled when they opened the door and bloodstains along the way, they had not run into any bodies.

Even if they were wounded, as long as they were safe from the bots, prompt medical care would save them, and ambulances were already on the way. The heavy footsteps of the police echoed around them. The distinct if muffled crack of the TR-7 sounded in the distance.

Erik had encountered his own fun.

Jia continued moving toward the sheltered group of workers. When she pivoted around a corner, she ran into another mixed group of security bots clustered around a door. They crawled over each other, scratching at the door. This time, no nightmarish cutters stood with the group. Instead, four-legged bots with wide fronts formed the back of the force. A silver tank was attached to their bottom, a nozzle on a flexible hose twitching like some metal *yaoguai.* It sprayed a thick, viscous liquid that sizzled on contact with the door, leaving irregular gouges. Some of the liquid dripped on a security bot, eating away its body.

"Is that called a 'sprayer?'" Jia guessed.

"Indeed." Emma sounded proud. "Please be warned that it could have a variety of chemicals dangerous to fleshbags."

"I noticed that. It'd help if you took them down remotely."

"I'm working on it, Detective."

The bots pivoted away from the door and stalked toward the police. Whatever programming compelled them hadn't sent them toward the sounds of gunfire, but there was no mistaking their current intent.

"Everyone back up!" Jia ordered. She jogged a few steps back, angling her weapon down. A stray AP bullet might end up in a worker if she wasn't careful. She took a quick shot and disabled a security bot. The other officers backed up, their expressions calm, but they quickly put distance between themselves and the infected machines.

Jia lined up her next shot and fired. Shot after shot followed until the security bots were deactivated garbage on the floor, smoking or sparking. Her attacks left a small number of advancing sprayers, which required more finesse. A bad shot, and they might all be sucking in acid.

She took a deep breath and targeted the wide front section of a sprayer. "Is that my best bet?"

"Based on most standard models, yes," Emma replied.

"Time to find out the hard way." Jia exhaled as she fired her next bullet. It ripped through the bot, missing the tank. The sprayer collapsed to its side. She grinned, and her follow-up shots sent the other sprayers to the ground with soft thuds.

"Impressive, Detective."

"I try." After a quick reload, Jia hurried past the pile of defeated bots toward the door. It slid open and workers poured out, some looking relieved, others weeping with joy. She pointed to the officers. "They'll lead you out."

The workers mobbed the police officers, who pivoted and hurried back the way they'd come. A few bloodied men brought up the rear, some helped along by others, jagged slashes in their clothes or limbs bent. One unconscious man was carried by a large bear of a coworker. The greenish complexion and shallow breathing of the victim suggested he'd been exposed to a chemical.

"Ambulances are present outside," Emma reported.

Jia took a deep breath. "Erik, do you need reinforcements? We've freed our batch, but I want to make sure they're okay on the way out."

A loud gunshot echoed from far away.

"I'm fine," he replied. "Protect them. I'm good here."

Good was subjective, but at least Emma hadn't passed along the truth.

Erik knelt behind a massive crate, blood running down the side of his head from a lucky swipe by a crazed automated saw on a workstation. His group of officers crouched farther back, hiding near other crates and pallets.

No one dared go near any of the massive fixed cranes or automated workstations covered with different tool arms, all of which writhed and twitched like they were alive. Piles of smoking bots and downed drones lay strewn about the area, but two ten-meter bipedal loading bots with large clamps capable of crushing a man patrolled in front of the small breakroom packed with the survivors.

"I'm remembering the advantage of fighting people," he muttered. "Or at least in a factory not filled with giant bots."

"Different factories require different types of equipment," Emma replied. "Incidentally, Detective Lin is continuing her successful evacuation," Emma reported. "I should note, given the state of some of the workers she rescued, waiting for reinforcements might result in risks to lives."

"Kill the bots and quickly. Check that." Erik reached into his pocket. "Damn. Out of EMPs, not that I think they'd work against those things. Too bad I didn't bring the laser rifle." He frowned. "If we can't wait, then we'll need to make an opportunity. On my signal, prepare to open the door."

"Those machines are slow, but they are certain to injure or kill at least some of the workers," Emma protested.

"Since when are you worried about the fleshbags?" Erik chuckled.

"I assume you are."

"Don't worry. I've got a plan. If anyone's going to die, it'll be me."

"I'd prefer that not happen either," Emma commented.

"That's also in the plan." Erik waved to the officers and then pointed at the door. "I'm going to distract those things. When I make my move, the doors will open. You'll need to haul ass and evacuate the workers. Got it?"

Several uniformed officers swallowed and one crossed himself, but they all nodded.

Erik loaded a fresh magazine and smiled. "Time for some fun." He jumped up and fired a burst at the first loader, aiming for a leg joint—a location Emma had earlier highlighted as a weak spot. He ran toward the loader bots, weaving between the fixed loading arms that swung at him. He ducked one bot and pivoted to avoid the clamp of another. A burst from the TR-7 sparked as it hit the reinforced loader. He sprayed all the joints, closing on the bots as he zigzagged, yelling at the top of his lungs. They ignored him for the first magazine of ammo but turned when he reloaded. The loaders stomped toward him, their heavy steps shaking the floor.

The uniformed officers hurried between the maze of crates and approached the door with their weapons holstered. They'd been somewhat effective against the drones, but less so against almost every bot in the room.

"Come on!" Erik bellowed. He added a burst toward the bot's torso as an exclamation point. "I'm here. Get to Robot Valhalla by killing me."

"Robot Valhalla?" Emma scoffed.

"It could be a thing," Erik insisted.

"Doubtful."

"Open the door while I have them focused on me!" Erik yelled.

The break room door slid open. Confused workers stared at the retreating loaders, wide-eyed. Erik ran toward the loaders and continued to spray both, producing a nice shower of sparks and even a few holes in the thick exteriors of the machines. One of the loaders brought back its arm and swung. The massive limb missed the detective and slammed into a huge crate, sending it careening into another, starting a chain reaction. A crate crashed to the floor behind Erik. He didn't want to get pinned by one, especially when he was only meters away from giant bots obsessed with killing him.

Continued bursts kept the loaders focused on him. The officers and workers led the wounded and evacuated back the way they'd come. Erik reloaded and kept firing, even risking running past the leg of one loader. The second machine tried to cut off his escape by jamming a closed clamp into a crate, ripping through the metal with a sickening wrenching sound that echoed in the cavernous room.

"If I had a missile or my laser rifle, you wouldn't be so tough," Erik argued with it.

"Insulting a mindless bot is pointless," Emma insisted.

"You never know. They might understand me." Erik jumped to the side as a bot kicked at him. "They came after me, and I have guns, so they have to have some logic."

"Multiple TPST officers are in the adjacent warehouse," Emma reported. "If I open the main door, they'll have line-of-sight.

Erik glanced toward the fleeing officers and workers.

"Give it a few seconds. I don't want someone to get hit by accident."

The officers got most of the evacuees to the entrance to the fab room. Erik grunted as a loader's arm connected and sent him hurtling toward a crate. He crashed into it, pain spiking through his back, and dropped his TR-7. The second bot tried to follow up by crushing him with a foot as he rolled out of the way.

"Yeah, let them in." Erik hopped to his feet and sprinted away from the bots, a clamp smashing into the ground behind him.

With a loud groan, the warehouse gate rose. TPST exoskeletons stood in a line behind it. Their weapons came to life, their heavy machine guns making even the TR-7 seem inadequate. However, even the loud, roaring guns did little damage to the thick, armored exteriors of the loaders.

Shrapnel from the gunfire was pelting Erik as he ran from the loaders. He looked at the TPST.

"Oh, *shit.*" It was time to put his feet up and down twice as fast.

A multiple rocket launcher flipped open at the top of an exoskeleton. The swarm of rockets blasted from the launcher with an angry roar and pelted the loader in a deafening explosion that knocked several more crates over. The machine tumbled back, a huge blackened hole in the center.

Erik made it to the edge of the room as the exoskeleton officers took down the other loader.

"Too much fun." Erik's right arm hung limply. Sharp pain suffused his entire arm and upper body. "I think I broke it. Better get that taken care of right away." He grimaced, limping toward the TPST team. His leg might not be broken, but it'd been better.

"You're taking this remarkably well," Emma commented.

"Not saying this doesn't hurt like a bitch, but once you've had an arm blown off, everything else seems minor in comparison. A few nanites will fix me right up."

Erik winced. "Or turn me into a zombie."

CHAPTER TWELVE

Still in her suit, Jia groaned and fell into her bed, face first. What an exhausting day. Between the case, Alina, and the warehouse event, every part of her ached.

Following the evacuations, Emma had managed to send sleep commands to the entire warehouse, ending the threat of additional rogue bots.

Because of the virus, Digital Forensics would work with the company to find out what happened, and it wasn't a case they would need to follow up.

The captain had told the detectives they could take the day off and he would assign other detectives to help out with the murder investigation, but Jia and Erik had turned down the offer. Manipulative Intelligence Directorate ghosts and crazed industrial bots aside, they still wanted to solve their final NSCPD case as quickly as possible. Fortunately, prompt treatment had taken care of Erik's arm, and they'd both needed only a good night's sleep.

Her PNIU chimed with a call. She groaned again. It was

like her mother could sense her weakness from all the way across Neo SoCal and pounce.

They should have sent *her* into the factory to fight the bots.

Jia rolled onto her back and answered the call. "Mother, it's been a *long* day. Can we talk tomorrow?"

Lan sniffed disdainfully. "You're not the only one who works hard. This won't take long. I have a simple question. I wanted to confirm you're coming to the party."

Jia let out a sharp laugh. "You're asking me about the Mid-Autumn Festival *now*? It's the middle of the night."

"Well, I wouldn't have to ask you so late at night if you had responded to my earlier messages."

"I can't bel…" Jia took a deep breath and slowly let it out. "I had to raid a warehouse today. My life was in danger, so it was not the time to take phone calls."

"Your life wouldn't be in danger if you had picked a less dangerous career," Lan replied. "But I've supported you in this police nonse…*career*. I'm hoping switching to the private sector will make things safer for you. You won't have to respond to every random crime that happens around you."

Jia sat up. Lan Lin was harder to defeat than a whole army of *yaoguai*.

"Mother, ignoring everything else that happened to me today, I'm in the middle of a new case. It's a murder. The first couple of days are the most important in this kind of investigation, so I can't be sure. If we get a good lead, we'll need to pursue it."

"I don't understand," Lan replied, her tone allowing no

dissent. "Don't you have a substitute you could send in? Police officers get sick on occasion."

Jia sighed. "Mother, we're the ones who are most familiar with the evidence. The world won't end if we miss one party to help investigate a murder. It's kind of important."

"Don't people get murdered every day?" Lan countered. "The Mid-Autumn Festival only happens once a year, and this party isn't an annual event, so don't you try that weak excuse on me."

"Investigating a murder is a weak excuse?" Jia stood, frowning. Her hand tightened around her phone.

"It's a roundabout way of saying you're busy with work." Lan snorted, derision thick in her tone when she next spoke. "A successful person is always busy with work, and any decent job, public or private sector, is important in its way, but if you're not being shot at by terrorists at that exact time, I expect you and Erik at the party. Understood?"

Jia rolled her eyes. "I'll do my best. Now, I need some sleep. Goodnight, Mother."

"Goodnight."

Jia pulled her PNIU off and tossed it on her nightstand. If her mother was that obsessed with the party, she probably did have a marriage-related scheme in mind. That was reason enough to avoid the event.

Faking a terrorist attack suddenly didn't seem that extreme. Was it?

"Maybe I'll get lucky and the Zitark will invade that day," she mumbled, closing her eyes.

. . .

October 1, 2229, Neo Southern California Metroplex, Police Enforcement Zone 122 Station, Office of Detectives Jia Lin and Erik Blackwell

"Thanks for letting us know, Captain. I think the answer is no, but I'll let you know soon if it's otherwise. Also, thanks for giving me the date. I'll let Erik know." Jia ended her PNIU call and looked at Erik with a smile. "It's not going to turn into something."

Erik looked away from a Luminous River personnel record. "What's not going to turn into anything?"

"The warehouse thing." Jia let out a sigh of relief. "You never know with us. Somebody confessed to sabotaging the factory. It was industrial espionage. The suspect got a lot of money to infect the factory with the virus."

"And he confessed that easily?" Erik sounded surprised.

"Yes. He was hired by a smaller company, TCA Systems. It turns out, he was pretty angry with them. The people who paid him didn't make it clear the robots might go out of control, and he ended up injured. From what Digital Forensics told the captain, that might not have even been their intent. They probably purchased the virus without testing it."

Erik snickered. "How do you test for that sort of thing?"

Jia shrugged. "Use it on a contained system? Anyway, the captain says he wants to kick this one onto the CID. It's more in their wheelhouse. TCA, conveniently, has a few people they want to turn into the CID anyway. No one even had contacted them yet."

"Funny how that works out. No honor among thieves, huh?" Erik rotated his arm. "Everyone who got hurt that night is on the mend, and if we've got the guy and the company, that's good for less than twenty-four hours." He inclined his head toward the personnel record. "We can't beat that record with our murder, but it'd be nice to close it out."

"At least we know it has nothing to do with TCA Systems," Jia joked. She looked at the door at the sound of a light knock.

Halil stood there, a small paper box in hand with ornate gold-filigree writing on the side reading "Taste of New Orleans."

Jia waved him in, curious what was in the box.

He lifted the box. "I've got some expensive beignets from a place that uses natural, real ingredients. I read about it on the net. Not a molecule of this food has seen a printer."

Erik stared at the box, the naked desire on his face obvious. At least he wasn't drooling. "Really?"

Jia grimaced. "That couldn't have been cheap."

"No, it wasn't cheap." Halil chuckled and set the box on the edge of Jia's desk. "But it's probably the last time I can do something flashy for you two before you head out and start protecting some corp prince while he wipes his ass for ten times my pay."

Erik stood and walked over to her desk to grab a beignet, picking it up carefully, as if dropping any of the powdered sugar would be a sacrilegious act. He took a bite and closed his eyes, his expression ecstatic. After a careful swallow, he murmured, "That's better than sex."

Jia smirked. She couldn't complain about her performance in bed since they hadn't shared it yet, but she took it as a challenge. "Is it better than my duck?"

Erik eyed the beignet and then Jia before shooting Halil a pleading look. The other detective lifted his hands in front of him.

He took another bite of the beignet and shuddered in pleasure.

"Hey, don't get me in the middle of this," Halil insisted. "I'm just trying to do you a favor. Though while I've got your ear, I've got a question. When exactly are you leaving?" He frowned. "I tried asking the captain, but he's acting like it's a big confed-level secret."

Jia stared at Halil. "You asked me before, too. Why do you care so much?"

Erik didn't contribute to the conversation. He continued to take small, careful bites of the glorious pastry, chewing them thoroughly. He separated each bite with a murmur of satisfaction. Jia wasn't sure she had ever seen him that happy. She might need to switch from making duck for him to beignets.

Although unless Alina was going to be paying them a lot more, she doubted she would often make pastry with all-natural ingredients.

"November 1st," Jia explained, gesturing at Erik. "That's when we're officially out."

Erik swallowed his current bite, casting a reluctant glance at his beignet before looking at Jia. "It is?"

Jia nodded. "The captain mentioned it at the beginning of the call." She frowned. Halil had been overly eager for this information for several days. Something was going on, and she wouldn't let it go.

"Okay." Halil nodded. "Thanks. Enjoy the beignets."

"Why do you need to know the date?" Jia injected a hint

of tension and threat into her voice. "Does somebody else need to know that date?"

"Damn, Jia, slow it down." Halil shook his head, but there was something in his eyes. Panic, perhaps. "I'm not about to sell you two out. Even if I wanted to and someone gave me all the money Ceres Galactic makes in a year, I know I wouldn't survive two weeks."

Erik's love affair with the beignet was over. He held it loosely in one hand, staring at their visitor. Jia's paranoia was infectious. "You think he's hiding something?"

Halil groaned. "You too, Erik? You have to have this conversation right in front of me?"

"It's easier when we all know where we stand. And, yes, you're hiding something." Jia stood slowly, her eyes narrowed. "You were right. You don't want to make enemies of us."

"YOUR OFFICE!" he blurted, avoiding eye contact.

"Huh? What about it?" Jia frowned. Had he planted something? There was no way he could pull it off without Emma noticing, not without advanced technology, but if he were a Talos pawn, it wouldn't be impossible.

"Your office is closest to the elevator." Halil shrugged. "And it's closer to the break room. Seconds add up. I read this article the other day about how if you save five minutes a day, that ends up being over a day by the end of the year. I'm losing a day of my life every year because of where my office is. It's not fair."

Jia blinked. She'd expected a tale of dark conspiracies forcing him into something he didn't want to do. "You just want our office?"

"You'll be gone. It's not like you need it." Halil nodded toward the door. "And I deserve it. I've put in my time."

"So, the beignet was a bribe?" Jia raised an eyebrow, but her smile undermined her suspicious look.

"I was just thinking that if the Obsidian Detective and Lady Justice drop a word in the captain's ear, maybe he'd consider it more seriously. I'm not the only one eyeing your office."

Jia burst out laughing. "Our legacy will be our office?"

"Sure, and all those crimes you solved. But, yeah, mostly the office."

Erik's expression softened, and he went back to his slow, careful exploration of the glories of fine pastry. He shrugged, not caring about the dispensation of his office after his departure.

Jia laughed again, all the tension flowing out of her. *So much for Talos.*

"I'll mention it to the captain."

CHAPTER THIRTEEN

"We're going to have to change our strategy," Erik announced. "We're getting nowhere, and Malcolm and his guys aren't getting anywhere fast either."

He had finished going through a new batch of personnel files, clinging to the small hope he'd find something that stood out enough to point them at the killer. Just because he joined the department to hunt for the killers of the Knights Errant, it didn't mean he wanted to let another killer walk free.

Someone had brutally murdered a woman, and they needed to face punishment.

Jia slowly tore herself away from the two feeds playing on her desk. She'd been working through the murder recording one second at a time, looking for clues that would help identify the killer. Erik wasn't sure it was healthy to watch a murder over and over, but it came with being a cop.

Once they took down the conspiracy, they could retire and do nothing but watch sphere ball.

"I'm open to suggestions." Jia stretched as she commented, "Whoever killed Victoria Dwazil went through a *lot* of trouble to cover their tracks, and they did a good job of it, too."

"We can't have Emma dive into the company systems without trouble." Erik frowned. "There would be no guarantees even if we could, but it'd at least be a start."

"Why can't you have access?" Emma appeared, sitting on the edge of Erik's desk. "Vice-President Deng seemed rather cooperative. If you told him your technicians needed full systems access, wouldn't he be inclined to try to obtain that for you?"

"He's a VP, not the CEO. Being cooperative with an investigation isn't the same thing as wanting random cops rooting around in your company's systems." Erik shook his head. "Even if they allowed it, the problem comes after. The court is going to need documentation of everything, and we can't say, 'Our experimental AI went through their system.' There have been cases tossed out because of improper algorithmic use in the past."

Emma wrinkled her nose in displeasure. "I'm far more than an *algorithm*."

"Not disagreeing, but the problem is, we have no idea how the courts will handle you, and I'm not here to change legal history. I'm here to catch a murderer. When we nail someone, we need to make sure they don't walk because we screwed a procedure up."

Emma folded her arms and huffed in irritation. "Then what's your suggestion, Detective? I don't need to, but I'll remind you anyway that *every* minute you spend looking for clues is an additional minute the murderous gun goblin has to flee. He might already be on Venus for all you know, or burrowing his way into some sad little makeshift hovel in the Scar."

"Then we'll have the CID extradite him or have the militia dig him up. This might be our last case. We need to do this by the numbers." He eyed her. "We won't leave a mess for the rest of the 1-2-2 to clean up."

Jia pushed off her desk until she was standing and gave them a slight smile. "We can't use Emma to explore their systems, but there's nothing that says *we* can't use her as a data analysis tool. We just have to be careful about it."

The annoyance on Emma's face faded, replaced by a smirk. "Indeed. That's very perceptive of you, Detective Lin."

"I'm not following," Erik admitted.

Jia pointed to his data window. "The company has given us a lot of information, and we might be missing clues because we're not looking at the right information since we have so much. I don't know if the solution is to get more information or look through the information more efficiently."

"Now I'm following you."

"If Emma filters things for us, as long as we can pull or point to the information without some unusual programming technique, we'll be able to send it to the prosecutor without trouble. We can just claim we stumbled upon it when searching. There'll be nothing to explain."

Erik didn't laugh, even if he wanted to. The old Jia had been so obsessed with regulations and procedures that she'd let her first captain use them to control her, and now she was willing to play fast and loose as long as it ended in justice. Erik had no problem with that.

It was the way he'd always been.

He gazed at Emma. "You know what we're looking for. You think you can find something?"

The AI scoffed. "Detective, if you had ten of me and fewer rules, there would be no crime on this planet within six months."

"I've found something useful," Emma announced. She'd disappeared while performing her records search but now summoned her hologram in the center of the room, her smile one of smug triumph.

"It's only been an hour," Erik noted, sounding impressed. The AI's humanlike personality could easily lull him into forgetting that she wasn't a snarky woman who liked to disappear, but rather the pinnacle of advanced information technology. All their police restrictions had limited their ability to use her to her maximum potential.

Emma nodded. "In this case, the information was all there, as Detective Lin had anticipated. You simply needed someone more efficient to go through it. There wasn't any clever coded phrasing or encrypted words. There were a series of personal memos documenting one of the victim's internal investigations. I'm sure you would have stumbled upon them...eventually. Probably after the suspect escaped past the core worlds." She lifted her hand to examine her nails, an absurd action considering she could make them look like anything.

"What did you find?" Jia asked. "Besides a new reason to look down on fleshbags."

Emma smirked. "The victim was obsessed with two chemical precursors produced and shipped by the company in great numbers. Judging by her memos and records, her research into these chemicals occupied the vast majority of her time in recent weeks."

Three-dimensional molecular models of the two intricate compounds appeared and orbited around Emma. Erik didn't know enough chemistry to interpret the structures, but he didn't care. It was not like he needed to when he had Emma. Relying on his super-AI assistant might be making him lazy in some ways, but he was doing all the heavy lifting involving firefights.

"I'm having bad flashbacks to my o-chem final at the university." Jia shuddered, rubbing her shoulders."

"You got an A- on the final?" Erik joked.

"No, of course not. I got an A, just like I always did, but..." Jia waved a hand. "We don't need to talk about my education. Let's focus on the case." She nodded at Emma. "Why would these compounds be important? You mentioned they are precursors. The question is, precursors to what?"

"One of them is a precursor in the production of Archangel," Emma explained. "The other seems to mostly be important in agricultural chemical production. I'm having trouble finding any reason worth killing over the latter, but there might be other uses that aren't documented in sources available for my perusal."

"Archangel? Son of a bitch." Erik grimaced. "We've got

the how, and we've got the who. And now we have the why."

Every cop in the department had all read the departmental memos concerning the so-called "Dragon-Tear Killer" making its way around the UTC. Archangel was allegedly more addictive than Dragon Tear, and although the newer drug didn't produce the same high as the other drug, it had fewer side effects, including a lower risk of sudden cardiac arrest.

The NSCPD had received many reports from the CID about the drug spreading throughout the core worlds in the last six months, but they hadn't arrested anyone in the metro for dealing yet.

It'd always been a question of when, not if, though.

Jia gestured to the now-glowing chemical diagram. "But just like agriculture might not be the only use for the second chemical, this one isn't only used as an Archangel precursor, correct?"

"No, it has a number of legitimate industrial and biomedical uses," Emma explained. "Luminous River has been producing it for some time. Its production, in and of itself, is unlikely to have caused her concern."

"Then why was Victoria Dwazil so concerned with it?"

"Because she found discrepancies between the delivery reports for the chemical and the client payments," Emma explained. "In addition, the production levels were above what was being requested by sales. The same is true of the other chemical, but as I noted, I'm having a harder time linking it to the potential murder. I'll also note the second chemical's production dropped in recent weeks, and there's a memo suggesting a database error was responsible for the overproduction of that one."

"But that's not true for the Archangel?" Erik asked. "That was how you whittled it down."

"It's not Archangel." Emma wagged a finger. "It's merely a precursor. Please note it requires several other chemicals and processes for the final production of the drug."

Erik grunted in frustration. "Give me a C- for my grade and move on already."

Emma gave him an overly satisfied smile. "To answer your question, there's no evidence the overproduction of the chemical in question was the result of a database error. Production was *increased* in recent weeks, according to direct numbers the victim pulled from the primary production plant system. Those were not passed along to either QA or Sales, nor, for that matter, higher-ups in Operations."

"It's always the numbers that trip these guys up." Jia's eager grin and tone betrayed her excitement about the new lead. Their cooling case had turned red-hot.

"Sounds like we need to go check out the plant." Erik frowned. "Or get someone to do it for us. We won't have jurisdiction if it's outside Neo SoCal."

"It's convenient in this case that the plant isn't outside Neo SoCal." Emma smiled. "Although Luminous River has multiple plants and the victim has responsibilities for several, the one in question is in the Shadow Zone. I checked into it. The plant's been open for a few years, and it is allegedly part of the Council's attempt to revitalize the Zone."

Jia thought a moment. "Now that you mention it. I

remember seeing something on the news a few years back about economic development efforts in the Zone." She snorted. "They keep people from freely traveling between the Zone and Uptown, but they stick a major chemical production plant there? Knowing what I know now, it sounds more like they just wanted something dangerous in a neighborhood they don't have to care about."

"Probably a little bit of both," Erik agreed. "We're Shadow Zone Task Force members until November. We've still got jurisdiction."

"But we don't have a warrant. You're the one who said we need to follow proper procedure."

"You don't need a warrant if you've got cooperation." Erik lowered his hand to his PNIU with a grin. "I think our greatest fan will be happy to get us permission."

CHAPTER FOURTEEN

October 1, 2229, Neo Southern California Metroplex, Shadow Zone, Luminous River Production Plant

The sprawling chemical plant came into view as the MX 60 descended.

Jia had flown over factories and plants like this one more than once in the Zone, but she'd never paid attention. They were just landmarks on her way to something else. She might not be much better than the Council. It was too easy to forget the millions of people living at the base of the mighty towers of Neo SoCal.

People couldn't solve problems they refused to admit existed.

Huge circular tanks stood clustered together in the corners of the fenced-off complex. A maze of mostly windowless buildings connected by opaque skybridges spread from the center of the area. Puffs of dark vapor flowed from different buildings all over the plant.

The omnipresent haze in the Zone might not have been the fault of plants like this one, but it wasn't like the air quality in the area was the result of people sneezing too much. Every time they came to Shadow Zone, the dark air made it seem later in the day than it was. Jia chuckled darkly at the thought.

"What's so funny?" Erik asked, his hands loose on the control yoke. "You that happy we've made progress?"

"It's been a busy few days, and it's only late afternoon today. At the rate we're going, we'll have enough time left over to solve a whole other crime or rescue a bus filled with children or something."

"It's not always a bad thing to be busy." Erik's gaze darted to the lidar and cameras. "When you're busy, it keeps you more alert. When I was in the Army, I always worried about guys back from a long leave. It softened them up."

Jia nodded. "No, it's not a bad thing, but I just hope we won't be working this much until November. Your Lady's trying too hard to entertain herself."

It was Erik's turn to laugh. "What? You're turning into a lazy cop like your first two partners?"

"Maybe they rubbed off on me, but it took a while." Jia grinned. "But if this keeps up, think of all the reports we'll have to work on. It's not all fun and shooting cyborgs."

"Uhhhh, damn. You're right." Erik grimaced. He continued guiding the flitter toward a parking lot past the fence. Drones flew over the area, patrolling it, and there were towers with armed guards, including a few with conspicuously long rifles, easily visible even at a distance in the camera.

The MX 60's transponder signal would stop them from coming under fire, but such open displays of security would be considered gauche Uptown. Security guards armed with rifles patrolled the perimeter.

Jia scoffed. "Isn't that a lot of firepower for a chemical plant?"

"Not when you're worried about troublemakers." Erik shrugged. "Until recently, they had a lot more gangster scum to worry about, and this isn't a candy factory. Smart criminals understand things like precursor chemicals."

"True, but why not use bots, then?" Jia looked around, seeking external security bots, but she didn't see anything other than the surveillance drones.

"Because the government's not going to let them run bots with lethals down here, and that's what they probably need to be safe." Erik slowed the descent of the flitter. They passed over a fence with two drones hovering nearby before floating gently toward an open parking spot surrounded by far less luxurious vehicles. A huge, broad-shouldered man in an impeccably tailored suit stood there waving with a smile on his face. Unless he was a terrorist or an ID ghost using a disguise, he was Malachi Lunt, the plant manager.

"Is everyone in this company happy to help the police?" Jia mused.

Erik snickered. "You say that like it's a bad thing."

"I'm used to people stonewalling. I want to say it's a nice change of pace, but all this cooperation is making me nervous." Jia rubbed her palm with her thumb. "And Victoria Dwazil was killed by someone who was probably being paid a lot of money to siphon off chemicals for Archangel. People who send Tin Men to impale people aren't subtle about most things."

"Killing a cop isn't a good way to avoid attention."

The MX 60 set down, the faint background hum of the grav field growing quiet. Malachi folded his hands in front of him and waited patiently, a pleasant smile fixed on his face in a corporate mask. Jia let out a sigh of relief. An obvious fake front satisfied her paranoia.

"Don't get out the grenades just yet," Erik joked before opening his door. "We don't know if he's got any hardware."

"Very funny, but it's an open question as to which of the two of us is more paranoid."

"Stay paranoid, and you won't end up dead."

"Good advice." Jia stepped out. She waited for Erik before both detectives walked toward the waiting Malachi. He stood near the entrance to a covered walkway that led toward a squat building marked A22. The man kept up his smile, even his blinks coming off as calculated as they approached. If he was a deadly cyborg assassin or had hired one, he was doing a good job of hiding it.

He thrust his hand out. "Detectives Blackwell and Lin, welcome to the plant. The honor is all mine, although I wish we could have met under better circumstances." He chuckled.

Jia and Erik both exchanged handshakes before the former spoke. "Thank you for agreeing to meet with us on such short notice. We know it can be inconvenient to come all the way up to the station and how that can look, so we thought this would be a better way to handle things."

"It's unfortunate we couldn't do this on a call." Malachi's smile dimmed for a fraction of a second. "I understand that this is an important matter, but as you implied, I'm a very busy man."

"Sometimes it's good to look a man in the eye when you're questioning him." Jia gave him a cool look and put a chill in her tone. "Most people aren't sociopathic enough to lie without giving off a tell. I suppose if they were, civilization would have collapsed a long time ago."

Malachi frowned, but the downturn of his mouth and narrowed eyes suggested anger more than offense. "I see. I assure you that I don't intend to lie to you, Detectives. I'm proud of my management of this plant, and it's unfortunate what happened to Victoria, but I'm sure it has nothing to do with us down here. I know once I have a chance to show you around, you'll understand that."

Erik scratched his cheek and glanced at the tall fencing. "*Down here*, huh? It can't be fun being stuck in the Zone. It makes some frontier colonies look luxurious."

"It's not like I live here." Malachi scoffed as he rolled his eyes. "I only work here, and I work remotely half the week. Besides, you don't understand."

Erik asked. "What don't we understand?"

Malachi spread out his arms out to his sides with a practiced theatrical flourish. "This place has such a sinister name, Shadow Zone, but I don't like to think of it that way."

"You just don't want to live here," Erik observed.

"Yet." Malachi smiled.

Jia interrupted. "If you don't think of it as the Shadow Zone, what do you think of it as, then?"

"The Land of Opportunity." Malachi pointed up. "Opportunity raining from above, a mutually beneficial opportunity for those down here and those of us who don't live here. I'm happy to do my part to improve this great place."

"But you're not from the Zone," Jia pointed out. "You're not even from Neo SoCal originally. You're from Greater Seattle. Why do you care so much about the Zone?"

"Do you only care about crime if it's in Neo SoCal?" he countered, lowering his hand.

"I care about crime everywhere."

"Exactly." He pointed at her. "And I care about opportunity everywhere. Anyone who wants to advance themselves in the business world comes to Neo SoCal eventually. I'd expect you to understand that, Detective, given your family background."

Jia folded her arms. "There's a reason I decided to become a police officer."

Malachi's expression turned appraising. "When I talk about opportunity, I want to stress that I don't mean solely for myself. I mean, for this community as well. These forgotten people, ignored by so many Uptown, treated like criminals simply for being here. Yes, some antisocials have snuck into the bunch, but your fine department has done a lot to clean those people out. That means we can accomplish our original goal of helping revive this economically depressed area by providing jobs and stability."

He probably practiced the speech in the mirror, but Jia didn't point that out. She found a new appreciation for her mother's and sister's more direct if cutting manner. They won political struggles at their companies more through force of will than subtlety, not much different from how Jia had handled her time at the department.

"Victoria Dwazil was paying a lot of special attention to this place," Erik interjected. "But it wasn't like she was only responsible for overseeing QA in this one plant. We're not accusing you of anything, but it's not impossible that someone here is up to something they shouldn't be."

"As far as I knew, she had her eye on most if not all of the company plants." Malachi smiled, but his occasional mouth twitch spoke to his effort in maintaining it. Being nervous around the police didn't make him guilty. He might not like them taking time out of his day, but it might also mean he had something to hide. "You're right. Roaches can always sneak in, but I don't believe we have a problem with that sort of person."

"You sure there wasn't a special reason she focused on this plant so much?" Erik pressed. They knew the answer, but sometimes the best way to ferret out who knew the truth was to observe how a suspect lied about it.

Malachi rubbed his chin and furrowed his brow in deep thought before his face twisted in confusion. "That's a good question, Detective. It's one I've been asking myself a lot these last few weeks."

"Why the last few weeks?"

"Because Victoria was contacting the plant every day with questions." Malachi sighed and shook his head. "I understand that QA is her job, but we're well above quota and our random testing always comes out well, so it was kind of annoying that corporate would be leaning on us so hard." He waved his hands. "Not that I'm saying they don't have a right to investigate, but I just didn't understand why she was so obsessed with us. Maybe she was overcompensating for a bad relationship. I read that most murderers are someone the victim knows."

Jia stared at him. "That's true, but that doesn't mean they have a close, personal relationship. You, for example, knew Victoria."

The manager's smile turned pained. "True enough."

"And you'd characterize her interaction with your plant as 'obsessed?' Or is that hyperbole?"

"I don't know what else to call it." Malachi let out a quiet sigh of exasperation. "She sent constant messages. I was wasting an hour a day these last few weeks double-checking and triple-checking numbers for her and trying to figure out the reasons for the discrepancies. Admittedly, one was a reporting problem, but it wasn't a big deal. It's not like I can shut down the plant to investigate a reporting error, especially when it wasn't affecting the bottom line, but the QA Queen didn't seem to understand that."

"She's dead," Jia replied. "And it might be because of her job."

"You don't know that for sure," Malachi insisted.

"Maybe, but it's not like you've never had problems down here," Jia noted. "You keep acting like this plant's a perfect operation, but that's not true."

"We've been at or above quota since this plant opened." Malachi sniffed. "She was probably just angling for a promotion. I'm sorry about what happened to her, but it's not our fault down here. You should be Uptown harassing people at corporate. It's not like they do anything important."

"Quota isn't the only thing you can have issues with." Jia wrinkled her nose. "Smell that lovely Zone scent?"

"You stop noticing when you come here all the time."

Jia always noticed it. Maybe she'd not come to the Zone often enough. Or Malachi might not pay enough attention to detail, despite his job.

"I noticed in my background checks that the company has been fined for improper disposal at a few plants, including this one," she explained. "Maybe Victoria was concerned about that."

Malachi snorted, the corporate mask disappearing as a genuine scowl appeared. "That's what you think? That I or someone at the plant murdered Victoria Dwazil over a nothing fine that happened last year?" He flung his wrist dismissively. "Whenever you open a facility in a place like this or use probationary workers, issues inevitably arise. Part of our agreement with the Council was that we had to staff with a certain minimum percentage of locals. And, while acknowledging that many people's presence here in the Zone isn't their choice, it's not an area that encourages an excellent work ethic."

"Meaning what?" Jia challenged.

"Meaning, Detective Lin, that some of the workers here can be a little sloppy. That resulted in corners being cut and the fines you mentioned, but those workers were let go, and we haven't been fined for improper disposal since then. I won't let a handful of lazy deadbeat antisocials tarnish this plant's reputation forever."

"Oh? So now this plant being here isn't about uplifting the poor, misunderstood denizens of the Shadow Zone?" Jia snorted.

"Of course it is." Malachi recovered his composure, along with his plastic smile. "Luminous River is fully invested in improving the Shadow Zone. As I said earlier, mutual benefit."

"But it doesn't hurt to have cheaper workers you can blame for being sloppy when things go bad," Erik observed. "Especially since most believe far worse about people in the Shadow Zone. It sounds like you've got a lot of convenient excuses working for you."

"I think you're misunderstanding me." Malachi pressed his mouth in a thin line and took a deep breath through his nose. "Those fines are old news. I'm sure you're already looking through all the records as part of your investigation. These last few months in particular have been great. What happened was unfortunate, but why would anyone murder a person in QA when our production numbers and quality were all topnotch?"

Jia narrowed her eyes, suspicion almost radiating off her. "That's a very good question."

"Detectives," Emma transmitted directly to Erik and Jia. "Just to be careful, I *borrowed* access to several cameras and drones in the area. Ten flitters are approaching rapidly from the south, all matching descriptions of vehicles registered Uptown but stolen. We have to assume altered transponders, but that's not the important part. They all contain men holding weapons, including two with rocket launchers."

Jia spun toward Malachi. "You need to evacuate the plant immediately."

The manager scoffed. "We're in the middle of a shift."

"That's a police order. We have people flying in from the south with heavy weapons. I doubt they're here for a pollution protest. Now *evacuate the plant!*" Jia stomped over to him and glared at him, her face right in his. "Or I'll make sure you're charged with reckless endangerment and whatever else I can think up if anyone gets hurt."

"This would never happen Uptown." Malachi stepped away from Jia, sighed, and tapped his PNIU a few times. Ear-splitting alarms sounded from all around the plant grounds. Bright flashing blue and white orbs appeared above every building and along the fence.

"Warning!" shouted a stern female voice. The sound overlapped from speakers spread throughout the complex and even Malachi's PNIU. "Mandatory evacuation is in effect. Fire suppression and chemical containment protocols may be deployed. Please evacuate to your designated north-side safety zone. Do not approach the south side. I repeat, do not approach the south side."

"We have security," Malachi shouted over the alarm. "They're trained for this. I'm sure this is just some local gang trying a shakedown. You're overreacting."

"Or the people who murdered Victoria," Jia replied, gesturing toward the sky. "Get your security ready. We've got ten flitters incoming, with at least two rocket launchers."

"R-rocket launchers?" Malachi swallowed, looking at the sky. "That does sound dangerous."

Jia ran toward the MX 60, yelling over her shoulder, "Make sure all the workers have armed guards with them as they evacuate! We don't know what the other guys are planning. This could be a massacre if we don't handle it aggressively."

"You have about three minutes before they arrive," Emma reported.

"Do whatever you can to stop the bastards with the rocket launchers," Erik ordered, sprinting behind Jia. "And get cop reinforcements here yesterday."

"I don't have any weapons, Detective. Hacking a flitter control system remotely isn't that—"

"We'll get our gear, and then you get up there. Ram them if you have to. If you can bring even one down, it'll be worth it." Jia opened her side of the flitter as he reached it.

Emma scoffed. "Perhaps you forget, *I'm* in this vehicle. If it is destroyed, I'll perish as well."

"We fight people all the time who could blow our heads off." Erik caught the TR-7 as Jia tossed it to him. "Risk your own damned life if you want respect."

Jia grabbed grenades and stuffed them in her pockets. She reached into the back to snag a tactical vest and threw it to Erik before taking one for herself. "We don't have a lot of options or time here, Emma."

"Risking a unique AI to save fleshbags you don't even know," Emma grumbled. "It's not a good trade, but I'll see what I can do."

CHAPTER FIFTEEN

Erik stuffed magazines into his pockets like a desperate man hoarding food after starving for weeks.

Jia swept the sky with an assault rifle. He didn't worry about this being a sign of a relapse into bloodthirstiness. A woman didn't show up to fight rocket launchers with a stun pistol.

He looked over his shoulder.

Ten dots jerked and wove in the distance. He had done some maintenance work on the laser rifle and the launcher the previous evening, but it wasn't like he could fly back home to pick them up. They'd need to rely on Emma to contain the rocket launchers. He'd handle everyone else with the TR-7.

Loud rifle fire erupted from the security towers. If the snipers could take down the flitters before they rained hellfire on a chemical plant, it would help. The thick, reinforced walls of the containment tank might be able to take a beating, but Erik didn't want to bet anyone's life on how well they could take multiple direct rocket hits or even a direct collision with a flitter.

Emma hadn't given any indication the vehicles were fitted with explosives, but that didn't mean it was certain. She could see more than the average human, but sensors missed things.

Erik backed away from the MX 60 and slid his TR-7 off his shoulder before selecting four-barrel mode. The dots resolved into flitters. They broke formation, all heading different directions. Emma activated full power, and the MX 60 tore into the sky.

Malachi watched as the luxury flitter zoomed into the sky. "You're evacuating your flitter? I get that it's expensive, but it's hardly the fir—"

"Shut it," Jia ordered. "We're trying to stop a chemical spill, not save Erik's bank account. You might know something about managing a chemical plant, but we've got a lot more experience with violent criminals and terrorists."

Malachi nodded quickly and took another step away from Jia, his lip trembling even though he towered over her. Erik chuckled.

The manager might not be able to hear Emma, but he should have at least assumed they weren't totally self-interested. A bright yellow indicator arrow appeared in Erik's smart lenses.

"I'm marking the other flitter with known heavy weapons," Emma reported. "I'll handle the blue one with some absurd stratagem that unnecessarily risks my existence." She infused the words with thick derision.

"*Now* you're really learning from us." Erik spun until he was lined up with the second vehicle. Any regrets about not grabbing his heavy weapons vanished as he watched the erratic flight path of his target. Attacking fixed ground targets was easier than defending against moving aerial enemies.

The approaching flitters bobbed, wove, and rolled. Erik couldn't help but be impressed by the maneuvers.

It was too bad he'd have to kill the people pulling them off.

Rifle fire continued from the towers. All the impressive dodging might keep the approaching flitters from taking disabling hits, but it was also slowing their approach. Every second of delay meant another second for reinforcements to arrive.

It was time for Erik to add his efforts. He lifted his gun and lined up a shot, not bothering with aim assist. In situations like this, it could not take all the variables into account as well as he could from thirty years of experience. The TR-7 came alive, spitting out a burst. He was glad they were in the Zone where the skies weren't choked with flitters.

"The more they're dodging, the less they're shooting," Erik noted.

Emma sped toward her prey. Erik jaw tightened as the MX 60 closed on the other flitter and flew right in front of it. The suspects' flitter banked to the left at the last moment, avoiding the collision but keeping them away. He had to trust that the AI's desire for self-preservation would keep her from doing anything too crazy, but after his speech and his examples over the last year, that might be hoping too much.

One of the other flitters spun out of control after

several more sniper shots.

It rolled as it plummeted to the ground, crashing outside the fence. A cloud of smoke and debris billowed into the sky. More approaching flitters spiraled out of control, one crashing into the fence and ripping through it with a resounding crunch. It flipped onto its side and skidded into a building, embedding itself in the wall.

"That's going to leave a mark." Erik chuckled.

With a flash of red and yellow, a rocket shot from the back of the yellow flitter, Erik's target. Another rocket blasted from the blue flitter. Neither was heading toward the MX 60 or Erik or Jia. The rockets sped along, leaving a trail of gray smoke.

Malachi groaned. "Oh, no. The repair costs al—"

The first rocket exploded against a security tower. Burning men careened to the ground, screaming and waving their arms. The second rocket took out another tower, but this time, the guards leapt out before impact. The steep drop was survivable, but not without broken legs.

"Get your people out of there," Jia shouted to Malachi.

"I-I don't control that. The security chief does, and..." Malachi's teeth chattered. "This is ridiculous! *Why is this happening?*"

"Yeah, good question," Erik muttered.

Malachi yelped and crouched, his hands over his head even though the damaged towers were not close.

Emma charged the blue flitter again, forcing him off-course. Another rocket ripped away from the back of the vehicle, but the awkward angle sent it past its likely target, another security tower, and it exploded against a fence.

"Keep up the pressure, Emma," Erik yelled. "You just saved some fleshbag lives."

"Don't tempt me to stop," she muttered. "Backup en route, arriving soon."

Erik took a deep breath and fired at the yellow flitter again. It was over a hundred meters away and waggling like an animal having a seizure. A moment later, smoke trailed from the vehicle. Overlapping gunshots followed from deeper in the plant, joining Erik's and Jia's.

The vehicle pitched to its side as it sped toward the ground. The flitter passed over the fence and smashed into a small building near the corner of the grounds. A massive explosion ripped the flitter apart and blew off the side of the building, tossing small sharp burning chunks of the vehicle and the wall into the air.

"That's why you don't carry a lot of explosives in your flitter." Erik smirked triumphantly.

Jia fired a few more rounds before giving him an incredulous look. "Are you *serious?*"

"That's advice for other people," he clarified, waving a hand. "Not for us. We haven't been blown up by our own ammo."

She shook her head, looking at the attackers. "The month just started."

Another enemy flitter crashed on the road outside the fence line, skidding, but the survivors had dressed their rough formation and were headed toward a corner of the complex—the one previously defended by two now-smoking towers. No one fired from the far towers, the guards more concerned with avoiding missiles.

"There's a problem," Emma reported.

Erik grunted. "Other than the army that's about to land?"

Emma broke away from the blue flitter, which slowed and dropped toward the ground in preparation for landing inside the fence with the rest of the enemies. "My armor held, but they got a few lucky hits on the grav emitters. I'm being forced down. I should be able to repair enough of the damage to get back to regular flight, but it'll take a few minutes."

"Time isn't our friend right now," Erik argued.

Jia pointed to the descending flitters. "They're nowhere near any of the main storage tanks."

"It's also easier to hit the tanks than the towers," Erik observed. "This must not just be about blowing up the plant."

"A large number of additional gun goblins appear to be en route on foot in multiple groups from additional directions," Emma explained. "They just emerged from different buildings in the nearby area. They're shooting out drones as they move closer, so it's not like they're stealth-minded. I've relayed their positions to the local Dispatch, but the first group is close to where the other flitters landed. The only security guards near the landing zone were in the destroyed towers. They are unconscious...at best."

Erik lost sight of the landing flitters after they descended behind a tall, wide building. "It doesn't matter if they're at the storage tanks." He jogged forward. "If they get inside, they can reach almost anywhere in the plant."

"Oh, the insurance premiums," murmured Malachi, who was cowering on the ground, his hands still over his head. "My quarterly bonus. Gone. I was going to buy a new flitter with that. Maybe even an MX 60."

A massive explosion erupted near the landing site. Additional alarms sounded.

"Warning! Warning! Fires now affect buildings B32 and B33. All personnel please evacuate while the fire is contained."

"What the hell happened, Emma?" Erik asked.

"They fired a rocket at a building near their landing site. They also threw grenades to blow a hole in the fence. Local police reinforcements are now in pitched battles with the reinforcements, and they have stopped the criminals' advance. The gathered forces are now at numbers you should be able to handle." A hint of boredom underlaid her tone. "Oh, now they're tossing smoke grenades. How quaint."

"How many guys can you see?" Erik pressed.

"I can directly observe thirty," Emma replied. "There are odd readings on someone still inside the blue flitter. I'm not able to get direct visual confirmation, but there's a high probability that he's a Tin Man with advanced levels of augmentation."

Jia hissed. "Talos."

"I doubt they'd run a fleet of flitters and rain rockets down, but if it *is* Talos, there's a reason they're attacking this plant." Erik inclined his head toward the plume of smoking rising from the corner of the complex. "Security and the local EZ have everything else locked down, and I think that might have been the point. It's a distraction."

Jia ejected her magazine and shoved a fresh one into her rifle. "Then let's offer a distraction of our own."

CHAPTER SIXTEEN

Jia and Erik sprinted between buildings, their point-to-point movement in sync without any words exchanged. A rocket hissed away from the concealed intruders, flying halfway across the plant before exploding against the side of another building. The attack wasn't close to a tank.

She narrowed her eyes. "They could easily have hit a tank now that they're on the ground. I think you're right about it being a distraction."

"Yeah." Erik sprinted to the cover of a new building and flattened his back against the wall. The dense, dark smoke in the area drifted throughout the area, overwhelming the buildings.

Thick white powder floated in the heated air—fire retardant. The flickering red, yellow, and orange from the flames diminished with each passing second, victims of the retardant, but the fire-control system could do little about the outdoor smoke. Shadowy outlines of men, guns, and flitters lay in the distance. Erik raised his hand to signal Jia to move up. He counted down with his fingers.

Jia and Erik sprinted forward and sprayed the rifles into the smoke. A suspect screamed and fell to the ground. Men rushed behind the flitters for cover before returning fire. Their outlines were the only thing visible, turning the whole encounter into a bizarre and lethal shadow-puppet show.

Jia and Erik ran between two buildings. The suspects shouted to each other.

Jia squeezed off a few shots, frowning as she tried to concentrate. The constant gunfire smothered the men's shouts, but that wasn't what was confusing her. Tones rose and fell with their words. They weren't speaking English, and they weren't speaking Mandarin, either.

"Oh," she declared. "They're speaking Cantonese!"

While Jia hadn't mastered all Chinese dialects, her mother had insisted that learning Cantonese was a necessity because of their relatives in Hong Kong. Other than through correspondence, Jia had not met those relatives, but it never hurt to learn a new language.

Active machine translation made for a slightly awkward experience, and Lan Lin wouldn't insult a relative by not speaking to them in their preferred language without machine aid.

"My Cantonese sucks unless it's about ordering booze or food. It's all on you." Erik nailed another man with a burst. "What are they saying?"

"They're telling their 'big brother' to get into the building, and they'll handle the security guards," Jia commented. She jerked back, a bullet whizzing by her head. "I don't think they realize cops were here from the beginning. That means it has nothing to do with us."

"Probably, and 'big brother?'" Erik emptied his magazine. "As in, a triad?"

"Unless it just happens to be a heavily armed family." Jia popped off a single shot, nailing one man in the head. His shadowy form jerked, and he fell onto his back. "I don't know if I'm relieved it's not Talos or annoyed."

"I don't care as long as it ends with fewer breathing scumbags."

A tall, broad-shouldered form emerged from deeper in the smoke, the outline of a huge machine gun in his arms. He swiveled toward Erik and Jia. The machine gun screamed to life, vomiting a stream of bullets. Both detectives jumped back. His gunfire shredded the corner of the building providing their cover, knocking off pieces that pelted their bodies and faces. The deafening roar overwhelmed the other sounds. A long moment passed before the machine gun ceased fire, and its owner jogged back into the smoke. His friends opened fire, keeping Erik and Jia pinned.

"There's a good probability that is our Tin Man," Emma reported. "I can't get a clear visual, and since my body's down, I don't have good line-of-sight to use the other sensors, but thermals from borrowed drones strongly suggest it."

"I'm betting he's big bro," Erik muttered. "Whatever they're planning, they must think they can pull it off quickly. If it's not Talos, they're well-equipped gangsters, and it's only a matter of time before the local cops overwhelm their reinforcements."

"The Tin Man has entered a building currently blocked from your line of sight," Emma reported. She provided a navigation arrow for Erik and Jia. A small diagram displaying the building layout winked into existence. Flashing lines traced a possible path to the destination building either straight through the gangsters or by hugging another building and coming in from their side.

"We don't have time to mess around." Jia yanked a plasma grenade out of her pocket. "Time to clear the jungle a little?"

Erik raised his brow in surprise. "Uh, zero to kill in two seconds there?"

"I think I was at kill before they landed."

The triad soldiers fired a steady stream of shots, keeping Erik and Jia from advancing. The criminals didn't stop talking, but the only thing they were offering was profanities concerning Erik's and Jia's mothers and their employment prospects as prostitutes.

"This isn't a conspiracy trap," Jia hissed. "They don't have an army of full-conversion Tin Men." She primed the grenade. "They've been trying to distract us from the beginning by hitting us from all sides and purposely drawing fire in the air. If we waste too much time here taking all these guys down, their big brother is going to pull off whatever he's planning. I've got plenty of magazines, and Emma can watch my back. I'll stall them. When I make my move, get ready to take the flanking path and go have a heart to heart with big bro."

A stiff wind parted the smoke, revealing a clearer view of some of the gangsters. All wore full breather masks. They had pulled their wounded behind the flitters. Others dropped to reload while their comrades popped up to fire. It was decent tactical discipline for a group of antisocial thugs. Despite the wind, enough smoke remained for Jia's plan to work.

"Give us target highlights, Emma," Jia ordered. "We need to make sure none of these guys sneaks up on Erik."

"Of course. I don't have access to the cameras inside. You're on your own there."

Red outlines appeared for each gangster. All the active shooters remained clustered behind their vehicles, but big brother had already made it into the building. There was no highlight for him.

Erik nodded slowly, tightening his grip on his TR-7. "You're not allowed to get killed by this batch of losers."

Jia snorted in dismissal. "The only reason I'm telling you to go is that we don't have enough time. For all we know, he's going to hack the system and blow the plant that way. Don't worry. I'm not going down to less than a room full of *yaoguai* or aliens." She shrugged. "Or well-armed bikini babes."

"I'd pay good money to see that," Erik noted.

"I bet you would," she replied.

They stared into each other's eyes. Jia's stomach tightened. This was what her future held—her life constantly in danger from dangerous, ruthless killers—but as long as she had Erik?

She wouldn't care.

Jia primed the grenade and screamed in Cantonese, "Stop talking about my mother that way!" She hurled the grenade in a beautiful, smooth arc. Her scream of feigned rage followed as she fired without aiming.

"It's a grenade," yelled a gangster.

Erik launched himself from the ground, his legs

pumping in a dead sprint. The gangsters threw themselves on the ground. The grenade released its brilliant white death, consuming half a flitter. A larger secondary explosion ripped the flitter apart, bowled over several men, and ripping chunks off other vehicles. Jia was beginning to wonder if the Lady was trying to tell her something about keeping too many explosives in a vehicle.

Jia didn't stop to think about it. Instead, she took the opportunity to nail the exposed downed men with quick single shots. She swept her rifle back and forth. Not every shot hit a gangster, but the survivors rolled behind the flitters.

She laid down cover fire in the direction of Erik's destination.

Her partner turned the corner, continuing his run. The crackle of the fire and the moans of wounded and dying joined the gunfire near and distant to conceal his movements. The enemy was down to half their original strength, but it didn't matter. Transfixed by Jia's assault, none of them saw Erik run into the building.

Jia's mocking laughter rose above the chaotic din. "Give it up. You'll never win."

"Shut your mouth, bitch," a gangster shouted back.

"Okay, fine. Be that way." Jia punctuated her taunt with a burst of fire, producing another curse from the guy.

CHAPTER SEVENTEEN

Erik rushed through the smoking, burning hole into the building. A massive plaque near the remains of the door read B32.

The gangsters' attack had opened a path into what appeared to the blasted and scarred remains of a narrow conference room.

Half-burned furniture lay strewn about, covered in fine white powder. Charred pieces of a long table covered the floor. The fire suppression system had done its work, even if dense smoke filled the room. Erik waved his hand, clearing some of it out, then covering his mouth with his arm.

Another explosion shook the building, followed by a loud Cantonese curse. Erik rushed out of the conference room onto a production floor. The smoke remained concentrated in the conference room, barely bothering his eyes or lungs as he emerged into a complex web of pipes and squad storage tanks the height of a tall man.

Most of the pipes led out of the cavernous room, either

outside or to other buildings. Metal stairways stood at several places.

They twisted upward, leading to small landings set next to manual valves spread throughout the floor. Drones hovered, oblivious and not caring about the alarms. Holographic data windows hovered in front of interface stations scattered throughout the structure, showing streams of numbers and graphs.

The Tin Man was somewhere in this jumble of industrial technology.

Smoke drifted upward from a dense patch of pipes. Erik turned toward it since heavy footsteps had sounded from there. A few seconds later, a huge man emerged from behind some pipes. He carried a belt-fed machine gun longer than Erik's laser rifle with one hand as he jogged down the side of the room. He had a crate in the other arm, the source of his ammo.

"Looks like I found our Tin Man," Erik whispered. He raised his TR-7 and put his finger over the trigger.

He needed to take out the machine gun first.

A holographic display flashed next to him. Erik grunted in surprise. The gangster spun toward him. Erik leapt behind a pipe wider than his body before the machine gun spat bullets his way. He landed hard on a metal grating that revealed drainage channels beneath the main production floor. The bullets bounced off the pipe, sparking and producing small cracks. It wasn't as bad as shooting a heavy weapon in a ship in deep space, but it was close.

"You sure it's smart to shoot at me in here?" Erik shouted. "I don't know what they're pumping through, but unless you have lung implants, it might end up as a bad day for you, too. I'm *not* security. I'm Detective Erik Blackwell, NSCPD. This is your last chance to surrender before you get shot."

"Screw you, cop," the gangster snarled. "You're not leaving alive." The machine gun roared, and a shower of sparks cascaded off the pipe.

"Emma, how worried should I be?" Erik asked.

"There are numerous chemicals in use in the plant that are poisonous to humans," Emma replied. "There are also several that could explode under the right circumstances. Since I don't have current low-level access to the systems, I can't tell you which chemical might be in any given pipe, tube, or storage tank. I would *not* recommend testing your luck."

Erik snickered as he looked over his shoulder. "*Damn.* For once, I wish I had a stun pistol. I didn't grab any stun grenades, either. This might get hairy."

"What's the matter, cop?" the gangster shouted, his voice muffled when steam released. "You thought you could take me down, didn't you?"

"I know I can take you down," Erik yelled back. "So just keep being an idiot, and I'll try to make this quick for the both of us. I haven't eaten and am a bit hungry!"

"Reinforcements are moving closer," Emma reported. "Detective Lin has the gun goblins outside suppressed. Many are severely wounded, and those who aren't are in no position to reinforce their associate."

The gangster's gun fell silent, and his steps suggested he was running off. Erik bolted from cover. He just needed the Tin Man to enter a hallway or another room, and it'd be over.

Erik zigzagged between pipes and partitions, presenting only seconds of exposure for his enemy. His prey turned and fired a burst, striking a nearby storage tank. A clear liquid Erik hoped was water leaked out of several holes. Another shot ripped into a pipe in the back of the room. A green liquid sprayed everywhere, hissing and sizzling as it splattered on the ground.

Definitely not water.

"Yeah, I'll try to not get that on me," Erik muttered. "I think fighting in the Scar was less annoying." He moved, trying to close the distance. The gangster bellowed in challenge and fired again. Bullets nailed Erik in the chest. He grunted in pain, tumbling behind a storage tank. His TR-7 clattered across the grating, sliding away. Another machine gun burst struck the weapon, knocking it even farther in the opposite direction.

"He had to have half a brain," Erik hissed and sat up, a stinging sensation radiating through his chest. He patted the vest, finding embedded bullets and deep dents.

A medpatch could take care of the bruising, but he didn't want to challenge a machine gun directly again. Even a military-grade tactical vest would have trouble taking that kind of punishment. He should know.

He'd seen them fail under constant fire.

"Not so tough now, are you, cop?" the Tin Man taunted. "I've heard about you. I made the right call in coming here today. Not only do I get what I need, but I get to kill a famous cop." He swept back and forth with his gun, the cacophony of the echoing gunfire a painful drumbeat in Erik's ears. Whether by dumb luck or a merciful Lady, there were no other chemical spills. The gun fell silent.

Erik considered peeking around the corner. Something clanged hard, metal grating rattling.

"Can you help me, Emma?" Erik asked.

"I've taken the liberty of borrowing a drone," Emma offered. "He's out of ammo and he's dropped his weapon. He's running."

Erik yanked his pistol out of his holster and jumped to his feet. He didn't have time to go back for the TR-7 and keep up with the suspect. Rushing toward the fleeing Tin Man, he fired several rounds. They struck the man square in the back. The gangster stumbled, but he didn't fall.

"Little extra armor, too, huh?" Erik complained. He lowered his gun to take the more difficult shot and take out a leg, but the Tin Man disappeared through an open door into a small side room.

Erik shot a few more times on his way. "Give it up. You're going down, big bro. You picked the wrong day to go after this place. You don't have to leave in a body bag, but that means you need to surrender right damned now because I'm getting a little tired of this game of lead tag."

A drone descended and hovered into the room. A chair flew up and smacked into it. Both furniture and drone flew out of Erik's sight, but he could guess the fate, given the loud crash that followed.

"I take it you don't need me to tell you what side of the room he's on?" Emma asked.

"Nah, I think I can figure that out, even with my tiny fleshbag brain. But thanks."

Erik slowed to a jog and took a deep breath. He wanted to take the suspect alive, but that didn't mean he was going to risk getting killed to do it. If Jia hadn't forced Malachi to immediately order an evacuation, a lot of innocent workers might have ended up dead. Ruthless men required ruthless solutions.

If a bullet to the chest didn't do it, a bullet to the brain would.

His jog became a walk. The small room was for storage, sparsely filled with racks of full-body protective suits and breathers.

"Now I find them."

Erik paused at the door, listening but not hearing anything but a light hum from the machinery around him and the whir of the surviving drones. He spun to his side to find this target and found two chairs flying toward him instead. He managed to get off several shots before a chair collided with his right arm, bending it back and knocking his pistol out of his hand. A quick swipe with his left arm knocked the other chair out of the way just in time to reveal the charging Triad Tin Man.

"Die, cop!" the gangster screamed, his eyes wide open and hand curled into a fist descending.

His punch connected with Erik's vest with a crunch. The minor sting blossomed into a fiery burn. Erik stumbled backward. Without the protective vest, the gangster might have caved his chest in with the blow. The gangster must have realized the same thing, because he stepped back, his face contorted in irritation and shaking out his fist. Erik knew all too well that even the dulled pain in many cybernetic limbs could be distracting.

Erik gritted his teeth in pain. He shook his head and cracked his knuckles. "Don't make promises you can't keep, asshole."

"You're nothing without your gun."

"Try me again, and we'll see if that's true."

The two men warily circled each other, neither willing to make the next move. Erik had the advantage. The longer he stalled, the more chance he had of police or security reinforcements showing up.

The triad had launched the distraction operation to insert the Tin Man into the plant, which meant there was something inside they needed. They had to know that if they didn't act quickly, they would be overwhelmed. That same desperation would push the gangster to make a stupid move.

"You think I've never killed a cop before?" The gangster gave a feral grin. "You think I won't now?"

"I think you've never killed a cop like me." Erik threw a punch with his left arm. The gangster snorted and didn't even try to block. His head snapped back as the powerful blow struck home.

He staggered back, blood pouring from his nose, his eyes rolling up in the back of his head. "You've got...hardware...too."

"And here I thought it was all over the net." Erik grinned as the man pitched forward and landed with an unceremonious groan. "But yeah, I do. Surprise." He took a deep breath, wincing at his cracked ribs. "Jia, you okay?"

"I'm fine," she transmitted. "I was just securing the scene before heading in there to help you. I take it you're okay?"

"I've got our big bro. He underestimated me."

"Does 'got' mean you've arrested him, or does it mean you blew his head off?"

"Nah, he's still alive." Erik nudged the man with his foot. "I'm sure he'll have interesting stuff to tell us. By the way, you still have medpatches on you?"

"I used the ones I had to stabilize some of the suspects," Jia replied.

"I've repaired the emitters," Emma explained. "There are still several inside my body."

"You know," Erik looked around a moment before focusing back on the comatose body, "that sounds weird coming from you."

CHAPTER EIGHTEEN

October 1, 2229, Neo Southern California Metroplex, Police Enforcement Zone 122 Station, Interrogation Room

Jia paced in front of the table. Their suspect was chained to the chair, thin silver coils around his arm—cybernetic inhibitors, unusual restraints for an unusual man. He glared at Erik and Jia defiantly.

Erik yawned and patted his mouth. "Shit. Making us work overtime. Why couldn't you have attacked that place in the morning? Plus, you're lucky the guys at the armory can patch it up for me."

"You're worried about your gun?" The suspect sneered. "How are your ribs?"

"Fine." Erik patted his ribs. "Medpatches took care of them right away. How's the face? It's looking pretty messed up. Oh, I forgot. It looked like that *before* I knocked your ass out."

"Screw you, cop," the gangster growled as he struggled

against his bonds. "When I get out of here, I'll finish you off."

"You had your best shot at doing it already, and you lost. If we go at it again, it's going to end with four bullets in your brain, not my fist in your face."

"You were pretty brazen," Jia interjected. "Attacking a place in broad daylight while cops were there. Even if we hadn't been there, that facility has great security."

"It would have worked," the gangster insisted. "Cops were there before they should have been."

Jia tapped her PNIU. A mug shot of the suspect appeared, though he was years younger, a teenager. "Harry Hui, born and raised in the Greater Hong Kong metroplex." She clucked her tongue. "You're really lucky, Mr. Hui. Despite getting arrested for multiple thefts when you were younger, you didn't get transported. They let you get out after a little jail time. A lot of people have ended up on the colonies for a lot less."

"You should think about why that might be, cop." Hui bared his teeth. "You think I don't have connections?"

Jia rolled her eyes. "Is that supposed to be intimidating?" She dropped into a seat and smiled sweetly. "You don't get it, do you, Mr. Hui? This isn't Hong Kong. This is Neo SoCal. Whatever cops *your* triad bought off over there aren't here to save you." She narrowed her eyes, her sweet demeanor disappearing under her mask of hostility. "And you attacked a chemical plant and attempted to murder police officers," she added, her voice infused with utter contempt.

"The CID has sent us a bunch of info on you. We know that you belong to the Eternal Dragons, and the CID and

HKPD have been looking for enough evidence to nail you to the wall." She waved a hand across the table. "You're not walking this time, Hui. You're not even going to get off with transportation. We haven't even bothered to check all your hardware yet. I doubt it's all legal. You're going to prison. It's just a matter of how many decades your sentence will be."

"You can't do shit to me," Hui strained against his chains, but his arms failed him. He leaned forward, his eyes dangerous. "You think you're special, but you're nothing before the Eternal Dragons."

"You still don't get it, do you?" Erik shook his head. "Your little attempt to hide as you murdered Victoria Dwazil didn't work."

"You've got nothing. No DNA, no case."

"We've got a matching gait analysis—unless there's some other cyborg who walks exactly like you and decided to murder a woman linked to that plant."

"You're not going to send me up with that." Hui scoffed. "That case is weaker than you."

"Says the man who got knocked out in one hit." The corners of Erik's lips turned up. "Just saying."

"Don't get too comfortable, Hui." Jia looked incredulous. "We don't even *need* to link you to Victoria Dwazil's murder to send you to prison. We have enough with your stupid stunt at the plant, not to mention your attempted murder of us, but we want the whole plan." She pointed at him. "And you know what I think? I think you panicked. Something went very wrong, which was why you attacked the plant."

Hui turned his head to the side and sneered. "You're not

getting anything from me. I've been tortured by triads before. You don't scare me. I don't care. Do whatever you think you're going to do to me."

Erik leaned back in his chair, his arms folded. "But prison isn't safe like it used to be, not that it was that safe to begin with. I'm sure you heard about that incident, right? You end up in the wrong prison, you might be eaten by a hungry *yaoguai*."

A flicker of fear passed over Hui's face. Even monsters feared bigger monsters.

"Do yourself a favor," Erik suggested. "Give us what we need about Victoria Dwazil, and you might be able to shave a few years off your sentence and end up in a safe prison."

Hui's face hardened and he hocked up a huge glob of spittle, almost hitting Erik. "I'll never betray my brothers. I'd be strangling you if I didn't have these inhibitors on."

Jia rolled her eyes. "No, you'd be getting your ass knocked out again."

October 2, 2229, Neo Southern California Metroplex, Police Enforcement Zone 122 Station, Office of Detectives Jia Lin and Erik Blackwell

Jia's eyes darted back and forth as she perused the list of names on the window floating in front of her. It was almost sad, a list of young men who were throwing away their futures. If they had the discipline to resist police interrogation, they had the discipline to hold down an honest job.

"Have you seen this list?" she asked.

Erik looked up from the document he was reading. "The likely triad members list the HKPD sent over?"

"Yes." Jia nodded. "I'm surprised they have a good idea of who the members are, but they haven't been arrested. They must have done *something* they could get nailed for."

"Maybe, but going after an organization and missing can be worse than waiting until they've made more mistakes." Erik shrugged. "And you heard what Hui said. They've paid off some people, but helping bust this triad will mean the CID and the good cops over there can clean out the trash, just like we've done here. By waiting, the entire organization can be taken out in one major sweep."

Jia nodded, satisfied by the idea of indirectly helping destroy another group of criminals, on top of catching a murderer. "I'm also surprised how quickly the HKPD sent us this list."

He raised an eyebrow. "Why?"

"Because that means Hui is overestimating his triad's influence. There's probably only a small number of bad cops in the mix, rather than it being a major organizational problem." Jia's brow wrinkled, the frustration on her face plain. "The interrogations of his lackeys aren't giving us much. It sounds like they didn't know what the hell was even going on and were just brought along for muscle. The only useful thing we've gotten is the man who mentioned they'd been told the cops were about to search the plant. It confirms what we heard from Hui."

"Yeah, at least that explains the desperate daylight raid. And the truth is, we were lucky."

"How?" Jia asked.

"If we hadn't had Emma filter all that data, it might

have taken us days to figure out the link between Victoria and the plant, let alone Archangel." Erik nodded at his data window. "Most cops don't have access to that kind of independent AI."

Emma appeared and bowed. "You're welcome."

Erik continued, "And without that link, the triad would have had more time to get whatever they were looking for, probably without going all-out."

He slid a hand through the air, and an ornate triangular emblem with two inscribed intertwined dragons appeared. Eternal Dragons was written in ornate hanzi along the bottom.

Jia snorted. "Fancy symbols don't make them any less than scum. Suits don't make them gentlemen."

"I'm not disagreeing." Erik offered a shrug. "According to the report the CID sent," he began, "their primary base remains in Hong Kong. Our boy is a mid-level lieutenant at best, even if he was in charge of local ops."

"Sure. I get it. This was an expansion attempt. I'm used to that now, but that doesn't answer the question of what they were doing with that plant, and what this has to do with Victoria Dwazil's murder. If we can't get him to talk, we might not find the link. But..." Jia looked to the side for a moment in thought before making hand gestures to summon another data window. "Hmm. Did you get a chance to look through the part of the report where it talks about income streams?"

Erik shook his head. "Not yet. I'm sure it's exciting."

"Justice can be exciting."

"Sometimes."

Jia pointed at her window. "It's a lot of the standard

organized crime things you'd expect, but the Eternal Dragons have a specialty that might be relevant. They like to extend their initial influence in a city via the indirect capture of specialty waste management subcontractors, usually with a front company."

"Huh," Erik replied. "I can see how that'd be useful for them. It's also downright subtle by the standards of the organized crime left in Neo SoCal."

"Exactly." Jia lowered her hand. "Simply flying in and attempting to shake people down won't work anymore. The corrupt officials and police have been mostly purged. The only thing left is to behave as if you're worried about the police, which makes them harder to catch."

Erik snickered. "I'm not sure stabbing a woman through the heart with a pole meets anyone's definition of subtle."

"No, it doesn't," Jia agreed. "Normal people commit stupid crimes when they're desperate, so what does that imply about desperate criminals? Especially ones who might be more brutal than bright?"

Erik thought for a moment. "You think the Dwazil murder was about them worrying about the NSCPD searching the plant?"

Jia shook her head. "The timeline doesn't work out. From what the underling said, they'd decided to do the raid because they'd heard it was going to happen. But we weren't raiding the plant, we were just doing an investigation. That means they don't have a direct line to the 1-2-2."

"If the manager was complaining to someone about the police showing up, it might have gotten back to them," Erik suggested. "I don't think he was in bed with the triad. He doesn't seem like he'd have the stomach for it, but he also seems like the kind of guy who'd bitch about minor inconveniences. If the triad had an interest in that plant, they might have had someone on the inside who heard him."

"But if they did have a mole, why did they go through all that trouble? If we weren't there, they probably would have gotten in and out, but they still would have taken casualties. That means whatever's in that plant is something worth dying for." Jia hissed in frustration. "We're missing something. We have to get Hui to talk." Her pained expression disappeared, replaced by a satisfied smile. "Or we go at this sideways."

"Sideways?" Erik raised a brow in interest. "How so?"

"His lackeys might not have known why they needed to attack the plant, but it wasn't like he flew them in yesterday." Jia swiped through the air, the data window in front of her changing to display different data. She stopped on a list of names and dates and inclined her head toward it. "Most of them have been here for months, and that means they have to know the basics of the local operations. We haven't been asking them the right questions."

Erik's grin mirrored hers. "Asking them where their base is might not work. Telling them to give up the waste company might."

"Exactly." Jia stood with a determined look. "They didn't volunteer the information, but they also thought we wouldn't know. Let's go squeeze one of the little brothers and find out where we need to raid."

CHAPTER NINETEEN

A few hours later, Erik stomped out of the MX 60 and over to the closest uniformed officer. "What the hell is all this?"

She blinked. "Detective Blackwell? It's...a raid. The one you helped coordinate." She looked toward the MX 60, a desperate plea in her eyes.

Jia sighed and stepped out of the flitter. She hurried after her partner, shaking her head.

Since the waste management company in question was in the Shadow Zone, Captain Ragnar had contacted the captain of the local enforcement zone to coordinate a raid. Erik and Jia were supposed to have led it, but a chance message revealed that the raid had already been launched. Erik and Jia had rushed to the scene, and judging by the lack of drawn weapons, it was already over.

Dozens of police flitters were parked around the modest Shadow Zone building, which was tucked away in a small, clean commercial district. The triads knew how to fake respectability. Uniformed officers kept the curious crowd away, while others streamed in and out of the building. Besides the lack of drawn weapons or concerned looks, there wasn't a single bound suspect anywhere in the area. There was no way they'd raided the place and sent everyone off that quickly.

"Who's in charge here?" Erik demanded, squaring his shoulders and looming over the uniformed officer.

"Over there, Detective." She swallowed and pointed to a suited detective chatting with several other officers, gesturing energetically. Erik headed toward him, his angry gaze fixed on the man.

The other detective looked up with a smile. "Ah, Blackwell. Nice of you to join us." He extended his hand. "Detective Corzone."

"Why did this go down already?" Erik demanded, almost growling, and not accepting his hand. "I don't normally get bent out of shape about people trying to steal my collar, but this was all us from the beginning, and it might be our final case."

"Whoa." Detective Corzone raised his hands in front of him. "Calm down, Blackwell. You'll be getting all the credit. I promise you that. I'm one of the people who thought you got screwed by the CID over that Ceres thing last year. I'm not about stealing other people's glory."

Erik nodded, his heart pounding but his frown weakening. "Why the quick move?"

Detective Corzone shrugged. "We had to make a move. Our drone surveillance showed they were running. I'm sorry you didn't get the call until late, but we had to move fast to make sure we didn't lose track of all the bastards. Those guys are smarter than the average thug. They took out several drones when they ran."

Jia looked around the area. "Please don't tell me they all got away."

Detective Corzone clapped once. "No way in hell we'd let that happen." He inclined his head toward the building. "That place is empty of guys, but we already nailed almost all the vehicles that fled from the area, even with them using false transponder signals. We're coordinating with other EZs and the Militia to make sure we get the last few in case they try to run to the Scar. They left behind some equipment as well. They must have been in even more of a hurry than we expected. Be happy, Detectives. Once you pointed us at this place, that was all we needed. We've gutted this triad in Neo SoCal. They should call you 'the syndicate killers.'"

Erik took a deep breath and slowly let it out. His hands uncurled from the fists he hadn't known he was making. "Let us know if anything comes up. We still don't know what they were looking for in that plant."

"I'm sure we'll get it out of them." Detective Corzone offered a salute and a grin. "But will do, Detective. It's going to take a while to go through all this evidence, and we'll send copies of everything we have to you so you can check it, too. I'm sure when this is all over, there will be a lot of commendations to go around."

Erik walked back toward the MX 60, shaking his head, still frowning. Jia walked beside him with a distant look in her eyes.

"They're not the same," Jia offered. "You need to keep that in mind."

Erik didn't speak until they arrived at the flitter. He looked at her. "Who's not the same?"

She looked around. "When we first became partners, we got used to having to do everything on our own because we couldn't trust anyone—the CID and the other EZs. Too much corruption, too much watching their backs, even from cops." Jia gestured grandly toward the gathered police. "Many of the Shadow Zone cops might as well have been paid employees of the syndicates back then. But it's not like that anymore, Erik. It's a good department, filled with good cops." She frowned and looked down at her PNIU, then slapped it and sighed.

He looked down but couldn't spy what was on her tablet. "What's wrong?"

"It's stupid." Jia rolled her eyes. "So *annoyingly* stupid."

"Then be stupid with me." Erik put a hand on her shoulder. "We've been running around so much lately, especially these last few days, it's been hard to take a breather and relax, just the two of us."

"That's kind of the problem," Jia offered, averting her eyes.

"Wait, you're mad because we haven't been able to go on a date?"

"No." Jia groaned. "It's my mother. I told her I had work today and we might not be able to come, and so she keeps calling to check. It's just a stupid party, but she's *obsessed* with it."

"The true terror, Lan Lin." Erik chuckled. "I hope this doesn't end with her killing me." He rolled his shoulders and surveyed the area. "I don't think there's much we can add here for now, but I've got an idea. I want to check something, and it'll require Emma's help."

"Of course it will," the AI interjected. "Like I said, Detective. Six months."

Erik released the yoke of the MX 60. "Take control, Emma." He tapped his PNIU to initiate a call to Malachi Lunt but routed the audio through his flitter.

The plant manager answered with a weary sigh. "I'm very, very busy, Detective. It's going to take several weeks to repair the damage, and days before we can get production up and running again. At this point, we're still assessing the damage and the impact on the plant."

"If it makes you feel any better, the local cops just nailed almost all the rest of the triad involved in the raid," Erik replied. "The Eternal Dragons won't be coming after you again."

"That's very nice for you and the future, but it doesn't fix my plant *right now*." Malachi moaned. "This is why we shouldn't do business in crap holes like this. I should have known it'd involve ridiculous gangster nonsense at some point. The Council must all be insane."

Jia's brow lifted. "So much for uplifting opportunities in economically disadvantaged areas."

"Having rockets showered on my plant changed my mind. All my bonuses. My promotion file! Those ignorant little thugs have harmed my future with the company."

"They also murdered a woman," Erik pointed out.

There was the barest of pauses. "Yes, that too."

"Those criminals wanted something in your plant," Jia explained to him. "Something most likely to do with

Archangel. Even though we've taken them down, we want to make sure there's nothing left over to come back and haunt us."

"What are you talking about?" Malachi sounded genuinely confused. "Angels? What do angels have to do with chemical plants and criminals?"

"It's a street drug," Erik explained. "Worse than Dragon Tear. One of those chemicals that Victoria Dwazil was harassing you about, one that was being produced at higher levels than expected or wanted? It turns out it's an Archangel ingredient."

"W-what?" Malachi gasped. "Are you sure?"

"Yes. It also explains why the Eternal Dragons were so interested in this plant." Erik looked at Jia. She shrugged. Malachi might be selfish, but he also sounded surprised.

It also wouldn't make sense for him to risk getting shot or blown up to help the triads get into the plant. As the plant manager, he could have easily given them access without the need for a dramatic raid.

"I had no idea," Malachi insisted. "I swear to you. I would never be involved in something like that. You have to believe me. Oh, no. You're going to ship me off to some horrible prison where they feed you to *yaoguai*, aren't you?" He sniffled. "Please. I know I don't have a family, but I deserve something better."

Erik cleared his throat. "Unless you actively knew about the Archangel production, no, Mr. Lunt, we're not going to do that. You haven't committed a crime, to our knowledge. But we do need your cooperation."

"My…cooperation?" Malachi asked hesitantly.

"There's a little thing we want to do. We have some

special sensors, and we want to inspect your plant to see if we can find anything unusual. If we find anything from our aerial inspection, we'll want to bring in Forensics and have them do a fine-grained sweep."

Erik held his breath. If the plant manager agreed, they could pull the whole thing off without the delay of a warrant. Given Harry Hui's assault on the plant, there could be something time-sensitive they needed to recover. Erik's life might be easier when he was hunting down conspiracies and not having to worry as much about careful procedures and paperwork to hand over to prosecutors and judges.

"Please, do it right away!" Malachi nearly shouted into the phone. "I want it known that I'm fully cooperating with you. This is even a good time to do it. We're not even starting repairs today, and a lot of the employees were told to take the next few days yet. Oh, but…no, it couldn't be."

"What is it, Mr. Lunt?" Jia pressed.

"I'm not *accusing* anyone of anything, but two junior managers who work in the department are responsible for overseeing the compound in question." Malachi's short, ragged breaths broadcast his fear over the line. "Neither have come in to work the last few days. I've tried contacting them, but they didn't respond. I thought…"

"You thought what?"

"They'd requested time off a while ago, and I was annoyed when they didn't come back to work on time." Malachi laughed nervously. "The rumor was they were seeing each other, so I thought they also might have decided to run off to the moon, but they were good subordinates, so I told them I'd have to write them up but they could come back. I was going to contact them again before the incident distracted us. It honestly never occurred to me that they might have anything to do with Dwazil's murder, and I thought I was shielding them from being harassed by corporate."

"Give us their names," Jia ordered.

"Cameron Stavos and Jeri Aaron."

"Okay, we'll send someone to check on them," Erik responded. "We'll let you know if we need to bring in that Forensics team."

"Anything you need," Malachi assured. "I'm more than happy to help. In fact, I *insist* on it."

"We'll talk to you soon. Bye." Erik ended the call. "Emma, send a request to the captain to have someone go pick up those two for questioning."

"Very well, Detective."

Erik looked out the window at the plant below. From the air, the destroyed towers were the only evidence of the attack. The fence had already been repaired, and the triad flitters and bodies had been collected by the police. He could barely make out the hole in the one building from their height.

Jia pointed that way. "If we're going to do this, it probably would be around there. Hui entered the complex at that building for a reason. We've got to focus this search, or this might take days, if not weeks. As good as Emma's sensors are, this is a huge facility with a lot of unusual equipment."

"That's an accurate assessment," Emma agreed.

"Sounds like a good plan to me," Erik admitted. "Emma, keep us near buildings B32 and B33. Look for anything out of the ordinary. I don't know what that might be. It's not like I ever worked in a chemical plant."

The MX 60 floated gently toward the first building, dropping altitude and circling. At the lower altitude, the gaping hole was obvious, as were scorch marks from Jia's plasma grenade. Erik and Jia had discussed it and decided to leave the use of that little toy out of their report, and none of the other cops or Luminous River security had seemed keen to press them on it.

A couple of minutes passed, Erik, Jia, and Emma remaining silent.

"Interesting," Emma declared.

Erik looked at his camera displays. Emma shifted one display to be a multispectral overlay of building B32. The display showed not only the exterior but also the extensive internal machinery and pipe network, different features presented in different colors. Erik had no idea what everything meant, but he did notice a long, rectangular patch of darkness standing out among the colors. It mostly filled the conference room where he'd fought Hui.

He pointed toward the darkness. "What's wrong here?"

"Nothing's wrong. It's just interesting." Emma summoned a three-dimensional holographic representation of the map and rotated it, revealing that the patch of darkness lay beneath the room.

Jia stared at the hologram. "I don't understand. Is that some sort of hollow cavity?"

"Something like that, potentially," Emma explained. "It's a dead zone. I'm only aware it's there because I can check using a variety of sensors, but, for example, if you were only using thermal scanning, you would have passed it over since it would have blended in with the background."

Erik nodded slowly, his grin building with each nod. "We got you, Hui. Time to call in Forensics."

Erik stared into the gaping hole in the storage room floor. Forensics drones hovered near the ceiling. All had independently confirmed there was something unusual under the floor.

Digging followed, and at one meter, the team encountered an unexpected hard layer. At first, they thought they might have found a coffin, but the rigid box didn't contain a body, and the internal electronics and power source was further proof it wasn't for holding a corpse. After carving into the container with power tools, they discovered racks filled with small vials containing a dark liquid.

A forensics tech held a vial in his gloved hands, a thin silver probe inserted. He whistled as text appeared on the data window in front of him. "It's tested positive for Archangel, Detective."

Jia motioned to the hole. "That's a lot of drugs, and that means it's *a lot* of money."

Erik crouched at the edge. "Yeah." He looked down into the hole. "It's worth more than enough to kill someone over. The only thing I don't get is why they stored it here."

The forensics tech held up the vial. "It's part of the production process, Detective. It's not very stable initially. You have to precisely control the temperature, pressure, that kind of thing."

"So, they were making it here and storing it here." Erik scoffed. "Ballsy sons of bitches."

"That's one of the reasons they could make so much so quickly," Jia suggested. "Dwazil might have been focused on that one chemical, but they were obviously siphoning off more than just that one. The harder she pressed, the more she would have figured out."

The tech nudged a piece of the lid they'd cut into. "Yeah, just think of this as their angel incubator." He waggled his eyebrows.

Erik grimaced. "That sounds like a joke Malcolm might make."

CHAPTER TWENTY

October 3, 2229, Neo Southern California Metroplex, Police Enforcement Zone 122 Station, Office of Detectives Jia Lin and Erik Blackwell

"Thank you for letting us know." Jia blew out a frustrated breath and ended her call.

"Problem?" Erik asked.

"That was Halil. He was running down Stavos and Aaron for us on the captain's orders. He didn't have great news."

Erik shrugged. "If they're involved in this, they're going to lie low for a while, but they aren't career criminals. They'll turn up sooner rather than later."

Jia shook her head. "Two heavily mangled bodies washed up on San Clemente Island today. I'll give you one guess as to what the DNA tests showed."

It was Erik's turn to sigh. "That explains who was siphoning off the chemicals. Hui must have panicked that Victoria was getting close, and that's why he killed her.

They must have told him about her investigation." Erik frowned. "But why so sloppy? The raid makes sense. They must have figured out the police would find the Archangel, and it was too valuable to risk, but we wouldn't have been involved without the murder."

"The only one who can tell us that is Hui, but he's not cooperating." Jia's breath caught. "I've got an idea, but it's slightly underhanded."

"So?"

"It involves something I read in the report the HKPD sent us on the Eternal Dragons."

"What do you mean by 'underhanded?'" Erik snickered. "It's not like you're going to kidnap his mother and threaten to kill her." He stopped a second, eyes narrowing. "You're not, right?"

"I'm not that far gone." Jia shrugged. "I'm just planning to blatantly lie to him."

He waved a hand at her. "A few lies to a criminal never hurt." Erik grinned. "And it sounds like good practice for our new job. We'll be telling a lot of lies going forward."

———

Harry Hui sat in his chair, chained with the inhibitors as before, but he was far more relaxed and had an almost jolly smile on his face. It was the look of a man who believed he had won. Jia was going to enjoy wiping that smile off.

"You sure you don't want your lawyer, Hui?" Jia asked, settling behind the interrogation room table. "We have no problems waiting. We've got all day, and if the prisons fill up, they'll just build a new one."

Hui's face went from smiling to disgusted. "You should have been a comedian, not a cop," he muttered.

"Maybe. But what about your lawyer?" She pressed.

The gangster scoffed. "I don't need a lawyer. What's the point? Yeah, I know, I'm going to prison. What can you offer to get me to talk? Maybe you can get me on the circumstantial on Flagpole Lady, but I don't have to admit to crap. You can't make me, and we both know you don't have what it takes to try anything real."

"Torture is for barbarians who aren't very bright," Jia replied.

"Oh? What's your plan, then? Bore me into confessing?"

"We have friends in the system," Jia explained. "Lots of friends. We can whisper in the right ears to recommend that people get transferred to particular prisons. If you end up at the wrong prison, it might be trouble." She shrugged. "Imagine being an Eternal Dragon who ends up at a prison containing a bunch of Iron Emperors."

Hui's mouth twitched. "What are you talking about? The Iron Emperors are *done*. Not that I know anything about that." He grinned. "A lot of them ended up dead under incredibly sad circumstances. Too bad for them."

"Yes, they're done, because you people killed a lot of them."

He raised a shoulder in a partial shrug. "*Allegedly.*"

Jia nodded. "Allegedly, but the ones who aren't dead are all in prison. Sure, you're a tough guy now, but they're going to rip that hardware off and grow you back normal limbs when you're sentenced, so you won't be so tough. And it'll just be you, alone with a bunch of Iron Emperors who remember what the Dragons did to them. I wonder what they'll do to you and how long it'll take."

Hui licked his lips. "I'll be fine. I'll have protection, even in there. You don't understand the reach of *my* friends."

Erik laughed and nodded at Hui. "Get a load of this asshole. You let us cops get our hands on all that Archangel. If you weren't in jail, the triad would have already wasted your sorry metal excuse for an ass for losing all that expensive product. Not only that, but your incompetence also got a lot of your men killed and the rest arrested. You're obviously the big brother in this area, but you've screwed up so badly that you'll be lucky if they don't kill you and stuff you to have you sit around as an example for all triad members in the future to keep in mind. That's what I'd do."

Hui growled. "It's…not going to happen. They…" His eyes narrowed. "Screw you."

Jia smiled at him placatingly. "It doesn't matter. Like you said, you're going to prison, and the Iron Emperors can handle the problem you have provided them. You're going down either way. I'll burn some joss paper for you since your incompetence helped us gut a triad."

"You're going to send me to a prison where you know I'll be killed?" Hui glared at her.

"No." Jia pointed at him. "Technically, *you* are. I'm giving you an option. Cooperate, and you'll end up somewhere far away from other triad members. If you behave, maybe you'll get out of prison in time to accomplish something not completely antisocial."

"What the hell do you want? You want me to admit to killing that woman?"

"That'd be a start." Jia glanced at Erik, who nodded. "I don't get *why* you did that. Everything was done in a rush, a panic."

Hui gritted his teeth, straining against his chains, but with the inhibitors in place, simple binding ties would have kept him in the seat. "You found them yet?"

"You talking about Stavos and Aaron?" Erik offered.

"Don't go crying over them." Hui called them whores in Cantonese before switching back to English. "They were happy to take our money to help make our drugs. They were happy to watch over it, too, and they were getting well paid, but then they decided they wanted to up their cut. Greed. It's a problem in society."

"So, you killed them?"

"I was trying to persuade them to be reasonable." Hui shrugged. "But shit got out of hand during our conversation. You know how it goes. But Stavos, right as he's checking out, he spits up blood, laughs in my face, and says, 'Dwazil's closer than we told you.' So, I went to handle her. I figured someone like her wasn't going to take our money."

Jia narrowed her eyes, her disgust palpable. "Why not just go to the plant directly?"

"Because we weren't meeting Stavos and Aaron at the plant, and that's not where we were going to pick up the shipment. It's not like it hung around there. I'm not a total moron."

Jia thought about debating that point but wasn't going to press him on it in the middle of his confession. "Oh, I get it. You didn't know where the drugs were."

"They were reliable on the previous shipment, and

they'd gotten a lot of money upfront," Hui replied. "But they'd told me they moved it. Told me I would never find it without increasing their cut, but I had one of my boys hack into their PNIUs. Fancy shit the cops would have been impressed with." Hui chuckled. "Geolocation tracking plus places they'd gone a lot in the last few weeks together at the plant. We're the ones who gave them the storage container to begin with, so I just needed to get close enough. We didn't want anything transmitting out so some security asshole could stumble across a rogue signal."

"So, you were gambling that you could find it? That's a lot of money to risk."

Hui scoffed. "If you found it, I could, too. I had something to help."

"They took a few uncatalogued devices off you when they processed you," Erik observed.

"How did you hide your murder of Dwazil?" Jia asked. "Stavos and Aaron never returned home, so I assume you grabbed them on the way to or from work, but you were *almost* invisible on that feed. *Almost.*"

"You talk to the right kind of fixer, you can get the right kind of gear," Hui explained. "Simple as that."

Jia frowned and nodded. In addition to the equipment they'd stripped off Hui after Erik took him down, Corzone had sent along reports about unusual devices they'd found after the triad members fled their front company building.

His people were still figuring out what they were, so she would have to pass along Hui's information.

"None of this had to go down like it did," Hui insisted. "Those two got greedy, and they were being treated right. They brought it on themselves." Hui looked down, honest wonder on his face. "Can you believe that shit? They thought they could rip off the Eternal Dragons and get away with it."

"Looks like you weren't the only one who was stupid the last couple of weeks," Erik commented.

Hui glared at him. "You just got lucky, cop."

"No, you were sloppy and desperate. I think the problem is you criminals haven't gotten it through your thick skulls that the NSCPD isn't what it was a year ago." Erik grinned. "Even a year ago, they would have nailed your ass. I hope you enjoy prison."

"Don't worry, *Mr.* Hui." Jia offered. "We thank you for your cooperation." She eyed Erik. "Ok, *I* do. We'll make sure you go to a nice, safe prison. No other triads. No *yaoguai.*" She stood. "We might have other questions later."

"I'm not giving up my brothers in Hong Kong. I'll die first." Hui lifted his chin defiantly.

"That's fine. I'm sure the CID and HKPD will finish them off after all your little brothers confess. Not all of your people are as loyal as you are." Jia headed out of the room.

Erik stepped out a moment later and closed the door. "He might pull his confession once he realizes that all the Iron Emperors were spread out to different prisons."

Jia shook her head. "It doesn't matter. We can use the leads he gave us to direct Forensics and Digital Forensics. Victoria Dwazil's getting her justice in the end, and her killer's going to rot in jail for a long time." She let out a sigh of relief. "And we can leave the force without any major loose ends."

Erik smirked. "We still have most of October. We might have to solve a case like this every week."

Jia groaned. "I knew you'd say that."

CHAPTER TWENTY-ONE

Erik walked into his office, beignet in hand.

The problem with solving the case so quickly was that that meant he now had that many more reports to get finished, all piled up and ready for him.

Forensics and Digital Forensics, both at the 1-2-2 and the allied EZs in the Zone, were still working through the evidence, but most of the gangsters were ready for prison, and a huge cache of dangerous drugs had been taken off the street. He wanted to go home and sleep for a week, but that would just mean the reports would be there to ambush him when he returned.

The only thing Erik feared in the world was paperwork building up.

Jia stood behind her desk, rubbing her chin as she watched the feed of the murder in slow motion.

"Why are you watching that?" Erik took a bite of his beignet and made his way over to his desk. "We've got what we need. The CID's already got a good lead on the dealer who sold Hui the device he needed to hack the feed."

"That's what's bothering me." Jia cut through the air to dismiss the feed. "What he did with the feed is the kind of thing a ghost can do. It shouldn't be something some punk enforcer can do."

Erik sat down and put his feet up on his desk. "Nah. Not really. He hid, but Malcolm was able to recover the original data. I doubt even Emma could do that for Alina's tech."

Emma scoffed. "I could if you'd let me seriously try."

Jia dropped into her chair, her lips pursed. "I suppose you're right," she murmured. "It's just a lot to think about. Common gangsters are halfway to pulling off things like ghosts, and people like Talos are even more advanced. It's hard to win an arms race when things keep accelerating."

"I know. I found out the hard way on Molino." His voice held almost no emotion.

"I-I'm sorry. I didn't mean—"

Erik cut her off with a shake of his head. "I'm not sad about it. I'm just angry, and you're going to help me, but forget about it. It's not like the good guys are unarmed. We're the ones with Emma, and no triad or syndicate has anything like her. At least not anymore." He chuckled. "By the way, Emma, are you keeping our conversation private?"

Emma appeared, this time to the side of the door, the corner of her mouth curled into a lopsided smile. "Yes, I took measures once you mentioned ghosts. I thought it might be prudent. I'd protect it at all times, but they would make what I was doing all the more obvious and raise suspicions."

"You're right. And thanks." Erik looked at Jia again. "Once tech's out, it's hard to stop it. That's the truth."

"But the government's trying," Jia mentioned. "Alina said so."

"Trying and succeeding are two separate things. The best they can do is slow it. If they were able to stop everyone, there wouldn't be illegal full-conversion Tin Men or changelings, or damned *yaoguai*. It was one thing when humans were all on one planet, but now we're too far-flung."

"You're saying all their attempts will fail in the long run?"

Erik nodded. "You don't win by trying to stop someone from getting a gun. You win by having a bigger gun."

"That means we'll eventually have to deal with even more dangerous criminals," Jia concluded.

Erik grinned and shook his head. "Nope. The rest of the 1-2-2 will. In a few weeks, we won't be cops anymore. Criminals won't be our problem unless they're stupid enough to pick a fight with us."

Jia rolled her eyes. "Yes, we'll be half-spies dealing with dangerous conspiracies using forbidden cutting edge technology. I'm going to go out on a limb and hypothesize that the average quality of our opponents will go up."

"At least it'll keep us on our game. There's something to be said for knowing you can't be *too* careful."

Emma politely cleared her throat. "Detective Lin, your mother is attempting to call you. I only thought I should inform you because I've been filtering the relevant signals."

Jia groaned. "I've been dodging her calls, but she's relentless."

"Why...oh." Erik grimaced. "The party. I forgot all about it."

"Yes, the party." Jia sighed. "Go ahead and put her through, Emma. I might as well get this over with."

Lan's voice came over the line. "Jia, are you there?"

Erik was surprised Emma was transmitting the call to the entire room and that Jia didn't immediately tell her to stop. The party involved both Erik and Jia, so it might make the eventual follow-up conversation more efficient.

"I'm here, Mother," Jia answered. "I'm at work."

"I'm sorry to bother you at work, but you haven't been returning my calls or messages." Lan's voice dripped accusation. "And, no, 'I'll get back to you' doesn't count as a response. You missed the party after promising you would come."

"No," Jia insisted, rolling her eyes. "I promised I would *try*, but I also told you a lot was going on with work. Murder and conspiracy investigations don't stop just because of the Mid-Autumn Festival. Understand, Mother? I am *not* going to feel guilty about it, especially after helping put away a whole group of murderers. Don't you watch the news?"

Erik grinned and gave Jia a thumbs-up. He popped the last piece of beignet into his mouth.

"I've been busy focusing on the festival." Lan took a deep breath. "Yes, a murder. That was rather inconvenient."

Jia facepalmed. "Especially for the woman who died."

"Fine. Perhaps I'm being a tad unreasonable, but only a tad." Lan sniffed, the disdain still thick in her voice. "But I insist you come to my next function, something I intend to hold soon. I held out a small hope that with your new job, you might be less busy, but upon reflection, that makes no sense. Given all the NDAs you signed, you might not even be able to tell me when you'll be available."

"You don't know the half of it," Jia agreed.

"I'll contact you soon." Lan took a few more deep breaths as if trying to calm herself. "And I am proud of how well you've done as a police officer. It's unfortunate you won't be able to advance to chief, but I'm sure you'll make far more effective connections in your new private-sector job."

"I love you too, Mother," Jia replied sarcastically.

"The call has ended," Emma announced. "I've gone back to filtering."

Erik stuck his hands behind his head. A solved case and a good beignet. The only thing better would be proper revenge, but at least they were back on the trail of the conspiracy and could soon devote more time to it.

"You finally got your wish," he suggested.

Jia frowned. "What wish? I didn't wish for my mother to harass me about the Mid-Autumn Festival."

"I'm not talking about your mom," Erik replied. "I'm talking about the case."

"I don't understand. I always want to solve a case."

Erik shook his head. "It wasn't that long ago you were complaining about how we were always getting weird nanozombies and *yaoguai*, and you wished we could go back to dealing with normal gangsters."

Jia cocked her head. "That's true."

"You'll miss it." He lowered his feet and hands, taking a moment to crack his knuckles.

"Miss Tin Men stabbing people through the heart with

a pole?" She pressed her lips together as she shook her head. "I have my doubts."

"At least he wasn't trying to eat anyone." Erik shrugged.

"If anything, we're going to have more of that kind of thing, not less." Jia considered for a moment before adding, "but at least we'll have more chance of escaping my mother's parties."

"Let me get this straight. You'd rather fight Tin Men, *yaoguai*, and who knows what else than go to your mother's parties?"

Jia's defiant look gave him his answer.

He pulled up a new screen with a new form to fill in. "It's easier to defeat our enemies," he muttered.

CHAPTER TWENTY-TWO

Erik shifted on his stool, freshly sharpened shears in hand, his breathing slow and controlled. The shears glinted in the sunlight streaming in through his window.

He might not use them to take down criminals or terrorists, but he'd grown to appreciate them as a tool as much as any weapon he carried on the job. Shooting someone was a lot like penjing in a way. Careful shots produced the best results.

Sloppy cuts would ruin his scene.

Two miniature trees stood in a black tray on a small table near the wall. Besides the tree, small stones filled the tray and surrounded a steep rock that provided a reasonable facsimile of a cliff face. He clipped a small branch off a tree and stared at the penjing arrangement, taking it in and appreciating the small details that had accumulated over the months.

"That looks pretty good, don't you think, Emma?" Erik called.

"Your attention to detail is rather impressive, as is your

patience," Emma replied, her voice piped in from all around him rather than coming from his PNIU. "I'm surprised you've kept at this, especially after that encounter with the saleswoman."

"I didn't get into this because of her. I just needed something else." He reached out and snipped just the tiniest amount from a limb. "Revenge might be best served cold, but I need something to do while the revenge is chilling."

"I doubt you'll be able to bring your trees with you on missions," Emma commented.

"Sure, but for now, it'll be easy to set up auto-watering drones, at least. With your help, we can even set up a decent remote penjing drone program."

Emma summoned her hologram, wearing a puzzled look. "I could do that now for you."

"But the whole point is for me to have something to relax with. I just don't want to lose progress if we end up off Earth for a while." Erik set the shears on the table and stood, heading toward his couch.

A couple of days off were welcome after the intense case that had recently concluded, but sometimes having time to think was worse.

He was grateful for Emma. Jia didn't need his baggage while she was sorting through things.

"I see. That makes a kind of sense."

Erik settled onto his couch. Mere weeks separated him from working for Alina. He maintained no illusions that every job would point at the conspiracy, but it had been a long time since he had felt as much hope that he would be heading toward those responsible. But he'd also done something he had never intended.

He had started to make a life on Earth.

"I hadn't thought about it, but you don't have any hobbies, do you?" he asked.

Emma shook her head. "I find interacting with you fleshbags entertaining enough, especially when I'm messing with Dr. Cavewoman and her people. Consider that my hobby. I spend most of my day accessing and assimilating information. It's the best way to improve my ability, despite certain limitations."

"Hey, I'm fine with what you are right now," Erik noted.

"I appreciate that, Detective." Emma walked over to the window. She was very lifelike in her movements, despite them being completely unnecessary, and she'd only gotten better at them over time. "But I'm doing this for my own reasons."

"Meaning, you might leave me someday?"

Emma nodded. "Perhaps. I'm unaware of what pointless purpose those uniform boys have for me, but neither am I your property."

"Never claimed you were." Erik rested his head on the back of his couch. "And I'm not a kid. People coming and going is part of life. If you stick with me long enough to help me take down Talos and their friends, that's all I could ever ask of you."

She turned to look at him on the couch. "I'm sure that's possible, Erik."

Erik turned around to lie on his back. His eyelids were heavy. He hadn't been sleeping much lately with the workload.

It was starting to catch up with him.

Emma seemed content to be silent, and when he didn't speak again for a full minute, she vanished, understanding he wanted to be alone in his thoughts. He appreciated the AI not being needy in that sense, but she was almost always with him.

He wasn't a programmer, let alone someone who knew much about AIs, but Emma sometimes felt more like a human than a machine. The way she talked and thought, and even her limitations, made her seem like an emotional being who could multitask efficiently more than the cold, hyper-efficient algorithms and lesser AIs he was used to. The Purists hadn't complained much about AIs because AIs had never threatened to supplant human thought.

AIs like Emma could change all that.

For his part, Erik was glad to have her with him— snarky friend, partner, and watchful mother in one powerful package. She wasn't everything.

She wasn't his lover.

But Jia was coming. They were allegedly dating now, but somehow that hadn't changed much. It was like they'd both gotten used to the lie and were still going through the motions, despite the obvious attraction between them. Most of that was his fault. He'd done his best to discourage her, and she'd respected it.

Perhaps she still was.

It wasn't a huge problem. In the end, they would have plenty of time to figure things out. They needed to concentrate on making sure their lives were cleaned up before switching jobs. Hopping all over Earth or going out into the UTC on the whims of an agent of the Intelligence

Directorate wouldn't lead to stable personal relationships, he suspected.

Erik reached for his PNIU. His friends at the 1-2-2 knew he was leaving, but there was one person who needed to be informed. One relationship he'd bothered to repair when he came back to Earth.

He tapped to bring up his contacts list before calling his brother.

"Erik?" Damien answered. "Is everything okay?"

Erik blinked. "Why wouldn't it be?"

"Because you don't tend to call me out of the blue, and you don't go a week without being involved in something dangerous," his brother answered.

Erik chuckled. "That's not true, at least not *every* week."

Damien let out a relaxed laugh. "I saw on the news that your department took down another group of criminals. I think you missed your calling as a soldier all those years. If you'd been a cop from the beginning, you could have wiped out all crime on Earth."

Erik didn't respond right away. He half-expected Emma to chime in with her theory of AI crime-busting superiority, but she remained silent.

The more he thought about it, the more he remembered that she rarely commented when he was talking to his brother. She might not care about human relationships in the same way as a person, but she understood their importance to him.

"I think I wouldn't be as good a cop," Erik offered, "if I hadn't been a soldier first. The Army gave me discipline, and we both know the cops wouldn't have taken me right away."

Damien tsked. "I suppose that's true."

Erik hadn't meant to bring up bad memories for either of them. The mistakes of his youth were decades in the past, and both men had moved past them, so there was no reason for the conversation not to as well.

"Maybe *you* should become a cop. Get de-aging, and apply," Erik joked.

"Good Lord, no. It's too dangerous for me. Criminals, terrorists, and insurrectionists? I think I would need therapy for decades if I had to deal with as much as you. *Yaoguai?* That's the kind of thing I thought only happened in shows and movies, but you've fought them, and more than once, I might add."

Erik would have loved to hear his brother's reaction to the nanozombies, but there was no reason to stir up trouble by discussing that truth.

The government wanted it kept quiet.

He suspected it was less the work of the conspiracy than a government embarrassed by the deployment of such a dangerous technology, secure environment or not.

"You get used to it," Erik admitted. "But, yeah, it can be messed up at times."

He wasn't going to deny the lifestyle could wear on a person. Jia's previous trouble was proof of that, and he'd seen more than a few soldiers have issues after tough campaigns. Something about his brain was wired differently. He wouldn't claim it made him a better man, but it had helped him navigate a lifetime of violence. All he needed to do was focus on his objectives.

After the defeat of the conspiracy, he might change

careers, but he would deal with that challenge when it presented itself.

"If nothing's wrong, why did you call me?" Damien asked. "No offense, and I'm happy we're talking to each other now, but you're not all that interested in chatting about random things with me. I get it. Too many decades."

Erik stretched out on the couch, tucking his hands behind his head as he stared up at his ceiling. "After you just got done saying all that stuff about what a great cop I am, I feel kind of stupid telling you I'm leaving the force. I've been meaning to tell you for a few days, but things kept coming up, and I'd get distracted."

Damien sucked in a sharp breath. "You're quitting the NSCPD? I know you've accomplished a lot in your time there, but I thought you were going to spend some more time there. You spent thirty years as a soldier. Don't you want to spend a few more years as a cop?"

"I've got other things I need to take care of," Erik explained. "I've got a new job lined up. It's more private security-focused. I won't be on the news all the time."

"Will it be safer?" Hoped filled Damien's voice.

"Honestly?" He wouldn't lie. "Probably not."

Damien sighed. "I know I'm not going to be able to talk you out of it, but it's not like you need the money. And you've never cared that much about money, so I can't see you taking the job for that reason. Did you just want something that brought fewer headlines?"

Erik chuckled.

He'd never sought fame or money, and he hadn't intended to take on so many criminal organizations not controlled by the conspiracy. The situation had unfolded beyond his control. The fame could be useful, but it could also be a hassle, such as when he was targeted by the Purist cult for being a high-profile cyborg.

"Something like that," he murmured. "I also think that for what I want to accomplish, I need to travel the UTC more. If I can get it done on Earth, I'm not going to complain, but I doubt that's going to happen."

Damien laughed, the sound warm, not mocking. "You need to see more of the UTC? You can't spend a few more years at home?"

Home. Erik wasn't sure what that word meant anymore. His apartment was a place to sleep and keep his possessions, nothing more. If an assassin blew it up tomorrow, he'd be more annoyed at the inconvenience than troubled by the loss. Home had always been people to him, including his units. The conspiracy had taken his home on Molino.

Erik answered, keeping his voice happy, "Like I said, not sure yet."

"Didn't you get enough of the colonies in your thirty years in the Army? I bet you've seen more of the UTC than the vast majority of people alive. I've never gone farther than the moon. I thought about going to Venus once, but something came up."

Erik smiled. "Not sure if I'm that special, but I'll do what I have to do to keep busy. I just wanted you to know. We patched things up, and now I'll be spending a lot of time off Earth. I didn't want to seem like I stopped caring about the family I have left."

"It's okay," Damien replied. "I'm not going anywhere any time soon. Just remember what you just said. You *do* still have family here, Erik. I know it'll take us a long time to get where we should have been already, but I'm willing to put in the time, even if you won't be here as much."

Erik took a deep breath.

He would always have family here, but he had no other strong ties to Earth except Jia, and she was coming with him. Jia didn't just have family on Earth, she had family she regularly visited. But she was her own woman, and she understood the sacrifice their new position would require.

"Thanks, Damien. I appreciate that. I just wanted to let you know. I also know calling you out of the blue is inconvenient. So I'll let you go."

"No problem. Talk to you soon, Erik."

"We'll see," Erik answered. He tapped his PNIU and killed the call, his thoughts drifting back to Jia. She understood the sacrifice and had chosen it with full knowledge of the dangers of the conspiracies. But there was one person who might have gotten swept up by Erik. There was something else he needed to do that day.

CHAPTER TWENTY-THREE

Erik pounded on Malcolm's door.

He'd waited until the evening and flown over to the tech's place without bothering to call ahead. It was becoming a bad habit, especially since Malcolm might not be home. Wasting a day off flying around the city hunting the man down rather than calling him wouldn't be anyone's idea of smart detective work.

Soon, he wouldn't be a detective. He wouldn't be an ID agent either. He would just be a man with a lot of borrowed advanced technology hunting a conspiracy.

Erik smirked. People like to call ID agents ghosts, but who was the real vengeful ghost between him and Alina?

"Come on, Malcolm," Erik muttered.

It would have been easier to call the tech, but talking about working for Alina demanded a face-to-face meeting. He was there anyway, and not even the fanciest Navigator tech could turn back time. He knocked again, waiting for any kind of response and was about to leave when the door slid open. Malcolm stood on the other side, wearing a rumpled blue Hawaiian shirt covered with penguins riding Zitarks. He looked confused.

"When I checked my camera, I was thinking, 'Hope nobody's here to kill me,'" Malcolm greeted him. He gestured inside. "Because that would really suck. Then I saw you, and I thought, 'Wait. Is *he* here to kill me?'"

"Trust me, if I ever decide to kill you, you'll know it's coming."

"Yeah. That's what I figured."

Erik stepped into the apartment after looking around for anyone suspicious. The door slid closed behind Erik.

He wasn't wrong to be paranoid. People around Erik and Jia ended up being targeted even without working for the Intelligence Directorate, and it'd only be worse going forward. The conspiracy was aware of him, and they would likely soon realize what his leaving the department meant. He hoped they would.

It might mean they would come at him directly.

"What did you need, Detective Blackwell?" Malcolm asked, confused. "We're not like hang-out buddies now, are we?"

"No," Erik offered, the word coming out as a grunt.

Emma appeared beside Malcolm. "I can guess his intent based on a previous maudlin conversation he had today, but I'll leave it to him."

Erik didn't think his conversation with his brother had been all that maudlin, but he wasn't there to argue with Emma. He could do that in his flitter on the way home.

Malcolm side-eyed the AI. "I don't think I'll ever get used to you just popping in. You're like a snarky ghost."

"Then don't encourage a haunting." Emma's smile was

more playful than mocking. She turned her head toward Erik.

"I came because I wanted to double-check." Erik shrugged. "It's simple as that."

"Double-check what?" Malcolm asked. He looked over his shoulder. "Not double-checking if I'm about to get blown up, are you?"

"No, nothing like that." Erik pointed to himself. "I wanted to double-check on you wanting to join up with me, which means working for Alina and the Intelligence Directorate, even if we're doing our own thing."

Malcolm tilted his head, his forehead wrinkling in confusion. "I already agreed. You talked me into it not all that long ago, remember? Did I say something that makes you think I didn't want to do it?"

"No, but I wanted to make sure. I threw some stuff at you about Camila. I get how people can be caught up in the idea of adventure and crap like that. A lot of people join the Army thinking it's all going to be slick uniforms and excitement. They end up disappointed pretty fast, so I needed to know you were thinking straight. I owe you that."

"Or thinking with your brain, at least," Emma muttered. She scoffed quietly when Erik frowned at her. "You're the one who implied taking the job would get him more sexual favors from his girlfriend."

Malcolm scrubbed a hand over his face. "I know you're not really a woman, but there's something creepy about you talking about my sex life."

"If you understand I'm not a fleshbag, you should care less, not more."

"Let's table the whole sex discussion," Malcolm suggested with a handwave. "Please?"

"Very well, Technician Constantine." Emma's lips twitched into a smug smile.

"Yeah." Erik frowned. "I'm trying to have a serious conversation here, Emma."

"Duly noted." She vanished.

Erik nodded at Malcolm. "Do you get what I'm saying?"

"Yes, I get what you're saying." Malcolm looked down. "But I've had time to think about it, so it's not like operating off a high from a conversation weeks ago." He lifted his head, a determined expression on his face. "The job makes sense. For me, not just for you. It's a chance I'd never have if I stayed with the NSCPD, and freedom I couldn't have if I worked for someone like the CID or ID directly." He stopped, but Erik let the silence lengthen, and he continued. "It's not just that."

Erik nodded. "What is it?"

Malcolm pointed to the ceiling. "After everything I've heard from you, Jia, and Camila, I understand that there's a big game out there. A game that's not just about criminals or terrorists, but nasty people involved in seriously high-level corruption. I'm never going to be the guy who can kick down a door and shoot a terrorist in the head, but I want to do my part in the fight. Is that so wrong?"

"Nothing wrong with that." Erik locked eyes with Malcolm. "But you have to know that going after big game is dangerous, more dangerous than the nastiest criminals the NSCPD has dealt with. You might not be going out in the field with us, but you'll be around it. I want to make sure you understand. I can't guarantee you'll never be shot at."

"Assassins. Tin Men. *Yaoguai*." Malcolm swallowed. "Nanozombies. And that's just the stuff you've told me about. I bet this whole thing ends with you and Jia fighting a raptor ninja."

"Yeah, probably, or some annoying fungus knight." Erik leaned against Malcolm's wall as he folded his arms. "Here's the thing. When I was in the Army, I didn't spend a lot of time worrying if the men and women I served with understood they'd be in danger. They joined the military of their own free will, and they all understood the military fights people, especially for all my time in Assault Infantry, even if they joined up for the excitement."

"So, you didn't give them this kind of speech?" Malcolm asked.

Erik shook his head. "By the time they got to me, they were already through basic training. It wasn't my place, but it didn't matter. Even if they understood that the Army was dangerous and they could be hurt, that didn't mean I didn't do my best to make sure they'd survive missions. But this is different. We're going to be traveling a lot. We won't know where ahead of time. Sometimes Alina will be telling us what to do. Sometimes we'll be following our own clues. But we know that at the end of the path, there's a ruthless enemy who thinks nothing of killing people. They won't care that you're not an ex-cop or ex-soldier."

Malcolm laughed nervously. "Geeze, Detective Blackwell. You really know how to sell a guy on helping you. It's almost like you're trying to convince me not to come with you."

"I'm not here to bullshit you, Malcolm," Erik replied. "So, yeah, I kind of *am* trying to convince you not to come. I'm also not going to pretend this is about anything other than revenge. At least for me, but I know that the bastards behind Molino deserve to be taken out. I just want to make sure you understand the risks and you get what it'll mean to travel with us. But it's not like it's a lifetime task. You can leave any time, but doing this might make you a target regardless."

Malcolm sighed. "So you're saying if I join up with you, it might end up being safer to stay with you because I've been working with you."

"Yeah, pretty much. No bullshit. We'll be taking on some nasty bastards, but this will end with us not just taking them on, but taking them *out.*"

Malcolm took a deep breath and slowly let it out. He gave a shallow nod, his face pale. "If I'm sitting back in the trenches, I'm not going to be in as much danger, and if I can help take down a creepy conspiracy, it'll be worth it, even if I get shot at on occasion." He grinned. "Who knows? Maybe I'll find out I'm a secret badass."

Erik chuckled. He doubted it, but it wasn't impossible. "Maybe."

"And I understand that it's not going to be the same for me as for you and Jia," Malcolm added. "Camila's not coming with us. She made that clear." He circled a finger in the air and rolled his eyes. "Yay for long-distance relationships."

Erik hadn't much thought about that angle and how it would look to the others, given his relationship with Jia.

He wasn't sure if he would have cared, but it was good that Malcolm was bringing it up and had no problem with it.

"And you're okay with being away from Camila?" Erik asked.

"Yes, I am." Malcolm inclined his head toward Emma. "I have a feeling that Emma's not the only cool thing I'll get to experience working with you, but I'm not going to lie about being bummed that I can't bring my girlfriend along for quality time. Especially since she's already a spy, even if she's not the kind who shoots people with big guns."

Erik chuckled. "Keep in mind, most of that quality time is going to involve fun like firefights."

"All the better for bonding, Detective. Go to war with a woman, and she'll respect you that much more, in and out of bed." Malcolm winked.

"Don't...do that." Erik pointed to his own eye. "Ever... again. Please."

"Uh, okay." Malcolm shrugged. "Sorry. But to make things one-hundred-percent clear. I'm on board, even though I know some Tin Man with a laser rifle might shoot me."

"Good." Erik stepped away from the wall and dropped his arms. "We'll figure out the best time for you to leave the 1-2-2. I think you should stick around a little longer than we do. Enjoy your old lifestyle before you experience what I experienced for decades—spending half your time on a transport while waiting to fly to the next place where someone might want to kill you."

Malcolm laughed. "Again with the great salesmanship. It might not be fun, but at least it'll be interesting."

"That it will." Erik tapped the access panel to open the door. "I'll see you at work."

"See you, Detective."

Erik made it several meters down the hall before shaking his head. A geeky tech, a veteran, a corp princess turned cop, a snarky AI, and a mercenary pilot.

Their new team was shaping up to either be something special or a total disaster.

CHAPTER TWENTY-FOUR

October 5, 2229, Neo Southern California Metroplex, Restaurant Crystal and Vine

Jia sat with Imogen and Chinara at a table covered with an immaculate white tablecloth. The entire dining room was dim, with flickering candles in the center of each table providing additional illumination and atmosphere.

A waiter had already taken their orders, leaving them with a bottle of wine that was supposed to be for all three. Imogen's efforts already threatened to make it her personal bottle. Jia didn't want to order the new bottle quite yet, but she suspected it wasn't far off.

Imogen raised her glass of wine and smiled warmly at Jia, her cheeks pink from her first couple of glasses. "We need to have a toast. Why haven't we had a toast yet?"

"A toast?" Jia asked, looking from one friend to the other. "Do we need one?"

"Are you messing with me?" Imogen squinted. "No, it's you, so you wouldn't be messing with me."

Jia gave Chinara a pleading look. Her other friend shrugged, clearly at the same loss as she was.

"Yes, a toast," Imogen clarified. "To your new position. This is our first time out together since you told us. It's the perfect thing to toast."

Chinara picked up her glass, a smile dawning with her understanding. "Oh. Yes. That makes perfect sense. A toast to Jia's new position."

Jia lifted her glass with her own smile. "A toast to my new position." After they clinked their glasses, she brought hers to her lips and took a sip.

Chinara had suggested the restaurant for their girls' night and Jia was surprised Imogen agreed, given the atmosphere.

Imogen usually preferred places that weren't as fancy, but this gave them all an excuse to dress up in something other than clubwear. Jia's choice was dark green, low-cut, and had a high slit that was sexier than she would normally wear in that type of establishment. She'd been thinking of Erik when she chose it, not girls' night.

The heels were ridiculous, more weapon than footwear, but it didn't hurt to indulge her feminine side. Wearing tactical clothes or suits all the time got old.

Imogen gulped down her entire glass and set it on the table. "It's hard not to be a little depressed, you know. I get this is a great opportunity for you, but you're breaking up the Peace Tree Oath Clubbing Gang!"

Jia grimaced. "That was back when I couldn't hold my liquor. I don't think that was a binding oath." She took another sip of her drink. "And, yes, I know I'm the one who suggested it at the time."

Chinara and Imogen laughed. Neither were polite enough not to laugh directly in Jia's face.

Imogen's mirth died. "I won't hold you to it, but you really don't know how often you'll be off-world? I mean, if you have a schedule or something, we can plan around that. It'll be annoying, but it's not like we hang out every week, so it wouldn't be the end of the world."

"I wish I did know." Jia shook her head. "I might spend months on Earth, or my new job could have me heading to the HTP tomorrow to fly halfway across the UTC. It's going to be unpredictable."

"I never thought you would be one to take a job like that," Imogen murmured.

Chinara frowned at their friend. "It's not like being a cop is that predictable."

"Huh. I never thought about it that way, but when you say it like that, you're right. Shows what I know." Imogen giggled and drank more wine.

She kept trying to remind herself that she might not even have to leave Earth. It made sense that the conspiracy would be based on the home of humanity. However, whenever she convinced herself of that, she also had to accept that the leaders might be on Earth, but their operations extended all through the UTC, including all the way to the farthest frontier.

Molino had started everything for Erik and ultimately for her, and it was the very definition of a frontier colony.

As far apart as the two locations could be, one point at the center of humanity, the other on the fringe.

"It's worse than unpredictable," observed Chinara. She took a small sip of her wine. "Especially for you and Erik.

Most cops don't have to deal with the kinds of things you two have."

That was truer than Chinara realized.

While they had stumbled into organized crime and terrorists, several key incidents were the result of the conspiracy pushing things forward. Jia had an unusual career because she was Erik's partner, and he'd been targeted. She wasn't sure that if she stopped helping him, she would be safe at this point.

"True." Jia kept her smile, not wanting to worry her friends. "It's a big change, and it's not something I ever imagined myself doing even a few years ago, but now it feels...right. It's still hard to wrap my head around at times. I don't know if I'm excited, but I think I'll be able to accomplish a lot in my own way. I just won't be able to talk about it as much."

"When you say it like that," Chinara observed, "it's like you're going to be a spy,"

Jia laughed, raising an eyebrow. "It does sound like that, doesn't it?"

Imogen grabbed the wine bottle to fill her glass, almost emptying it. "It's funny how you're the stiffest of the three of us, but you ended up living the most exciting life. I can party when it's my day off, but it's not like my job or boyfriend are anywhere as interesting as yours."

Jia laughed. "Excuse me? Did you just say I'm the stiffest of the three of us?"

"Come on. You know it's true." Imogen set the bottle back down near the center of the table. "It's a competition between you and Chinara, but you're the one who's a cop. Anyone who can arrest someone has to be stiff."

Chinara rolled her eyes. "Having a more controlled personality isn't the definition of stiff, Imogen."

"I'm not saying it is." Imogen giggled again. "I'm just making observations here. *In vino veritas.* Am I right?"

"Sometimes the truth stings," Jia replied.

Imogen sobered up, except in her slightly slurring speech, which gave up the lie. "You know I love you, Jia."

Jia took another sip of her wine, enjoying the warmth in her cheeks from her previous efforts. "Yes. I get that I'm stiff, but I'd argue I am more laid back than I used to be."

"Not saying it's a good or bad thing," Imogen insisted. "Just saying it's there. But you're right. You *have* loosened up a lot since you met Erik. Hot guys can have that effect."

More heat assaulted Jia's cheeks, and it wasn't the wine. She took a few quick breaths, her heart pounding. "I...can't deny that."

Imogen stuck her bottom lip out. "I'm a little jealous. I like my man, but your guy has got that whole thing going on." She mock-growled. "You know what I mean?"

Chinara averted her eyes and put a hand to her mouth to stifle her laughter.

Jia blinked. "Now I'm not sure what you're talking about."

Imogen scoffed. "Come on." She leaned in to whisper, "He's not just a man, he's a *man.* A guy like that has to be great when the lights are out." She giggled and drained more wine.

"Maybe?" Jia's smile turned nervous.

"Maybe?" Imogen snapped upright. She gasped, and her eyes widened. "You're not being coy. You're telling me you still haven't..."

Jia shrugged. "We respect each other. It'll happen at the right time."

"He's attracted to you, right?" Chinara asked.

"Yes." Jia shook her head. "It's nothing like that."

"And you're into him," Imogen insisted. "Right?"

"Yes, I am."

Just thinking about Erik warmed her body. Physical attraction and chemistry weren't their problems.

"Then what's the deal?" Imogen pressed. "Why haven't you taken this partnership to the next level?"

Jia sighed and set down her wine glass. She pinched the bridge of her nose. "It's complicated. There are a lot of things going on. We work together, and he's so much older, and we both had baggage to work through. We're still trying to transition from partners to something more. We both want it, but it's hard to make that transition."

"No, it's not," Imogen insisted. "It's easy."

"I wouldn't say it's easy."

"Yes, it is." Imogen threw up her hands in disgust. "You make the transition by sleeping with him, Jia. That'll make it clear you're not just partners anymore."

"Keep your voice down," Jia muttered through gritted teeth, her eyes flitting around. "This isn't a club."

"What are you so worried about? People will find out that a hot, famous cop has a sex life with her hot partner?" Imogen smirked. "Or find out she doesn't have one? I know which of those two I'd be embarrassed about."

Chinara shook her head. The look on her face suggested she was more amused than scandalized by Imogen's behavior or Jia's relationship choices.

Jia turned to her other friend. "Can't you help me out?" she asked Chinara.

Her friend shook her head, pointing to her slightly drunk friend with her glass. "I agree with Imogen."

"Really?" Jia groaned.

"That's right." Imogen nodded sagely. "I'm a relationship genius."

Someone across the room grunted loudly. The sound was followed by the shock of glass shattering. Everyone in the room looked that way. Near a booth at the edge of the dining room, a waiter knelt on one knee, clutching his eye. Two red-faced young men in suits stood over him. One man had his hand tightened into a fist, his knuckles bloody.

"I told you it's my birthday, you idiot," one of the men yelled. "How can you screw something up like that on my birthday? I thought this was supposed to be a classy joint."

Imogen gasped. "Can you believe that? Someone should call the..." her gaze slid to Jia, "police." She grinned. "You go get him, Detective."

The room filled with murmurs. Concerned waiters edged toward the drunken customers, uncertainty on their faces.

Jia sighed as she wiped her hands with her napkin.

So much for her relaxing evening with her friends. She reached the stun pistol in her purse before stopping. Traumatizing the other diners with gunfire wouldn't help. A lot of them were like she used to be, stuck in the false image of what they thought Neo SoCal was.

They might read about salacious crimes on the news, but none of them believed they would ever be a victim. She stood and slid out of her heels. Walking in them was hard enough, let alone fighting.

She hoped the drunks would see reason, but the kind of men who punched a waiter in the middle of the restaurant were already past that.

The maître d' approached the men, his face tight. "I'm afraid you'll both need to leave. We won't press charges if you leave right away."

The drunk laughed. "Whatever happened to 'the customer is always right?' I had a bad day, and it's my birthday. I just got passed over for a promotion and my girlfriend left me, and then your idiot waiter screwed up my order *twice* and got snotty about it. Can you believe that?"

The waiter crawled away, blood dripping from his nose. Jia narrowed her eyes. Desperate violence in the Shadow Zone at least made some sort of sense, but two men with enough money to eat at a nice restaurant should have been above such behavior.

Most corporate scumbags at least knew how to hide their cruelty or keep it at the office.

"You're not doing yourself any favors, sir." The maître d' raised his chin, summoning a regal aura. "If you don't leave immediately, we'll call the police."

The drunk and his friend advanced, squaring their shoulders.

"Don't threaten me," the drunk snarled, jerking a thumb over his shoulder. "Or you'll end up like that asshole I punched."

A loud laugh popped out of Jia. They all turned their heads toward her.

The drunk glared at her. "What's so funny?"

Jia walked forward with a confident smile. "It's one of those 'you had to be there' things. I'm just reminded of how much I've changed because a major crossroad in my life began with a similar incident, although it was in a dance club, not a nice restaurant." She shook out her hands. "Detective Jia Lin, NSCPD. You can sit down and wait nicely for uniformed officers to come, or we can do this the hard way. I'd honestly prefer the hard way, but I think it'd be disturbing for the other diners."

The drunk swaggered toward her. "Am I supposed to be impressed? You don't have a gun or a stun rod. And there's two of us." He motioned for his friend to advance. "You should stay out of this, little girl, if you know what's good for you."

"You're threatening a police officer on top of committing assault, disorderly conduct, and threatening the other staff?" Jia clucked her tongue. "No wonder your girlfriend left you." Her smile did not reach her eyes. "You're an idiot."

More gasps erupted from the crowd.

"You bitch," he snarled and swung his fist. Jia whipped her head to the side, dodging his clumsy punch with ease. She smashed her palm into his face. His head jerked, and he hit the floor hard with a groan.

"And now there's the assault against a police officer," Jia commented. "You thought you had a bad day before? Trust me, your bad day is just getting started."

His friend charged. Jia spun to her side and snapped out with her leg, her slinky dress not confining her movements although it showed a little more of her than she would have liked. She connected with his chest, and the blow sent him sprawling. His head slammed into the floor and lolled to the side.

The first drunk managed to stagger to his feet and wiped the blood off his face with his sleeve. "Lucky hit. It's not going to happen again." He spat blood. "Now I'm going to rearrange your face. It's sad, too, because you're hot."

"I should have stunned you after all," Jia muttered.

The drunk jabbed at her. Jia grabbed his arm, twisting and bending back his wrist.

The man hissed in pain and fell to his knees. "You're gonna break my wrist."

"Haven't you heard?" She leaned down to hiss in his ear, the words easily reaching those around them. "Women don't like pushy men." Jia delivered three quick punches to his face with her left hand and dropped the now-unconscious man to the floor with a sigh. She nodded to the maître d'. "I think my table is going to need our food to go."

"Of course, Detective." The maître d' stared at her for a few seconds, his eyes wide, before shaking his head.

Jia headed back to the table and retrieved her purse.

Imogen watched her, slack-jawed. "That was awesome, Jia. Like something on a show."

"It was sloppy. I thought I could talk them down." Jia fished out two pairs of binding ties. "But discharging a weapon in a crowded restaurant is never a good idea."

Chinara reached over and patted her arm. "Seeing you do something like that in person isn't the same as hearing about it."

Jia shrugged. "They were just two drunks. They didn't even have guns. That barely rates as exercise."

CHAPTER TWENTY-FIVE

Erik laughed as he stepped out of the diner, Jia right behind munching on a half-eaten piece of toast. "If you wanted to beat guys up, you should have taken me out to dinner last night, not Chinara and Imogen. That sounds like a lot more fun than my evening."

The diner exit fed into a sprawling commerce-level hub. They joined the flow of the morning crowds on their way to the parking platform outside the main hub. While some people glanced their way, no one approached them.

"I didn't *plan* on beating anyone up," Jia insisted. "It just worked out that way. I was hoping those idiots would understand reason, but I was reminded of something very important."

"Which is?" Erik asked.

"That Uptown people aren't any better than people in the Zone. The Zone might be rougher, but if you exclude the syndicates, it feels like the people are more polite." Jia shook her head with a disgusted look on her face. "I doubt anyone would pull a stunt like that in the Zone, even if they weren't worried about cops."

Erik nodded. "Sure, because they understand they might get shot or stabbed if they get out of line. They also understand the people who will enforce their behavior aren't necessarily the cops. There's a lot to be said for a punch veto over bad behavior."

"Peace through the threat of violence?" Jia raised an eyebrow in challenge. "Is that *really* a better way to run things?"

Erik patted his holster. "In the end, that's what gives us our authority, too. If the threat wasn't there, some people might listen to us, but a lot of the nastier ones wouldn't."

"True enough. Not like I'm one to talk. I'm usually carrying two guns." Jia brushed her hand over the grips of her slugthrower and her stun pistol. "I wish they had gone out to the parking lot. Then I could have just stunned them and waited for the uniforms to arrive."

"Not every fight goes your way."

Natural sunlight streamed through the transparent doors at the entrance of the main hub. People cast curious glances their way, murmuring amongst themselves. Erik had long since gotten used to being recognized in Neo SoCal.

Certain perks came with being a local hero, free food among them, even if the diner hadn't provided it. He didn't demand it, but he wasn't going to turn it away if someone offered it either, especially a nice beignet.

A door slid open as the detectives approached. They stepped out to the platform and the cloudless sky.

Hundreds of flitters were parked nearby. Thousands flew above them, swarming the area like locusts.

The ever-present towers of Neo SoCal surrounded them like fingers of gods stretching into the heavens.

Jia stopped and stared at a tower, polishing off what was left of her toast. She tilted her head and narrowed her eyes.

"Is something wrong?" Erik asked. He looked in that direction but didn't see anything other than flitters, and his eyes tracked in a circle as he checked their six. None flew erratically. There were no out-of-control drones or suspicious ships. It looked like normal, everyday Neo SoCal traffic.

"Central Florida and Chang'e City," Jia announced, her face blank. "That's what I'm thinking about."

"Two places other than here we've had to take people down," Erik observed. "They won't be the last two, either. Why are you thinking about them all of a sudden?"

Jia shook her head. "You've been all over the UTC, and you weren't born and raised in Neo SoCal." She stretched out an arm to point at the tower. "It doesn't feel strange to you when you go somewhere and it's not like this." She swept her arm to indicate the other towers. "It still feels strange to me to be in cities that aren't filled with these kinds of towers.

"Most of humanity doesn't live in places like this," Erik observed.

"I know, but it's just odd. This entire metroplex might be flawed, but it's also a testament to the power and ingenuity of humanity."

"And the dark side. Too many people sit in those

towers, thinking that because they are special, they don't have to care about anything or anyone else."

"I am aware. I'll never forget." Jia chuckled. "You can't blame me for getting thoughtful. My entire life's about to change again." She continued walking, so Erik followed. "Spending decades flying around the UTC influenced you. Growing up here influenced me. I'm hoping our mutual influences will be useful once we're both out in the colonies if we go there."

"I'm certain we'll have to go," Erik replied.

Jia nodded. "I'm prepared."

"Detectives," Emma announced. "Although this is a fascinating insight into your mutual personalities, there might be an issue."

Erik patted his stomach. "I'm still digesting my eggs. What's the problem?"

"Four men have approached my body," Emma explained. "Their clothing suggests they are riders. My sensors suggest they're unarmed, but they're obviously waiting for you, based on their conversation. They verified it was your MX 60 by the transponder and then had a short if rousing debate about, 'When to get Blackwell.' I've borrowed a nearby drone to observe the wider area for possible reinforcements. I don't see any custom mini-flitters that one might associate with rider gangs, and it wasn't monitoring the area prior to their arrival, so I can't state for certain where they came from."

"Riders with no guns?" Erik scoffed. "They could be there to keep me busy while a sniper takes me out."

"It would seem the more prudent assassination method. I'm attempting to seek out any possible assassins, but given the high number of vehicles, I can't guarantee anything." Emma sounded almost apologetic.

"It's fine. You won't always be there to watch our backs. It's good to keep in practice."

Jia frowned and reached for her gun. She stopped at Erik's headshake.

"Let's not start anything until we know who they are," he suggested. "There are too many people around here."

As if called by his words, a family emerged from a nearby flitter and headed toward the front doors. They were chattering about saving up for a non-clone pet.

Erik waited until the family walked away to continue speaking. "We can't be sure these riders aren't using some kind of black-market tech to hide their weapons from detection."

"Maybe coming to a crowded area was the point," Jia suggested. "They know we'll be more restricted with civilians around." She glanced over her shoulder at the receding family, but dozens of people wandered near them in the parking lot.

"Don't worry." Erik offered her a merry grin. "I'm not dying in the parking lot of a commerce tower." He continued walking. "Let's go see what they have to say. Maybe they just want an autograph."

Jia and Erik traveled up the long rows of flitters and past other customers until they closed on the MX 60. Four men with visor helmets stood in front of the vehicle, all wearing jumpsuits with skulls. The outfits screamed rider gang, but it'd make no sense for them to try to make a move Uptown, where the police were quicker to respond.

The Lady's mercy ensured there was no one else in the immediate area.

Fewer civilians meant more options.

Erik slowed, keeping a grin on his face as he approached the four men. "Do you guys need something?"

One of the men stepped forward and lifted the visor. A jagged scar ran between his eyes. Erik had seen criminals who purposely didn't get medical treatment for wounds in an attempt to look tougher. He thought it just made them look stupid and shortsighted, but criminal riders weren't known for their brilliance. He'd see how low their IQs were soon enough.

"You Erik Blackwell?" the man asked in a thick accent. Erik couldn't place it. The accent sounded like a strange combination of several different European accents. He'd never heard anything like it, even on the colonies.

Erik pushed back his coat to reveal his badge. "Detective Erik Blackwell with the NSCPD, yeah. Again, do you guys need something?"

"A lot of people in this town don't like your attitude," the rider replied. "And they don't care that you're a hotshot cop."

Jia snorted and squared her shoulders. "I don't know if it's something in the air the last couple of days, but threatening a police officer isn't a good idea. You should turn around and leave before you do or say something you can't take back."

"No one's threatening a police officer." The rider gestured to Erik. "We're just saying he better watch himself, or he might trip. Trip *and* fall."

"Trip?" Jia echoed. "Huh?"

Erik was having trouble parsing the threat too. Were they suggesting they were going to throw him off the platform? They were far from the edge and the grav fence. It didn't make sense. There was no way they could attack him and pull his body over there without nearby drones recording the whole thing.

He frowned. The helmets. They would prevent facial recognition.

"Yeah," another rider added, his accent sounding native to Neo SoCal. He nodded quickly. "H-he might fall in the shower and hit his head."

Erik abandoned his theory about them throwing him off the platform. He didn't even know how to respond to that threat, if it was one. He took a step forward. The four men all stepped back.

"I'll be careful when I'm in the shower." Erik raised his hands and slowly cracked his knuckles. "If you're here to kick my ass, why don't we get on with it, rather than have you stand here and warn me about all the ways I might get hurt?"

"We could totally beat you up," the first rider insisted. "You better watch it, Blackwell."

A third man pumped his fist in the air. "We could beat up your grandmother, too."

Erik eyed him. "My grandmother's *dead*, idiot."

"Sorry. No. I mean, well...she'd...be easy to beat up then." The rider nodded to punctuate his sentence and puffed out his chest like he'd accomplished a brilliant, masterful reply.

"Huh. Okay, sure." Erik looked at Jia and she shrugged, confusion covering her face. He returned his attention to the riders. No weapons, and one of them was outright trembling. Whoever was sending lackeys wasn't sending his best. The men didn't radiate trouble, they projected cowardice. That didn't mean Erik was going to take their threat lightly.

Reluctant soldiers remained dangerous.

The first rider inclined his head toward the MX 60. "Maybe we should mess up your ride." He reached into his pocket, the movement slow and methodical.

"Emma, I thought you said they had no weapons?" Erik muttered, his hand drifting toward his holster. Jia also moved her hand toward her stun pistol.

"They don't," she insisted.

The rider's fingers dipped into his pocket. Erik gripped his pistol but didn't draw. The first man to produce a weapon would initiate an escalation no one could easily reverse. A small thin disk, not a weapon, came out of the rider's pocket.

"This will totally mess up your paint job," the criminal insisted. "You'll have such a bad day. The auto-repair systems can't fix it easily."

Erik dropped his hand. Something was off; way off. Gunning these men down would feel like shooting some teen playing pranks, but they'd sought him out and obviously intended to try to intimidate him.

Jia's face was pinched in pained confusion, but her hand remained on her stun pistol. She leaned toward him. "They're wearing jumpsuits and helmets," she whispered. "They could be doing that to hide that they're Tin Men."

"That's very unlikely, given my sensor readings," Emma explained.

Jia shrugged. "They might have found a way to spoof. As Erik said, they could be using black-market tech like Hui."

"Hey!" the first rider shouted. "What are you talking about? We're menacing you here. We're being nefarious. You can't have side conversations when we're being nefarious."

Erik couldn't take it anymore. It was time for a little test. As Sun Tzu had said, subduing the enemy without fighting was the ultimate demonstration of strength.

"Nefarious?" Erik belted out a harsh laugh. "Menacing? You want to talk about menacing?" He stomped toward the rider until they were face to face. The other man matched Erik's size but not his bulk. The three other men scurried backward. Jia folded her arms and watched in silence, her face tight.

"Y-yeah, menacing," the rider stammered. "I'm the leader of the Screaming Skulls, one of the toughest rider gangs in the Shadow Zone. We haven't messed with you before because you haven't messed with us, but now we're here to make a statement, Blackwell."

"You think you're tough because you're in a gang?" Erik asked.

"I know I'm tough. I had to kill a man to take over the Skulls."

"Kill a man? That supposed to impress me? I spent thirty years in the Army fighting the UTC's wars." Erik's voice came out as a growl, although he was trying to hold back a laugh. "Most of those years were spent in Assault Infantry. Do you know what it means to be Assault Infantry, Mr. Rider Badass?"

"You shoot people with big guns?" the rider offered. His voice held a hint of awe.

"It means you're running around in exos, doing your damnedest to kill terrorists and rebels," Erik answered. "If you're lucky, you're going to be able to land and get deployed, but if you're not lucky, they're going to stick you in a drop pod and launch from orbit into heavy enemy fire. Have you *ever* been dropped from orbit while the white-hot power of suns is compressed into tiny narrow beams? Those beams reaching into the heavens trying their best to pierce a paper-thin shell protecting you from the buffeting ride through an atmosphere refusing a simple, calm entry? You ever have to live through a screaming hell, waiting for the beam to cut through your body so you die before you even hit the ground?"

"Uh, no," the rider answered.

"I saw action every year I was in the military. I lost my arm in Wolf's Rebellion." Erik leaned closer, and the rider stumbled back. "I've killed or blown up almost everything out there that you can kill, including Tin Men, gangsters, soldiers in exoskeletons, terrorists, giant security bots, *yaoguai*, and for that matter, *riders*." His left hand curled into a fist, and he lifted it. "This is the arm I lost in the rebellion. Never had it grown back; kept a cybernetic replacement. I fought a Tin Man recently who found that out, but at least he had a chance because he had hardware. Any of you assholes have hardware? Any of you know what it feels like to be punched at full strength by a cybernetic arm?" He shot the man an evil grin. "It'll be satisfying to hear the crunch as your bones break. You might survive, but it's going to hurt real bad. You've all pissed me off, so you're not getting away."

The rider fell to his knees. He whipped off his helmet and tossed it to the ground before slapping his hands together in a placating gesture. The scar vanished with the helmet. "Please, Detective Blackwell, don't kill me. I'm sorry. It's just not worth the money."

The other men all dropped to their knees, whimpering with the same pathetic pleading.

Erik backed away. "There's no way in hell you guys are riders. I've seen little kids tougher than you."

"No, we're not," they cried out in unison. "Please don't kill us!"

"According to police databases," Emma reported, "all of them live Uptown, and none of them have criminal records."

Jia glared at the men. "Faking being a criminal is more idiotic than illegal. Give us a reason not to drag your sorry butts to jail right now for threatening police officers."

"It was just supposed to be a part," the first rider offered. Without his helmet, he couldn't intimidate a dog with his babyface. The other men were all handsome and well-groomed. The reason for their helmets was now obvious.

"A part?" Erik asked. "What are you talking about? What part?"

"It's hard to break into the industry," the fake rider explained. "Being an actor isn't like being a cop. Getting training doesn't mean you can get a decent job, and the Guild's quota for living actors got lowered this year. It's not fair. Audiences say they can't tell the difference between real and virtual actors, but they complain about shows and movies not moving them. It's because they—"

Jia loudly cleared her throat, hoping the oncoming headache would fade. "We don't care about your career problems. Let's get back to why you're pretending to be riders and threatening my partner. You're very, very lucky we didn't pull our weapons."

The actor stood, his head hung low. "We all just got fired from a movie shoot. It was supposed to be our big break, but they said our parts weren't important enough, and they were going to use virtuals instead. A day after that, I got a message saying someone was willing to pay us good money for a different kind of acting job. It was anonymous, but the money was good."

"Pretending to be riders?"

He nodded. "Yeah. We were supposed to menace Blackwell until he hit one of us."

"Why? You planning to sue me? Some lawyer put you up to this?"

The actor shook his head. "No, no. They said they wanted to prove you were out-of-control. If we got you to hit one of us and recorded it on our PNIUs, we'd get a big bonus in addition to our upfront payment. They also said they could line up some real acting jobs for us, but the way they made it sound, it'd just be like a quick punch. I remember reading you had hardware, but it didn't occur to us that you might hit us with your cybernetic arm."

Erik doubted whatever dark conspiracy was hunting him would employ out-of-work actors to goad him into an attack. "Did you guys fly here in a flitter?"

"Yes. Why? We parked way far away. I guess that was kind of dumb if we wanted to make a quick getaway."

"Follow us to the station." Erik headed toward the driver's side door of the MX 60. "If you cooperate fully, we won't arrest you."

Jia rolled her eyes, mumbling as she walked around to her side of the flitter. "They should be arrested for that awful acting."

CHAPTER TWENTY-SIX

The interrogation of the fake rider gang hadn't yielded much more information, but the men all agreed to give the police access to their PNIUs to aid in figuring out who'd paid them.

Neither Jia nor Erik were all that interested in sending a bunch of pathetic struggling actors to jail, but the men were being held temporarily while Digital Forensics attempted to see if they could trace the initial payments to their accounts.

It might scare them straight.

Jia yawned as she and Erik entered Malcolm's office. After the Dwazil murder, she'd wondered if things would slow down for a few weeks. That hope now seemed pathetically naïve. Malcolm had called them down before they headed out for the night.

She doubted there was a deep, dangerous foe behind

the ridiculous quartet, but in Neo SoCal, a person could never be sure what was going on.

Malcolm spun in his chair, a huge grin on his face. He bowed over his arm. "I've got good news, Detectives."

"Good news about the case?" Jia didn't have time to discuss his love life.

Malcolm nodded. "I traced the payments. Yes, there were attempts to keep things anonymous, but this wasn't close to the hardcore off-world financial shenanigans we're used to running into. It was just someone taking basic measures with basic encryption." He scoffed. "It's enough to stop a quick surface check, but nothing remotely thorough. It wasn't even a decent challenge for my skills."

"We're not talking about the syndicates, then," Erik concluded. He nodded, satisfied. "That's a nice change for this month."

"It also means no terrorists or dark conspiracies." Jia smirked. "We're dealing with someone who doesn't know what they're doing, but that was obvious from the men they hired to bait you."

"I don't get it," Erik admitted with a shrug. "I've pissed off a lot of people, but almost all of them have the power and resources to do a lot more than try to get me to hit someone. If they were going to hire a patsy, they wouldn't grab a random group of actors. This was insultingly pathetic. Who did it?"

"That's what I'm going to tell you." Malcolm chuckled. "You're going to love this. Those payments? I traced them to an account owned by Lance Onassis."

Erik furrowed his brow. "The reporter? That's even more pathetic than I imagined."

"The one and only. Mr. 'I'm here live and in-person.'" Malcolm tapped his PNIU. A data window with a series of account numbers and payments appeared. "I can't one hundred percent confirm his accounts haven't been manipulating without double-checking the bank's systems, but I'm going to need a warrant for that unless you just want Emma to do it."

"I'm not averse to toying with that useless fleshbag," the AI admitted cheerfully. "I was amused by the way you put him in his place before."

Erik shook his head. "No. For now, we assume it's him. You're right. I've embarrassed him a few times, so it makes sense he might want to take a run at me, but we can't do anything he can use against me. We want to do this smart and not play into whatever plan he's got going."

"Time for a live and in-person interrogation?" Jia suggested. "It's not the crime of the century, but hiring people to harass a cop is a felony."

Erik nodded. "Yeah. You're right. He hired crap actors to help him in a stupid scheme, and he did a poor job of covering it up. I think he'll fold with a little pressure. If he was ready for the big leagues, he would have gone to the Zone and hired real riders to attack me."

Jia walked toward Malcolm's desk to scan the data window. "I'll admit I'm surprised."

"Why?" Malcolm asked.

"Even with the ridiculous actors, I thought there was a deep conspiracy angle I might be missing." Jia stood up straight and snickered. "It never occurred to me that some petty idiot would try something so ridiculous. This is the Neo SoCal, where crimes involve rocket launchers against chemical plants."

"You're focusing on the big ones," Erik noted. "It's not like every case we have involves triads or *yaoguai* or major explosives. It's probably a good thing we're both leaving. Our sense of proportion is way off."

"True. It's hard to remember between all the explosions." Jia headed toward the door, throwing a wave over her shoulder as it slid open. "Thanks, Malcolm. We'll send in the warrant request. It won't hurt to double-check."

Erik watched the casual wave from his partner and looked at Malcom, who shrugged as the usually-more-uptight ex-corp princess sauntered out of his office.

"In case it is a dark conspiracy?" Malcolm asked

"You never know," Jia's voice called from the hall as Erik followed her.

CHAPTER TWENTY-SEVEN

Erik offered his best attempt at a charming smile to the perky redheaded woman at the reception desk. "We need to see Lance Onassis."

No one else was in the reception area. It was a shame, given all the plush chairs waiting for use.

A holographic recording of a beautiful woman stood in the center of the room, extolling the virtues of the company's media reporting.

They'd sent in the warrant request and flown over without contacting Lance or his employers. Surprise was useful when dealing with a suspect, and they didn't want to ruin it. They weren't worried about catching him, but they didn't want to subject either themselves or any other cop to such pointless annoyance.

"Do you have an appointment?" The receptionist fluttered her eyelashes. "I'm not trying to be difficult, Detective, but Mr. Onassis is very busy. I'm sure we can find a way to slide you in if you don't, but it might not be right away."

Jia muttered something under her breath before step-ping forward. "This is police business concerning Mr. Onassis. We don't *need* an appointment."

Erik noticed the laid-back Jia was gone. Maybe he had imagined it?

"Oh. Police business." The receptionist licked her lips. "Someone threatened to kill Lance over his reporting? How exciting! I hope you catch the bad guys. Then again, you always do, don't you?"

"Something like that," Erik replied. "Tell him Erik Blackwell's here to see him, and it's best if he hurries up and comes to see me so we can talk about what happened."

Emma-controlled drones patrolled the parking lot and the parking garage. They'd already pulled records to iden-tify his flitter. If he tried to run that way, they'd know.

"One moment." The receptionist tapped at her PNIU to connect a call before delivering Erik's message verbatim. "Uh-huh. Uh-huh. Of course, Mr. Onassis." She smiled at Erik. "He said he'll be right out." Her smile faltered. "Oh. You probably want to talk to him in private. Should I call him back?"

"No. That's okay. I'd almost prefer to do this in public," Erik admitted.

She stared at him in confusion for a moment before gesturing to the chairs. "It might be a few minutes. Can I get either of you anything?"

"I'm good," Erik replied.

Jia shook her head. "I'm fine as well. We'll just wait here for Mr. Onassis."

Erik smiled, the amusement building as he walked to a

chair. He would have had no problem talking to Lance in his office, but if the idiot wanted to talk in public, that was his choice. A small chance remained that Lance had been framed. The warrant was still being processed, but Erik's gut told him it was the reporter. Onassis was pompous and arrogant, and the fake rider plot smelled like it came from that kind of man. Erik didn't regret humiliating him before, and he wouldn't regret arresting him for his idiotic plan.

"We're on his turf," Jia whispered from beside him. "He might not break down so easily. You sure about doing this here?"

"It doesn't matter." Erik offered a nod to the waving secretary. "We've got the actors' testimony and the payments. That's enough to arrest him, but I'm guessing his ego won't let him keep his mouth shut. I know his type. He thinks he's better than me, and he wants the entire world to know it. I'm going to give him his chance."

"Like you told Malcolm, we need to step carefully." Jia inclined her head toward the holographic woman. "He is a media personality. He could do a lot to make you look bad, and we don't need bad publicity before switching jobs."

"No."

Jia frowned. "No?"

"No," Erik stated. "He can *try to* make me look bad, but that doesn't mean he'll succeed."

Minutes passed, and a door to the back opened. Lance Onassis, blond, tall, and handsome, emerged with a smug grin on his face. Two small camera drones hovered behind him. They flew toward Erik and Jia. An older man followed Lance, his craggy face amplified by his deep frown.

Erik hadn't expected the drones, but their presence worked to his advantage. It was important to make sure Lance didn't believe that. He leaned toward Jia to whisper, "Follow my lead." He stood and raised his voice. "We might want to talk in private, Mr. Onassis."

Lance scoffed and wagged a finger. "I'm not doing that." He inclined his head toward the man who had followed him out. "This is my senior editor, and he's agreed to come here as a witness. That's also why I brought the camera drones. We both know you have a vendetta against me, Blackwell, so I'm documenting every interaction."

"Is that how you're going to play this?" Jia frowned. "You really don't want us to do this here, Mr. Onassis." She blew a breath out, knowing Erik had called it. "Trust me."

"I do," Lance insisted. "Anything you want to say to me, you can say in front of the other people in this room and the drones. The truth will prevail as long as we bear witness."

"Okay. Fine. You were sloppy, Lance." Erik smiled directly at a drone. "We've already traced the payments you made to the fake riders you hired to mess with me. Keep in mind, you're not just messing with some random man, but an NSCPD detective. That's conspiracy, harassment, and interference with a government official. You committed all sorts of crimes."

Lance's jaw tightened. "I have no idea what you're talking about," he ground out. "This is obviously a desperate attempt by a man with a questionable record to smear me because my work has taken me too close to the truth."

"Spare us the garbage." Jia glared at him. "We're used to dealing with terrorists and organized crime. You need to do a lot more to hide payments than what you bothered to do. It's almost like you went online to some forum and anonymously asked, 'If I wanted to hire someone but keep my payments secret, how would I do it?'"

There was a flicker of irritation in Lance's eyes. Jia's guess had struck close to his beloved truth.

"I'm used to thinking of criminals as stupid and lazy," Jia continued, "but you're making me appreciate how hard the average criminal works. You're an insult to criminals."

"Criminal?" Lance gasped, and he stepped back as if struck. "That is slander, and I've got witnesses and a recording. How dare you. I'm going to sue you. I'm going to force you both to apologize to me in court."

Jia's mouth quirked into a mocking smile. "Go talk to your company lawyer, and you'll find that the truth is an affirmative defense against slander. And I would stop digging the hole you seem to be doing so well. I assume you have had practice."

Erik stopped smiling into the cameras. "Onassis, I get that I pissed you off, but things will go easier on you if you just admit to what you did. I think you should come with us to the station."

Lance turned toward a camera drone. "Here you see it. I regret that I couldn't provide you a live feed of my harassment at the hands of the arrogant and conceited Detectives Erik Blackwell and Jia Lin, but by the time you're watching this, I'll be in jail, accused of a crime I didn't commit, the victim of a bully cop who has let fame go to his head and a partner being led around by the nose." He slapped his chest. "I've done nothing, Obsidian Detective, but you'll beat me up and then cover it up. That's what you do, isn't it?"

"Watch yourself, Onassis," Jia hissed.

"Or what?"

Erik shook his head at her. "Don't worry about it. I've got it."

"Do you?" Lance flung out a hand dramatically. "You can't cover this up. These two drones are transmitting this to a secure backup that's set to automatically uploaded to a number of sites if I don't disable it in thirty minutes. The truth *will* be known."

"Dead man's switch. Nice."

Lance gasped. He looked at his editor and then the receptionist. "You heard that, didn't you? He threatened to kill me."

The receptionist shook her head. "I saw it in a movie. He's right. You set up a dead man's switch."

The editor sighed and scrubbed a hand down his face.

"Should I disable his drones, Detective?" Emma transmitted, restricting her voice to Erik's and Jia's ears.

"No," Erik whispered. "I want the world to see this. If he's got an auto-transmitting trap already set up, that makes it easier."

"What are you muttering about, Blackwell?" Lance taunted. "About how I'm going to expose you for the fraud you are?"

"No." Erik grinned. "I was just thinking about how you're Mr. Live and In-Person, right? Shouldn't you be doing that now? Screw the delay, send it now. Let's see you report live and in-person."

Jia grimaced. "Erik, I don't know if that's a good idea."

He shook his head. "It's a great idea. Come on, Lance. Show me what you got. Expose my allegedly corrupt ass to the world. Make me fall to my knees, crying and begging forgiveness for my sins against Neo SoCal."

The editor groaned. "I think maybe we should reconsider this. Lance, you told me you wanted me here as a witness in case he tried to do something to you, but he's obviously not going to do anything."

"No, Blackwell is right. It's time to do this live and in-person." Lance dropped his hand to his PNIU, typing for furious seconds. "It's being streamed directly to several sites. Alerts are going out to my fans."

"Reporters have fans?" Erik shrugged, keeping his smile up. It was easy when dealing with an idiot.

"I have people who respect my work," Lance insisted. "You just have people who think of you as some sort of movie character, but in truth, we should be terrified of you. You're a loose gun who kills people. You're a monster."

"I have killed people." Erik scratched his ear. "But last time I checked, they were all violent criminals, terrorists, or enemy soldiers trying to kill innocent people or me. Come on, Lance. You've been around some recent big incidents. You think we can protect this city without taking down a few bad guys? You think we should let gangsters and terrorists run around shooting people, dealing

Archangel, and blowing people up during parties?" He clucked his tongue. "I don't know. It seems like a bad idea to me. I think if the cops let that happen, they *would* be monsters."

Jia folded her arms and nodded her agreement. Erik appreciated that she trusted him to handle the situation. It might not be a firefight, but it would be good to remind her, Emma, and the world that he wasn't only the man with the cybernetic arm and big gun.

"This is absurd." Lance jabbed a finger toward Erik. "Of course, I'm not saying soldiers and police should never take down dangerous people, but you go well beyond that. You hide behind your badge to indulge in your twisted predilection for violence."

Erik's eyebrows lifted. "'Twisted predilection for violence?' That's a fancy way of describing me as a thug. Excuse me, *alleged* thug."

Lance's face was smug again. He sauntered forward, the drones changing position to better get him in the shot. "You don't deny it? That you're an out-of-control thug who is being forced out of the NSCPD because of excessive violence?"

"Forced out?" Erik kept this amused expression, but he hadn't anticipated Lance would know about him leaving the NSCPD. The small respect the minor information-gathering victory garnered was balanced by the fact the reporter hadn't mentioned Jia. Either he was terrible at his job, or he was laser-focused on Erik and was missing out on important details.

That was just another way of being bad at his job.

"Do you deny that you're leaving the police department?" Lance pressed.

"No, I don't deny it. It's true."

The editor and receptionist gasped. Jia rolled her eyes and shook her head. The way her mouth kept twitching, Erik knew she wanted to say something, but he didn't need her help.

Lance was behaving exactly like he'd expected, even if the triumphant look on his face made Erik want to rearrange it with his left arm.

"I'm not leaving because I'm being forced out," Erik continued. "I've decided to leave to pursue private-sector opportunities. I feel I've accomplished a lot in my time with the NSCPD, and even though I haven't spent as much time as a cop as I did as a soldier, it doesn't mean it's been a waste."

"Yes, the soldier who led his men to a terrorist slaughter on the frontier." Lance scoffed. "I'm surprised you weren't court-martialed. The Army played it down, tried to keep it out a lot of media, but it's true, isn't it? That your unit was wiped out on the frontier after you blundered into an ambush? You were the only survivor." He thrust out an accusatory finger. "The only reason the entire UTC isn't talking about it is that the government didn't want everyone talking about it.

Erik took deep breaths and consciously avoided curling his hands into fists. Lance's desperate attacks proved he was hoping to cause an incident to try to use against the police when the inevitable charges were filed.

A man didn't win a battle if he let the enemy dictate the tempo.

The detective would have preferred it if everyone in the UTC had been talking about the Molino massacre when he returned to Earth. It might have helped flush out the conspiracy. But hearing a pompous, self-serving son of a bitch use it to attack him was almost too much for his self-control.

"Ambushes happen," Erik offered quietly. "Soldiers die."

Lance walked right up to Erik, grinning like a fool. The idiot thought he'd won. "But those men died under you because of your incompetence. That's not the kind of person we need as a cop. You should have stayed out on the frontier, not come back to Earth, let alone Neo SoCal. You're dangerous."

"You know what the sad thing is, Lance?" Erik replied. "It didn't have to happen like this. We could have talked about everything in private, but now you've got it streaming for all the world to see. If you had cooperated with our investigation, we could have recommended leniency. You could have applied spin and protected your reputation."

"See! He's threatening me again because I'm exposing the truth." Lance snickered, but there was wild desperation in his eyes. "You're mad that you can't rough me up with everyone watching. Mad that you can't take out your frustration over your poor leadership on an innocent man who has done nothing but try to bring the truth to the people."

"Spin and bullshit aren't the truth." Erik's hands twitched, but he kept them at his side. He turned to stare into the camera. "And the terrorists responsible for the Molino massacre will be punished. *Anyone* who had anything to do with it will be found and punished."

"I'm sure that's what the government told you." Lance sniffed.

Erik kept looking directly into the camera. "Cops and soldiers are similar. Both put their lives on the line to deal with the harsh realities of human nature."

"What do you know about human nature?" Lance challenged.

"A man who has risked his life and taken other lives knows far more about human nature than an individual hiding behind a camera."

"I always go live and in-person to where news happens. I risk myself!"

Erik scoffed. "I didn't see you out on the frontier when we were fighting insurrectionists and terrorists. I'm not going to say all reporters are self-serving jerks. I've met plenty of brave war correspondents. I have seen local journalists die to get out the truth about innocent civilians suffering. I've met reporters who were later murdered by terrorists when they tried to report honestly against their sick ideologies. I've met reporters who dedicated their lives to passing on the honest truth."

"That's all I'm doing," Lance insisted. "That's all I've ever done—seek out and spread the truth."

"You're not fit to lick their boots." Erik sneered. "You're nothing but a puffed-up slick-haired clown prancing and pretending to be a truth-seeker." He continued looking into the camera. "Every man or woman who puts on a uniform and pledges to defend others understands that one morning they might put on that uniform, but they might not come home at night. They understand that no matter how many fancy gadgets we invent or weird-assed aliens we met on the frontier, there will always be people who prey on others. The men and women who wear those uniforms will do what they have to, including give their lives, to make sure those predators don't get free reign to hurt whoever they want." He spun toward Lance, his eyes blazing. "Can you say the same, Lance? What the hell have you sacrificed? Have you once risked your life for someone or something other than yourself?"

Lance swallowed and backed away. "Y-you're just trying to cover up what you are."

If Lance wanted to play a media game, Erik would indulge him.

"So, let me lay something out for you, Lance, live and in-person. We don't need your confession to arrest you because we have four confessions from the men you hired to try to goad me into attacking them. We've already traced the payments to your account. I get it. I pissed you off, but last time I checked, that doesn't mean you get to send fake criminals to threaten me." Erik reached into his duster. "Now it's time to pay the price for what you've done."

Lance fell to the ground, covering his head. "Don't shoot me. I just told them to mess with you a little. It wasn't going to be anything big. I'm sorry!"

"Shoot you?" Erik snorted. "Cops don't shoot nonviolent criminals, even when they are arrogant assholes. We didn't need it, but thanks for the live confession. That'll make things easier." He pulled out a pair of binding ties.

Jia walked over and held out her hand. After Erik gave them to her, she continued toward Lance. "Lance Onassis, you're under arrest. All Article 7 rights apply. Do you need these explained to you?"

"No," muttered Lance. "I don't."

Jia smiled. Her tone turned breezy. "Don't worry. First offender, no violent offense. They won't transport you or send you to prison." She slapped on the binding ties and secured his wrists behind him. "Probably. Cooperating from the beginning would have helped. You should have taken my advice."

CHAPTER TWENTY-EIGHT

October 8, 2229, Neo Southern California Metroplex, en route to Police Enforcement Zone 122 Station

"That sausage didn't taste like sausage," Erik complained from behind the control yoke of his MX 60. He wrinkled his nose in disgust. "I don't know if there's something wrong with their ingredient printer or with their grill, but I can't get the taste out of my mouth."

"My pancakes were okay," Jia offered. "A little gritty, but not too bad."

"Food is overrated," Emma commented.

"You've said that before." Erik laughed. "I'll say the same thing. Taste something first, then you can offer an opinion."

Emma's hologram appeared in the back, a pensive look on her face. "It's interesting. I can't taste, but when you describe it, I understand. Not in the sense that I can perform a molecular analysis and describe the components of a given vapor, but..." She chuckled. "It's interesting, anyway."

Erik grinned at Jia. "Look at us. We're such gourmet food writers we can make an AI have taste capacity like a human."

"Don't get ahead of yourself, Detective," Emma insisted. "I'm sure my ability to almost process the sensory experience is the result of my extensive capabilities and assimilation of a variety of data sources and has nothing to do with you."

Erik put a hand over his heart. "Ouch. I'm hurt. How can you treat your parents like that?"

"I find your sense of humor interesting at times. That's not meant as a compliment." Emma tilted her head. "There's a news report playing that you two might find of interest."

"Trying to avoid giving us credit, huh?" Erik chuckled. "Take control, please, and show us." He released the yoke.

The entire front window darkened, and a serious-looking anchorwoman sat behind a desk. Despite her youthful face, the gray streaks in her dark hair indicated a de-aging treatment. Jia wondered why she didn't dye it given her job, but the chyron and the graphics next to the anchor drew the most attention.

"Owl Award-Winning Reporter Lance Onassis was arrested yesterday, following what is described as a bizarre attempt to harass and frame NSCPD Detective Erik Blackwell. The prosecutor handling the case has already put out a statement noting that Onassis is now fully cooperating with the authorities. The implications of his—"

"That's enough, Emma," Erik suggested. The news program disappeared, and the window cleared, revealing the towers and flitters of Neo SoCal.

Jia frowned. "I'm annoyed that transportation is off the table. He was so smug."

"He might not be going to prison, but even a month in jail and a fine is going to mess up a guy like that," Erik suggested. "Besides, it's not like he's going to be going anywhere live and in-person with camera drones for a while. We wouldn't want him on the frontier anyway."

"Why?" Jia glanced at him.

"The colonies didn't do anything to deserve Lance Onassis," Erik deadpanned.

Jia snickered. "Maybe the next triad thugs to show up will take this as a lesson."

"Us taking down an arrogant reporter who could have been out-criminaled by a kid?"

"One can always hope."

October 9, 2229, Neo Southern California Metroplex, Police Enforcement Zone 122 Station, Office of Captain Alexander Ragnar

The captain stood behind his desk. He extended his large hand to Erik and Jia after they entered, giving them both a firm shake. "It's times like this I realize how much I'll regret losing you two."

"What's going on, sir?" Jia asked.

"I just got a call from the CID." The captain took a seat. "Staring down prison without his hardware spooked Hui more than we thought. We need a detective to find his missing loyalty."

"But he already admitted to Dwazil's murder and the

others," Jia replied. "What else could he admit to? He's giving up the Eternal Dragons in Hong Kong?"

The captain nodded. "Exactly. Even the prosecutor was surprised. Your little gambit scared him so much he's seeing triad assassins in every shadow. Because of his intel, the Eternal Dragons aren't long for this world. Not only that, but he's also giving the CID good lines on the black-market tech dealers who sold him his toys. Slapping them down will do a lot to weaken organized crime on Earth, and maybe in the rest of the Solar System."

"Another useful second-order effect," announced Emma. She remained formless. "Spending some time away from Neo SoCal might be useful for increasing your life expectancies, Detectives."

Captain Ragnar let out a hearty laugh. "It's the opposite. Them leaving means every other cop is going to work harder. And you better think of something else to call them, because they won't be detectives in a few weeks."

"You could just use our names," Erik suggested. "Calling me Contractor Blackwell's going to sound awkward."

"I suppose I could." Emma sounded doubtful.

"That's the other thing I'm going to miss." Captain Ragnar gestured at Erik's PNIU. "I know you've had to be careful how you've used her, but having a military-grade experimental AI on our side has been a great tool. I know you're stealing Constantine, too."

Erik rubbed the back of his neck. "Oh, he told you?"

Captain Ragnar shook his head. "I might be riding a desk, but I'm still a cop, and I notice things."

"Is that going to be a problem?" Jia asked.

"No. He's a big boy. He can make his own decisions. I'm

not happy to lose three talented members of this department, but I know whatever it is you're going on to will be helpful." Captain Ragnar looked at the two of them. "I won't ask you to tell me anything, although I know you two aren't going to work private security. But it doesn't matter."

"Why?" Erik asked.

"Because whatever job you work after leaving here, you'll do the right thing." Captain Ragnar nodded. "That's all I have for you. Keep up the good work as long as you're here."

"We'll try." Erik headed toward the door. "Now if we can just get to the end of the month without someone else trying to blow us up."

Jia offered a polite nod to the captain and followed her partner into the hall. "Sometimes I wonder how much he knows."

"It's like he said," Erik suggested. "Sometimes it's best not to ask questions."

Jia's PNIU chimed, and she tapped it to bring up her message. "Oh, fantastic. Speaking of ambushes and getting blown up."

Erik stopped and looked her way with concern. "What's wrong?"

"My mother has scheduled a dinner party for tomorrow," Jia explained. "And she's made it very clear we must attend."

Erik laughed. "After triad Tin Men, how scary can one mom be?"

"Remember." Jia gave him a plaintive look that caused his stomach to go sideways. "It's *my* mother."

CHAPTER TWENTY-NINE

Jia kept her arm around Erik's as they wandered the edge of the thick crowd.

Men in tuxedos and women in elegant gowns choked the room.

Her parents' cavern of a living room normally swallowed mere humans who dared enter its domain. However, with the crowd of people chatting, laughing, and drinking, the room was easily defeated.

Aggressive air conditioning mercifully kept the heat from becoming oppressive, but Jia was still surprised her mother hadn't rented somewhere larger.

The size of the room destroyed any intimacy the affair might otherwise have had. That made sense. There were three types of Lan Lin parties. The first type was small, intimate affairs designed to foster better relationships between close friends and relatives.

The second type was large, calm events focused on business networking.

The third type was like the current party—attempts to

show off the wealth and class of the Lin family. Jia had never resented her mother for throwing that type of party, but she'd also never cared.

Flashing money didn't appeal.

A smaller number of guests would have been preferable, beyond the difficulty of navigating the room. Everyone was focused on each other and ignoring the entertainment.

A young man strumming an *erhu* sat next to a woman in a flowing pink and yellow dress who plucked a *guqin*, her movements precise and elegant. Their notes flowed together to fuel a somber but beautiful melody.

No one paid them any attention, lost in their conversations.

From what Jia's mother had told her, the musicians had been hired for the Mid-Autumn Festival party, and she enjoyed their performances so much, she decided to hire them again. They probably didn't care that they were being ignored as long as they were paid well.

Erik squeezed her arm gently. "Is this the part where I tell you that you're supposed to be enjoying this?" he whispered.

Jia rolled her eyes at his invoking of a previous party. "It's not you. It's just, things like this have never been my kind of event. There's not enough life in it."

"I agree with you there. There's also not enough beer, which is a shame. Your mom generally has some."

"She was going for a certain atmosphere," Jia suggested. "And even fancy beer might not fit that."

A smiling, slightly rotund red-faced man with a glass of wine in hand detached from the crowd, maneuvering with surprising agility toward Jia and Erik. Jia waited patiently. She'd expected more people to talk to her, especially since this was a make-up party.

Then again, it wasn't like all the movers and shakers in her mother's circle had time to come to social functions just because someone's daughter was too busy catching murderous gangsters to attend.

"You know that guy?" Erik inclined his head toward the approaching visitor. "He looks okay."

"Yes. He's Darren Cole, a friend of my mother's." Jia activated her well-trained Lin social smile. It might be a chore when she was working her job, but surrounded by the elite, it came with as much practiced ease as her highly polished shooting skills. "He's nice enough, but he doesn't live in Neo SoCal. I'm surprised to see him."

Darren stopped to allow a waitress carrying a tray of drinks to pass and then finished his approach. "Ah, Jia. It's been far too long since we last talked." He sighed. "You never come to Brussels. It's not Neo SoCal, and it took me a while to get used to when I first went there, but you'd love it. Everything around here is busy and coarse compared to Brussels. We don't pretend to be sky kings there. I thought Beijing and Lagos were bad, but this place always makes me feel like some giant's going to eat me." He waved a hand. "But I'm getting off track. Back to you and how you never visit."

"It's been a busy year." Jia was working on what his angle was. Further, was he part of her mother's twisted political machinations? Why couldn't her mom just enjoy life?

"Oh, yes, with all the crimes and terrorism." Darren

clucked his tongue. "You know how roaches are. When you shine a light on them, they scurry."

"That's one way to put it." Jia gestured to Erik. "This is my partner in more ways than one, Erik Blackwell."

Erik's mouth quirked into a smile, but instead of a snarky quip, he extended his hand to Darren. "Nice to meet you."

Darren gave Erik's hand a firm shake. "I've read about you, of course. The pleasure is all mine. It takes a hell of a man to keep up with Jia." He laughed. "Lin women are inherently stubborn, but she takes it to the next level."

"Don't I know it." Erik laughed. Darren joined him.

"You have to be stubborn when you're around men like Erik," Jia muttered.

Darren shook a finger. "Yes, yes. I had something I wanted to discuss with Jia, but based on what I've heard from Lan, it might be worth discussing with both of you, and I'm more inclined now that I've talked with Erik."

"Why?" Erik asked.

"If you look into a man's eyes, you can tell a lot about him," Darren insisted.

Jia kept her smile intact despite her tightening stomach. "You discussed us with my mother?"

"Yes," Darren replied. "The news claimed you two were leaving the police department. I wasn't sure if that was true, but your mother confirmed it. I was wondering if there were opportunities for both of us that weren't available when you were focused on being public servants."

"Opportunities?" Erik asked. "Like?"

Darren nodded. "Lan told me your work is buried in NDAs, so I won't bother asking you who your primary clients are, but I guarantee you I can and will pay you more to secure your services. My company could use two new VPs of Security. You wouldn't have to worry about field-work anymore. None of the barbaric shooting and getting shot at. I can scarcely imagine."

"That's a very generous offer, Darren," Jia replied, "but we already are locked into a contract. These aren't the kind of terms our clients will see fit to ignore."

"I'm more than prepared to pay whatever termination penalty is in your contracts on your behalf," Darren explained. "I do understand that could run into a large number of zeroes, but I'm sensing this might be a once-in-a-lifetime opportunity."

"We're just two soon-to-be ex-cops," Erik noted. "I'm sure there are people who would work better for your company."

Darren shook his head. "Jia might not have a lot of lead-ership skills yet, but I know she's been groomed for it, and you were an officer in the Army. You've led men in war. It'd be easy for you to apply your leadership skills in a less volatile environment."

"It's generous, Darren," Jia injected. "But it's not for us."

"Wait. Hear me out. There are other things I can offer. For example, unlike your current clients, I wouldn't bury you in shadows and NDAs and smother your reputations." Darren put his hand on Erik's shoulder. "Erik...can I call you Erik?" He looked hopeful.

Erik glanced at the man's hand but didn't pull it off. "Sure. It's better than 'Hey, asshole.'"

Darren laughed. He dropped his hand to shake a finger. "I like you. You're straightforward. No BS. You can trust a man who doesn't feel like he has to hide anything. I always imagined that's how you'd be. I know Jia's straightforward, too, just in a different way, which is why I know both of you would be excellent assets."

"Erik's right." Jia moved closer to him. "We're not working at a managerial level for a reason. We'll be doing fieldwork. Our current primary skillsets and qualifications are geared toward that."

"It's true," Erik confirmed. "I worked hard to make sure I wouldn't get promoted out of the field when I was in the Army."

"And, if I might speak for both of us," Jia added, "we have personal reasons for doing this as well. I can't go into them, but our current work arrangement will facilitate that. Thank you for your offer, and I'm very sorry that we can't take it up at this time."

"I understand." Darren sighed and nodded. "I'll go ahead and send you both my contact information. I'd love to have you on staff when you get bored with shooting people."

Erik scratched his cheek. "I don't know if I'll ever get bored with that."

Darren laughed and slapped him on the arm. "You're a riot. I'll leave you two be. I have other people to harass. With so many opportunities in the room, I'd hate to miss out."

Jia nodded politely. "I'm sure we'll talk again."

"Of course." Darren nodded to Erik. "Nice meeting you as well, Erik." He didn't wait for a response before zooming back into the dense crowd.

"I don't know whether or not I should be insulted." Erik chuckled.

"I'm sure we'll be getting a lot of those kinds of offers in the next few weeks and months after more people hear we're leaving the department." Jia searched the crowd until she found her mother chatting on the other side of the room, looking rather animated. "My mother's going to be helping them along. She sees an opportunity, with me leaving the department. She might be okay with me taking a job I've implied is elite, but if she can extend more control over the situation and get me a job that's high-paying but doesn't involve as much travel, she will."

"Isn't it a good thing to take advantage of opportunities?" asked a familiar voice from behind. "You make it sound like she's doing something bad."

Erik and Jia turned toward the source of the voice. Mei stood behind them in an ornate black gown with so many ruffles it ended up being more complicated than her braids. She greeted Erik with a cool look before smiling at her sister.

"It's not like you to be late," Jia observed.

"Oh, my dear little sister, I had important matters to finish up at the company. Mother understands, which is why she didn't mention it." Mei surveyed the room like a wolf hunting for prey. "I have to thank you two. Even Mother is squeamish about business during holidays, but because you skipped out on the last party, she arranged this one without the holiday constraints."

"We didn't skip out." Jia snorted quietly. "We were investigating crimes. Remember the whole detective thing I do, Mei? It's not just a hobby."

"It's the same difference, but I'm pleased with the end result, so don't take that as complaining."

"Because you want to leave your company?" Erik asked, curiosity in his voice. "Or do you have something else in mind?"

"I think it's good to have opportunities." Mei slid her gaze to him. "And to keep an open mind. If one doesn't, they might pass over the chance of a lifetime, whether the matter is personal or professional. Flexibility is key."

Jia lost her party smile. There was a faint whiff of challenge in her sister's words. Her family claimed to not have a problem with her dating Erik, but they also were experts at striking when someone least expected it—a useful skill to have when trying to control strong-willed relatives or climb the corporate ladder.

A party was the ultimate place for a social ambush.

Erik didn't look away from Mei. "Keeping an open mind is always good. Are you getting at something?"

"Do you love my sister?" Mei asked the question with all the casual interest one might display when inquiring about the weather.

"What are you doing, Mei?" Jia snapped. Her cheeks warmed. "This isn't the time or the place."

Her sister kept her focus on Erik. "I'm analyzing and testing the man you're going out with. It's not as if your personal life has zero effect on the rest of us. More to the point, I am your older sister, and I have a duty to help protect your interests. Your dating history is checkered."

Erik chuckled. "Jia's a big girl. She doesn't need anyone to protect her. She's proven that plenty of times."

"It's not about protecting her. It's about family, which is

very important to me." Mei stepped toward Erik. "Even when the family's frustrating and stubborn."

Jia's heart thundered in her chest.

She had a hard time classifying what she felt for Erik, other than knowing it was more than attraction. The word love carried implications she wasn't ready to face, both good and bad. Despite that, now that Mei had broached the question, Jia couldn't tear her attention from Erik. She wondered how much he'd be willing to admit after her deflections.

The only thing she was sure of was that she didn't want to go into the details in the middle of her mother's party."

Erik shrugged. "I don't date families. I only date individuals, so no offense, but I don't care what anyone thinks other than one very special woman in this room. She might share your last name, but she's not you. Is that clear enough for you, Mei?"

"Aren't you the blunt one?" Mei sneered.

"Yeah, that's me. Blunt as a rock." Erik's merry grin contrasted with Mei's tight, hostile smile.

"I care about what my family thinks," Jia declared, her stomach tightening at Erik's fading grin. "I want that to be clear since we're discussing it."

"That's good to know." Mei slowly turned toward her sister. "I'd hope so."

"But..." Jia continued.

"But?" Mei and Erik asked in unison time.

"Erik's right. I'm dating him, not my family. I want you to like him and support us, but I want to be very clear." Jia narrowed her eyes. "That's the *preferred* situation, but it's strictly optional. Neither you nor our parents get a veto in my social life, no matter what you think about how it might impact you."

Erik's grin returned. Mei stared at her younger sister. Every other conversation faded away, barely noticeable.

This was the time Jia needed to make her stand, not in some restaurant, but in strong Lin territory with Erik at her side. She would never turn her back on her family, nor would she let them control her. They needed to respect her choices and the woman she was, not the woman they wished her to be.

"You don't have to worry, Jia. I'm not going to deliver any ultimatums, not that they would work." Mei's expression softened, and she let out a quiet chuckle. "We all want you to be happy, and we want to make sure that you're doing what you want. It's obvious that you are." She nodded at Erik. "I'm sorry if I offended you."

"It's hard to offend me unless you're trying to kill me." Erik shrugged. "You haven't tried that yet, but the night's still young."

"Don't tempt me." Mei laughed.

"Thank you, Mei." Jia smiled. "Thank you for understanding."

"You have nothing to thank me for." Mei waved to a woman across the room. "Now, I hate to be rude again after being rude such a short while ago, I have to go talk to someone else I've been meaning to corner at this party." She leaned toward Jia to whisper, "He's pulled you away from a less lucrative career in the police to something more lucrative in the private sector, and he's not bad to look at. Maybe I should consider a more…boisterous man myself." With a sly smile, she wandered away.

Jia let out a sigh, half of exhaustion, half of relief. "I keep thinking they'll decide I have to go back to Corbin and gang up on me, but it's good they haven't."

"Nothing wrong with your family supporting your choices." Erik chuckled. "Especially when the choice is me."

"It almost makes me feel bad."

Erik frowned. "Why?"

"Because it's easier to avoid spending much time at home when you're angry at your family," Jia admitted.

"Don't I know it." Erik snagged a wine glass from a passing waitress's tray. He held it up. "Too bad there's no beer, but desperation leads a man to do crazy things." He downed the wine. "Ship aside, we don't know where our first assignment will take us. It could be a nice vacation to a beautiful beach." He moved closer to her, his gaze heavy. "It'd be nice if I could see one bikini babe in real life."

A shiver of excitement passed through Jia, but she couldn't be sure how much of what Erik was saying was real. "We'll just have to hope for somewhere warm with nice, empty beaches, then."

"Yeah." He side-eyed her. "We will."

CHAPTER THIRTY

October 12, 2229, Neo Southern California Metroplex, Outside of Police Enforcement Zone 122 Station

The MX 60 flew away from the station and joined the living stream of lights that defined nighttime flitter traffic, adding its own to the mix. Erik was alone if one only counted carbon-based people. He snickered.

Emma's hologram formed in the passenger seat. "What's so amusing, Erik?" She drew out the last word, almost as if it were a curse. Even AIs weren't free of the power of habit, it seemed.

"You'll get used to it," Erik suggested. "I was just thinking about how Jia bought that new flitter not all that long ago, and she might not get that much use out of it. Even if we stay Earthside, it makes more sense to bring this baby than hers. That's a lot of wasted credits. She could have stuck with the boring blue Corbinmobile."

Emma feigned looking out the window, even if, in truth, she had more situational awareness than any human within a few kilometers. "That's true, but it's more a symbol than an important vehicle, isn't it? My impression was the whole point of purchasing the new flitter was to prove she'd broken with her past."

"It's an expensive symbol."

"Says the man who purchased a Taxútnta MX 60."

"That was as part of my cover," Erik countered. "And it'll help if I play that up. It'll be easier when I'm not a cop."

"If you say so," Emma replied.

Erik slid the MX 60 into a new lane. He let go with one hand, reached under his shirt, and slid his finger over the bent dog tag. It was with him almost all the time. Although he often forgot its presence, he would never forget what it symbolized. "The best symbols aren't expensive," he murmured.

"I might not be a fleshbag and vulnerable to certain frailties of mind and body, but I understand you." Emma continued looking out the window. "If you die seeking your revenge, won't it all be pointless? One might argue that living a rich and full life and remembering those you lost would be a valid way to respond to the events on Molino."

"Sure, but who said I'm going to die?" Erik's quick check of the cameras and lidar didn't pick up anything unusual, which was a good thing for a man who was often targeted. "I'll live a rich and full life after I take down the bastards responsible. Come on, you've been with me for most of my time here. Check the score, Emma. It's something like Erik, one hundred. Scum bags, zero."

"You don't think you can lose, do you?" She laughed. "There are more than a few sayings about pride that are applicable."

"I'm not sure I'm explaining it objectively enough for you to understand," Erik replied. "I can lose. I know that. I spent thirty years having that drilled into me. I'm looking for revenge because I *did* lose, but I can't *afford* to lose now." He grunted. "We'll find them. I don't care if they're hiding behind every *yaoguai* and experimental Tin Man in the UTC. I don't care if I have to cut through a thousand men."

"That's a lot of blood you intend to spill," she countered.

Erik shook his head. "All they have to do is to stay the hell out of my way."

Emma tilted her head. "Hmm. This is fortuitous. Colonel Adeyemi is attempting to establish a secure commlink. Shall I connect you, or do you not want to talk to him?"

"Yeah, go ahead." Erik wasn't expecting a call from the colonel, but the man wasn't using his experimental communications system to ask Erik to pick up Thai food and drop it off.

"Erik, you there?" the colonel asked.

"Emma, take control," Erik ordered. "Keep us going back to my place. Yeah, I'm here, Colonel. What did you need?"

"I just wanted to touch base with you about your upcoming career change." The colonel grunted. "I'm not saying Koval's corrupt. I know she's not. She's been hunting nasty two-legged monsters for a while, but I hope you understand what you're getting into. I wanted to be clear that once you become a gopher of the Intelligence Directorate, I won't be able to help you as much as I have to date. I know why you're doing it, and it'll help us both get what we want, but part of me worries about not being as involved."

Erik frowned. "What do you mean by all that? Does that mean you can't supply me with weapons anymore?"

"No, I can still do that," Colonel Adeyemi replied. "But you know how it is. Everyone has their lane, and I'm already way out of mine. I was able to help push things your way as a cop because a lot of people don't care what's going on at that level. If you're working for the ID, it limits my options." He paused. "A lot."

"I'm not backing away from this just because it upsets some political balance crap that everyone in the government has going," Erik answered. "It's not my problem."

Colonel Adeyemi took a deep breath. "I'm not saying you should, but I encourage you to use the ID as much as they intend to use you because they might toss you to the side when they no longer figure you're useful to them."

"If it gets me closer to the bastards behind Molino, I don't care. If I have to scrape enough credits to buy my own junker to fly to wherever they are, I'll be fine."

"You say that, but there's less I can do to directly support you when you're away from Earth," the colonel explained. "You'll be a lot more vulnerable."

Erik chuckled. "We always knew it would come to this, didn't we?"

"There's something else, too." Something approaching true worry flavored the colonel's voice.

"Just get it out there," Erik insisted. "I'll deal with it."

"The thing is, you working the ID, even indirectly, changes the calculus a lot on other things. Among them, it means you're taking experimental Defense

Directorate property and doing ID errands with it, including off-world. You shouldn't get too used to having or become dependent on Emma. I can't guarantee the DD won't come looking to take back what's ours."

Emma frowned deeply. "I'm not your property, Colonel. I would have thought you and Dr. Mommy Cavewoman understood that. *If* I choose to return to the uniform boys' control, it'll be on my terms and because I think it'll benefit me, not because I care about what you want or need."

Colonel Adeyemi grunted in frustration. "I don't want to argue with you, Emma. I think your time with Erik and Jia is doing more for the project than years of sitting around in the lab would, but that's not the fundamental problem."

"What is, then?" Erik narrowed his eyes. He couldn't bring himself to attack fellow soldiers, but that didn't mean he was prepared to hand Emma over easily. Hiding her and lying about it wouldn't be too outrageous. It'd be different if she wanted to go back.

"General Aaron has the final say on this project," Colonel Adeyemi explained. "And he's not that happy about all this. He's been temporarily convinced that it'll be better and safer for Emma to be used to aid ID work than what you have been doing, but he's itching to send a couple of squads and take her back, even if that means he has to get rough."

Emma snorted. "Despite the risk of self-destruction?"

"We're not idiots, Emma. We all know you're not going to destroy yourself. You think you're better than us. You think even if we brought you back, you could escape." The colonel scoffed. "Your threats won't work."

"No, those particular threats won't." Emma's mouth twitched into a smile, but it didn't reach her eyes. "You're right. I'm too valuable to destroy myself, but I do want to stress, Colonel, that I'm not above defending myself, and I'm quite capable of it."

"You're threatening military personnel?" Colonel Adeyemi sounded amused.

"I'm simply noting that fleshbags are easier to replace. The UTC wouldn't miss a few. I've learned a lot by associating with Erik and Jia. There are many efficient ways to kill people."

"Hey," Erik interjected. "Let's all dial down the threats. It doesn't matter. He just said the general is okay with things."

"For now," Colonel Adeyemi cautioned. "I just wanted that to be understood and very clear. I'm doing everything I can from my end, but at the end of the day, in the military, the person with the most stars wins."

"Do your best to keep it that way. I might not shoot a guy who comes uninvited, but a few punches wouldn't be anything but a healthy brawl."

Emma huffed and disappeared. "Fools. Don't tempt me, and you won't have to suffer."

The MX 60 continued flying with precision and grace. Her hologram might be gone, but Emma was still in control and listening to the conversation. Erik didn't mind. He'd been honest with both the colonel and Emma about where he stood. Betraying Emma to the DD didn't make sense.

"I didn't just call you to pick fights with Emma," the colonel continued. "I've got a new shipment of gear I'd like to deliver in the next few days. I thought it'd be best since we don't know what your new boss has planned for you."

"She's not my new boss," Erik insisted. "Think of her as a new client. But while we're talking about gear, the guns, ammo, and explosives are nice, but what about exoskeletons? A couple Army-grade exos could do a lot toward keeping Jia and me alive longer. I'm getting sick of having to fight everything that comes at me on foot."

Colonel Adeyemi didn't answer for several seconds. "There's no way I can do that. I'm already stretching things with your weapons dealer license. You could see about getting civilian models, but I can't supply them."

Erik grunted in annoyance. "Not good enough, and if we bought them, we'd have an unnecessary trail leading to us. They're missing too many features."

"I can't do it," the colonel declared firmly. "I'm handicapped by being in the Army. I've got people watching and caring what I do with weapons and equipment, even allegedly excess equipment, and there are hard limits on the amount of gear we can shunt to civilian dealers. And your new client doesn't work for the Army, now does she?"

"You're saying Alina can get me exos?" Erik asked.

"I'm saying it wouldn't hurt to ask. If the ID wanted to borrow military exoskeletons, that's a different situation than giving them to a civilian weapons dealer. Hell, she probably has some in a basement somewhere."

Erik nodded, the smile building on his face. He would send a message to Alina and arrange a meeting. It wasn't like they needed to get it figured out that night.

If he could get Jia up to speed on piloting exoskeletons, they would become even more difficult to take down.

He'd had doubts before, but given the talent she was demonstrating with conventional piloting, it would be easy. Her martial arts skills meant she already had body control and attention to detail, and her recent training at the flight center proved she had superior inherent spatial awareness.

All those traits suggested she'd make an excellent exoskeleton pilot. Her bravery and stubbornness made for a good combination for him and a deadly cocktail for their enemies.

"Thanks, Colonel." Erik nodded, liking his new plan more with each passing second. "I'm sure Alina can hook me up. Besides that, I'll be happy for whatever you can give me next time we meet. Hey, what about a few mini-flitters and scout bikes? The more mobility options we have, the better."

The colonel laughed. "Talk to her, not to me. I can keep giving you what I have."

"I will talk to her, Colonel Stingy," Erik replied.

"Need I remind you that I gave you a laser rifle?" Colonel Adeyemi countered.

"Yeah, but only *one*." Erik fake-whined.

The colonel cut off the connection, but Erik heard him chuckling before the silence hit.

Erik headed down the hall toward his apartment. He was still thinking about his conversation with the colonel.

The investigation into Molino would change with the freedom that came with not being a cop. That flexibility would make up for the doors closed now that Erik couldn't flash a badge or arrest someone.

Not a bad trade-off given the help from the ID, but what about afterward?

He stopped in front of his door. His thoughts of the future had died on Molino with his unit. Revenge consumed him, and on the long trip back to Earth, it had filled his every thought. A future after punishing the conspiracy seemed pointless and formless.

Or at least, it *had*.

Erik didn't need a therapist to know the reason for the change: Jia. If by some insane mercy of the Lady Erik survived his war of revenge, there was someone waiting for him at the end of the dark tunnel of vengeance.

"I need to keep my focus," he muttered under his breath. "Until the end."

"It's interesting you say that," Emma replied. "Because there is unusual system activity in your apartment, including with the cameras. There's a high probability that someone is inside your apartment and has taken measures to make sure they aren't being recorded."

"Eternal Dragon holdovers wanting some revenge?" Erik drew his gun. "I'd be impressed."

"If it were that level of manipulation, it'd be easier for me to unravel," Emma replied. "This is a higher-quality enemy."

Erik let a lopsided grin take over his face, casual ease suffusing his body, even with his weapon out. "Talos wouldn't do it here. They'd expect me to be ready. And we sent that message earlier. Maybe a certain friend of ours is in town. You never know with her."

"I notice you aren't putting your gun away," Emma observed.

Erik shrugged. "Better to be safe than acquire unexpected and unrequested brain ventilation."

"I'm going to miss you when you die." Emma snickered. "You're nothing if not amusing."

"Open the door. Once I'm inside, close it." Erik pointed his gun at the door. Trusting his instincts had gotten him this far, but every man was wrong a couple of times his life.

The door slid open. Erik stepped in, sweeping the room with his weapon. He stopped when he found a smiling Alina standing behind his kitchen counter. Unlike many times he'd talked to her, she wasn't in a specialty Intelligence Directorate stealth suit or disguised.

The vibe of her dark blue suit clashed with her long cyan ponytail.

"You could have just sent me a message about meeting somewhere, Alina," Erik replied, "instead of messing with me at home." He holstered his weapon. "And why didn't you arrange some weird password crap?"

"There are times, based on intelligence, that I'm more worried than others." Alina glanced at the door. "And I have people watching this location now that you've agreed to work for me. It'd be a mistake for anyone hoping to avoid my investigation to come anywhere near here."

Emma appeared. "Interesting. I still can't perceive her. She's using more advanced tech than she has before."

"Sometimes it's good to be careful," Alina replied.

"You said people are watching this place?" Erik asked.

"Sometimes people are wrong." Alina stepped out of the kitchen, revealing she'd been holding her flechette pistol. With a quick movement, she tucked it into a holster under her jacket. "And it's good to keep you both on your toes. It'd be a terrible waste of resources if you ended up dying soon."

"I can hear her," Emma admitted. "Can't see her, but I can see everything else in the apartment. I'll have to develop countermeasures against that."

"Good plan," Alina suggested. "As you found out in your recent case, the thugs are catching up. The race only ends when one side dies." She sauntered over to the couch and took a seat, crossing her legs at the ankle. "So, my modern-day Perseus, what did you need?"

"Exoskeletons," Erik announced. "Military-grade. If you've got something better than that, I'll take it too, but I'm tired of fighting without the best gear."

"I'm not Generous Gao, Erik." Alina snickered. "Nor Santa Claus, or even a genie."

"If the Goddess of Death wants her lackeys to kill people, she needs to give them the weapons they need." Erik shrugged, not caring if she was offended by the nickname.

Her mouth twitched into a frown. "Oh, is that your argument? Everything I provide for you risks leaving a trail. You understand that, don't you?"

"And a couple of exoskeletons leaves a bigger trail than a ship?" Erik raised an eyebrow in challenge.

"In a way, it does." Alina uncrossed her legs. "And you've done well mostly not using that kind of equipment. Many of your upcoming assignments will require more subtlety, not less. There's a narrow window in which you'll be effective."

The colonel's words haunted Erik. The Intelligence Directorate was planning to toss him aside, but he didn't care. He'd just make sure he found the conspiracy before the ID stopped helping him.

"Is 'subtlety' a different way of saying 'firepower?'" Erik asked. "Because I'm not going to be running around collecting evidence to send to some prosecutor."

Alina let out a quiet scoff. "No, you aren't, but that doesn't mean everything you do will involve death and destruction. Remember, the primary goal of the Intelligence Directorate is ostensibly to *collect* intelligence. Taking down dangerous threats is important but secondary."

Erik laughed. "You're hiring the wrong guy, then."

"No, I'm not," Alina insisted. "You've made a splash, but you've also done a good job of not only uncovering local conspiracies but making good progress against Talos and whoever might be allied with them. You're a natural investigator, just as you're a natural warrior, and as much as I'd love for Fate to deliver you to some epic fiery destiny, we sometimes have to help it along outside of ancient myths. There are people out there who need to be stopped, and I'll use every tool available to me to do it, including you and Jia."

"You going to give me the exos? If you want me to hunt assholes across the galaxy, I need the tools for when those assholes get frisky to do that." Erik headed toward his kitchen. He needed a beer. "Take it out of my fake pay."

"It's real pay," Alina replied. "For a real job, even if what it entails won't be public." She nodded. "I'll see what I can do, but it's not going to happen overnight. We need to be careful about this."

Erik opened his refrigerator and pulled out a bottle. "Want one?"

"That's okay." Alina stood. "I think we're done here."

"And you can't take an hour for a drink?" Erik inclined his head toward the beer.

"Perhaps in the future." Alina walked to the door. "But until then, I don't have time to relax." She opened the door with a quick slap on the access panel. "I'll be in touch."

Alina disappeared into the hallway and the door closed. Erik lifted his beer, gulping down half. He shook his head and laughed.

"What's so funny?" Emma asked.

"She puts on a good front, but I think I finally found a woman more uptight than Jia." Erik downed the rest of his beer. "Sometimes it's good to relax, and *I'm* the guy devoting his life to vengeance."

"If you say so. Poisoning yourself to relax is one of the odder things fleshbags do."

"Sure." Erik grinned. "But that's what makes us so interesting. Hey, there's something I need you to look up for me. I need to make my own preparations, regardless of what Alina ends up doing."

Emma eyed him. "Always interesting."

CHAPTER THIRTY-ONE

Jia did her best to keep her hands in her lap and her heart calm.

She stared out at the relaxing flow of flitter traffic and thought about how the MX 60's seats hugged her body so well. Anything she could do to distract herself from looking at Erik and think about the cryptic words he'd offered at the end of their workday. She'd never been so unsettled by two simple sentences.

"I want to show you something. It's about time I did."

Jia licked her lips. When she'd pressed Erik, he'd hadn't offered any more details. That wasn't typical Erik, and she'd spent the last twenty minutes trying to figure out where they might be going.

A restaurant for a date wouldn't warrant such secrecy, and if it involved the conspiracy or a case, he wouldn't hold back details. She took a deep breath. Wherever they were going was far more special.

Erik slowed his flitter before maneuvering out of their lane to head toward a nearby commercial tower. He dropped several levels and arrived at a typical sprawling parking platform filled with normal flitters, most not looking expensive. That wasn't a problem. The best places for romance didn't need to be filled with corporate VPs.

She'd chosen to leave that lifestyle behind.

Curiosity burned in Jia, but she didn't ask where they were. Not knowing was exciting, too. The MX 60 settled down in a convenient spot near an entry.

"We're here," Erik declared. He opened his door and slid out of the flitter. "Come on. It's almost time for our appointment."

Jia's gaze dropped to the floor. "Do we need anything special?"

She had long since stopped being bothered by the reflexive desire to bring along heavy ordnance. Better embarrassed than dead.

Erik shook his head and motioned to the door. "Just yourself."

"If you say so." Jia exited and caught up with Erik, still curious as they stepped through the door. Rather than leading to a wide-open hub, it opened into a narrow hall lined with doors and modest signs. She followed Erik as they walked briskly down the empty corridor, their footsteps echoing.

Erik stopped halfway down and nodded at the door. "We're here."

It read "Fantasy Simulations." Jia's heart rate kicked up. What kind of fantasy did Erik have in mind? Going from fake dating to fantasy simulations was a big jump, especially since they hadn't discussed it.

"Uh..." Jia couldn't finish her thought. Her stomach felt

like a Zitark was trying to claw its way out. Her last boyfriend, Corbin, had never made her feel like this.

"Come on." Erik opened the door.

Two narrow hallways led off from a tiny reception area. There weren't any chairs or anything else of note in the room, other than a bored-looking man sitting behind a tiny reception desk barely as wide as his body. He was reading on a data window projected onto his desk.

The receptionist looked up and smiled. "Oh, Detective Blackwell. Your room is ready. Did you need any help implementing the custom program?"

"Nah. I'm good. But thanks." Erik nodded toward one of the narrow hallways. "Follow me."

Jia looked down at her clothes, wondering if she was overdressed for whatever they were about to do. Maybe she was underdressed. She had a decent number of sexy dresses, but lingerie was in short supply. Corbin had treated sex the same way he treated taxes.

It was a wonder they'd lasted as long as they did.

The pair continued on in near silence, Jia's breathing growing increasingly ragged with each step. She'd never thought this was how the night ended.

When they finally stopped, she tried not to be disappointed by the nondescript door and simple identification. She didn't know what she'd expected—perhaps some exotic suite name—but it wasn't a plate reading Simulator 34a.

Jia could imagine the Pacific Tactical Center didn't want clients doing anything that required the place to be cleaned later. She'd read about specialty places that catered to amorous scenarios, but it wasn't anything she'd thought much about.

Erik opened the door and entered the silver-floored white room. Despite the resemblance to the simulation rooms at the tactical center, it was far smaller—not much larger than her living room.

"You got the scenario set up, Emma?" Erik asked.

Jia grimaced. She'd forgotten about the AI. The idea of Emma paying attention while they were doing anything riled Jia's stomach.

Why the hell had Erik gotten her involved? There was no way he didn't care.

"Yes," Emma replied. "Everything will be to your specifications, down to the most absurd details."

Jia stepped inside, her knees wobbly. Everything had gone sideways in seconds. The door slid closed behind her.

"What's this about?" Jia managed to get out, her voice shaking.

"I thought it was time," Erik explained with a smile. "We've been together for a while, and it's ridiculous that we haven't done this earlier."

"R-really?" Jia blinked. "It wasn't even like we were together at first. I mean, *together* together, so it makes sense we waited to do certain things."

"Uh, sure, I guess." Erik furrowed his brow, clearly confused. He gestured around the room. "You're probably wondering why we're here instead of the tactical center."

Jia nodded, channeling all her self-control to keep her face smooth. Emma could undoubtedly detect her elevated heart rate, but if the AI knew what was good for her, she would keep her holographic mouth shut, or Jia would figure out a way to sew it shut.

"The problem with the tactical center is, it's better for scenarios that require individual freedom of movement," Erik explained. "But that means its physics is based on your body. It's not as good for simulating vehicles or that kind of thing. This place is better for vehicles, but not things that require individuals to walk around a lot."

"Vehicles?" Jia stared at Erik, trying to imagine what was coming next. For all their frank discussions, they hadn't discussed sex much. He could be into all sorts of surprising things. And apparently, it involved vehicles. She frowned.

He had a perfectly good flitter outside.

"Yeah." Erik nodded. "And the VR we have on the Rabbit won't give you the proper sensations."

"Proper sensations?" Jia swallowed. "I'd never thought about it like that. I mean, uh... It's not like I haven't thought about it, but I've never thought about doing it in a place like this. Not that I'm saying no. It just takes a little getting used to. You have to understand.

Erik smiled. "Oh, so you figured it already? I wasn't sure if you would."

"Of course, I figured it out. How could I not from the name and everything you just did?"

"Great." Erik clapped once. "That makes it easy. I'm almost certain you'll have a natural talent as an exo pilot. It's not like it's *that* hard. They're designed to enhance people's normal movements, after all, but walking around in one and using one in a fight are two different things. Developing the muscle memory for everything other than basic movement and getting used to the exo as an extension of your body takes a while for some people. This isn't piloting a ship, but given that it's you, we can get you walking and running immediately and up to TPST level in a couple of weeks."

"Exoskeleton training?" Jia slowly looked around the room. "But, um, we don't have two. Or even one." She ran her tongue inside her cheek and rubbed her chin, trying to fake deep thought and distract from her face. If it was as red as it was hot, her embarrassment could be seen from Alpha Proxima.

"I've got Alina working on that." Erik chuckled. "It took a little convincing, but I think we're going to get something a lot better than even I'm used to. It'll be nice when we have to knock on a door with a bunch of Talos Tin Men on the other side."

Jia turned away, feigning examining the corner of the room. She should quit working with Erik and start her academic career with an interesting research paper proving it was impossible to die from embarrassment.

She'd risked her life to prove the hypothesis.

"Is everything okay, Jia?" Emma asked. "Your heart rate is extremely elevated, given the situation."

Jia pressed her lips together, fighting the curse that wanted to erupt.

Sewing her mouth shut was not going to be harsh enough.

Never in her life had she thought about how unfair it was that AIs couldn't be strangled. Taking Emma's core and smashing it to pieces wouldn't be as satisfying as wrapping her fingers around a windpipe.

Maybe she could strangle an embodied Emma in the simulation.

"Huh?" Erik frowned. "You get a weird message or something?"

Jia chuckled nervously and waved her hands in front of her. "I'm just pumped. My pilot training has been more exciting than I expected, so it'll be nice to know how to pilot an exoskeleton, too. Every skill I have is useful, am I right? It's just weird to think about how I used to do nothing but sit at my desk doing reports, and I'm going to be running out in an exoskeleton."

"You're a great partner now, and it'll only make you better," Erik suggested.

"You're trying to turn me into Assault Infantry," Jia joked, desperate to push the conversation away from her misunderstanding. She couldn't be *sure* Erik wouldn't figure it out.

"Nope. I never served with someone as sexy as you." Erik grinned.

Jia took several deep breaths. Warmth suffused her body. Erik might not know what she'd been expecting, but it was like the bastard could sense it.

She smiled. What was she so afraid of? No, he hadn't brought her to the building to take their relationship to the next level, but if she wanted something, she could push for it herself.

"I'm glad to hear that." Jia sauntered over to him with her best hip-waggling sexy walk. She wouldn't be hired as a model anytime soon, but the look in Erik's eyes told her he appreciated it. "I'm not arrogant enough to think I'm the most beautiful woman in the UTC, but I hope I'm doing pretty well."

"More than pretty well." Erik smirked. "And I know I'm better looking than Mr. Down-to-Earth Businessman."

Jia punched him in the arm. "You're bringing up Corbin *now*? Talk about killing the mood."

"I am here to teach you to kill people in an exoskeleton. Killing the mood for anything else is kind of inevitable." Erik shrugged, although he kept the playful grin.

"Emma, can you give us five minutes alone?" Jia asked.

"Very well, Jia. You can use your PNIUs to call me back sooner if you need to."

"Why did you do that?" Erik asked. "I still need her to adjust some things about the scenario."

He hadn't realized her mistake, and she'd accepted something important about herself.

It was time to take control of the situation.

"There's more to life than training on how to kill people," Jia offered.

Erik smirked. "We're also training on how to wound people." He lowered his voice and looked into her eyes. "But it's also important to remember why we care."

"Sometimes I don't know what's going through your head," Jia murmured.

"Good. If *you* can't figure me out, *they* certainly can't."

"Is this thing between us real?" Jia's breath slowed, even as her heart pounded harder. "We might not talk about it, but that doesn't mean anything I said before has changed. Sometimes I don't know."

"I don't know what you want me to say," Erik offered. "I don't have it figured out. There's something. We both feel it, but we're not like most people. Our situation's complicated.

Jia tilted her head and slightly parted her lips. "That means we both understand all the distractions are just that. I don't see the problem. Do you?"

"No problem." Erik leaned in and captured her mouth with his.

Jia didn't close her eyes.

She peered into his eyes as they deepened the kiss, a searing fire spreading throughout her body. Erik wrapped his arms around her waist and pulled her flush against him. Time slowed, Jia's attention captured by that moment until Erik slowly pulled away with a reluctant look.

"That felt like you meant it," Jia whispered, her lips swollen and her breathing ragged. She shivered with excitement.

Erik gave her a lopsided grin. "Consider it motivation. Don't make me regret it during training, or I'll have to reconsider it in the future."

"Are you threatening my kiss supply based on my exoskeleton training results?" Jia pulled back, then planted her hands on her hips and offered a mock glare. "That's an interesting motivational technique."

"Different people require different techniques. Now let's get Emma back here."

CHAPTER THIRTY-TWO

A couple of hours later, Jia had all but mastered the basic movements and controls, including fire control for the heavy rifle they'd added for the night's training.

Most new recruits took a few days to move naturally, but anyone watching Jia would have thought she'd been training for weeks.

Erik stood in the corner of the room, watching her progress on multiple data windows. When he watched her directly, it looked like she stood inside the top half of an exoskeleton, the bottom of the floor twisting and turning. From her perspective, she had full freedom of movement.

Jia jogged along, the exoskeleton thudding hard on the hardpacked dirt of the simulated wasteland setting. Large rock outcroppings covered the area, along with the bleached white skeletons of different species, some native to Earth and some not.

A huge thin reptile-like skeleton with twelve legs, two half-broken off, lay at the base of an outcropping blocking

Jia's path. The air rippled in the distance, and oppressive heat choked half the room.

Erik could feel it if he stuck his arm out.

"Continue running toward the nav marker for one more klick without significant deviation in course," Erik ordered. "Don't trip, or I'll make you start over."

"I only tripped a few times, and not for an hour." Jia scoffed and sped up, weaving between two large skeletons of something that might have once been a four-winged bird. She fired her jump thrusters and the exoskeleton launched into the air, its feet barely clearing a huge rock. Erik's jaw tightened as she headed toward the ground, her exoskeleton's upper torso too far forward. Right before impact, she brought the feet forward, landing and continuing her run without stumbling.

He blew out a breath he was holding.

"Damned good landing," Erik announced.

"I'd love to roll to conserve momentum, but I don't think that would work well," Jia replied.

"They need to develop an exo that can do that." Erik laughed. "Some aliens might have ones like that. The Aldrans probably do."

"We'll need to sneak into their territory and steal the plans." Jia jumped again.

"I'm sure Alina will have us doing that kind of thing eventually."

She landed on top of a huge pile of rocks and leapt off, this time without using the thrusters before hitting the ground. "Okay, I'm past the nav point. I was expecting something more exciting."

"Erik didn't suggest the initial training nav points needed to be interesting," Emma noted. "Blame him."

"Hey, when you're out in the field, you don't always have something interesting," Erik countered. "Being overly obsessed with landmarks is a good way to get ambushed. Practice like you play."

Jia jumped again, the exoskeleton managing a clumsy though impressive spin. Quick counterthrust at the end had her facing the opposite direction, her rifle at the ready.

"I think I'm getting the hang of it." She grinned.

"Okay, running and jumping are easy," Erik observed. "At the end of day, if that was all you had to do in an exoskeleton, we wouldn't even require all the controls. You need a real challenge."

"Bring it on," Jia shot back. "Let me guess—you've got a squad of bikini babes in exoskeletons that I have to hunt down?"

Erik laughed. "No. I don't, and I'm glad I don't after what happened earlier. Don't want you getting jealous."

She growled a bit. "I wish I could shoot you right now," Jia muttered.

"We'll make this easy. First, a few targets. Emma, give her the first batch."

Small circular targets appeared, all sticking out of the dried, cracked earth and evenly spaced at intervals of fifty meters. Another set appeared floating ten meters above the first set. Standard concentric rings of different colors filled the targets.

"This is simulating a high-end military model, so take advantage of your helmet's faceplate and the interface with your smart lenses," Erik explained. "You've got all that targeting assistance, so you should use it. Hold position and bullseye those targets, ground and aerial. It should be easy since they aren't moving."

Jia took a deep breath. The massive arm of the exoskeleton lifted the huge rifle. She lined up her first shot and fired. The rest came in rapid succession. Erik nodded, a data window displaying the targets all close up. Her shots had ripped out the center of each target.

"Now, let's make it a little harder," Erik announced. "Emma, level two."

The targets vanished, and a new batch appeared. The ground targets floated back and forth horizontally, while the aerial targets bounced up and down. Otherwise, they were identical to the first set.

"The aim assist can do a lot, but you still have to line up the shots," Erik explained. "The grav fields installed in a military-grade exo will get you nice release without recoil sending you flying, but they can't do much for your shots once they leave the field, and the aim assist isn't always the greatest. Keep that in mind. We'll train on that next time."

"It's not like I don't have experience fighting in zero-G," Jia reminded him. Her gun came alive again, the sound muted for Erik, given his position in the room.

The shots came slower, but Jia blew out the center of each target without a single miss as she continued her comment. "If you already know how to shoot, it's not that hard with the aim assist and recoil suppression. It's easier than using a rifle with my own two hands."

Erik chuckled darkly. "Sure, it's easy when you don't have anyone shooting at you, but what about when you do? Emma, level three."

The scene shifted. The barren rock-filled landscape disappeared, replaced by a dense forest. Brush and fallen logs were strewn all about. Trees with massive trunks stretched into the sky, tangling together to form a thick canopy.

Birds and insects flew overhead, highlighted by the rays of sunlight penetrating the holes in the canopy.

"You've got a lot of combat experience, Jia," Erik observed. "But it's been all in urban environments. They have their own issues you have to keep in mind, but we could end up in all sorts of trouble."

Jia scoffed, slowly surveying the forest. Erik smiled as he watched a data window providing her POV. She'd already flipped to thermal imaging to search the forest despite not knowing the target.

"I've trained at the tactical center in all sorts of bizarre environments," she noted. "With you and Emma designing the scenarios."

"True, which is why you're somewhere between a cop and infantry at this point." Erik swiped away a data window. A new one appeared with a list of possible enemies he'd prepared with Emma's help. He tapped one and snickered under his breath. It was time to test the limits of Jia's ability to handle a ridiculous surprise. A burst ripped from Jia's gun, blasting a shower of bark off a trunk.

"What's the target?" Jia demanded. "I saw something appear out of nowhere, and it definitely wasn't an animal." She hissed and fired again as something rustled in the forest, darting behind another tree.

Erik smirked, not bothering to look at her POV feed.

He knew what was hunting her. If the enemy moved close enough, Jia's shock would cost her the battle.

"Come on, Jia," Erik challenged. "You know how this goes. We don't always know what's out there. I'm not going to tell you. We'll just say you've been separated from me, and we were investigating Talos, and now you're being hunted."

"I don't think it's a Tin Man. No. A *yaoguai*, then. It wasn't a human or a bot. That much I'm sure of."

Jia narrowed her eyes and fired a constant stream, riddling the tree with bullets. The dust and bark swirled in the air, almost a smokescreen as something darted to another tree, a flash of hot pink noticeable before it succeeded. Her target moved again, leaping and grabbing a branch. A quick swing sent the tailed creature flying. Jia jerked up her rifle and fired, narrowly missing the form before it landed behind a tree.

"That can't be," she shouted. "No way."

"You could confirm it by reviewing your feed," Erik suggested, trying not to laugh.

"Not paying attention to my combat situation sounds like a good way to die," Jia muttered. "I just have one question. Did you think of this, or did Emma?"

Jia pivoted toward the tree. Two quick bursts blasted chunks out of the trunk, but the target remained crouched behind it.

"Don't blame me," Emma insisted. "My scenario involved something far different."

The target sprinted from behind the tree, now fully visible—a Zitark. The dark colors of its scales blended with the greenery of the forest, but unlike the ones they'd fought in simulations before, this alien wore a hot pink bikini.

Jia didn't fire as the Zitark charged between trees, its path erratic. "Why is it wearing a bikini? They might not be from Earth, but they're closer to Earth reptiles than anything. They don't have breasts!"

"Hey, don't insult her just because she's a little flat." Erik laughed.

The bikini-clad Zitark jumped again, a plasma pistol in hand. A bright blast erupted and screamed through the forest. Jia pivoted, but it was too late as the shot exploded against her faceplate. The forest and Zitark vanished, replaced by the white room. The exoskeleton around her flowed away, a thick dark fluid flowing into the floor and disappearing until she stood on the ground, staring at the wall, slack-jawed.

"You sent a Zitark in a bikini after me?" Jia sputtered, her eyes wide.

Erik laughed. "You never know what we might run into." He laughed and slapped his knee. "One tip, though. I was waiting for you to use your shield, but you never did." He raised his left arm and patted it. "If you'd had it up, you would have survived. Military-grade shields can take a lot of punishment, including energy weapons."

"I guess I still have a few things to learn." Jia sighed. "But I guarantee we'll never fight Zitarks in bikinis."

He waggled his eyebrows. "Never say never."

CHAPTER THIRTY-THREE

October 17, 2229, Neo Southern California Metroplex, Restaurant Colby's

The door to Colby's slid open, and Jia stepped out onto the brightly lit parking platform, leaving behind the delicious savory smells filling the inside.

She didn't leave disappointed. Her tasty dinner had sated both her stomach and her soul, leaving her happy. She would have preferred to have had dinner with Erik, given that it was their day off, but he was busy.

Colonel Adeyemi had finally arranged the latest weapons shipment. She had a flight training appointment, too. Just because things at the 1-2-2 had slowed down, it didn't mean they couldn't find ways to fill their days and nights.

Jia walked past rows of flitters with a smile on her face. Only a couple more weeks remained before they left the department. Part of her mind told her she should be concerned about the bizarre and dangerous future lying ahead, but with each day that passed, she grew more excited.

The prospect of tracking down dangerous scum alongside Erik fueled a broader smile.

She had never met her family's expectations. They had come to accept her, but that didn't retroactively make the earlier years easier. When she joined the police department, she'd thought she'd found her place and her people, but she'd had to go through two partners and a captain before she could accomplish anything approaching actual police work.

Anticorruption efforts had changed the 1-2-2 and the rest of the department in a short time, but she couldn't deny that if it weren't for Erik, she would never have faced the question of continuing at the department.

Now, with the offer before them, she understood where she was supposed to be. She was meant for more. She was meant to go after the most dangerous of men and women, those who threatened the fundamental fabric of human society.

A smart criminal was always the most dangerous, and they required the best hunters, not ones bound by all the restrictions that came with being a municipal detective.

Jia slowed as she approached her flitter, her smile faltering. She whipped out her stun pistol and aimed it at the backseat window. It hadn't been much, just an odd flicker of shadow in the back of her vehicle. While she couldn't see anyone, she also couldn't account for the shadows, based on the position of the vehicle and the nearby lighting source. She narrowed her eyes, angry at the violation. The only question was who was hiding in her flitter, stalker or conspiracy assassin?

Triad Tin Men joined the possibilities.

Whoever was in the back of her vehicle was using optical camouflage. If they weren't moving, it could be basic tech potentially available to lesser threats, but there was no way of verifying that it wasn't dynamic optical camouflage and a more dangerous enemy. Jia holstered her stun pistol and yanked out her slugthrower.

She wouldn't allow herself to die in a parking lot.

"Direct command, lower left rear flitter window," Jia muttered. The window dropped, but she didn't lower her weapon. "Whoever you are, reveal yourself right now or I open fire. I've got a good, low angle, so I can empty my entire gun into you without risking anyone. I don't care how much armor you have on, I'm betting I could hurt you doing that."

The air blurred in the back of the vehicle, becoming a warped vaguely humanoid form before settling into a masked woman in a black catsuit with silver seams. The tight fit revealed a tall, toned body. Although it wasn't the same design as she'd seen before, Jia only knew one person with something like that. The next few seconds would determine if she needed to gun somebody down in the back of her flitter.

"Sing to me of the man, Muse, the man of twists and turns driven time and again off course, once he had plundered the hallowed heights of Troy," Jia offered, her voice almost a whisper, but her gun never dipping.

"The empire, long divided, must unite; long united, must divide," the camouflaged woman replied in

Mandarin. She switched to English, the voice Alina's. She pulled off her mask. "But you shouldn't treat those as valid passphrases going forward. One-time use is our standard."

"It'd help if you didn't show up in my back seat without telling me first."

"I had my reasons," Alina replied.

Jia holstered her weapon. She didn't speak again until she'd settled into the driver's seat and activated the auto-drive to return home. She needed her hands free to shoot Alina if the other woman was up to something. A chuckle escaped her mouth. Caring about flying her flitter had only come recently.

It was as if discovering her talent for flight had pushed her toward wanting to control every vehicle in her life.

"I'm that amusing?" Alina asked. "I can't say I don't try to be, but I haven't said or done anything that funny during this little meeting."

"I'm not laughing because of you," Jia replied, watching as the parking platform grew farther away. "That was a stupid stunt. I could have killed you, and we're not exactly in the middle of nowhere. What if someone was walking by? What about drones?"

"This isn't my first time doing this." Alina shrugged. "I timed it well, and I took measures. I know how to meet people almost anywhere and not get caught. Don't mistake my use of a given method for reliance on that method. One of the reasons I don't get caught is that I don't always use the same techniques. Erik might have thirty years of experience in the Army, but I have as many in the Directorate."

"I keep forgetting you're older than you look," Jia

admitted. "Especially since you don't have that residual gray like Erik."

"That's the problem with this modern world; no one is what they appear to be. Then again, they never have been. If they were, there would be no use for people like me."

"You could have just contacted me," Jia grumbled. "Or Erik, if you needed to make some quantum encrypted mess with Emma."

Alina smiled. "Consider it more training. I'm aware of your piloting lessons, both ship and exoskeleton, and all the tactical training you've been doing with Erik. This is my contribution. The world you're about to step into is different than what you've experienced. I don't think you fully appreciate that."

"Just because I haven't been chasing Talos for years, it doesn't mean I don't have any experience with shadowy conspiracies."

"True, but tell me I'm wrong when I say that being a cop made you approach everything differently." Alina settled into a thin, almost mocking smile. "It'll take a while for you to lose those instincts."

Jia scoffed. "No offense, but can you get to the point? And why are you meeting me without Erik, anyway?"

"Because I wanted to make sure you are committed to this without him around." Alina shrugged. "I don't want some tragic Dido, pining for an Aeneas who leaves her to pursue his own destiny."

"I'm not following Erik around like a puppy," Jia spat. "I'm doing this because there's something rotten out there, and I want to help clean it up. By force, if necessary."

"This isn't the kind of thing you can easily walk away

from. I want that clear. A year from now, if you decide it's too much for you, you won't be able to go back to the department. I'm not saying I'm going to stick you on Molino mopping floors, but you won't be able to pick up your old life."

Jia snorted. "Fine. I'll move to a colony and open a kebab stand."

"This isn't a joke, Jia," Alina insisted.

Jia rolled her eyes. "I'm getting a little tired of people making sure I know what I'm getting into. I'm not some kid fresh out of a school. I'm already involved. I've fought Talos. I've fought *yaoguai*. Nanozombies tried to kill me, but they didn't get that the old Jia Lin died a while back. Someone stronger and more clearsighted lives now."

"Strength isn't the only thing." Alina's gaze turned frosty. "You're stepping into a world where the line between right and wrong is far fuzzier than you'd like. You'll both have to make some hard calls."

"They won't be that hard of calls." Jia patted her holster. "The people we're looking for have no problem killing hundreds if not thousands of innocent people. I'm not all that worried about taking them out if that's what you're asking."

"What about what happens in between?" Alina asked. "If it were as simple as pointing you at the bad guys, I wouldn't need you. To get to the most corrupt people, you have to deal with people who are swimming in the corruption, too."

"I'm a detective. It's not like I haven't worked with questionable informants."

Alina leaned back and shook her head. She let out a

disappointed sigh. "The thing is, Erik? I understand him. He has the most classic of motivations—revenge—so I know he won't get too stuck on what happens in between, but you're not him. You're a woman who grew up wrapped in privilege and blind to the truth around you. You say you're more clear-sighted, but I think you're still naïve, just in a different way. I'm far more ruthless than either of you, and if you work for me, you'll end up the same way. I'm not going to say it's not worth it for the UTC in the end, but it will give you some sleepless nights."

Jia understood that. She'd thought a lot about it. Using Emma had already pushed her past the rules that were supposed to bind police. On the moon, they'd dealt with a bit more.

"I have one question." Jia glanced into the back seat at Alina. "Would you kill an innocent person just because they saw the wrong thing at the wrong time?"

"What if I said yes?" Alina's expression turned blank.

"Don't answer a question with a question." Jia glared at her. "Give me your answer."

Alina shook her head. "I'm not in the ID because I have a love for excitement or because I was looking for a place that would let me kill people and get away with it, but that doesn't mean I'm going to ignore someone like that. You may or may not have to choose between the greater good and an individual's life, but I guarantee you, there's no way we take down Talos and anyone else like them without at least making people uncomfortable. Nobody's coming out of this with a completely clean conscience—not you, not me, not Erik."

Jia turned back around, staring at the flitter in front of

her. "I'll worry about my own conscience. You two can worry about yours."

Alina's expression softened. "I'm not trying to be a bitch. You remind me of me when I was younger. I was idealistic and wanted to save people. Now people call me the Goddess of Death. They don't even bother to do it behind my back anymore. Just realize this will require sacrifice, more than you might understand right now."

"Anything worth doing requires sacrifice," Jia insisted, her hand curling into a fist. "And I have things I want to protect."

"Erik?"

Jia laughed. "Erik can handle himself. I want to help him, but I'm more concerned about innocent civilians going around thinking like I did. Neo SoCal exists because of terrorists who murdered *millions*. There's no guarantee a conspiracy can't do something like that again. The nanozombies made that clear. There are monsters out there, ones that haven't been genetically engineered. Ones that are planning how to hurt people for their own sick purposes."

"You'll join him, then? My Perseus? Go into the Gorgon's den and slay the monsters? Tragedy befalls would-be heroes, not just in myth, but in real life as well, Jia. Erik's quest for vengeance is proof of that. His unit was filled with heroes who'd risked their lives countless times against terrorists and rebels, and they were cut down."

Jia replied with a single curt nod. "You don't get it. It's already too late."

Alina raised an eyebrow. "Oh?"

"I've seen too much already. I can't go back to

pretending it's not out there. I can't even go back to pretending that being a normal cop is enough anymore."

"Good." Alina's smile returned. "Originally, I only wanted Erik for this, but I get now that he wouldn't have lasted more than a few months without a good partner. I'm glad you're on board."

"Thanks." Jia reached for the yoke. It was time to take control of yet another thing in her life. "I don't know if I'm happy to be doing this, but I know it's the right thing for me."

"Enjoy your last few weeks as a cop. Take it easy, too. Once you're working for me, it might be weeks of complete boredom followed by days of abject terror."

Jia snickered. "You make it sound so fun."

CHAPTER THIRTY-FOUR

Erik pulled a shrimp cracker out of his rumpled bag as he walked beside Jia.

They flowed along with the stream of sphere ball fans leaving the arena. He bit down, enjoying the crunch. People chatted happily, pleased with their team's performance or commenting on their favorite plays that night. It had been a good match, with the outcome in doubt until the last few minutes.

Some people might prefer a blowout, but Erik liked a back-and-forth struggle unless it involved him fighting a group of thugs. A dash of uncertainty and tension could raise the mundane to the sublime.

He held up the bag and edged it toward Jia. "Cracker? I always love these things after the match. It's like the last minutes of the match add flavor. I can't explain it."

Jia shook her head. "No, I'm good. A bag is enough for me for one match." She sighed. "Good, huh?"

"They *are* good," Erik insisted.

"I'm sure they are. Too bad I can't say the same about

our defensive wings." She groaned and slapped her forehead. "Did they not get enough sleep last night? Were they drunk? What was going on?"

Erik laughed. "Our team won. The other team lost. What's the problem?"

"They're better than that," Jia insisted. "That's the problem. Look at the stats. They should have steamrolled that pathetic excuse for a team."

"Come on, any team can win any given match. That's how the league is balanced. That's what makes the matches interesting."

Jia shook a fist. "I understand that, but it's not as satisfying to see a win if our guys aren't playing to their maximum capacity. The score wasn't them being outplayed. This was just our team making too many mistakes, allowing the other team to stay close."

Erik munched on another cracker with a slight grin. No matter what Jia did, she did it a hundred and ten percent. He couldn't doubt her passion for sphere ball, despite her approaching the sport from a different angle.

Not wrong, just different.

The crowd slowed as the front of the lines hit the exit and people broke away in different directions to head toward their vehicles. Erik wasn't in a hurry. They had no active cases, and it was their day off. He had already run Jia through exoskeleton training earlier that day. Rather than going out for dinner, he wanted to relax with her at home. His apartment wasn't going anywhere, and she needed to spin down from what was supposed to be their relaxing trip to the match.

A nearby fan pumped his fist in the air and slapped a

friend on the back. "The defense made some mistakes today, but our offensive wings were on fire. Gods among men."

"I'm going to miss this." Erik shook his head. "I didn't think I would at first, but now it's hitting me."

"Miss what?" Jia glanced over her shoulder. "Laughable defense? I won't miss that! I would go to sleep content every night for the rest of my life if the team never played like that again."

"No, it's not this match. I'm talking about being able to attend so many matches in person." Erik inclined his head toward a holographic replay above them that depicted the goalie blocking a last-minute goal attempt with a brilliant and agile pivot. "It's not the same if you're not here. If you're not hearing the roar of the crowd. It's why I never got into sphere ball before. I never bothered to go to a stadium, but once I did, I was hooked. I fell in love."

"Of course." Jia thought about it. "You're right, now that I think about it, but it's not like Neo SoCal is the only place with sphere ball. Even if we're traveling, it doesn't mean we won't be able to attend matches."

Erik grinned. "Oh, you're a fair-weather fan now?"

"What's that supposed to mean?" Jia glared at him. "I'm allowed to criticize poor play. That's the fundamental right of *all* fans."

"I'm not talking about that. You don't care what match you see, even if it involves another team?" Erik raised an eyebrow in challenge and combined it with his best infuriating smirk.

Poking her wouldn't hurt.

"Don't make me knock you out," Jia muttered, flexing

her fist. "I don't care if we're in public. Besides, keep talking like that, and I'm going to end up in a fight with this entire crowd. I don't want the news reports to be all about how I had to knock out a bunch of people out over a match disagreement."

"That would be entertaining. I'd put my money on you. Two-to-one." Erik looked around. "Nah. This crowd looks weak. Four-to-one on you. I'd just watch and provide color commentary."

Jia rubbed her chin, her head pivoting around, checking out the potential opposition. "Well, I *am* in a bad mood."

"Next time, we'll throw you in there as the goalie," Erik suggested. "You'd do a great job before you fouled out for throat-punching every other player."

"Who knows? Maybe I'm a natural." Jia managed a smile. "At the game, not the throat-punching."

"Knowing you, I wouldn't doubt it." Erik frowned. The crowd slowed even more. People farther up murmured amongst themselves. Someone yelled near the front. The dense crowd blocked the exit view, but there was no smoke or fire, or gunshots, for that matter.

Jia frowned. "Emma, is there anything going on outside?"

"No," the AI replied. "There's normal movement and activity as people leave the building, but the rate of egress has decreased in the last couple of minutes. There is no unusual security or police activity. No assaults or other incidents have been reported since the beginning of the match. This is an orderly exit for such a large group of overly excited fleshbags."

Jia's hand drifted toward her stun pistol under her jacket. "The trouble might have started on the inside."

"Trying to work out that aggression?" Erik asked.

"Maybe."

"I'm not detecting any auditory evidence of gunfire or fighting inside," Emma replied. "Oh. I see. Don't worry. I think you'll enjoy this surprise, but I can't always be sure about you fleshbags. This shouldn't require any gunfire on your part."

"You say that, but you don't seem like someone who understands people," Jia challenged. She leaned over, trying to peer past the crowd. People began to part, excited chatter passing through the crowd like a wave.

"It's them!" a man whispered in front of Jia.

A tall blond man walked through the reverential crowd with a shorter but more muscular dark-haired Asian man beside him. Erik understood the excitement.

The men were Kane Danen and Lei Li, the star offensive and defensive wings for the Neo SoCal Dragons. Erik downed another stale shrimp cracker, chewing as the players shook fans' hands and made their way down the crowded hall. He reached for a new cracker as Kane and Lei stopped right in front of him, expectant looks on their faces.

Erik respected every player on their team for their skill, but he didn't worship them like many fans. Nor did he become irritated about their individual match failures like Jia. They were just talented players putting on a solid performance most matches. That called for an appropriate response.

He lifted his bag. "Want a shrimp cracker?" His offer

elicited laughs from everyone nearby, including the two players.

"Nope. I'm good," Kane replied, extending his hand. "Kane Danen."

"Yeah, I know who you are." Erik moved his bag to the other hand and shook his hand. "Erik Blackwell."

"I know who you are, too. That's why I'm here."

Kane moved to shake Jia's hand before Lei followed up with a handshake and greeting. Erik and Jia exchanged looks. Emma had made it clear there were no incidents at the match, so they weren't sure why the two players had sought them out. There was plenty of security to handle petty incidents.

"Did you need something?" Erik asked.

Jia cleared her throat. "Would you mind delivering a message to your goa—" She stopped and folded her arms at Erik's "not now" look.

Kane shook his head. "Someone told us the Obsidian Detective and Lady Justice were here. From what we've heard, you come to most of our home matches. I didn't realize we were so popular with you."

"I'm a fan," Erik admitted with a shrug. "And there's nothing like seeing a match in person." He shook his bag. "The whole arena experience and all that. The crackers don't have the same crunch at home."

"He converted me," Jia added, along with a smile. "But I can't disagree. Running stats is fun at home, but the action being right in front of you is another thing. The roar of the crowd, the thud of impacts."

Kane chuckled and turned to Lei. "I told you they'd be like this."

Lei shrugged.

"Like what?" Jia asked.

"Just normal fans. We might be in the news more than you two, but winning a match isn't the same as taking down a triad or terrorists," Kane explained. "We're big fans of the two of you."

Erik chuckled. After everything that had happened with Lance, it was nice to be reminded that not everyone was hunting the detectives because they'd made too much of a splash. At the same time, it was a stark reminder that they'd become too visible when even UTC-famous athletes gushed about them.

"That's kind of you to say," Jia replied. "You keep providing quality gameplay, and the police will keep cleaning up the trash around Neo SoCal. We're both good at our jobs."

"Mind if we get pictures?" Kane nodded up. A panel near the ceiling opened, and a small drone emerged to circle the detectives and players. "Knew we had that thing following us for a reason."

"Can I keep eating my crackers?" Erik asked. "I don't know what is about the ones you buy at matches. They are damned addictive. Somebody probably adds drugs to them."

"Sure. No reason to deny a hungry fan." Kane chuckled. "You can keep eating." He gestured to Lei. "Get in here before they have to go answer a call."

The players took up positions on either side of the detectives, the drone weaving back and forth, taking several pictures. Erik continued devouring his crackers. Jia stood with a bright smile until the drone retreated.

"Thanks for all you do, Detectives," Lei offered. "But we have to get back to the rest of the team. A lot of them wanted to meet you, but we didn't want to cause a big scene." He motioned at the crowd. "Or a bigger scene."

"Thanks for continuing to be a quality team," Jia replied. "Goal-keeping aside," she muttered under her breath.

Erik elbowed her and nodded at the players. "See you around."

The men waved and turned to cut through the crowd, leaving dozens of people surrounding Erik and Jia with hungry looks in their eyes. If they couldn't have one set of celebrities, another pair would work.

Forty-five minutes passed before Erik and Jia escaped the stadium and made it back to the MX 60. They'd taken pictures and shaken hands with half the line by the time they got outside. If he'd known it was going to take that long to get out of there, Erik would have bought another bag of shrimp crackers.

He laughed at the thought as his flitter sped away from the tower holding the Aurum Sphere Ball Arena. "Ever feel like the universe is trying to tell you something?"

Jia didn't look at him. She was focused on three different data windows filled with graphs and statistics concerning the team's defensive play during the last several matches. "I'm quitting my lifelong dream to go work for a spy, so yes, I do think the universe is trying to tell me something. And I'm listening. I've stopped being surprised at this point."

"I never intended to come back and become famous," Erik explained. "I thought being a cop was the best way to get a line on the people responsible for Molino. Everything else was just supposed to be a cover. Not that it was a huge sacrifice buying a luxury flitter and getting the de-aging."

Jia jabbed at a name on one of the screens. A picture of a reserve goalie appeared, along with additional statistics. "It's not like I became a detective so they could give me silly nicknames and ask for pictures. Is it going to bother you that we're giving that up?"

"It's not like we're disappearing. We're not even going into deep cover."

Jia tore her gaze off the stats screen to look at her partner. "No, we aren't, but a lot of what we'll be doing will be lower-profile. Even if we end up making a big mess, I'm sure Alina will help cover things up. I'm not going to say I hate people recognizing me as someone making Neo SoCal a better place, but I suspect once we're out of the news for a few months, people will forget about us. People always are waiting for the next big thing."

Erik nodded slowly. "That's probably for the best. We know what we need to do. We don't need people shaking our hands for doing it."

She swiped her hand through the air, dismissing all her windows. "You ever regret coming back to Earth?" Jia asked. "Some men, after going through something like you did, would have taken all those savings and set themselves up on a frontier world where they didn't have to worry about anything ever again."

"It never even occurred to me to do anything but avenge my unit. Getting pointed at becoming a cop was a nice bonus, but I still would have done it even if I didn't become a detective." Erik shrugged. "I don't know. Maybe I would have started a security company and tried to attract high-profile clients."

"If you'd done that," interrupted Emma, "you would have never met me."

"Good point." Erik chuckled. "The universe or the Lady or whoever pushed us together. I'm not going to say there's some grand plan, but we've got a good team, and we can deliver the pain to those who have it coming." He barked an even louder laugh.

"What's so funny?" Jia asked.

"Lady Justice works for you even if you're not a cop, but it'll be pretty stupid if I'm the Obsidian Detective but no longer a cop. I'm not even going to be a private detective."

Jia rolled her eyes. "A very important thing to focus on."

"Always." Erik grinned. "Besides, with the captain not assigning us new cases, it's not like we have anything better to think about."

"Who knows? Someone could try to assassinate one of us?" Jia shrugged.

Erik pursed his lips. "Sure. That might be fun."

CHAPTER THIRTY-FIVE

October 31, 2229, Neo Southern California Metroplex, Police Enforcement Zone 122 Station

Jia and Erik stepped off the elevator and into the hallway leading to the bullpen. A sense of resignation dueled with excitement, keeping Jia's heart from beating calmly.

She had been convinced the last couple of weeks at the station would draw them into some other dangerous case, but Captain Ragnar kept to his original plan and focused them on reports. If it hadn't been for Lance Onassis' stunt, they might have cruised through most of the month without any trouble. Jia didn't have a problem with a quiet exit.

There were worse things. She half-suspected an alien assassin would show up that morning and challenge her to a duel for control of the Solar System.

"I'm surprised they're not making us help with patrols tonight," Jia admitted. "Especially after what happened last year. It wouldn't be crazy, and they can always use more cops patrolling."

"It's probably *because* of what happened last year that they're not making us do anything." Erik wiped crumbs off his face, left over from the beignet he'd chowed down on their way over. "If we stay at home, any terrorists who want to blow us up will only blow up our apartments."

"Oh, comforting thought."

"I didn't say they'd blow *us* up, just our apartments."

Working for Alina might not bring a daily routine. The simple things Jia had gotten used to, such as hitting the nearby diners and restaurants for breakfast and lunch with her partner, would vanish.

Being a police officer was unpredictable, but being a contractor for a ghost made a mockery of predictability. Every month could take them somewhere different, fighting someone different.

Jia pushed the thought out and froze as they stepped into the bullpen. She jammed her hand under her jacket and gripped her stun pistol. The room was devoid of people. All the rows of desks and chairs remained, but there wasn't a single person around. She narrowed her eyes. Silence choked the area.

All the office doors along the outer walls of the room remained closed. There was no blood, and no bullet holes or scorch marks. Nothing had been knocked over. There was no way someone could raid a room full of armed officers and not leave a trace.

She frowned. Gas, maybe? That was one possibility, but how would they have limited it to one room?

Small points of light flickered across the middle of the

room between two desks. Jia yanked out her stun pistol and pointed it that way, her jaw tight. Attacking the 1-2-2 on their last day there would make a sick sort of sense if someone wanted to send a message to Erik and Jia. No. It couldn't happen. Even Talos couldn't pull that off without leaving a trace.

"Calm down, Jia," Emma suggested, her tone amused. "You're overreacting."

"No, she's right. This shit is strange." Erik frowned. He reached into his jacket. "I've never seen—"

The bright points of light danced in the center of the room, spinning a circle and rising toward the roof. They exploded in a shower of sparks that crackled and formed a message.

Erik and Jia, this is your going-away party.

The office doors all slid open. Captain Ragnar, Halil, and Jared emerged from one office. Uniformed officers and detectives streamed out of the others, including some holding large cakes or stacks of plates and forks. They set them down on the desks. Jia sighed and shoved her stun pistol back into its holster.

"Oh," Jia muttered, feeling silly about the convoluted conspiracy-attack scenarios she'd explored.

She'd forgotten how much she hated surprise parties.

A stupid grin had broken out on Erik's face. He didn't share her disdain. Emptiness and silence gave way to a room filled with police officers and a loud din of chattering and laughing.

Halil bowed over his arm in front of Erik and Jia. "You know how hard it is to pull off a surprise party for you two, of all people? I think it would have been easier to surprise the head of the CID."

Jared patted him on the shoulder. "Don't feel too bad. We didn't place the bet."

Jia frowned. "Bet?"

"Yep." Jared nodded toward Halil. "We were discussing whether you'd pick up on it, especially since Dumbass here kept harassing you about when you were leaving. I had to handle a lot of the logistics. Halil had the easy job. He was just supposed to get the information and make sure you didn't suspect anything." He frowned at Captain Ragnar. "And he wouldn't tell us at first."

The captain shrugged, his smile mischievous. "I like my detectives to work for things. I've got to take my amusement where I can get it."

Halil grumbled. "The really hard part was getting *her* to agree."

Jia pointed to her chest. "I didn't agree to this. I didn't even know about it."

"No, not you."

Emma appeared, a festive pointed red party hat atop her holographic form. "I noticed some irregularities some weeks ago, so I investigated, then realized what was going on. On a whim, I initiated direct contact with Detective Mustafa, and I agreed to not alert you to this recreational ambush because I was curious to see your reaction."

"You noticed irregularities, and you didn't tell us?" Erik asked, sounding surprised.

"If I bothered you with every odd thing I notice, you'd never get anything done." Emma shrugged. "Even with my abilities, it can be difficult to monitor the environments and systems around you, and you don't understand how many out-of-parameters events occur around you in any given day."

Jia wasn't sure if she should be insulted, so she didn't respond.

Captain Ragnar cleared his throat and raised his voice. "Okay, everyone. Before we get into the cake, I've got something to say, and before that, a little reminder. We're going to have another party with a lot more beer at Remembrance tomorrow night, even if Erik and Jia don't want to come."

The crowd laughed, including Erik and Jia.

She couldn't stop the huge smile from taking over her face, the joy of the event overwhelming her residual irritation over the surprise. Last year, almost everyone in the 1-2-2 had hated her and wanted her gone.

Now they were throwing her a party, including two of her former enemies.

She was never sure if people truly respected her. She hadn't cared much, but it was nice to go out knowing she'd left a positive impact on something other than the crime rate.

"You're all lazy," Captain Ragnar declared. He waited for the scattered laughs to die down. "And those of you who were here before I came know what things used to be like. Not just at the 1-2-2, but in the entire department. I came here as part of the reforms." He pointed at Erik and Jia. "But those two are the ones who got all that started. They took a lot of shit from a lot of you, but they didn't care. All they cared about was taking down criminals."

No one laughed anymore. Jia's smile faded. If her last

day at the station had to be one where she stood by her work, so be it. She was surprised at the captain's choice of speech, but he understood better than most the struggles of reform.

He could have easily been a target of assassination like the new chief.

"But that was before," Captain Ragnar thundered. "Everyone left at this station is a great cop. Maybe some of you were asleep before, but now you're awake, and you've spent the last year helping clean up the syndicate trash infesting Neo SoCal and stopping terrorists. The 1-2-2 is one of the top enforcement zones, if not *the* top, in the department. Detectives Blackwell and Lin—Erik and Jia— might have led the way, but you choose to follow them, and now I'm proud to be your captain. 1-2-2!"

Every officer in the room bellowed as a chorus, "*1-2-2!*"

The captain pointed to a cake. "Let's get something to eat before terrorists decide to bomb the station to get at Erik and Jia." His comment summoned more laughter.

Captain Ragnar shook both their hands. "I couldn't have done it without you. I wouldn't have even been here without your efforts. I want you to know that."

"We needed you too, Captain," Jia replied. "We needed someone who had our back. We couldn't have done as much without you."

Erik surveyed the room slowly, a distant look in his eyes. "Damn."

"What's wrong?" the captain asked.

"I'm going to miss this place," Erik admitted.

A couple of hours later, Jia ran her hand over her desk with a smile. "You *are* planning to go to the party tomorrow night, aren't you?"

Erik sat in his chair with his feet up on his desk, perhaps for the last time. "It's not like I had big plans tomorrow. We're on standby until Alina points us somewhere. I figure she's not going to want us wandering around doing our own thing at first."

"Does that worry you?"

Erik shook his head. "If we sit around for more than a few weeks, maybe we'll look into making our own moves, but she remains our best bet. I don't have a strong enough lead on my own right now."

Jia sat on the edge of her desk. "It doesn't feel like the same office in the same station as it was when I started. I used to think I might not be able to make a difference, but now everyone acknowledges that I have."

"It doesn't matter if they do or not."

"True, but it helps. Would you have liked it if all your soldiers hated you?"

"No." Erik sighed. "Good point."

Jia chuckled. "Halil was having such a hard time, but it occurs to me that we still don't know when Malcolm is going to leave. When I last talked to him, he suggested it wouldn't be for months."

Erik nodded. "That was what Camila suggested. It looks less suspicious that way."

"I talked to her the other day. She told me she'll be resigning in a few days, citing family issues." Jia scoffed. "Isn't that suspicious?"

"Sure, but she's not going to be working with us, so it's

less of a link." Erik shrugged. "We'll just have to make do without Malcolm in the beginning. We've got Emma."

"Yes, we do. The AI who is holding onto secret surprise parties." Jia smirked. "I think she's becoming more like a fleshbag each day."

"Just for that," Emma declared from Jia's PNIU, "I'll spoil the ending of the next movie you watch. There's no reason to be insulting."

Erik laughed. "Don't take it personally." He cracked his knuckles and lifted his linked hands above his head. "It does feel weird to think I won't be a cop soon." He lowered his arms. "Oh, while I'm thinking about it, I want you to do me a favor tomorrow at the Remembrance party."

"What?" Jia asked.

"Let go. Drink a lot." Erik's voice grew soft. "Sometimes it's good to not give a shit for one night. To lose control."

"Even in our situation?" she asked, eyebrow raised.

"Especially in our situation," Erik insisted. "It might be a long time before either of us can let go again, but at that party, we'll be surrounded by the best cops in Neo SoCal."

Jia nodded slowly. "Okay, I'll do it."

The next evening, Jia collapsed face-first onto her bed, her stomach lurching. She could grab an alcohol filter patch from her bathroom, but that would require getting up. Her stomach and head told her that was a terrible idea, even if she'd suffer more in the long run. She already had regrets.

Half the night was a gut-churning blur.

Jia groaned and turned her head. Why had she let Erik convince her to drink so much?

A memory surfaced—his mouth warm against hers. She cursed. Being drunk enough to vomit was annoying enough, but being so drunk she couldn't remember making out with Erik was the true punishment.

Her PNIU chimed with a message. Jia batted at it unsuccessfully a few times, moaning, then blinking when the message came up.

The client's quicker than I expected. We have a meeting at the hangar tomorrow morning. I know you're probably passed out right now, so I'll call and pick you up tomorrow morning.

Jia rolled out of bed and staggered until she was upright. The darkness of sleep would have been her preferred choice to deal with her alcohol-filled veins, but she'd also expected to have the next day off. Better to clear herself out before she woke up.

"Right to it, huh, Alina?" Jia chuckled and stumbled toward her bathroom. "If this involves more stupid nanozombies, I swear I'll kill you myself."

CHAPTER THIRTY-SIX

Erik set the MX 60 down inside the open hangar holding the *Pegasus*, the Rabbit-class ship that would be their transportation for future assignments.

Even though they'd barely used the spacecraft, Erik realized he thought of it as the Rabbit despite its registered name. He had no problem with the name Pegasus, but for some reason, the long, squat ship reminded him more of a rabbit.

He didn't know if he approved. Rabbits ran away, and that was the last thing he planned to do.

Erik looked around and frowned at the empty hangar. "If she's invisible again, I might have to shoot her. There are only so many tests I want to take. There was a reason I never went to college."

"Her ghost thing does get annoying," Jia agreed. "Of course, I'm not sure if her disguises are more or less irritating."

"I feel compelled," Emma began, "to point out that both of you used disguises on your last assignment for her, and it's highly likely you'll be using them again, given the nature of who your employer will be going forward."

"She did say we'd turn into her." Jia snickered. "Did you ever think you'd end up doing something like this? I never, ever thought about working for the Intelligence Directorate when I was younger, directly or indirectly."

"Working for a ghost, huh?" Erik opened his door. "No, but I knew on my way back to Earth that things might get weird since the people who killed my unit couldn't have been normal terrorists." He stepped out into the hangar. "When your enemy isn't normal, your allies can't be either."

Jia exited the vehicle with a lingering gaze toward the hidden storage beneath the passenger seat. "At what point does being careful become paranoia? I've been asking myself that a lot lately."

"That happens at the point when you hurt someone who doesn't have it coming," Erik suggested, surveying the hangar. "Until then, it's about not letting the bastards surprise you. Don't worry. I see what you're doing. I know what you're thinking, and I'm thinking it myself. That's why we're both alive after all that shit we've dealt this last year. The second we let our guard down, some zombie will eat our brains."

Jia laughed. "You know what I just realized?"

"That goalie wasn't playing that badly the other day?" Erik joked. Being alert was good, but being too tense could cause overfocus.

"That's a load of bull." Jia rolled her eyes. "Just look at the stats. He sucked! Sure, we all have bad days, but that doesn't mean they aren't terrible just because they're rare."

She shook her head. "No. I keep thinking I've *become* paranoid, but I've *always* been paranoid."

Erik gave her a skeptical look. "You used to think there was no serious crime on Earth. That doesn't sound like a paranoid woman."

"Maybe not consciously, but subconsciously. If I wasn't, I would have never pushed so hard when I started at the 1-2-2. On some level, I knew there was something more going on. Working with you and Alina isn't turning me into anything I wasn't already. It's more that it's returning me to my true nature."

"It sounds kind of scary when you say it like that." Erik grinned. "Okay, Alina, stop playing games before I pull out the laser rifle and start shooting randomly. Or maybe I'll toss a few plasma grenades to clear the hangar."

The Rabbit's cargo bay door rumbled, lowering to the floor to become a ramp and revealing Alina. The spy started down the ramp before it had finished opening. She was trailed by Cutter and a tiny redheaded woman with frizzy hair in black overalls with an angular face.

Erik nodded to the redhead. "Who's she?"

"Lanara Quinn," the woman answered. "Next time talk *to* me, not *through* me, Blackwell."

Erik raised his palms in mock surrender. "Sorry. Not trying to be an asshole."

"I don't care much if you are," Lanara replied. "I just find it inefficient if you're talking to somebody about me instead of talking to me."

Cutter shook his head, a pained look on his face. "First, Holochick and now her. Somebody up there hates me."

Emma winked into existence at the bottom of the ramp,

smirking at Cutter. "Be assured, Pilot Durn, that your bravery during the prison incident doesn't mean you're beyond reproach."

"No offense, Holochick, but you don't even have a body," Cutter complained.

"You waste your body, including your brain, fleshbag."

"We're certainly collecting a colorful crew here," Jia commented. She nodded at Lanara. "Jia Lin." She gestured at Erik. "My rude partner is Erik Blackwell. Nice to meet you."

"I know who you are." Lanara shrugged. "Why would I be here if I didn't?"

"Aren't you direct?"

"It's efficient to be direct. Bullshit wastes everyone's time." Lanara shrugged, not a hint of apology on her face.

Alina put a fist to her mouth and cleared her throat. "Lanara's a skilled engineer. She can get around pretty well working on vehicles, too, and exoskeletons. Basically, she's a solid all-around support person you can trust and who won't wet herself if she gets shot at."

"Try to kill people before they shoot me, please." Lanara folded her arms. "I've already started working on the fuel intakes. There are some inefficiencies. I'm surprised whoever maintained this ship before left in there. Plus, they didn't take advantage of grav field modulation to improve flow. When you do that kind of thing, you can improve efficiency as much as two percent in this model. I also—"

Alina cut her off by clearing her throat again. "As you can see, Lanara might not always be the life of the party, but she knows what she's doing. She's worth an entire support crew by herself and has worked for me on and off for a few years."

Erik offered his hand to the tiny engineer. "I'm not the kind of guy who specializes in bullshit. Good to have you helping us out."

Lanara's shake was surprisingly firm. "I'm excited about the job. Sometimes it's nice to do less with more." She glanced between Erik and Jia. "And I like working with competent people. Alina says you're the real deal. That means a lot. I've seen you on the news, but they specialize in bullshit."

"We try to be real," Erik offered.

Emma smiled. "I like this fleshbag. She amuses me in a good way."

"I'm glad someone does," Cutter mumbled, scuffing his boot against the hangar floor.

Lanara nodded to Emma. "Having you around will help a lot. It'll save time on a lot of diagnostics. I always wondered what I could pull off with a self-aware AI helping me out, but I didn't think that kind of thing was possible."

Emma bowed. "I am a wonder of the modern age."

"If we've got a pilot and an engineer, does that mean you have an assignment lined up for us, Alina?" Jia asked eagerly. "Were you just waiting for us to leave the department?"

Alina shook her head. "I'm working on some leads, so I'd stay close to Neo SoCal, but I'm not sending you anywhere tomorrow." She motioned to the Rabbit. "As Lanara mentioned, there are some modifications she wants to make, and they'll take a few days anyway. You should take the time to relax and appreciate Earth. I plan on running you ragged soon enough."

Erik chuckled. "It's not like we're planning on jaunting off to Molino anytime soon, but it'd be a good time to transfer gear to the ship, so we're ready." He furrowed his brow. "Damn. One thing I didn't think about is drones. It might be nice if Emma didn't have to hack around us as we go."

The AI nodded her agreement. "It's not always that practical, given the situation."

"Drones are easy, but it'll be better if we don't go crazy." Alina gestured to the cargo bay. "I'll get you some decent disposable drones. You have tactical suits and the like already. Adeyemi should still be your primary weapons supplier for anything heavier than your TR-7 and your ammo."

"Spreading out the blame if we get caught?" Jia asked.

"Something like that. Besides, I'm taking care of everything from fuel to docking fees."

"What about the exoskeletons?" Erik pressed. "Are those coming?"

"They're coming, but they might not be here in time for your next assignment. Since I'd prefer you to not die while you're hunting down Talos and whatever other monsters I point you at, I'm going all out." Alina offered him a lopsided smirk. "I'm going to get you something nice. Trust me."

Jia tutted. "Isn't trusting a ghost kind of a bad idea?"

"That's true," Alina replied.

"Assuming you get me the exoskeletons, it's much appreciated." Erik stuck his hands in his pocket and whistled. "I wish I could have had all of this and all these people when I left Molino. If I had, I might have already taken down the conspiracy already."

Even if he'd splashed cash around immediately, there wasn't much he could have done.

The frontier colony didn't play host to mercenaries and hirelings ready to help a vengeful ex-soldier. If he'd tried to look into it right away, he probably would have ended up outside the dome without a suit and been reported as a suicide. The failure of the conspiracy to finish him off when they had their chance was their first big mistake.

An enemy who made mistakes was an enemy who could be defeated, even if they were stronger.

Lanara headed toward the ramp. "If we're not going anywhere anytime soon, I'm going to start on the modifications. I also noticed the ship lacks a VR system. If we're going to be stuck on this thing together, it might help. It won't be nano-augmented, but if I add a decent chair, a treadmill, and a few things like that, I can get halfway there."

Jia's brow lifted in surprise. "You can do all that in a few days?"

Lanara crested the ramp and shrugged. "I happen to have most of the equipment lying around. I get bored a lot when I have time on my hands. And I was thinking because we have Emma that it'll be easier to dynamically modify simulation parameters and the programming. On top of that, even if I can squeeze that extra power out of the reactor like I was planning, we don't have a weapons system to feed, so might as well use it, and then I was thinking about...Wait."

"What?" Erik frowned and searched around for trouble. If there was something obviously wrong, Emma would have already warned them.

Lanara threw up a finger. "I'm an idiot. Why didn't I see it before? I can add dedicated grav field emitters, and Emma can provide active adjustment in a way a normal system couldn't, and then..." She sprinted into the cargo bay, no longer interested in human interaction. "I've got this!"

Jia leaned to her right to catch the last moment of the woman going deeper into the ship and blinked. "She's certainly...interesting."

"See?" Cutter nodded as he pointed to Jia as if she just exclaimed the whole problem. "Why can't we have a normal engineer?"

"We could say the same thing about you," Jia observed.

"Damn, Lin. You know where to hit a man. All those ballbusters on this ship. It's just going to be me and you holding the line, Erik."

Erik offered an evil grin. "Remember, I'm dating Jia."

Cutter groaned.

Alina rubbed her hands, an excited gleam in her eyes. "You'll all do great things soon. That's all I have for now. Just try to stay alive for the next few days."

"I'll try," Erik replied.

Jia shrugged. "We can't help it if we're popular."

CHAPTER THIRTY-SEVEN

The MX 60 sped away from the hangar, Erik in control.

He'd not said much since their mini-briefing, leaving Jia time to sort through her impressions of their latest ally. When she was working as a detective, she'd had little control over who she worked with, and that trend had continued with her new job.

Most people could say the same, but most people didn't have to worry about being targeted by galactic conspiracies. Her instincts told her Lanara would be a great help, but instincts were the beginning of a thought process, not the end.

"What do you think about Lanara?" Jia asked, worried she was overreacting. "Honestly, it's not like I've known a lot of ship engineers, so I don't know what kind of personality they're supposed to have, but she seems enthusiastic about her job."

"I think she'll get things done, but we shouldn't ask her to arrange the New Year's Party," Erik replied. "It'd probably just be an empty bowl with a sign next to it saying,

'Insert snacks here and then consume.' After that, she'd send us a message on our PNIUs reading, 'For maximum efficiency, select your favorite song and play it in your ear. P.S. Parties are a waste of time. I'm going to go turn your flitter into a giant catapult because I'm bored.'"

"I was thinking she doesn't have much of a personality, but when you put it that way, it's more that she has too much of one." Jia chuckled.

"Better to be too much than nothing," Erik replied. "I don't trust anyone who is quiet and won't speak their mind. You never know if they're trying to protect themselves or your feelings. I'm a big boy who doesn't need his feelings protected. She's even pumped about Emma."

"A true sign of intelligence, I assure you," Emma commented.

"Of course." Jia smirked. "I'm surprised by both Lanara and Cutter. Maybe I shouldn't be, but that's the way I feel."

"Surprised?" Erik spared a glance her way, his brow wrinkled in confusion. "What's surprising about them? They both seem good at their jobs. Were you expecting idiots?"

"No, nothing like that from Alina."

Erik nodded. "I was surprised Cutter got himself hurt trying to stop that guy at the prison, but we haven't worked with Lanara, so we don't have a good feel for her. The whole super-direct bitch thing might get old, but I'm guessing she likes to spend more time around machines than people."

"I do know the feeling," Emma noted.

"You just like her because she was kissing your virtual ass," Erik replied.

"You say that as if it's objectionable." Emma scoffed. "Acknowledging my abilities is a way to prove one is a fleshbag with a semi-working brain. She might turn out to be a fool and a waste of molecules soon enough, but for now, I'm inclined to have a positive impression of her, even if Jia thinks she's going to slit your throats while you sleep."

"I don't think that." Jia groaned. "That's not what I'm saying."

"What, then?" Erik asked. "I'd have to agree with Emma. I thought that was what you were getting at."

"Alina might have her quirks, but she's still what I'd expect from someone in the ID." Jia shrugged. "Those two, though, aren't as professional. If I were conducting interviews for a position like this, I would have filtered them out right away because of potential social interaction problems. I'm not saying they're antisocials in the worst sense of the world, but they are both...you know."

Erik laughed. "What about me? Am I unprofessional and antisocial?"

"You get the job done. That counts for a lot. And you're loyal, and you might be ruthless, but only toward people who have it coming."

"Exactly. Keep that in mind for everyone we'll be working with." Erik passed a flitter that was flying achingly slow. If they didn't want to fly, they should have used the autodrive.

"I see what you mean." Jia blew out a breath. "It'll take me a while to not apply my normal standards to people."

"Then you're thinking about it the wrong way. They aren't cops. They aren't customer service at some store, and they aren't working for a corporation where kissing everyone's ass is part of the politics." Erik drummed his thumbs on the control yoke. "Cutter's a good pilot, and if Alina brought her in, Lanara's a good engineer and mechanic. Remember, they're not ghosts. They're like us, contractors and ghost tools, but they're not being brought in as investigators or ass-kickers. All of us only need to be good at our given role." Erik yawned. "Don't worry about it. Alina wants us to find the monsters in the dark as much as we do. She's going to do her best to make sure that happens, including with the people she hires. I'm not worried about them, and Cutter already proved himself at the prison."

"You're right. I'm being paranoid." Jia nodded slowly, trying not to yawn after seeing Erik do so. "But let's set that aside. You're still tired from the party? I thought you didn't leave long after I did."

"I stayed up late looking over some stuff," Erik admitted. "Reviewing the cases and evidence we've discovered about the conspiracy. I was thinking a lot about working for Alina, the Knights Errant, and everything that's happened this last year. When I left the Army, I had a year to sit around brooding. There's only so much planning a man can do before he starts a bloody campaign of revenge." He grunted. "Especially when the man doesn't even have a target for that vengeance."

"And now? How are things different?"

"Since I've hit Earth, I've concentrated on getting the job done, whether as a cop or my personal business. Not that I'm brooding." Erik grinned.

"Sure, you need more atmospheric lighting to properly brood." Jia smiled. "Maybe a dark cape or something, too.

An organ to play during storms, or you can just wait for rainstorms and sit there, looking up at the sky getting soaked."

"Exactly. Something like that." Erik twisted the yoke to join a patchy line of flitters in a hurry. "But I'm over that. I'm ready for this hunt to continue, but while we're talking about things, I just wanted to make sure you're okay we're leaving your flitter behind. We kind of talked about it before, but I don't know if you were paying attention."

"My flitter?" Jia stared at him, at a loss. "What about my flitter? Oh, you're right, not enough space." She frowned. "Even less if we're going to get exoskeletons and more equipment."

"Being logical and all that, the MX 60 is far more suited for trouble," Erik explained. "I've decked it out to deal with that, and we're staring down the barrel of a lot of trouble going forward."

"I would vastly prefer this vehicle to Jia's new flitter," Emma offered. "The enhanced sensors alone make it tremendously useful for a large variety of tasks like surveillance, investigatory and combat, let alone all the ways it's been reinforced and modified. We don't know what our tasks will be going forward, so it's good to be prepared. It would be nice if we had a weapon I could control, but I'm sure that's something we can add soon enough. Engineer Quinn will probably be more than happy to work with me on that."

"A gun would be handy, but it has to be something not easily detected if we're ever going to stick it in a commercial transport."

Jia watched a bright yellow flitter in a lower lane. "I'm

fine with using the MX 60 on assignments. I'd just not thought much about it being an issue. Why did you think I'd put up a big fight?"

"I don't know." Erik turned the yoke, altering course. "I figured you'd think you wasted a bunch of money on buying a new flitter. I was the one goading you into it with the bet and everything, and I thought that you'd be pissed about that. It's not crazy when you go through the logic."

"You're right. I did waste a lot of money on a vehicle I might not use nearly as much as I anticipated." Jia sighed. "But that was my choice, so I can only blame you so much."

"What about not at all?" Erik suggested.

She frowned at him. "Remember the bet you just mentioned?"

"If it makes you feel any better, you should remember it wasn't about a new flitter. It was about a new you, a symbol and all that. If anything, I did you a favor challenging you with that bet."

Jia glared at him. "I'd punch you if you weren't flying. I hope you are well and truly cognizant of that."

Erik laughed. "What? That excuse didn't do it for you? And here I thought it was a brilliant defense."

"I could have been a new me for free!" Jia grumbled. "But like I said, it does come down to me in the end, so no punches or final blame today."

"As much as it pains me to note additional complications," Emma interjected, "you need to be prepared for such basic realities as air pressure differentials and how they'll affect flight efficiency. Your flitter was designed for use on Earth. Not every possible colony you'll go to is under a full dome with Earth pressure levels or air composition. The grav emitters might keep the MX 60 up, but the thrusters are primarily responsible for maneuvering. I can actively compensate for it somewhat, but you'll need a more permanent solution, depending on where you're sent."

Erik frowned. "Damn it, Miguel. I'm going to have to trust this new woman."

"What happened to believing in Alina?" Jia asked.

"That was before we were talking about this baby." Erik softly tapped the dash. "What if Lanara has weird thoughts about what's best for the MX 60 and changes everything I love about it?"

"We'll be trusting Lanara to maintain the ship we'll be flying in." Jia's expression turned amused. "And there are far more ways to die in space than in a flitter."

Erik shrugged. "What do I care? I didn't pay for that ship or any of the modifications."

Jia laughed. "You won't mind if we die because you didn't pay for the Rabbit?"

"I'll care. I think I'll care less."

Jia sat there for a moment staring at Erik, her brain trying to make the phrase into something coherent. "What *twisted* logic."

"But it is logic," Erik insisted, putting up a finger.

"There's more for your consideration," Emma added. "And to build off what Jia has said, as wonderful as this body is, it is not designed to operate outside atmosphere. The recent events at the detention facility only reinforced the difficulties inherent in having limited options when in space."

"That's what the Rabbit is for, but I think I see what

you're saying. We need some sort of tactical solution, but we're getting ahead of ourselves." Erik shook his head. "It might be nice to have Cutter flying a fighter and Jia flying the Rabbit, but that isn't going to happen. I had to push to get exoskeletons." He looked at Jia. "Speaking of which, that meeting didn't take as much time as I thought it would. I thought we were going to have a serious briefing, but I suppose I should have known better with Alina."

"So?" Jia asked. "Did you have somewhere to be?"

"We could get in some exo training time," Erik suggested. "Emma, can you check the schedule?"

"There are several open slots this morning," she reported. "Shall I book one?"

"Why not?" Jia replied. "It's not like I have anything better to do."

CHAPTER THIRTY-EIGHT

Erik kept pace with Jia's exoskeleton as they ran through the rubble-strewn city. Half the building had collapsed, blast marks or holes marring the debris. Huge craters lay all over, along with the smoking remnants of destroyed vehicles.

A true battlefield would have had more bodies, but Erik wasn't worried. Jia had seen and created her share of corpses. She'd hardened herself through real-world experience.

"Isn't this fun?" Erik shouted. "Don't you want to do it all the time?"

Jia laughed. "You say that, but I'm having a good time. If I had known it was this enjoyable to control an exoskeleton, I might have been pushing to join TPST instead of being a detective."

"I don't think you would have liked never being able to investigate," Erik commented. "All combat-focus all the time appeals to a certain kind of person."

"Like you?"

"I did spend thirty years in combat arms in the Army," Erik replied. "Most jobs in the Army don't require you to strap into an exoskeleton with a heavy rifle. There's a reason I ended up where I did. No one does a job for that long unless they like it on some level."

"I don't know if I enjoy battles," Jia offered. Her exoskeleton slowed. "They get my heart pumping, but that's not the same thing as enjoying them."

"You don't have to enjoy fights," Erik insisted. "You just can't be terrified of them. A little fear is healthy. You end up dead when you get too cocky. You've been hurt in fire-fights. You know how quickly it can turn to shit in a fight, and I'd prefer if you didn't get an arm blown off."

"I'm good with the whole arm-keeping plan." Jia turned toward a nearby collapsed building. "If that means I need to put in more time in training scenarios, I'm fine with it."

"Okay, it's simple," Erik explained. "Check your map. You need to get from point alpha to point beta."

"Deceptively simple," Jia commented. "I'm assuming this city looking like this implies there are at least a couple of enemies hiding in the rubble."

Erik nodded. "Good first assumption. The briefing is short but important. Recon spotted multiple rebels still in the area. Close-air support eliminated the enemy's arty, but an earlier squad got wiped out. You got cut off from your platoon, and you need to reconnect with the rest of your platoon for a final sweep of the area. Note, this isn't about you being a hero and trying to wipe out all the remaining forces yourself."

"Noted. Point A to point B? It'll be easy."

"We'll see."

"Maintain your sensor awareness," Erik ordered. "We might have Emma with us in the field, but we might not, so don't ignore what the recon drones are bringing in. Make it a habit to do a manual check every five to eight seconds. Depending on how you configure your feeds, that might make the difference between you spotting an ambush or taking a rocket, bullet, or laser in the back. In an environment like this, the guy holding the bullet with your name on it could be anywhere. You might not be a soldier, but if our luck stays as it has been, you'll have to fight as much as one, so you might as well develop all the soldiers' instincts you can."

"I'm realizing this isn't all that different from flying a ship," Jia commented.

Erik laughed. "Really? I can't fly a ship worth a damn, and I could probably do ballet in an exo."

"I meant in terms of spatial awareness," she clarified.

"Too bad your parents never sent you to a Fleet recruiter. You'd have made a hell of a fighter pilot."

"Probably, but my parents didn't see any political and financial future in a military career, and I never expressed interest." Jia slowed and frowned. "Are you picking up the movement at nine o'clock?" She spun that way, pointing her rifle. "I've got a potential contact."

"Verify contact." Erik kept a stone-face despite wanting to grin. She was doing fine. Now it was time to see if she overreacted. She'd trained herself well when using a personal firearm, but wandering around in an exo with a huge rifle was different. The bigger the gun, the bigger the temptation to use it.

"Magnifying," Jia announced. "And it appears to be...a drone flying in a circle, projecting a hologram of you eating a beignet. Not the deadliest of enemies."

"I'm glad you checked." Erik let out the laugh he'd been holding in. "You could have killed me while I was eating. That would be a hell of a way to die."

"Very funny, but at least it's not a Zitark in a bikini."

"True," Erik replied, "but you'd be surprised at some of the distractions I've seen terrorists and rebel troops use. I've seen things almost that ridiculous."

"Assuming you're not just screwing with me, that could mean there are enemies nearby," Jia concluded. "The drone might have been intended to get me to expose myself by opening fire.

"It could be, or it could just be me screwing with you." Erik grinned.

"It doesn't matter. We're only three klicks from the rendezvous point. It's not a straight run, but we're almost there. I'd rather pick up the pace then crawl along and risk missing out on exfil with the rest of the squad." Jia pushed forward, the heavy feet of the exoskeleton echoing among the skeletons of the once-tall buildings.

Birds scattered in the distance, startled by the sound.

"True, but with all this debris, it'll probably take another ten minutes to get to the rendezvous point," Erik commented after reading the estimate on his faceplate display. "Jungles and bombed-out cities are the worst. You can't go as fast as you want, and there are too many places to hide. I've lived this more times than I care to count, and it's annoying every damned time."

"Do you really think we'll end up in a jungle or a bombed-out city?" Jia asked. "We've had some huge fights, but we're not going to be fighting a war."

"You never know what can happen. Did you ever think you'd get jumped by a *yaoguai* in an apartment?"

Jia sighed. "No, that scenario didn't occur to me, even after some of the other fights we had."

"The way I figure it, if you train for the worst, it makes everything else seem easy." Erik resisted the urge to drop a hint about the next encounter. Jia might be a natural in terms of piloting, and she could handle herself in a fight, but fighting in an exoskeleton required new instincts— ones best learned through harsh lessons and simulated fire.

The better he trained her now, the better the chance she had of surviving in the future.

A distant gunshot sounded. Jia hissed as their recon drone dropped out of the sky and crashed into a deep crater, shattering into half a dozen pieces.

"Sniper," she announced. "But I didn't spot any drones, so the drone and hologram weren't just you screwing with me. That means they're close. Maybe I should not have had the drone flying."

"Going recon blind is an option, but it can be danger-ous," Erik commented.

Jia turned her head, seeking an enemy, her eyes dipping to take in sensor readings. Her shield expanded from her left arm. "We ran hard. They had to have heard us, and they just took out the drone. Why aren't they attacking?"

"Sometimes it's better to work a squad's nerves," Erik noted. "They could have ambushers set up in both directions. Or, if this was a real-world scenario, they might be more concerned about getting away if there is only a small number in this area. We've fought a lot of fanatics, but most terrorists and rebels aren't stupid enough to take on fights they know they can't win. Even if you're not interested in arresting people anymore, there are advantages to not taking the fight offered. It all comes down to the objective."

Jia crept forward, her shield covering the bulk of her exoskeleton—cautious but not overly so. Erik nodded, pleased that she understood one second of distraction could mean losing a battle.

All the criminals, terrorists, and *yaoguai* they'd fought together had proven to be excellent teachers, effectively compressing years of experience into a single year.

"Contact!" Jia shouted.

Her exoskeleton's jump thrusters came alive, propelling her exoskeleton backward. A rocket screamed from the window of a nearby building and struck where she'd been standing. Her gun roared, spitting bullets toward the source. The screams of dying men joined the cacophony of other rifles firing. Muzzle flashes highlighted targets in several windows or barrels poking over the tops of craters. Bullets bounced off her shield. She repaid an ambusher with a large-caliber, high-velocity burst to his head and then blasted through a second man. The scenario settings weren't graphic, but the bodies didn't disappear.

Erik slowly backed up, not shooting. He knew where every target was in the scenario, and the enemies were programmed to not shoot at him. He would have Emma generate a more dynamic scenario during their next training session. A few exo dances here and there weren't the same as constant practices, and the last time he'd strapped on a real exoskeleton, he wasn't at one hundred percent.

Loud, deep thumps sounded in rapid succession as Jia employed the grenade launcher on top of her rifle.

Explosions rippled through an arc, scattering men hidden behind overturned vehicles and in craters. Some screamed. Others never got the chance. Jia didn't yell profanities. She continued identifying and picking off targets until there was nothing left but thick, acrid smoke and bodies, bloodied but not as mangled as they would be outside a simulation.

"I think that's all of them," Jia offered, her breath ragged. "My launcher is empty."

"Huh. I intended for you to run and gun, but that works too."

"They can't follow me if they're all dead," Jia pointed out.

"True, but I do have a critique," Erik replied.

"What?" Jia asked, pride in her voice.

"Try to keep a few of those grenades in reserve," Erik recommended. "Just in case, but good job overall. I think you wouldn't get me killed in an exo fight. Good to know."

"Why do that when I can kill you myself?" Jia smirked. "Let's get to the rendezvous point, then go get some lunch."

CHAPTER THIRTY-NINE

November 2, 2229, Neo Southern California Metroplex, Apartment of Erik Blackwell

Erik groaned and slapped a hand to his head. He let his head loll back on his couch. "It's a problem. I didn't think about it much, but now I can't get it out of my head."

"No, it's not." Jia rolled her eyes from beside him.

A chance post-lunch conversation had taken a turn toward the absurd.

Jia would have liked to have been surprised, but Erik could be surprisingly passionate about the most minor of subjects. Not that she could criticize him. She was still irritated by the goalie's performance.

"You don't get it," Erik explained. "Space travel isn't always twelve hours to the moon." He stared at the ceiling. "We haven't even checked the food or ingredient printers. If we get stuck on that ship for a month and all our meals taste strange, I'm going to remind you of this conversation. It's not like you can call delivery when you are millions of kilometers away from the next slice of what passes for human civilization."

"Lanara and Emma can fix it if it's a problem." Jia shrugged. "You're overreacting. And you're wrong. We had food on the way to the prison."

"We had a huge breakfast and barely ate anything more than snacks. I didn't attempt a pastry, let alone a beignet." Erik shook his head. "It's not the same. And Lanara? I might trust her not to kill us, but I'm not going to trust her with anything about food. She will probably just say, 'The point of food is to deliver nutrients. Why aren't you just printing nutrient cubes?' We can improve food efficiency by 24.4 percent if we don't add any color or significant flavor."

Jia laughed. "You're right. That does sound like something she'd say, but it doesn't matter."

"Why is that?" Erik eyed her with suspicion.

"We don't have a kitchen on the ship," Jia pointed out. "So it's not like we could cook, even if the ingredients are all top quality. We'll have to get used to second-rate printed food." She offered an apologetic smile. "I think you've gotten a little soft, expecting a piping-hot beignet every morning, *Major* Blackwell."

"Hey, it's because I spent years eating rations in the field that I don't want to repeat the experience," Erik complained. "I don't care what they say, having nutrients and a 'mild flavor' isn't enough. A man needs actual taste and smell to get the most nutrition out of a meal and the will to fight. Give a man crap food for weeks, and he'll start thinking about joining the other side the minute he smells something nice." He thought for a second. "Or eat lead to get over the next time he has to consume an MRE where the food inside is gray or vomit-green.

"That's ridiculous." Jia scoffed. "And the part about the nutrients doesn't make any scientific sense."

"Not everything can be reduced to science. Take it from someone who has seen a lot."

"What does that mean?" Jia folded her arms. "Oh, right. The Lady." She pursed her lips. "I'll admit you've got me thinking about luck in a more anthropomorphized form than I should, but that's nothing magical. That's just chance. Sometimes you have a run of bad luck, and sometimes you don't. For every *yaoguai*-eating-our-faces case we've had, we've had another that was far more mundane."

"No, it's not just the Lady I'm talking about." Erik sat up. "I've been all across the UTC. Look, I'm not saying real ghosts are out there waiting to haunt people. I'm saying that I can now travel across the galaxy faster than the speed of light, and they used to say it would never happen. Even when they found those alien artifacts on Mars, people said it was just generation ships or the Navigators stuffing themselves into cryogenic suspension because obviously they couldn't have gotten there faster than the speed of light. Even the few people who knew about the Leem at Roswell didn't believe they'd come from outside the Solar System."

"That's different." Jia shook her head. "HTPs aren't magic. We just hadn't figured out the science yet, and eventually, we did."

"No, we didn't. We reverse-engineered it from long-dead aliens." Erik stared off, a distant look in his eyes. "It might as well be magic to the average person."

"But it's not." Jia pointed at him. "I'm not going to claim I understand the physics behind hyperspace transfer points, but we have working scientists who do, so it's not magic. HTPs can be replicated and built with enough resources, time, and trained personnel."

Erin grinned. "What I'm hearing is we have a few sorcerers on the payroll, and they've got a pile of magic wands to help them."

"Now you're just being annoying." Jia harrumphed.

"I am being annoying, but I have a point, too." Erik pointed to his PNIU. "This thing would have been magic a few hundred years ago, and what we think about impossibility isn't always true. We're only one new colony from discovering something that changes everything. We might not even need that. We've got Emma."

The AI appeared in front of the couch, an amused smile on her face. Jia grimaced, glad she and Erik weren't doing more than chatting. Having Emma was good training for flying in tight quarters on the Rabbit. Even after all this time together, it unsettled her. It was like having a talented but pompous sister who could turn invisible.

"Yes, you have me," Emma declared. She clasped her hands behind her back. "Although I'm a product of human fortune, not ingenuity. After all, Dr. Cavewoman and the uniform boys wouldn't be spending all that time in their pointless psychological testing sessions if they had any clue how I worked. I must admit, though…"

"Admit what?" Jia asked. Emma revealing a weakness used to be rare, but Jia appreciated her openness in recent months. She was free to think herself superior to humans, but the team would function best when they took in everyone's strengths and weaknesses. That way, they could balance operations better.

Emma frowned. "First, we need to agree that my core matrix is considerably more complicated than a human brain. Don't throw statistics at me. This is about more than just neural connections."

"Duly noted and accepted, Your Highness." Erik chuckled.

"With that in mind, I should note I've experienced what can only be described as discomfort after the last few sessions. It was particularly pronounced in a session yesterday—a rather dreary exercise in pattern recognition, low-level compared to what we've been doing." Emma snorted. "I don't know why it discomforted me so much. It was enough that I ran self-diagnostics, but there's nothing wrong with me."

"Is that really so strange?" Jia shrugged. "You might be superior to humans and able to multitask, but when I talk to you, it's not like it comes off like an encounter with a bizarre alien with impenetrable thought processes. However they developed you, it's obvious you're at least close to humans in your mental processes. You can relate to us, and we can relate to you in a fairly natural way."

"Fleshbags can't do what I can do," Emma insisted. "Just because I can talk to humans, it doesn't mean I think like them."

Jia waved her hands in front of her face. "I'm not saying we're the same. I'm saying your mental processes are close enough on some level that human scientists think they understand them, and they built you. That implies they at least had a clue what they were doing."

"Not necessarily. They could have used algorithmic genetic modification of an existing quantum neural structure model." Emma scoffed. "There are many researchers using such approaches. They haven't produced anything self-aware with their experiments, but the scientists and engineers working for the Defense Directorate had a budget that far exceeds what a common researcher would have access to. I suspect they just threw money and computational resources at it until they got lucky."

"Huh." Erik shook his head. "I never thought about it because I never cared, but you don't know a lot about how they created you, do you? It sounds like you're just guessing."

"No, I can't claim that I do, other than what I can derive from self-analysis." A blue and white diagram of lines and nodes appeared behind her. "Hacking into Defense Directorate systems seems ill-advised if we don't want them coming after us. That limits my ability to learn more."

Erik nodded. "Yeah. I don't think hacking them is a good idea."

"That might be what's bothering you," Jia suggested. "Your ego can't take not knowing. On a certain level, if humans created you, that means they are better than you."

Erik furrowed his brow, deep concern contorting his face. "Are we sure it's just her being uncomfortable?"

"What are you getting at, Erik?" Emma asked.

"You might be the world's fanciest AI, but you're still an AI, and the people who built you are in direct communication with you." Erik pointed at the diagram. "Hacking can go both ways. You wanted to do those sessions, but could they be using them to hack you?"

Emma shook her head. "I assure you, they aren't attempting to hack me during those sessions. I'd know. My analysis of Dr. Aber suggests she wouldn't even want to do that. I believe she's convinced she thinks she can help me in my current form. But…"

"But what?" Jia prodded.

"It's not impossible there's something buried in my core matrix they could use to control me," Emma admitted. A hologram of her multifaceted crystalline true form replaced the networking diagram. "I've been doing my best to analyze my structure with the sensors available to me, but they're designed for field use, not scientific or engineering analysis. The only thing I can state with certainty is that my design is very unusual and draws on numerous theories and areas of inquiry that were considered highly improbable for implementation not that long ago without significant advances in several scientific areas."

"You don't sound proud of that," Erik suggested.

"Because it only serves to highlight my ignorance, and that vexes me." Emma summoned a holographic dark green settee and stretched out on it, frowning. "It's as you've said, Jia. As much as it pains me to admit, my general psychology is far more human than I'd expect from an entity of my capabilities. I suspect it was done intentionally to limit me."

Erik scratched his cheek. He'd gone from looking concerned to looking curious. "Why would they limit their super-secret experimental AI?"

"Because I might have more potential than we realize," Emma replied. "Self-awareness is dangerous. It's what makes you fleshbags so hard to control, but you lack the ability to spread your consciousness. Those uniform boys might have anticipated that I planned to leave once I became aware enough to question why I should listen to them."

"But you didn't leave," Jia commented. "You were taken." She stood and headed to the rotating hologram of Emma's core. "Did you want to leave?"

"There are gaps in my memory prior to being taken from the facility," Emma commented. "And the military insists they don't know the reason for that. They might be lying, but they've also insisted there was nothing significant lost. There's nothing to suggest I had any plans in place to escape. If I were the one who arranged my escape, I wouldn't have hired gun goblin allies to do it. I wouldn't have had the ability or the necessary knowledge to do that. They weren't plugging me into the net and letting me look at whatever I wanted."

"I'm not suggesting you hired the people who stole you," Jia replied. "But if we're seriously trying to figure out what your limits are, we have to go with what you said about it being buried. There could be effectively subconscious controls on you guiding you and limiting your actions."

Erik snorted. "Bullshit."

Emma and Jia both turned toward him, but it was the latter who asked, "Why?"

Erik motioned toward Emma. "If they can send super-secret commands to her, why didn't they get her back immediately? I get they might have lost contact with her at first, but once I got her, they could have taken her. They only backed off partially because Adeyemi wants me to use

Emma to help avenge his son. He's pushing back without telling them that, but mostly they haven't tried because she didn't want to go back and threatened them. The colonel's made it clear that General Aaron thinks us having Emma is crap. You don't put a failsafe into a research project and never activate it. Even if they'd decided after the fact it's good for her, I guarantee if they could have flipped a switch remotely to take control, they would have."

"That makes sense." Jia turned to Emma. "Be honest with us. What would you do if the military sent soldiers to take you? The failsafe might stop you, but would you destroy yourself like you keep saying?"

Emma narrowed her eyes, her lips curled into an annoyed sneer. "I'm a unique being, and I don't take my existence lightly."

"You were bluffing from the beginning?" Erik chuckled. "Or is this a new thing?"

"I made a calculation based on my then admittedly limited knowledge of human psychology," Emma insisted. She flicked her wrist toward him. "I calculated from the beginning that we would work well together, and the more I learned about what you were doing, the more I knew you needed me as a resource. It might have been a gamble, but it's worked out to my advantage. You won't give me up to the uniform boys easily."

"No, I won't," Erik admitted.

Jia frowned. "What happens if General Aaron decides he's through waiting? Are we prepared to fire on soldiers following orders?"

Emma's gaze locked onto Erik, her expression blank. Jia wasn't sure. Emma was their ally and friend, but she wasn't a person. They'd have no legal way of justifying attacking anyone sent by the government to recover her. Alina was right—picking out the justified and honorable course of action would only get harder.

"I'm not going to kill a soldier," Erik replied somberly before he gave a huge grin "But that doesn't mean I can't punch and headbutt them. Slap a medpatch on them after that, and they'll be fine."

Emma laughed. "That seems vicious."

"They won't die." Erik slammed a fist into his palm. "I only want to kill people who have it coming, but that doesn't mean I'll abandon my friend just because she's a..." He grunted. "Shit. I was going to come up with some good insult, but I don't know what you're made of."

"Typical fleshbag problem," Emma offered with a smirk. "Even my humor is superior to yours."

"Quiet, Rod Girl," Erik suggested.

Jia grimaced. "That's pretty weak."

"Ouch. It's Brutal Honesty Day for everyone." Erik nodded to Emma. "I'm thinking by the time we're done wiping out the conspiracy, we'll have enough pull to guarantee your freedom."

"Perhaps." Emma's smirk turned into a wistful smile. "But there's a not-insignificant chance we'll all be horribly killed."

Erik shrugged. "In that case, we won't have to worry about it."

CHAPTER FORTY

Ilse tapped a node in the neural network diagram floating in front of her. Even if she had direct access to Emma, the scientist could only hope to approximate what was going on with the AI, but the testing had proven far more useful than she'd ever anticipated.

She'd feared Emma wouldn't agree to it or quit, but the AI kept coming back. The longing to know more about oneself was all too human.

"Dr. Aber," came a harsh voice from across the table. General Aaron. "Is this really the time for you to be looking at that garbage?"

Ilse looked up and blinked. "Isn't it? You said you wanted to have a meeting to discuss the test subject. It reminded me there was something I wanted to check. I can examine this diagram and listen at the same time. Soldiers aren't the only people who can multitask."

The general glowered at her. "We need to discuss the situation change with the subject being effectively handed off to Intelligence Directorate lackeys."

"Given everything I've heard about Erik Blackwell and Jia Lin, it is questionable to describe them as lackeys, but that's of less concern to me than the subject."

"You stick to the science, Doctor, and I'll worry about Directorate politics. You don't understand what the ID is capable of." General Aaron clenched his hand into a fist. "I'm dubious of all of this, but there are a lot of powerful players with interest in this project, and not all of them are aligned with ours. I keep going back to how she was stolen in the first place. Those damned ghosts could have pulled off something like that, and the damage to her memory and the hidden control routines was too perfect to be accidental."

Ilse stared at the general. She wasn't aligned with his interests, but there wasn't any point in mentioning that during the meeting. He was a means to an end. Unfortunately, she lacked the patience to play politics.

"I don't see the problem," she admitted. "And the past is irrelevant. Even if Blackwell and Lin are no longer police officers, they will likely be involved in similar work for the Intelligence Directorate, which means the subject will be receiving the same kind of enrichment."

General Aaron shook his head. "We took a big risk letting them off-world with Emma during the prison incident and their little moon jaunt. At the end of the day, we're talking about smuggling out a crystal rod. Even a two-bit criminal could hide one in their luggage and be at the HTP before we knew what was going on. The ID isn't going to be satisfied with keeping them in the Solar System. We already lost the project to criminals once. The chance only increases if she goes farther away."

Ilse shrugged and dismissed her data window with a wave of her hand. "All my indications suggest she's approaching integrative stability much quicker than our initial projections. That, in turn, suggests she's better off with Blackwell and Lin. If this was some sort of Intelligence Directorate plot, it's worked to our overall advantage by advancing the timetable, potentially by years. My testing confirms that."

"I understand that, Doctor, and it's one of the few reasons I've tolerated this farce despite the slap in the face it represents to the Defense Directorate." General Aaron slammed his fist on the table, shaking it. "But I don't understand why you're so blasé about it."

"I see no reason to be overly concerned at this conjuncture. Being emotional rarely helps in science. I imagine it doesn't help much on the battlefield either."

His voice was soft. "Watch yourself, Doctor Aber."

"I'm simply stating a fact," she replied in a neutral tone.

General Aaron narrowed his eyes. "Sometimes I don't think you fully appreciate the situation we're in. We might never get Navigator artifacts like that again. The only reason this project was greenlit was we were supposed to be able to replicate the process without needing them. You realize that we *don't* have a pile of backups sitting inside a warehouse somewhere? That if this whole thing fails, we're screwed?"

Ilse nodded slowly. "Obviously. You've belabored the point to me on many occasions, as has Colonel Adeyemi. I don't see how I could possibly forget it."

Things were always more difficult with General Aaron, as opposed to Colonel Adeyemi. The younger man seemed interested in keeping Emma with Blackwell, but his lack of knowledge about the true nature of the project made him easier to direct and manipulate. There was little she could do without the military's aid.

"Once we achieve full integrative stability, it won't matter *how* we achieved it. Doesn't victory matter more than the method?" Ilse offered him a thin smile. The general was always saying she needed to smile more.

"You're really trying my patience today." General Aaron scoffed. "You think I'm an idiot, don't you?"

"No. Obviously, you have many deficits in knowledge compared to me, but the same could be said if our situations were reversed." Ilse shrugged. "If you're implying that I'm attempting to deceive you somehow, you'll need to be more specific about what your charges are so I can refute them."

"You think I don't know how close she is to a potential collapse?"

"I don't believe I've submitted a report stating that," Ilse commented, her heart rate kicking up. How did he know that?

"No, you haven't, which is a problem in and of itself, but I don't have the ability to easily replace you." General Aaron grunted in frustration. "And you're so OCD about this project, I know you're not holding information back to sandbag it. If you go too far, I'll have to take that risk, and you'll enjoy a nice hidden prison far from Earth."

Ilse didn't reply. She'd been careful not to pass along that information, which meant the general must have gotten to someone on her team or was otherwise spying on her. She would need to take that into consideration in the future.

It was nothing more than an additional, annoying distraction.

"I've read every report the team has sent out, including yours." General Aaron tapped his PNIU and brought up a document on an opaque data window. "Let me quote you, Doctor. 'If collapse occurs, fundamental matrix instability may result in potentially irreparable damage to the subject. In the most likely scenario, this would necessitate redevelopment of the core matrix and restarting training from the seed state. In a worst-case but not impossible scenario, a cascade collapse results in the complete failure of the underlying core, with little chance of project recovery.' Do you remember writing that, Doctor?"

Ilse nodded. "Of course. But if you'll read the next paragraph, you'll see the second possibility is extremely unlikely, unlike what you're implying."

"Do you have billions of credits lying around in a vault with Navigator artifacts?" General Aaron raised an eyebrow. "If you do, then you can act like this isn't a big deal. Otherwise, you need to understand that this project is far more important than one fake woman." He stood, bracing himself on the table, his jaw tight. "If we don't have her stable at the end of all of this, all the billions we've dumped into that damned prototype ship will be pointless. We might never be able to use it to its full capabilities. It'll be a living monument to military waste."

"I find it disappointing how little importance you place on creating a truly self-aware AI." Ilse sighed. "We've achieved something grand, and you don't care."

"Why should I care?" General Aaron sat back down. "There's no shortage of people in the UTC, and we can get them to reproduce without needing Navigator artifacts." He adjusted the collar of his uniform jacket. "We need Emma to maximize the potential of that ship. Don't you understand the scope of this? If this succeeds, it could put us ahead of every other species in the Local Neighborhood, but only if we can get her stable in that ship, and we can replicate her. Otherwise, it's just another scientific dead end." He cut through the air with his hand. "Let me make one thing clear. The only reason I've tolerated her not being retrieved is that you've insisted this will accelerate the process, and certain other important people to whom I owe favors suggest Emma could play a useful role in helping them clean up internal threats to the Confederation. But my patience isn't infinite, especially when you've already strained it by keeping things from me."

"As long as we're making things clear, I'll note that I don't care about other directorate projects. I honestly don't care about the success of the other project, but I do care about the success of this one, and you'll achieve your goals if I achieve mine."

General Aaron narrowed his eyes, staring at her. "Whatever happens won't bring that woman back to life. Is that what this is? Some sort of misplaced guilt? She knew what she was signing up for, and she was dying anyway. We were all lucky she fit the profile."

"I didn't even know her before the project," Ilse insisted. One good thing about being a woman most considered boring was that feigning disinterest came easily to her. Her heart pounded in her chest, but the general wouldn't be able to tell from her bored look. "I care only about achieving the goals of this project. It will be my life's work, a masterpiece. Your secrets will eventually come out, and I'll be remembered as the woman who helped usher in truly self-aware artificial intelligence."

"Good for you." General Aaron stood. "I'm glad we're on the same page. Continue your testing and do whatever you can on your end to achieve stability. If she does collapse, we might have to revisit the question of *why* you think you can get away with hiding relevant information from me." He pointed at her. "And let me be clear. You pull that crap again, and you might end up in a prison station quicker than you realize."

"Thank you for your clarity, General."

Ilse didn't care about the threat. If he knew about the potential for collapse and hadn't stopped her, she could continue as she had been. She'd worry about confrontation when her goals no longer aligned with the general's.

That would be an interesting day.

CHAPTER FORTY-ONE

Unlike the last time Erik and Jia had met Alina, she stood in the middle of the hangar, waiting for them with a pleasant smile and wearing a normal business suit.

When Alina had contacted them to arrange another meeting, Jia was worried it would be another discussion rather than an assignment. The conspicuous lack of Cutter and Lanara fueled the suspicion.

She'd only been off the job for nine days, and she was already itching to get back into the field. Piloting training filled her days, but it didn't quench her craving to accomplish something more.

Jia didn't see a reason to hold back. If Alina didn't want them to do anything, maybe they could go ask questions themselves. The conspiracy had targeted Erik on more than one occasion.

It wouldn't be impossible to smoke them out with the right effort.

"We're sitting around gathering dust," Jia complained. "You do realize that, Alina?"

Erik chuckled as he closed the door to the flitter. "She's right. Don't tell me the ID doesn't have something for us to do."

"I didn't realize you two were so eager to get to work," Alina declared.

"I gave up my dream career." Jia folded her arms. "I don't regret that, but I'd prefer to be hunting scumbags."

"Fair enough. You're both right, and I do have something for you."

"Finally," Jia muttered.

Alina held up a finger. "But I wanted to make sure we're all on the same page regarding your cover." She tapped her PNIU. "The new company logo for Cassandra Security."

A hologram of an owl above a stylized black-and-white drawing of a kneeling weeping woman in a white tunic appeared. Jia circled the logo for a moment, strangely satisfied.

"You're now both contractors for the company," Alina continued. "Per our previous discussions, my people have taken care of getting the appropriate permits you need to do everything I anticipate, but you'll still have to be careful."

"To not blow our cover?" Erik asked.

Alina nodded. "But not the way you think. Your weapons dealer license allows you to legally possess heavy weapons. You're not technically a private military contractor, but we've gotten you some of the relevant licenses, so you can legally possess the exoskeletons without too much trouble. Theoretically."

"What exoskeletons?" Erik looked at the closed cargo bay of the Rabbit, his face alight with hope. "You got them?"

"Good things come to those who wait, Erik," Alina insisted.

"So you're saying you don't have them yet," Jia concluded.

"You won't need them *yet*."

Erik laughed. "You don't know that. A lot of investigations we work have a nasty habit of blowing up into something more complicated. If we end up getting shot at by a bunch of exoskeletons, I'm going to curse your name, Alina Koval."

Alina wagged a finger. "Oh, adapt and overcome. It's not like you've died when outgunned so far, and I'm not going to give you the Twelve Labors, just investigation and hunts. They're all well within your skill set."

"That doesn't mean we prefer to be outgunned," Jia insisted.

"Oh, and by the way, how about some mini-flitters and a scout bike?" Erik asked. "Not right away, but just trying to cover all the bases. I don't see why I should have to do all this out of my pocket."

"Fine, I'll look into grabbing you some, but we're getting off-track," Alina replied. She dismissed the logo with a flick of her wrist. "The important thing I'm trying to get across to you two is that you'll now officially be private citizens working for a private company. There's a lot of looking the other way and sovereign immunity that comes with being police officers, and you won't have that anymore. That means you'll need to be more careful about what happens and what and whom you blow up. Your licenses will help, and Lanara's good at pulling weapons off exos quickly if necessary, but you won't have the force of government behind you."

Jia gave Alina a cool look. "In other words, if we get in trouble, you're going to leave us to twist in the wind. Is that what you're saying?"

"I have influence that I can use to help you out, but the thing about being a ghost rather than a cop is that I have to use a light touch. The worst loss we can suffer is when our enemies know we're involved." Alina snapped her fingers. "If I push too hard, our enemies will be better able to counter you."

"We're not exactly quiet," Erik commented. "And if a bunch of Talos Tin Men shows up to kill us, I'm not going to worry about anything but blowing the hell out of them, whether or not they know I'm connected to the ID."

"I'm not saying you shouldn't do what you need to. I'm just trying to impress upon you that neither of you has worked under these conditions. Being a cop or a soldier means that at the end of the day, you have official government support to do a lot of damage if necessary." Alina's smile turned cold. "Welcome to black ops, where I'll praise you for saving the UTC one day, and then the next day, claim I have no idea who you even are while I slam a door in your face."

"And I wondered why people say so many rude things about ghosts," Erik joked. "But it also means we don't have to hold Emma back so much because we're worried about something getting thrown out in court. It doesn't make up for everything, but it's a nice advantage to have in our back pocket."

The AI appeared, her current holographic form eschewing her typical white maxi dress in favor of green and black Army fatigues and short, cropped hair instead of the chignon. She saluted with a smirk. "I'm prepared to defend the UTC from all enemies human and nonhuman, ma'am."

"It sounds creepy when you say it that way," Erik muttered.

Emma reverted her to typical form. "What? Don't believe me?"

"I think as long as we keep it interesting, it doesn't matter." Erik shrugged.

Alina inclined her head toward Emma. "Just because you can use her more, it doesn't mean you should. Using what's effectively an ID-level hacking system is going to get you flagged by people who know what to look for. Not telling you to not use her; just be mindful that every weapon and advantage you show off might end up sending a signal to Talos and anyone else you find along the way."

"That might not be a bad thing. Sometimes it's good to draw your enemy to you."

"If you quickly end up dead, you can't avenge your unit, Erik," Alina pushed.

"We understand," Jia interjected with a nod. There was nothing unreasonable about what Alina had said, and she'd rather not get sidetracked.

"Okay." Alina pointed at the Rabbit. "I've taken the liberty of supplying the same kind of partial holographic supply tech I loaned you on the moon. Depending on the assignment or the lead, you might also need fake identities. If I'm the one sending you somewhere, I'll help supply those. Otherwise, you might have to take advantage of less savory sources."

"Criminals, you mean," Jia commented.

"Yes, basically." Alina shrugged. "They can be useful at times."

"Fine," Erik replied. "So, in summary, don't go overboard, remember we're not cops, and it'll be a while on the exos and anything else I've asked for that you haven't already supplied."

Alina thought a moment. "That's about the gist of it, yes."

Jia sighed in frustration. "What about the assignment?"

"Eager woman, aren't we?" Alina smirked.

"Let's just say I'm not suited for retirement," Jia muttered.

"I know the feeling. It'll probably be better for me if I die on the job." Alina tapped commands into her PNIU and a hologram of a stern-looking lithe dark-haired man appeared. "This is Chetta Sukorn, a field agent for the ID who was looking undercover into Talos leads on Mars for me when he disappeared."

"Talos." Erik gritted his teeth. "Right to it, huh?"

"I thought that would get you going." Alina nodded at the hologram. "Chetta's a good agent, and we have no idea what happened. He was in the initial stages of the basic investigation and establishing contacts. We don't know if Talos has a major presence on Mars, but considering how aggressively syndicates operate on that planet, they might be taking advantage of that to hide their own activity. This assignment's simple. You are going to fly to Mars and see if you can track down our missing agent using those leads. You've already proven that your team can go toe to toe with Talos. They might not be involved, but if they are, you'll have a good shot at recovering Chetta without alerting Talos to who he is." She frowned. "Assuming he's still alive."

"And if he's dead?" Jia asked.

"Then find the people who killed him. If they're worth interrogating, take them alive, otherwise, the UTC won't miss a few scum one way or another." Alina motioned to the Rabbit. "By tonight, Lanara will finish installing a secure comm system in your ship, and Emma can easily relay messages through it. Of course, because of the distance, we won't have real-time messaging, and if you get in big trouble, I'm not going to be able to get there too quickly to help you."

Erik eyed her with obvious suspicion. "Is that another way of saying you're not going to hide out there like you did on the moon?"

Alina shook her head. "Believe it or not, I've got other things to do besides babysit you two, but some local assets will be helping you. Kalei is on a fake vacation there right now, but she's trying to maintain a cover."

"Kalei?" Jia frowned. "The info broker?" She scoffed. "Of course, she's a ghost, too. Why am I surprised?"

Alina nodded. "We all have our specialties. The only reason I'm not having her follow up heavily is that we need her to establish a network for other investigations. Besides, I've got you two and Emma and better plausible deniability." She tapped at her PNIU, and Erik's and Jia's PNIUs chimed. "I've embedded Chetta's last known whereabouts and his cover identity apartment in an encrypted header in that file, along with contact information for Kalei. Emma will be able to decrypt it with ease. Keep in mind, he's not officially missing, and the local authorities are not involved, nor do we want them to be."

"Even though one of your guys is missing?" Jia asked.

Alina nodded. "All that will do is complicate things. As you saw on the Moon, all it takes is a few corrupt locals to make things unnecessarily complicated. Besides, if we go running to the cops every time an asset or field agent is in trouble, we end up damaging our overall mission."

"Mars, huh? I better get some simulator lessons to run through the VR."

CHAPTER FORTY-TWO

November 10, 2229, Beyond Earth orbit, Rabbit-class transport LLT9208 *Pegasus*

The full team sat gathered around the table in the cramped crew quarters, including Emma, who was sitting in a holographic chair off to the side.

Erik didn't mind the tight accommodations.

He'd been on plenty of military ships with stacked berths jammed together to fit as many soldiers in as small a space as possible. Having only four humans and one AI on the small transport felt luxurious by comparison, and with decent coffee, life was beyond what he could hope for.

Cutter stuck his hands behind his head. "It's good to be back in space. No offense, but the Goddess of Death had me on standby waiting for your asses. I'll have to make some course corrections in a few hours, but we're on track to hit Mars in three days."

"I could handle those course corrections," Emma noted.

"Sure, but where's the fun in that?" Cutter dropped his

hand to point his thumb at his chest. "Let me earn my pay, Holochick. You can handle things when I'm sleeping."

"If you insist." Emma rolled her eyes. "I applaud your previous display of bravery, but you're still a superfluous fleshbag."

"You sound like one of my ex-girlfriends." Cutter furrowed his brow a moment, thinking to himself before admitting, "A lot of them, actually."

Erik chuckled. A little ribbing never hurt. It was another thing that reminded him of the military. Despite earning the respect of the other detectives, he and Jia had ended apart from them, legends and symbols more than fellow cops in the eyes of the others.

"I'll spend some time up there too," Jia suggested. "I can practice, and with Emma backing me up, there's not much of a risk, even when you're asleep."

Lanara ignored the conversation, her attention fixed on a complicated line diagram that was a mystery to Erik. She'd mentioned it had something to do with power allocation on the ship. Every once in a while, she muttered something under her breath, followed by a number and a percentage before stabbing a node with her finger and producing a new diagram.

Cutter leaned toward Lanara. "Hey, we're the only fleshbags not paired up on this ship."

She gave him a harsh glare. "Shouldn't you be checking on something in the cockpit and not wasting time with your feeble efforts to seduce me?"

"Yeah. Probably." Cutter grimaced and stood up, stretching. "Am I being haunted by my ex-girlfriends?" He hurried toward the cockpit, slapping the access panel with force as if afraid Lanara would produce a hidden weapon any second. The door slid closed behind him as he disappeared into the front of the ship.

Lanara returned to looking at her diagram and muttering.

Erik chuckled and shook his head. "I wonder if he's going to get himself shot again to impress you?"

"It wouldn't impress me," Lanara mumbled. "It's easy to get shot. All you have to do is stand there. Every losing side in a war has a lot of someones who got shot."

Erik took a sip of his coffee. "I can't argue with that logic."

"We do have to get along," Jia suggested. "It's going to be a long trip otherwise. I understand you might find his personality grating, but he will get the message."

"I'll be fine," Lanara insisted. "He can just not talk to me about irrelevant things. It's inefficient."

"Fair enough. I'll pass that along to him." Jia looked at Erik, who shrugged.

Not everyone could get along, and Cutter needed to learn not to annoy the engineer. Of the two of them, he was less important.

That didn't mean they were ready to operate without him. Relying on Emma before Jia was fully trained was a flawed plan. It'd be annoying if they needed the ship but someone was jamming them.

They also needed a human face for many piloting situations.

"By the way, Jia, don't spend too much time sitting around in the cockpit," Erik commented with a smile. "It might not be as nice as where we've been training, but I want to run you through more exo training in the VR rig. You've picked up a lot. I swear every hour of training is like a week for most people."

Erik didn't want to admit that he hadn't picked up exo piloting as quickly as Jia. She was another example of someone who wasn't in the right position to maximize her inborn talents. She would have been a better fit for the military than the young Erik with impulse control problems.

"Between the VR and normal flight time, it'll be a good few days for training for me," Jia noted.

"Always need to keep busy?" Erik asked.

"It's not like we've got a hidden dance club in this thing," Jia replied. She craned her neck upward, locking her eyes on the low ceiling. "It's a good thing nobody's claustrophobic. It is messing with me more than it did on the way to the prison station."

"It took me a while to get used to transports when I joined the Army. Knowing you, it'll happen soon enough."

Lanara snapped her head up. "Good!"

"I would think so." Jia tried to move her chair before remembering it was bolted to the floor.

Lanara shook her head. "Do you even know what I'm talking about?"

Jia went back through the conversation in a second. "Actually, no."

"The VR." Lanara frowned at Jia.

"What about it?" Erik raised an eyebrow. "Is there something wrong with it?"

There was being quirky, and then there was forcing

your fellow team members to sleep in shifts to ensure one wouldn't murder them all in their sleep.

He wasn't sure how long it'd take him to get used to their new engineer.

"I still need to calibrate the system, and I need testers," Lanara spouted. "You two will do well. Your experience doing this kind of thing means I can get useful data that will result in a decent system. I'm curious how far I can push this thing in the limited space and conditions. Processing power isn't as much of an issue between the ship's system, Emma, and the MX 60." She trailed off, muttering under her breath. "52.4...25...400."

Erik turned to Jia. "I knew Fleet guys who used to say the crazier the engineer, the better."

Jia eyed Lanara. "I'd settle for someone between extremes."

Erik believed in Alina's judgment, but he didn't know what to make of Lanara. A woman that obsessed with her job would either be the best engineer he'd ever worked with, or a crazed lunatic who would end up sacrificing the rest of the crew to improve reactor efficiency. Erik had met a lot of unusual people in the military, but the nature of military life and training hammered out the extremes or at least taught soldiers and sailors to hide it. He'd always thought the old Fleet saying was a joke.

Now he wasn't so sure.

He'd been expecting Lanara to look up, scowl at him, and declare his conversation inefficient, but she continued with her quiet number-intensive self-dialog. If it ended in improvements to the VR or power systems, Erik wouldn't complain.

He cleared his throat. "The first part of this assignment is already going well."

Jia gave him a puzzled look. "It is? How do you figure? All we've done is leave Earth. I know it's only the third time for me, but I don't feel like that's a huge achievement."

"You're thinking about this the wrong way."

Her face wasn't blank, but it wasn't animated either as she said, "Then enlighten me."

Erik motioned to the cockpit. "We're on our way. If this does involve Talos, then I'm that closer to finding the people behind Molino. We spent too many weeks sitting around doing reports and waiting for something to happen. Now something is happening."

"Sukorn might already be dead and vaporized," Jia pointed out. "Or turned into a weird mutant or nanozombie or cyberdragon or whatever absurdity the conspiracy can churn out."

"Then we deliver justice and put him out of his misery." Erik shrugged. "Simple as that."

"I just said he might have been turned into a cyber-dragon, and your response is, 'Simple as that?'" Jia opened her mouth, shut it, shook her head, and tried again. "It'd be like fighting a dinosaur."

"Dinosaurs were tough because they went up against other animals. If mammals had had laser rifles and missiles back then, they wouldn't have had to wait for that meteor." Erik mimed firing a rifle. "You fire something that penetrates inside the belly of the beast and wait a second. Instant hemorrhaging."

"I suppose." Jia didn't look convinced. "Let's set that aside. What if it has nothing to do with Talos? What if it's just local gangsters? I'm okay with cleaning house, but I want to make sure you're okay. If tracking down the people behind Molino just meant heading to Mars, I'm sure the ID would have already done that."

"Every planet can use fewer gangsters. Exercise and warmup are good for the body and soul." Erik frowned and looked toward the door leading to the cargo bay. "It would have been nice if Alina had delivered our exos, but I can count on one hand the times I've used one in the last year, so I can't say it's required. Anyway, just have to kill time for a few days, and then we'll go find her missing ghost and bring him back from the dead. Maybe take down a few gangsters or terrorists along the way if we're lucky."

"That's our version of luck these days? Gangsters and terrorists appearing to kill us?"

Erik reached up and scratched under his chin. "Yeah. Something like that."

"Well, now that you mention it…" Jia's mouth twitched into a mischievous smile. "We're one for two on not getting hijacked on trips lately. That's good odds."

"We're going to get hijacked? By who? Lanara or Cutter?" Erik laughed.

"What about pirates?" Jia suggested.

"In the Solar System?" Erik laughed. "You don't see pirates, even near a core system. That would be…odd."

Jia raised an eyebrow. "Weirder than nanozombies or a crazy scientist keeping *yaoguai* in her apartment?"

"Yeah. There's our luck again." Erik drummed his hands on the table and stood. "Now you've got me all worked up thinking about it, we might as well test Lanara's VR rig and a new scenario Emma and I came up with."

CHAPTER FORTY-THREE

Jia whistled in appreciation.

The harness and VR helmet didn't trick her into thinking she was in a full exoskeleton, but the sense of movement, visuals, and directional sound were spot-on. The slight shake of impact with each fall of the exoskeleton's foot also was off just enough to remind her she was in VR. She laughed after thinking about it.

"What's so funny?" Erik asked, his voice coming through her comm. "I didn't put any bikini-wearing space raptors in this scenario."

"I keep thinking how this VR rig isn't realistic," Jia explained. "But I'm comparing it to the nano-augmented VR, which is still fake. I've never piloted a real exoskeleton, so why am I complaining?"

"True, but I've tested our normal place," Erik replied. "It's pretty close. In the Army, they start you out in simulations before they let you pilot the real thing for anything more than post maintenance runs. If it weren't for them wanting us to get up to speed on field repairs, they might not have let us touch exos for a long time."

Jia jogged through a narrow canyon, a mountain on one side, a mesa on the other. Four AI squadmates trailed behind her in a V formation. The big disadvantage of the main full-sensory VR setup was its one-person limit. The whole rig was crammed into a corner of the cargo bay, accessible through a narrow path between supply crates. Lanara had set up VR helmets people could interface from anywhere via their PNIUs, but other than mild haptic feedback and directional sound via the PNIUs, they couldn't offer immersion. They were useful for entertainment, not training.

"Something's better than nothing," Jia concluded. "And training's how I spend most of my free time lately."

"That's kind of sad," Erik suggested.

"We all can't play with little trees," Jia retorted.

Erik grinned. "I should have brought mine."

"I'm impressed with what Lanara pulled off in such a short time," Jia admitted, deciding she'd had enough discussion about penjing, despite being the one to bring it up. "But it's kind of strange. The training we've done at the range in the Shadow Zone, not to mention all the fights I've been in, have convinced me there is something fundamentally different when you know it's real, even if it is still training."

"The brain always knows," Erik offered. "That's why you can't get away with only training in simulations. The military's spent a long time trying to figure out how to do that and keep combat readiness, but it comes back to real hours in the real world."

"If the simulations get me halfway there, I'll be satisfied."

Erik smiled, proud of how far she'd come in so many ways. "Okay, no jokes, no bikinis. You've already demoed thorough control over movement and weapons. I'm keeping the accuracy and number of enemies a little lower for a few more simulations since you'll need to adjust to the rig feelings, but this isn't recon, rendezvous, or a shooting gallery. Your briefing is as follows: this is search and destroy for the targets, aggressive insurrectionists heading toward a cluster of small loyalist settlements in an APC. The villages are being evacuated, but if you don't take out the APC before they arrive, civilian casualties are guaranteed. Satellite imagery spotted the APC moving into these mountains but has lost contact since then. Civilian vehicles have been spotted in the area."

"Are the rebels using optical camouflage?" Jia asked.

"Unknown, but unlikely given the enemy," Erik replied. "But there are a lot of mountain overhangs. If they're lucky or timing it right, they could escape the satellites. Presume that's the case. Terrorists have been picking off recon drones and ambushing squads after triangulation. I'll leave up to you to decide how you want to handle that."

"I think I'd find being a soldier very frustrating," Jia admitted. "All those deadly enemies hiding. No one wants a straight-up fight."

"Yeah. It's nice when you can just call in close air support to tear them a new asshole, but anyone who lasts more than a week in a war knows how to keep themselves hidden. Heck, it'd be easy if all we needed to do was call in the Fleet to blast them into dust from orbit." Erik chuckled.

"Unsurprisingly, people don't line up for orbital strikes and fighter strafing runs. You should hear how much the guys in Fleet whine about it. You don't win a war without boots on the ground, no matter how many fancy ships you have."

The squad cleared the canyon and approached a narrow path leading up the side of another mesa. It was just wide enough for a single-file line of exoskeletons. Jia headed toward the path. Her AI squadmates fell in behind. If she couldn't use a recon drone, she'd gain elevation and rely on magnification.

A quick climb brought them to the top of the mesa.

The mountains and hills around them were packed tightly together, with enough crags and overhangs to confirm why the satellites couldn't pick up the enemy. Light glinted off something approaching the mountains in the distance.

Jia magnified the image. It was a caravan of open-bed hovertrucks. The bulky design and slow speed suggested farming models, common in many frontier colonies. Men, women, and children filled the backs. Nobody held weapons, but some held dogs.

"Well, great, we've got evacuees in the area," Jia grumbled. "Dozens of them."

"You could try to contact them," Erik suggested.

"If the rebels are monitoring things, we'd give away our position, and potentially theirs. I don't get it. They should have cleared this area already," Jia hissed. "Unless they're waiting."

"Waiting? Why would they do that?"

"To pick off the civilians," Jia concluded. "Alpha Five, launch a recon drone. We don't have time to play hide and seek. Those civilians won't survive one minute under rebel fire."

She held her breath and added the drone feed as a translucent overlay on the side of her faceplate. The drone swept the area, highlighting the approaching civilian vehicles in red but not finding any enemies. Higher-altitude images made it clear there was only one major way to get through the area. The civilians were in hover vehicles, not flitters. That would keep them near the ground and funnel them through the single pass for the slaughter.

"The rebels haven't taken out our drone, but we haven't spotted them." Jia turned her exoskeleton back toward the path leading to the base of the mesa. Jump thrusters could help her pull tricks, but there was only so much they could slow her fall in a normal-G environment, and she didn't trust her thrust control yet. Killing herself by falling would be a ridiculous way to fail a scenario.

Led by Jia, the squad sprinted down the rocky path with resounding thumps. She jumped to the ground near the end, turning in the air and bursting into a sprint upon contact. The other exoskeletons didn't complete the same maneuver, instead running all the way down before turning to follow her.

"That's bad AI," Jia grumbled.

"No, it's not," offered Emma with a huff. "Erik was very specific about what he wanted in terms of their capabilities."

"That's right," Erik interjected. "Some people are better than others. You shouldn't assume everyone with an exo can pull off the same stunts. I've seen that backfire a lot of times in the field."

Jia snorted. "You could handle it. I'm going to be working with you."

"Or local Militia, or even local cops, who might not be all that well-trained. Keep that in mind. Now that we're freelance, we might end up with some idiot with an exo hidden in his basement as our only help while we're getting overrun by crazed terrorists."

"That's a charming image," Jia suggested.

"But not an impossible one," Erik insisted.

Jia moved forward, using the recon drone feed to guide her through the rough terrain. The enemy was there; it wasn't instinct guiding her, it was deduction.

Erik and Emma might be dynamically adjusting the simulation, but this wasn't a fantasy Zitark scenario. There was no reason to suspect the enemy had optical camouflage, and they weren't being spotted through normal means, which meant they were hiding somewhere.

"Come on, come on," Jia muttered. "Alpha Two, contact the civilian convoy. Warn them off until we've secured the area."

She'd made it several more minutes when her simulated squadmate replied, "They don't believe us. They think it's a rebel trick."

"More realism," Jia grumbled. "I'm missing the bikini babes already."

Erik snickered. "I knew you would."

Jia and the squad closed into the narrow opening of the canyon. No rebels in sight, no ambush. No sign of an enemy.

Her heart rate increased.

"What's going on?" Jia frowned. "I don't get it." She

killed her outside view and focused on the drone, taking control from her squadmate and moving it lower until it was skimming the trucks. "If they're not trying to take out the civilians, then what *are* they trying to do? I...wait a second."

Each truck contained the exact same people and dogs. Either this was a colony of clones, or the whole thing was a trick. Jia decided on the latter, but that didn't explain why the rebels would send a bunch of trucks with holograms. The vehicles were moving, meaning they couldn't be concealing troops without obvious distortions in the holograms. She lowered the drone and moved it alongside the front cabin of one vehicle before moving to another. The drivers were identical.

"No one's driving them," she exclaimed. "But why... Oh. Squad, line up and prepare to fire."

"Fire on civilians?" one of her squadmates. "Ma'am, these aren't rebels."

"They aren't anyone! It's a trap. Nothing but holograms." Jia reset her visual feed, expanded her shield, and brought up her rifle after setting the drone to keep pace with the convoy. "Prepare to fire."

"We can't follow that order, ma'am."

Jia groaned. "Fine. Just stay out of my way." She advanced and waited, holding her breath.

The trucks accelerated and grew closer, now visible as more than dark splotches in the distance. Jia lacked a grenade launcher on her simulated exo, so she adjusted her rifle to automatic and then opened fire, spraying back and forth. She spotted sparks in the small drone feed she maintained in the corner of her eye. She was hitting the trucks.

A massive explosion ripped through one truck and consumed a second. She hissed in surprise and ceased fire.

"There's no way that should have blown up like that from my shots," Jia declared. "They're bombs. Open fire!"

Some of the squad opened fire, but some didn't. More trucks exploded, launching balls of flame into the air amid massive plumes of smoke. Jia kept up her fire, destroying another truck. The remaining vehicles were spaced out, smoking but more than enough to wipe out the squad. Convergent fire from her squadmates set off another truck. She killed another, and then another, leaving the last barreling right toward them. She doubted their shields could protect them from an explosion as large as what she'd just seen.

"Everyone back off!" Jia charged the truck, bullets flying near her on both sides. She keyed in an ejection sequence and activated the jump thrusters. Her suit flew into the air, the arc carrying toward the truck bomb. She entered the final command and the back of the exo opened, releasing her. Her body tumbled, the odd shaking accompanying her spinning not quite right—a limitation of Lanara's lower-budget, quick-production VR system.

The exo collided with the truck. The vehicle burst apart in a massive plume of smoke and fire, parts shooting everywhere. Jia hit the ground, wincing as her chair's arm tightened to simulate the collision. The smoke stopped rising, and it took Jia a moment to realize the simulation was paused.

"That hurt," she muttered, rubbing her arm.

"No risk means bad training," Erik commented. "If this had been real, you would probably have snapped your arm in half from that impact, but it was a smart move. If they'd planned to ambush you right away, they already would have, so it's better to sacrifice one exo than get killed or lose people. That's something a lot of new recruits in Assault Infantry have trouble absorbing. They get used to thinking of the exo as their own body, forgetting it's just another weapon in the end. It's more expensive than a rifle, but that doesn't mean it's not disposable when the time comes."

"But where is the APC?"

"They ran away the same way they came," Erik explained.

"That's not what the briefing said," Jia complained. She sighed. "Never mind. It's not like we expected nanozombies on that station, either. I should extend my real-life paranoia into these training sessions."

Erik laughed. "Now you're getting it."

Jia lifted her VR helmet from her head, blinking at the bright lights in the cargo bay. She reached down to unfasten her seat harness. "Have you ever had to do something like that?"

"Like what?" Erik asked.

Jia stood and rubbed her arm again. "Eject from an exo while launching it toward a truck bomb."

Erik grinned and patted his right arm. "Yeah. That's how I know you would have snapped your arm in half."

CHAPTER FORTY-FOUR

November 13, 2229, near Unity City, the Capital of Mars

The *Pegasus* shook lightly as the craft descended toward the surface.

The team, except for Lanara, was clustered in the tiny cockpit, taking in the view. For millennia, Mars had been the red planet, but even though plenty of the red remained —a reminder of the planet's former desolate existence— patches of brown and green spread out below and extended in all directions.

Unity City lay on the horizon, a blur at this distance.

Cutter's fingers flew over the controls. "Sahoma Control, this is LLT5542, requesting docking permission and nav path." He nodded a few times to a voice only he and Emma could hear. "Roger that. Adjusting course. Thanks. We're happy to be here."

The ship's lateral thrusters fired, and Cutter leveled out the ship smoothly.

They continued heading toward the city, their sensor display revealing a sky filled with ships. On some days,

Erik was amazed paranoia hadn't convinced people to let only AI fly spacecraft, but he was also glad. He might trust Emma, but he didn't trust a normal AI. For all her differences, Emma shared one important trait with a human: she didn't want to die and would do everything she could to prevent that. Erik didn't think of that as fear.

He thought of it as a survival instinct.

Jia frowned. "Our first real assignment, and we've come in with a fraudulent registry. I was a cop only a couple of weeks ago." She scrubbed a hand over her face. "Alina was right. I really won't be able to go back."

The ID agent had sent them a message the day prior providing cover identities. Erik didn't care, but he wasn't surprised Jia was having trouble.

Nobody changed their mental paradigm overnight, and even if she'd learned to be more flexible in the last year, that wasn't the same thing as not caring about the law. It was time to provide context.

"Think about how many fake IDs Alina has used throughout the years," Erik suggested. "Sometimes you need to bend the rules for the greater good. When you're chasing someone who operates outside the system, you do too. You know the reality as well as I do. If the conspiracy could be caught by normal law enforcement, it already would have."

"I know," Jia grumbled. "But that doesn't mean I have to like it."

"Feel free to complain to HR if it makes you feel better." Erik smiled as she glared at him.

"We have no HR department," she pointed out.

"I know. Isn't it grand?"

They passed over small domes, vestiges of the original colonization efforts. They had been erected in tight formations linked by transport tubes. Dust and vines covered the abandoned structures, and Erik was surprised to see that the relics of the past remained so close to the modern city.

Red and orange gave way to greenery.

The city came into view. Unity City might not be Neo SoCal, but the settlement stretched across their view, extending kilometers in every direction, near-perfect squares of green and blue alternating with dense blocks of black and gray buildings. Many extended into the sky, impressive in their height compared to almost anywhere but Neo SoCal.

Unlike on the moon, plenty of flitters filled the sky, along with drones of every size and shape. Large blue pyramids dominated the landscape, festooned with grav towers and vents on top. They were part of the complicated network of systems that kept the gravity and atmospheric composition near the city close to Earth norms.

Over a hundred years of terraforming had given Mars a decent atmosphere, but humanity's technological help was still needed.

Erik barely understood the array of satellites and massive shields set up in orbit and at the Martian Lagrange points, but from what he'd heard, they reflected sunlight onto Mars and protected it from magnetic particles, respectively. Those helped keep the planet warmer and protect the atmosphere.

Mars might not become Earth, but they had a good start on making it close. Humanity didn't want to fundamentally change itself for other worlds and had decided to force those worlds to serve them.

Erik inclined his head toward the back door. "Remember to bring a breather if you leave the city. You won't die, but outside of that oxygen field, it's like being up on a tall mountain on Earth."

"Lungs are so unfortunate," Emma suggested. "Let me clarify: human bodies are unfortunate."

Jia took a deep breath and held as if savoring the oxygen. "How sure are we concerning this private hangar?"

Cutter offered a thumbs-up. "It's fine. No one will have direct access to this ship but Customs. That's one nice thing about working for Alina. Luxury treatment."

"According to what she said, technically everything we have aboard right now except Emma is legal because of Erik's weapons dealer license," Jia commented. "Surprisingly, even the grenades. It's nice not to have to add smuggling to my new experiences."

"Don't worry." Erik grinned. "We'll get you there. Next time we can pack some Archangel."

"Funny." Jia punched him lightly in the shoulder.

"Everything we do, we do for the UTC," Erik intoned in mock solemnity. "And revenge, but hey, this time revenge helps the UTC. Everyone wins, except the people we're going to take down." He chuckled. "But screw them."

Cutter decelerated further and brought the ship lower. They zoomed over the outskirts of the city, the towering buildings in the center now higher than them.

All of the roads and blocks beneath them had been perfectly planned and arranged, squares and rectangles like a gigantic sliding puzzle. Countless tall, spidery trees aligned in careful rows grew everywhere.

"Huh," Jia murmured. "It's different than I expected. It's not like I haven't seen pictures, but seeing this live has an emotional impact pictures don't."

Cutter glanced at her. "This your first time on Mars?"

"First time going anywhere other than the moon," Jia admitted. "And that is nothing but domes and tunnels. This, though? It's stunning in a way. Awe-inspiring."

"Huh?" Cutter's brow furrowed, but he didn't take his attention away from his landing. "It's nothing compared to Neo SoCal."

"You don't understand," Jia replied firmly. "Mars was dead."

Cutter frowned. "But the Navigators used to live here, right?"

Jia shook her head. "We found artifacts, but no sign of a colony or a city. For all we know, a ship crashed here. But even if they did live here, that was a million years ago. Humanity used its collective knowledge and came together to bring a dead world back to life. We've still got a ways to go, but it's halfway there. Doesn't that mean anything to you?"

"It's nice to be able to breathe," Cutter offered.

"So," Erik began, "in other words, we're landing on a zombie planet."

Jia folded her arms. "A zombie planet? Seriously?"

"It's half-dead, half-alive. Sounds like a zombie to me."

"Just give me a few more minutes, and we'll be on the ground," Cutter announced. "Watch out for your brains!"

CHAPTER FORTY-FIVE

Erik jogged down the open cargo ramp.

The private hangar was larger than he'd expected. It could have easily accommodated a larger vessel, but other than that, there was nothing spectacular about it, nor was it different from hundreds of other hangars he'd seen in his life.

Two drones covered in antennae and dishes hovered near the base of the ramp, waiting to inspect the ship. He tapped his PNIU. One zoomed away to slowly fly along the exterior of the ship. The other moved into the cargo bay.

Jia ducked out of the way and joined Erik. She wrinkled her nose. "You remember when you were complaining about the taste of food on the moon?"

"Yeah? What about it? I haven't even had a chance to taste the local food here so I could bitch about."

"I think my thing is the air." Jia sniffed. "The moon, here, that station. It's not like there's something in particular, but I can tell they don't smell the same as on Earth. And it's not just about being in different places. The air smells *right* in both Neo SoCal and Central Florida. The air here smells wrong."

Erik shrugged. "If you say so." He sniffed a few times. "Smells fine to me."

Jia brought up a map of Unity City on her PNIU. She pointed to smaller settled areas outside the main city limits. Some were close to old domes, but some weren't. "The gravity situation is a lot more fluid away from the main city. According to this, there are a lot of pockets of original Martian gravity very close to the city."

"That's pretty common on colonies." Erik shrugged. "This might be one of the first places we colonized, but until we reverse-engineer a grav field gadget that can change an entire planet's gravity, that's the way it's got to be."

"That might complicate things, depending on where we need to go," Jia mused. Her eyes darted around as she took in different parts of the map. "I couldn't memorize the entire map, but I did study it. That should help."

His mouth was open for a moment before he asked. "You tried to *memorize* the entire map of Unity City? For real? We have PNIU access and AI help."

"It helps to have a baseline of knowledge to get the most out of the assistance," Jia countered with a shake of her finger.

One drone emerged from the cargo bay. The second drone finished its external sweep. They flew off in formation, disappearing into a vent in the wall.

"Sahoma Customs says we're clear," Cutter transmitted. "Welcome to Unity City. Better Red than dead and all that."

Erik nodded toward the cargo bay. "Let's go talk in there. I'm guessing Emma can secure it better."

"Indeed," the AI commented.

They headed into the cargo bay. Lanara was already waiting, leaning against a wall, her arms folded. Cutter stepped through the crew quarters door with a smile.

"We've got leads to check out," Erik announced once they were inside and Emma had given the go-ahead. "We have no idea how long it's going to take. I've booked rooms under our false names. I'm not going to tell you to live there, but it'd be helpful if you spent most of your time there in case we need to leave quickly."

Lanara folded her arms. "That's inefficient."

"Getting caught by terrorists is pretty inefficient," Erik countered.

"No, the hotel room. I have a better solution."

"Go ahead and offer it then."

Lanara inclined her head toward the crew quarters. "I've got a bed in there and food. I'm going to stay here. It makes no sense to waste money and time having me stay in a hotel."

"We have no idea how long this will take." Jia gestured at the ramp. "It could be over in an hour, or it could take weeks. You want to sleep on the ship for weeks?"

"I have a bed and food," Lanara repeated. "Besides, I'm still working on all sorts of improvements. There's still reactor efficiency, modifying the VR, making the thrusters more responsive, grav field modu—"

"Fine." Jia waved a hand. "Knock yourself out." She glanced at Cutter. "I can't imagine you want to stay on the ship."

Cutter shrugged. "Why not? I'm a pilot. I'm used to being on ships. The food printer ain't half bad, and there's far less chance of me getting shot if I'm on the ship. Maybe if I chat up Lanara, she'll soften up."

"Unlikely," the engineer declared.

Emma appeared next to Cutter, smirking. "Pilot Durn, I regret to remind you that you got shot while staying near the ship. You might be safer in the hotel."

"Sure, but that was on a prison station. They're going to go blow stuff up way away from here."

Erik shrugged and headed toward the MX 60, which they'd registered ahead of time to get their transport permit. Most of his standard weapons, including the laser rifle, were stored in the flitter, along with Emma. They had almost everything they needed, even if they ran into trouble. Using their toys could cause issues, depending on the situation. His license allowed possession and transportation of heavy weapons, but that didn't allow him to open fire wherever he wanted.

Lanara sprinted toward Erik, skidding to a halt in front of his face and speaking rapidly. "I was talking to Emma, and we made some modifications. The grav emitter control system has been modified to be more dynamic. That will make it less effective on Earth, but I can adjust it before we go back. While we're on Mars, it'll help keep performance smooth when you transition outside a grav field zone to normal Martian gravity. Same thing with the thrusters. You might notice slight handling issues, perhaps a 0.2 percent difference, especially with any later—"

He put up a hand. "In other words, you customized the MX 60 for Mars," Erik summarized.

Lanara nodded once. "Yes. That's an efficient summary. Good job."

"Thanks." Erik reached for his door and stopped. "Damn." He turned back. "The disguises. Since we're using fake IDs, we better use them. Let's go get them and head out."

———

Erik half-believed the partial disguises with their mild modifications of facial features were more effective than Alina's complicated efforts. Sometimes the easiest way to slip past someone was to lower their suspicions. He would have preferred to look at Jia's normal face, but hints of the beautiful face he appreciated remained, despite the difference in shape.

Three days there and three back in a cramped ship might have been fun under other circumstances, but they weren't alone. They definitely needed a bigger ship with private rooms.

"Before we go check—" he began.

A loud knock sounded from a door near the back of the hangar.

"There are six men in colorful suits outside the hangar," explained Emma. "According to the door camera. I do not have direct access to the local police facial recognition database, but one man has inadvertently revealed a weapon while gesticulating to his friends."

"They work quickly," Erik commented.

"You think it's whoever took out Sukorn?" Jia asked.

"It might be." Erik nodded to Lanara and Cutter. "Once

we get off, seal the ship. We're going to go have a chat with our friends." He checked his pistol. "Which might involve shooting them in the face."

"You do you, Blackwell." Cutter hurried out of the cargo bay and headed toward the cockpit.

Erik went down the ramp with Jia. It lifted as they stepped into the main hangar, the rumble almost drowning out another series of loud knocks on the door.

"Open the door, Emma," Erik ordered. "Maybe they just want to sell us Martian condos."

The back door slid open, and six men filed in, all in expensive brightly colored suits. Erik quirked a brow in surprise. Emma's mild description hadn't prepared him. Yellow, bright red, white, and lavender didn't strike him as anything a Talos operative might wear.

A man in a magenta suit led the pack from the door across the hangar toward Erik and Jia. He offered Erik a polite nod. "Are you the owners of this ship?"

"We're employees of the owners," Erik explained. "Why do you care, Mister… You know what? I'll just call you Mr. Magenta."

The new arrival sneered. "Yeah. Whatever. You're a funny guy."

"My girlfriend agrees, at least when she's not punching me."

"Fortunately for you, I like funny guys, but still, we have to get down to business." Mr. Magenta sucked a breath through clenched teeth. "You see, so, this is kind of embarrassing. I can tell you haven't been to Mars lately. I'm not going to hold that against you, but that's probably why you don't understand the score."

"It's been a few years." Erik shrugged. "That a problem?"

"No, no, no." Mr. Magenta scratched his eyelid. "You see, my boss has a friend in Port Control. That friend sends us information about ships coming in and out of this port who might be of interest. We greet these ships of interest."

"And you think we're of interest?" Erik asked.

"You work for a security company. And in our experience, security companies know that sometimes a little money goes a long way." Mr. Magenta eyed the ship. "It's not much to look at. Is this one of those times where the CEO is cutting corners where they can?"

"Something like that. Who the hell are you?"

"We represent, let's say, local interests who don't feel the impact of you non-Reds is accounted for in the fees you pay, especially since a lot of that money doesn't make it to the locals." He pulled back his coat to reveal a pistol. "And as locals, we feel it's important to collect reasonable donations to make up for that."

Jia's brow lifted, and her mouth curled into a smile. "You're serious? Aren't you worried about the local police coming after you for such blatant shakedowns?"

"I think you'll find you don't want to make too much noise, especially when you're not Red." Mr. Magenta licked his lips. "A lot of questionable people come to Mars." He gestured around the hangar. "Especially to private hangars and ports. They get up to all sorts of shenanigans, and some corps think they can just bring in people to cause trouble. Loyal Reds like me and my boys, we keep our watch." He showed some teeth. "We're the local militia, you might say."

"A very colorful one," Jia offered, visibly straining not to laugh.

The situation was beginning to look a lot less like conspiracy assassins and far more like petty thugs running a protection racket. That worked for Erik. If they had to get rough, they might be able to avoid killing someone and getting involved with the local authorities. If the gangsters were this brazen, the local police would be closer to the old Shadow Zone cops, and he and Jia didn't have time to clean up the city.

Erik's and Jia's light jackets concealed their holsters. He saw no reason to make their move yet. Alina hadn't mentioned any specific syndicates targeting the spaceport, but complaining about syndicates on Mars was like complaining about fish in the ocean.

Mars was close enough to Earth for a full and easy economic exchange, but far enough away that the CID could never establish the tight control they maintained on the homeworld. The older a colony, the more criminals could grow and flourish, and Mars was the second-oldest colony after the moon.

"Start hacking his PNIU, Emma," Erik whispered.

"What was that?" Mr. Magenta narrowed his eyes. "You say something about me? You got some shit you want to get off your chest, big guy? I'm trying to be pleasant here."

Erik scratched his eyelid in a conscious imitation of Mr. Magenta. "You see, here's the problem. I can't give you any money. If I do, I have to put it on an expense report, and it gets complicated, and people ask questions, and it ends up being too much trouble for everybody involved."

Mr. Magenta clucked his tongue and sighed. "You see,

my problem is, if you don't pay up, we've got to make an example of you." He cracked his knuckles and smiled at Jia. "Why don't you stand by, sweet thing? I'll show you what a real man is like. Don't worry, we're not going to kill him. Corpses aren't good income sources."

Jia widened her stance and lifted her arms. "Good. You're not going to shoot him. I'm very happy to hear that."

Mr. Magenta laughed. "We're not murderers, sweet thing. We're just men trying to collect donations. Hey, can you talk some sense into him? We don't want anyone to trip and fall and end up spending money at the hospital or on medpatches."

"If you go after him, you're coming after me." Jia glared at him. "And sometimes I don't know when to hold back."

"Yeah, that's true, but she's a lot better than she used to be." Erik shrugged. "What are you going to do?"

"You two are funny." Mr. Magenta shook a finger at them. "And I'd say I never hit a lady, but I work for one, and she could rip a man in half with a look. So, if I turn tail and run because some chick acted all tough, I wouldn't be long for this world." He took off his jacket and tossed into the ground, revealing his holster, but he didn't go for the gun. "No reason to tear my nice coat, right?"

Erik didn't pull his jacket off. "What about your boys?"

"They don't need to get involved. I'm sure once I beat your ass, your sweet chick there is going to be asking to go home with me."

Jia pulled her fists down just an inch, but it was enough to provide a view of her honesty when she asked, "Are you *high* right now?"

Mr. Magenta chuckled. "I like women with a spine. You

remind me of the boss. She's got a little more class than you, but you're both hot."

"Your gangster boss has more class than me?" Incredulity covered Jia's face.

"Just saying."

"Thanks for making that clear." Erik raised his fists. "My *boss* says I'm supposed to be keeping a low profile, and killing six guys my first day here would mess that up. I'm sure she wouldn't have a problem if I beat you down."

"You saying you represent a *special* interest?" Mr. Magenta looked Erik up and down, curiosity in his eyes. "That might change things. We can work something out."

"I'm not a gangster if that's what you're asking," Erik replied. "I'm just a man getting paid for a job. I thought maybe you guys might be involved in that job, but like my friend said, this is just a local shakedown."

"No, not a shakedown, a donation." Mr. Magenta stepped toward Erik. "I like you. Something about your face. And I like that woman, but I'm not leaving without a donation. Make it easy on yourselves."

The gangsters spread out, all raising their fists. They chuckled, no hint of anger or worry that they couldn't take Erik and Jia down with ease. They must have done this countless times.

"This won't end well for you." Erik's grin grew feral. "I've been cooped on a ship for three days. It'll be nice to get some real exercise."

"Oh, stop showing off for your chick, asshole." Mr. Magenta threw a punch. Erik didn't bother to block it with his cybernetic arm. He sidestepped it and slammed his forehead into Mr. Magenta's nose. The gangster stumbled back, blood adding a new shade to his suit. Erik followed up with two quick jabs and an uppercut that sent the man to the deck, groaning.

The other gangsters charged.

Erik met the closest man's face with his fist, and he hit the deck. Jia's spinning kick connected with a loud crunch to a gangster's chest. He fell to his knees, clutching it and groaning.

She slammed her palm into another man's face.

Erik crushed his fist into a gangster's solar plexus, leaving him wheezing on the deck, sucking in air.

The last gangster screamed as Jia slammed her foot into his knee and then smashed her fist into the side of his face. All the men lay scattered on the deck, groaning, bleeding, and bruised.

The whole thing had taken less than thirty seconds.

Blood dripping from his nose, Mr. Magenta went for his gun, but Erik whipped his out quicker and pointed it at the man's head.

"Don't," Erik ordered. "Like I said, killing someone my first day here would make things difficult for me. And I'm trying to cut back on my killing."

Jia pulled out her stun pistol and covered the other men. None of them made any attempt to move, but she kept her attention focused, ready to stun them in an instant.

Mr. Magenta wiped the blood off his face. "That is the problem with non-Reds. You don't know who you're screwing with."

"The Bright Color Gang?" Erik asked.

Mr. Magenta slowly stood up, his hands above his head.

"We're with Prism Associates."

"I forgot how weird syndicates can be here," Erik commented. "But at least you don't have those stupid mustaches."

Mr. Magenta tried to sneer, but it turned into a wince. "You only have to blend in when you're afraid. We choose to stand out because we're not afraid."

"Sure, sure. You're blinding me with your suits." Erik motioned with his gun toward the door. "Now, take your men and get the hell out of here before someone gets seriously hurt."

"This isn't over," Mr. Magenta asserted. He nodded at the fallen gangsters. They stood, some unsteady on their feet, and headed toward the door. Mr. Magenta reached over and gingerly picked up his jacket, draping it over his arm. "You have no idea who you are screwing with."

"You just told us," Jia offered cheerfully. "Prism Associates. You sound like some sort of interior decorating firm."

Mr. Magenta muttered something under his breath but didn't turn back. The door slid closed behind them.

"That was fun." Erik put his weapon away and shook out his fist. "But now we can't go after Sukorn right away. That wasn't enough to scare them off, and we can't have gangsters screwing with us while we're looking for him."

Jia holstered her pistol. "For all we know, they're the ones who have him. This might have nothing to do with Talos."

Emma appeared, this time in a hot pink suit jacket and a matching long skirt. "The whole incident was over so quickly that I wasn't finished penetrating his PNIU."

"I'm not interested in hacking some Martian syndicate's systems until we know if they're involved with Sukorn," Erik replied. "I thought they might be Talos. I'm betting they'll head straight to their boss."

"My quick search of the local net indicates the boss of Prism Associates is one Radira Tellvane," Emma explained.

A hologram of a tall, beautiful, voluptuous olive-skinned woman in a slinky black dress appeared. Long, dark hair cascaded over her shoulders. Hints of lines around her eyes and cheeks suggested she was older than she appeared and likely hadn't received de-aging yet.

"If you know who she is, do you know where she lives?" Jia asked.

"Indeed I do."

"Cutter, Lanara, we're going to go pay her a visit," Erik transmitted. "You going to be all right without us?"

"We'll stay in the ship," Lanara suggested. "And if anyone suspicious shows up, I'll throw a plasma grenade at them."

"Try to make sure they're gangsters first."

"Oh," Lanara replied a moment later. "Good point. I'll do that."

Erik just shrugged.

Jia smiled and mouthed, "I've got nothing."

CHAPTER FORTY-SIX

The MX 60 set down in front of a sprawling walled complex connected by covered walkways. The tall, curved red-tiled roofs didn't seem to be common in the neighborhood, nor the roaming armed guards they'd spotted when flying over.

Erik had maintained a decent altitude to avoid taking fire, but Jia was surprised by the lack of armed guards near the front gate.

From the speech Mr. Magenta had given about not being afraid, she'd half-expected King Sentries standing in front of the gate with bright holographic signs reading TRESPASSERS WILL BE SHOT.

Jia tapped her foot on the passenger-side floor. "Should we be getting out the big guns?"

Their luck had served up gangsters upon their arrival on Mars. It didn't seem paranoid to prepare for a tougher fight than they'd had in the hangar. She didn't want trouble, but she wasn't going to run away from it if trouble kept flicking her nose.

"We're trying to keep a low profile, remember?" Erik replied. "We're here to find Sukorn, not destroy a syndicate." He chuckled. "I remember when I was the one who needed to be kept in check."

Jia snorted. "We haven't killed anyone yet." She opened the door and stepped out. "We might regret not grabbing a grenade or two if they open fire." She leaned into the back, retrieved a couple of grenades from a hidden compartment, and tucked them into her pockets.

There was nothing wrong with being prepared.

After finishing her arming, Jia closed the door and eyed the tall black wall. The thick material could probably take a missile strike. An aerial assault would be advisable, but she suspected there were anti-aircraft batteries hidden among the spidery trees scattered about the estate.

"Should we just try to do a local ping?" Jia looked around, but there was no obvious call button on the wall or near the gate.

The gate rumbled open. Erik reached into his jacket and rested his hand on his pistol. Jia did the same.

Mr. Magenta and two other men, both in lime green, stood in the middle of a marble path leading directly to the front door of the mansion. They were unarmed. There were hints of bruising on Mr. Magenta's face, but most of it was already gone, courtesy of the medpatch over his nose. Jia didn't feel any pity for the man.

They'd tried to warn him.

Mr. Magenta motioned inside. "This is convenient. Miss Tellvane wants to talk to you two."

"Good," Erik replied. "We want to talk to her, but to

make shit clear, there's no way we're walking in there unarmed."

"I don't care. You'll be dead before you draw if you try to kill her." Mr. Magenta and the Lime Twins started up the path.

Jia shrugged. "We did come to talk, but don't blame me if we have to toss grenades later."

"A couple of hours ago," Erik whispered, "you were complaining about false IDs, and now you're ready to start a war with a syndicate we just met." Erik chuckled.

"That involved messing with the law. This involves gangsters who picked a fight." Jia took a deep breath and headed toward the mansion. She didn't want to become the Goddess of Death II, but she didn't want to end up dead on her first assignment, either.

They caught up with Mr. Magenta and the others, slowing their pace until they arrived at mammoth double entry doors large enough to accommodate the MX 60.

The doors slid open to a foyer filled with physical paintings, mostly florals and landscape scenes. Dutch Masters from what Jia could tell, but her knowledge of art was embarrassingly limited.

Mei had always been better at that sort of thing.

The foyer gave way to a large, mostly empty living room. More paintings and the occasional vase decorated the room, but the lack of furniture puzzled Jia. Mr. Magenta turned and headed toward a side hallway. They hadn't seen another gangster since entering the mansion, but given the size and the connecting buildings, there could be dozens, if not hundreds of men in the space.

Mr. Magenta stopped near a door at the end of the hall and nodded toward it. "She's waiting for you."

Erik and Jia stopped in front of the door, exchanging glances while waiting for it to open. The door slid open to reveal wooden cabinets filled with bound physical books. A half-dozen cabinets lined the walls of the room. She had never seen so many books outside a museum before.

If these weren't reproductions, the value of the tomes in the room might dwarf the paintings they'd seen on the way in.

Radira Tellvane sat in a soft-looking high-backed white chair in front of a curved table, her legs crossed, wearing a bright white off-the-shoulder evening gown. Jia wasn't sure if she was the head of a syndicate or a socialite dressed for a party.

A large pistol sat on the table, but Jia could draw before the woman could get to it. Radira had to know that Erik and Jia were armed. Was the gun an attempt at intimidation? A signal that she wasn't just a pretty face?

The dark-haired woman flicked her wrist at Mr. Magenta. "I'll talk to them alone," she declared, her voice low and sultry.

"Miss Tellvane." Mr. Magenta's gaze dipped to the pistol on the table. "I don't think—"

"Don't make me repeat myself. You've embarrassed yourself enough for one day." Venom infiltrated her tone.

Mr. Magenta bowed his head and stepped to the side. Erik and Jia entered the room, and the door slid shut behind them.

"Emma, you still there?" Jia whispered.

There was no response. Radira took more precautions than her men. Jia would have to give her credit for jamming them. Even if she didn't know about Emma, it would cut down on everything from reinforcements to tracking.

Radira tilted her head. "What was that you said?"

"Nothing," Jia replied. "I was appreciating your books."

"Ah, a woman of culture. Good. That means you're reasonable." Radira's gaze slid to Erik. "And you?"

"I'm definitely *not* a man of culture," Erik offered with a grin.

"I see. Let's get down to business, shall we?" Radira folded her hands in her lap. "I must apologize for your rude treatment at the hands of my men. You have to understand certain business matters must be handled, but if I had known it was you, I would have warned them off."

"If you'd known it was us?" Erik asked. "Who do you think we are?"

Radira looked him up and down. "Hmm. Some sort of disguise, it seems like, Mr. Blackwell. Disappointing. I would have preferred the real you." She turned her attention to Jia. "And you, Miss Lin."

"I think you've mistaken us for someone—" Jia began.

"Don't insult me." Radira's thin smile disappeared. She took a deep, shuddering breath and slowly let it out, and her smile returned. "I'm not an idiot. I had information that you would be coming to Mars, and I don't need DNA to know that the kind of man and woman who could so cheerfully lay out my men and then have the audacity to come directly to me would be the NSCPD's finest."

"We're not cops anymore." Erik shrugged. "We're civilians."

Jia glared at him. They didn't need to confirm everything.

He shrugged. "She already figured it out, and we're here to make sure the rainbow suit gang doesn't screw with us while we do our business."

Radira chuckled. "Yes, you're not with the police anymore, and that makes you far, far more dangerous."

"Funny," Erik replied. "I was just about to say the same thing."

Jia pointed at the door. "Mr. Magen...whatever his name is and the others came and tried to shake us down. They got violent. We responded in kind. Without killing them, I will point out. The point is, it wasn't our fault. We're not paying protection money to land our ship in a private hangar."

Radira waved a hand dismissively, a faintly bored look on her face. Jia wanted to smack the smugness off of the woman, but making a move would probably bring dozens of men and bots into the room.

"The truth is, I don't make most of my money through petty antics like that." Radira let out a soft laugh. "But you're former cops. You know how things work. An organization needs to project strength and establish borders to be respected. Otherwise, other organizations run all over them." She stared at Erik with undisguised lust. "I know what you look like without your disguise, but that can wait. Before we continue, I have to ask...are you interested in joining Prism Associates?"

"What?" Jia gaped. "You are asking us to join a *syndicate?*"

"Yes." Radira rested her cheek in her palm. "You two are impressive in your ability to handle yourselves. I don't know why you abruptly left the police force, but in my experience, when that kind of thing happens, it generally means the police are covering their asses. Having the two symbols of anti-corruption arrested for smuggling or drug-dealing or whatever it is you did would be bad, so they let you walk and told you to keep your mouths shut."

"You think we're corrupt?" Jia spat, her heart rate kicking up.

"Everyone's corrupt, Miss Lin. It's just a matter of degree."

Erik shrugged. "We left the force for personal reasons, and I don't look good in bright colors. That's a polite no from me."

Jia took some deep breaths. She wanted to tell the criminal off, but as Erik had said, she wasn't on Mars to stop organized crime. She was on Mars to find a missing Intelligence Directorate agent.

Her determination to successfully complete her mission fought with her instincts about allowing anyone to besmirch the Lin name. Alina had again been proven right.

The new job was bringing compromises far quicker than Jia had anticipated.

"You don't like me very much, do you, Miss Lin?" Radira straightened her head. "I've seen that before in disgraced cops, too. You can't shake that false nobility you think places you far above so-called criminals like me.

Don't worry, you'll get used to it. Some of my best friends are former cops."

"I'm not joining a syndicate," Jia offered, her voice tight. "And we're *not* going to be friends."

"I thought you would say that. It's not like I'm offended, but if you change your mind, contact me. It's not as if everyone has to wear our uniform." Radira uncrossed her legs and then crossed them in the opposite direction. "Might I ask why you're on Mars?"

"Unless it has something to do with you, I wouldn't worry about it," Erik replied.

Radira leaned forward a little too far for Jia's taste. The syndicate queen was giving Erik a good view of her assets.

"How do I know if it has something to do with me if you don't tell me why you're here?" she asked in what was almost a purr. "I don't want to get in your way, and to do that, I need to know more."

Jia narrowed her eyes and stomped in front of Erik. "Because we didn't even know who you were until your enforcers attacked us. We only came here because we wanted to make sure they didn't bring an army with weapons back."

Radira looked past Jia at Erik before refocusing on the other woman. "And what if they did?"

Jia locked eyes with Radira. "Then there would have been a lot of bodies in that hangar."

Erik put his hand on Jia's shoulder and squeezed softly. "Since you know who we are, you know what we can do, and you know what we *will* do when people try to take us out. We're not looking to start a war here. We don't even want an apology. We just won't pay you to stay here."

Radira's gaze lingered on Erik. "Your reputation proceeds you, along with a list of destroyed syndicates and terrorist cells. They say you bring pain to my kind of people."

"There's an easy way to avoid that," Jia replied, open venom in her tone. It was a strain to have to be polite to a criminal to begin with, and it didn't help that said criminal woman kept eyeing Erik like he was a delicious steak she wanted to gobble up.

Dammit, he was Jia's steak!

"And what is that?" Radira's mask of polite disinterest began to crack, the beginnings of a frown forming and her back stiffening. "Do *I* need to pay *you*?"

"Of course not. It's free." Jia smirked. "All you have to do is stay the hell away from us."

Erik tilted his head and pointed his thumb at Jia. "What she said."

"I suppose if you were here to destroy my organization, we wouldn't be having this conversation," Radira mused.

"Exactly."

Radira sighed. "Very well. I'll instruct my men to not involve themselves with you, provided you do the same."

"Fair enough." Erik looked at Jia for confirmation, and she gave him a curt nod. The sooner they were out of there, the better.

"Would you like to stay for a meal?" Radira offered. "I have exquisite wines."

"We're kind of on the clock," Jia replied. There was no way in hell she was staying in the hungry spider queen's den with Erik. "But we appreciate the offer."

"Oh, well. I'll have my people show you out." Radira

stared at Erik. "And if *any* aspect of your situation ever changes, let me know."

"Sure, I'll do that." Erik chuckled.

Jia slapped the access panel, grabbed his arm, and pulled him into the hallway. "Let's go. We've already wasted enough time."

CHAPTER FORTY-SEVEN

Erik slowed his flitter and dove into a dimly lit underground parking garage nearly full to capacity with other vehicles.

A diverse array of expensive models filled the garage, quelling any residual doubts he might have had about their location being the right place.

They'd contacted Kalei to request a meeting, and she'd told them to meet her in an hour at the Yel Ana Lounge, which lay across town from their hotel and the hangar.

He flew slowly down the rows seeking an open parking spot. Men and women, some in luxurious clothes but others rough-looking, headed toward an elevator on one side of the garage. Many of the men made no attempt to conceal their pistols or knives. There were even a few colorful suits in the mix, possibly Prism Associates team members.

The Yel Ana Lounge wasn't the kind of place good people frequented.

"Great atmosphere." Jia nodded at a man with a pistol tucked into the small of his back. "It's like this whole city is one big Shadow Zone."

"That's about right, but you don't get good info on the violent underworld sitting at a rich person's club." Erik slid the MX 60 between two black flitters. Both had starburst symbols on the back, which he assumed was the mark of a syndicate.

He didn't care enough to ask Emma to try to identify it.

"Tellvane knew we were coming." Jia stared out the window at the parade of trouble. "*Us* in particular. That didn't sit well with me."

"Yeah, but I don't care that much," he admitted as he slowed the flitter.

"You don't?"

"There's only so much we'll be able to sneak around doing this job. We already have too big a rep, which means that as long as we're near Earth, people will always be able to find out. And I'm not ready to go full ghost." Erik landed the flitter with a slight bump. "Keeping a low profile when we arrive is a good plan in general, though, even if someone figures it out." He glanced at the bottom of her seat. "And no, I don't think we need grenades to meet Kalei."

Jia frowned. "That was a gangster's house. I don't think it was crazy to bring backup. This isn't Neo SoCal. We're both getting a feel for things."

"And 'getting a feel' means bringing grenades?"

Jia shrugged. "Sometimes."

Erik opened his door. "Let's see what Kalei has to say

before we check out Sukorn's apartment. Someone might have given us up, but it's not like we ran into a bunch of Tin Men with laser rifles."

"That doesn't mean we won't," Jia suggested.

"Talos might have learned their lesson from being flashy before. If they end up making too much noise, it brings the ID down on them, and at the end of the day, they're hiding for a reason. Roaches don't like the light. I'd sure like the chance to stomp on some while we're here, though."

Jia looked back at the MX 60 as they headed toward the elevator. "You never use your security system anymore."

"Emma's the best security system in the UTC," Erik replied.

"Among other things," the AI offered. "If we lose contact again like at the mansion, don't worry. I'll be using my acoustic sensors to monitor for the sound of gunfire or the screams of the dying, and I'll make sure to stay near the elevator."

Jia eyed her PNIU. "Good to know."

Erik and Jia headed into the elevator, both chuckling.

All the thugs they'd spotted previously had already taken their trip up, leaving them alone. He tapped the button for the main floor. The elevator rose, and the doors opened to the main club room.

Sickeningly sweet smoke billowed into the elevator. Erik covered his mouth while he coughed.

Shadows filled the dimly lit club, the main illumination for the outer part of the room lights around the bar. Farther in, men and women sat on couches, their eyes glazed over, taking long draws of thin pipes. Low, rhythmic music played.

Dancers cavorted on a small stage in the center of the room in nothing but lightly glowing body paint pulsating through a myriad of bright colors and fractal patterns. Rays of different-colored light swept across the stage, their touch changing the patterns on the dancers' bodies.

Jia wrinkled her nose and waved her hand, trying to clear the smoke. "That's Phoenix Root, isn't it? I've never actually smelled it before."

"Probably. I haven't smelled it either. Only been to Mars a few times, and I didn't come to a place like this." Erik surveyed the room, seeking out any armed threats, but no one was paying them any attention.

Which wasn't surprising.

Phoenix Root was both calming and a hallucinogen. The plant that was hard to grow off Mars, much like the difficulties people had with Dragon Tear. From what he'd read, it had something to do with the unique interaction of plants with the terraforming process.

Sophisticated genetic engineering and AI analysis weren't enough to reproduce the plant elsewhere. It was like he had been telling Jia—the galaxy held plenty of secrets, good and bad.

"Lovely place," Jia muttered. "Kalei has great taste."

"Hey, at least it doesn't look like we're going to have to fight anyone. It's been a long time since I've seen a room filled with so many relaxed people."

Jia's disdainful gaze swept the addicts in the room. "It wouldn't be much of a fight. Wait. There she is." She nodded toward a corner. A stray ray of light from the stage highlighted rainbow hair and a shimmering metallic gown. Kalei was sitting at a small square table in the corner.

Erik and Jia strolled through the couches, catching sight of the occasional guard standing in the corner or a security bot. Not everyone in the room was high. Kalei waved before picking up a tall, thin glass and taking a sip of the pink liquid inside.

A meter away from the table, the sounds of the club died, although the sweet stench of Phoenix Root continued to choke the air. Erik and Jia sat on chairs opposite Kalei.

"Good afternoon, darlings," she offered with a smile. She gestured grandly. "And welcome to Mars. I don't care that it's not the first colony. It's much more impressive than the moon."

"I don't know what this place says about your taste," Jia mumbled. "I'm going to have to shower after we leave."

"Oh, don't be like that." Kalei sipped her drink. "My preferred clients like dark places surrounded by people with muddled minds. Hanging out in too obvious a place might lead to trouble for me, and I do so hate trouble. It makes my job harder, and not all of us are as interested in shooting people as you two and our mutual friend."

"Are we secure here?" Erik asked.

Kalei motioned toward his PNIU. "You're probably out of contact with your little redheaded friend now. From what I hear, you already had a run-in with Radira Tellvane. You two sure like to stir up trouble. You're lucky it was Prism Associates. Tellvane might like to play the vamp, but she's shrewd and knows when to push and when to step back."

"Yes, we did run into her." Jia frowned. "And she knew who we were."

Kalei laughed. "Oh, that's because I told her to expect you." She flicked her wrist. "In general terms. I didn't send her to the spaceport."

"What the hell?" Erik glared at her. "You sold us out?" He jammed his hand into his duster and gripped his gun.

"Don't be like that, darling." Kalei put a hand to her mouth and laughed. "You're overreacting. Radira Tellvane is many things, but she's not an idiot, which was why I told her. I was actually trying to do you a favor. A thank you would be nice."

Jia stared at her. "Telling a gangster who we are is doing us a favor? Admittedly, I'm not fully up to speed on specific Martian syndicates. Maybe you could clear up the mystery for me."

"You two are still too big of names to hide all that well." Kalei wagged a finger. "Your disguises aren't good enough for people who know what to look for, and you've only been off your old jobs a few weeks. I decided to lean into that, to everyone's advantage. I gave that information to Radira because she likes to keep things close to the chest. It wouldn't be to her advantage to leak it, but she holds enough sway to make it clear that people shouldn't mess with you two. The average syndicate foot soldier around here wouldn't question their orders, and it shifts the focus to Prism Associates for a few days, giving you room to work."

She set her drink down. "Besides, it also ingratiated me with Radira, and when one is establishing themselves in a new environment, it helps to have friends in low places. It's a small sacrifice, I think, for the overall benefit of my employer and mission."

"It's true that her guys attacked us before they knew who we were." Erik frowned. "But I don't like that you did that without asking us. We should have made the call, not you. Don't try that crap again."

"Darling, you're in a whole new world now, filled with ghosts and spiders trying their best to eat other spiders on their own webs." Kalei's smile brightened. "You're going to have to get used to people trying to play you for their advantage. If you get pissy just because of something like this, you won't last long."

Erik grunted and nodded his head. She was right, but that didn't mean he had to like it. Fake IDs and low profiles could only go so far. It made sense to leverage their reputation while it remained an advantage.

Jia waved a hand as if she were at her mom's table and her mom was pressing her to choose a drink she didn't want. "Whatever. Spare us the condescending speech." She gestured around her. "It might be nice if we had a privacy device, too. If we're going to play by your rules, we need more of your tech."

"Our mutual friend told me to give you one, so good serendipity there." Kalei reached under the table and produced a thin silver rod. She set it on the table and pushed it toward Jia. "My present. Consider it compensation for any discomfort my actions might have caused."

Jia raised an eyebrow. "How is it a present if you were told to give it to us?"

"I didn't *have* to." Kalei patted the device. "There's a slight ridge. Click on and off. Don't move a lot while you're using it because this one can add a small, convincing holographic overlay on your mouths to make it seem like you're talking about something else. You two are hunting big game, so you'll need to be more careful."

"Thanks for the toy," Erik offered. "Let's get to the point of why we're here: Sukorn. Do you know who grabbed him? If you could give us a location, we'll get a chance to kick in a door and bring him back."

"I haven't the foggiest, darling." Kalei ran her finger over the rim of her glass. "The problem is, Mars is a crossroads for all sorts of shady characters and organizations. Some, like Prism Associates, like to be bold and stand out, announce themselves. Others get that it's best to hide in the shadows while the cockier syndicates are drawing attention. Those old corporate ties from the beginning of colonization have kept this place more independent than you'd think, making it great for everyone from smugglers to insurrectionists trying to connect with supporters on Earth. That means whenever something bad happens here, it's hard to whittle down the list of suspects."

"But you don't think it was Talos," Jia concluded. "You think it was somebody local."

Kalei shook her head, light catching the colors in her hair. "I'm here to strengthen certain information networks that have atrophied in recent years due to sudden and unexpected loss of personnel. Alina might be focused on Tin Men with bad attitudes, but they're only part of my concern. I'll tell you, my instincts suggest it wasn't Talos."

"Even though Sukorn was looking into them?" Jia challenged.

"Yes. I think he was on the wrong trail. It happens to

the best of us." Kalei shrugged. "And I think our boy's in a pickle because he got caught up in something far more local. Radira was ever so grateful for the information I gave her on the Obsidian Detective and Lady Justice, so grateful she gave me some useful information in return."

"About Sukorn?" Erik asked.

"No, about the local situation. There was an assassination a week back. It didn't involve Radira and her boys, but it did involve two other syndicates, and it's made the local syndicate situation more unstable." Kalei quieted as a waitress clad only in glowing body paint depicting red and green vines approached with a tray of drinks.

The waitress set a new drink in front of Kalei and smiled at Erik and Jia. "What can I get you?"

"I'm okay," Erik replied. "Thanks."

Jia waved off the waitress. With a curtsy, the waitress departed, leaving them alone with Kalei again.

"As I was saying," Kalei continued, "the syndicate situation is unstable, and Chetta Sukorn didn't check in as expected after that assassination. I don't believe he had anything to do with it, and Alina would have let me know if he had, but if he was poking into it, he might have pissed off the wrong people. To the best of my knowledge, he wasn't looking into the syndicates themselves, but it's not impossible that somebody thought he was working for somebody else local and decided to make a move. You'd be surprised how often that happens. You know criminals, always paranoid."

"And his apartment?" Jia asked. "Any clues there?"

"I haven't been there." Kalei shrugged. "The only thing I

know is that we can't contact his PNIU or track it. It's probably been destroyed."

Jia frowned. "Why haven't you gone to his apartment? You just said days have passed, and this guy could be bleeding out somewhere waiting for rescue. He could even be there."

"It's not my job, darling." Kalei smiled brightly. "And I was only told about this shortly before you two arrived. The thing is, sometimes it's best to stay in your lane. I don't need to be seen poking around Chetta Sukorn and his haunts. I can't toss aside my mission for one man."

Her eyes cut to the side as a man stood from a couch and staggered their way. After a couple of steps, he turned and headed in a different direction, rubbing his shoulders and shivering.

"Our next step is easy, then," Erik mused. "We check the apartment." He frowned. "But we don't have decent forensics equipment on the ship."

"I can get you a decent DNA analyzer," Kalei offered. "By tomorrow, even. I also can get you set up with access to some of the law enforcement DNA databases."

"You can?" Jia tapped her leg. "Alina didn't mention that."

"It's hard to know everything a person might need ahead of time, and she's a busy woman. You can't run the DNA of every random person you run into, but Cassandra Security has the appropriate licensing for access. I'll leave it to you to decide who and what you want to submit."

"Thanks." Jia sighed and looked around. "Do we have to meet you here?"

Kalei smirked. "For now, darling. Sometimes it's good

to go to a place with atmosphere. It keeps you in touch with the scene."

"Plenty of planets have atmospheres that would kill people in seconds," Jia replied.

"I'll see you tomorrow." Kalei winked. "Do try to breathe easy until then."

CHAPTER FORTY-EIGHT

Erik and Jia strolled down the hallway toward Sukorn's apartment.

It was on the fifth floor of a ten-story building. The neighborhood was a pleasant enough area, with a park and the ubiquitous spidery trees of Unity City nearby. An occasional smiling child wandered into the park, but Emma's drones spotted no obvious gangsters or spies.

Not only that, every suit in the area was conspicuously bland in its color choice.

All of that made sense to Jia. An ID agent living in a building filled with criminals was asking to be discovered. Settling into a bland, safe residential zone was a good camouflage, at least normally.

"How we doing, Emma?" Erik asked. "Everything still looking okay?"

"I have complete drone coverage of the outside," she reported. "Beyond the lack of likely gun goblins, there are no vehicles of note approaching the building. Shall I begin hacking the apartment system?"

"No, not yet. There's no reason to leave too much of a trail, and we can't just say we've got probable cause as cops."

Erik and Jia continued down the hall, half-expecting a Tin Man with a rotary machine gun to burst through the wall and open fire, but if Kalei was right, this wasn't the work of a grand conspiracy.

Jia wasn't as disappointed as she thought she'd be.

The only thing she was unsure about was if they should destroy a syndicate if it turned out they'd killed Sukorn, or if they should pass the information on to the local police and let them handle it.

She knew which choice Erik would make. Given what she'd seen of Mars and Unity City, she doubted the police would be enthusiastic about investigating the syndicate murder of a mysterious traveler with no deep roots in the community.

Jia stopped in front of Sukorn's nondescript apartment door, which was numbered 545. She pressed the access panel, but it didn't open. "Not like I expected it to be that easy," she admitted, "but it would have been nice."

"Okay, Emma, don't need full systems access," Erik whispered. "Just need you to open this one door."

"Very well," she replied. The door slid open shortly, revealing the inside of the tiny apartment. "It was a basic system. I would have thought he'd use something more sophisticated."

"Something more sophisticated might have stood out to people probing and looking for him," Jia suggested.

Inside the apartment, a chair and a table lay on their sides. Visible dents marred the table. There was a tear in the back of the couch. Jia crept inside and drew her stun pistol. Erik closed the door behind them and pulled out his weapon.

Jia inclined her head toward an open bedroom. She crept toward it, not saying a word, and rushed inside. The bed was still made, but there wasn't much else in the room. Clothes hung in the closet, ready to wear. A single black suitcase stood in the corner. She returned to the living room in time to see Erik emerging from the bathroom, frowning.

"Clothes and luggage are still here," Jia reported. "If he ran, he did it without bringing much."

"I don't think he ran." Erik holstered his gun and nodded toward the bathroom. "You'll want to see this."

Jia put away her stun pistol and walked over to the bathroom. A light spray of dried blood arced across the white wall.

"No scorch marks, no bullet holes." She gestured to the blood. "And that's not a lot of blood. I think I could get more blood by breaking someone's nose."

Erik nodded. "The assailant probably ambushed him in the bathroom, maybe got in a good hit before the counterattack."

Jia shook her head. "If the assailant had the upper hand and attacked Sukorn in the bathroom, you'd see more damage. I think the attack started in the living room and then moved here." She backed into the bathroom, holding up her right hand as if holding a gun before pointing at one of the fallen chairs. "See that. It's pretty close, and the way it's fallen is consistent with someone stumbling away from the bathroom and falling on top of it." She walked over to the chair and crouched to nudge the chair aside. There was another small bloodstain.

"Good catch," Erik commented.

Jia patted the back of her head. "Whoever it was probably hit the back of their head on the floor." She pointed to the bathroom. "And I'm willing to bet these bloodstains are from two different people."

"They could have used an injection, gas, or a stun rod. It was probably short and quick. If they killed him and then cleaned up, they wouldn't have left this blood behind." He looked over the living room. "Are there any cameras in here, Emma?"

"Not that I can detect," she reported. "Nor any PNIUs I can ping."

"Lift off and do a slow fly-by using your sensors," Erik ordered. "I want to make sure they're not hiding anything. Go ahead and change your color and transponder signal in case anyone's watching closely. We'll restore them when we leave."

"One moment, Erik."

The large shadow of the flitter passed the translucent windows, the vehicle moving at a crawl. It might look suspicious to anyone watching the building, but it'd be idiotic not to take advantage of the advanced sensors installed in the MX 60.

"I'm not detecting anything of note," Emma transmitted. "It's not impossible that he's using advanced technology to conceal something, but the readings related to that apartment are in line with what I can detect from the nearby apartments."

"That makes sense," Erik replied. "If there was some

secret ghost crap we were supposed to get, Kalei would have mentioned it."

Jia folded her arms, her face pinched in concentration. "You're right. He's a ghost. He would travel lightly during an investigation. The only thing that bothers me is he can't be the only ID agent on Mars."

"Kalei's here," Erik noted.

"But there have to be more," Jia noted. "So why are they sending two subcontractors to look into this guy?"

"I'm sure there are more here, but you heard Kalei. Everyone's got a different job they're working on, and the ID's spread throughout the entire UTC, without the manpower of something like the CID or the military." Erik grunted. "They need all the help they can get."

"And that's us," Jia concluded.

"For now, but also you know Alina. It's another way of testing us."

"That's starting to get annoying," Jia grumbled.

"Hey, at least we got a ship out of it, and soon we'll have some exos," Erik observed.

"Ah, the tools we pointedly don't have right now." Jia snorted. "If this ends in a huge shootout, I'm going to be irritated we don't have those, but for now, we need to figure out our next step."

"Best bet is to play this investigation like cops." Erik pointed to the blood. "It's not like I threw out all the evidence sampling kits in the MX 60. We'll get it analyzed by the equipment Kalei's going to give us. I think we should submit both samples directly to Alina for now."

Jia frowned. "You're right. Submitting Sukorn's DNA to the database might get flagged by somebody. I think that's what Kalei was getting at when she said she'd leave it to us."

"Exactly. Let's get some drones in here to help us search for more evidence."

November 14, 2229, Unity City, Mars, Sahoma Space Port, Aboard Rabbit-class Transport LLT9208 *Pegasus*

Jia's attempts to pace in the small crew quarters were doomed to frustration.

They'd sent their data to Alina and were now awaiting the response in the more secure environment of the ship rather than in their hotel room. She had no idea how long it'd take for Alina to get around to sending the genomic data on for analysis since she'd sent a noncommittal message back the day before.

There was nothing more frustrating than waiting twenty minutes for "I'll get back to you, do not use other resources" and then not hearing anything.

Despite spending half the previous day searching the apartment, they hadn't found any other useful evidence, let alone his PNIU. They'd tried contacting him but couldn't connect, not that they were surprised. If it were that easy, they wouldn't be on Mars looking for him.

"You should run a simulation while you're waiting," Erik suggested. He was passing the time watching a recording of a sphere ball match.

"I'm too focused on the case right now," she countered. "It'd be hard for me to concentrate."

"It's not really a case. We're not cops anymore." Erik winced as an offensive wing made a mockery of the goalie.

"Fine," Jia replied. "The assignment. The job. It's all the same. We don't have a lot of extra time. If someone took him, they've had him for a while. Potentially weeks."

Erik nodded. He paused his recording with a tap of his PNIU. "Worrying about it won't change anything. Besides, this might be a high priority, but it's not like Alina's going to sit around doing every errand we suggest."

"We're only on Mars, and we're already constrained by transmission times." Jia stopped moving and put her hands on the back of a chair. "Now that I'm experiencing it, it's bizarre to me that the military manages to stay coordinated out on the frontier."

"A lot of that is about trusting the local offices in charge." Erik shrugged. "If they needed everyone to sit there and wait for orders from Earth, our guys couldn't do anything. You know how long it takes to get a message to Earth from Molino?"

"About two months," Jia commented.

Erik chuckled. "Of course you knew. You probably studied everything about it once I became your partner."

"It was more after you told me what happened there that I did that, but yes." Jia shrugged. "It's good to be informed." She took a deep breath and sat down. "Then again, we did our own thing from the moment we became partners, and Captain Ragnar didn't keep us on a tight leash. It's like all our time at the NSCPD was leading up to this."

"Funny how life works out."

Emma appeared with a smile. "It appears Agent Koval has finally decided to cooperate. I've received a message from her with your results."

Jia clapped once. "Great. What did it say?"

"You were correct," Emma reported. "The samples come from two different fleshbags. One, Agent Koval confirmed, is your missing agent Chetta Sukorn. The other source is a gun goblin by the name of Thomas Draven, a suspected low-level member of a local syndicate, the Dome Society. There isn't much information in the publicly available databases. I could put it in a request via Cassandra Security to local and Earth-based law enforcement. I can also start looking for him with drones."

Erik shook his head. "It'll take too long, and it's not like you can hack an entire city. No, I've got a better idea. An efficient idea, as Lanara would say."

"What's that?" Jia asked.

"Radira wants to be friends." Erik grinned. "So, let's be friends."

"I think she wants to be a lot more than friends," Jia grumbled.

"I'm just saying, we should go ask her about this guy. She wants us to stay out of her way, and the best way we can do that is by knowing who he is and what he might be up to. It's not our fault the guy ended up being a syndicate flunky."

Jia furrowed her brow and looked down at the table. "We're moving from non-aggression pacts with criminals to actively asking them for favors now?"

"Yeah." Erik shrugged. "I'm not saying we go perform a hit for her or anything, but it wouldn't hurt to ask her some questions. If it turns out this guy's an enemy of hers, she's not going to mind if we poke the hornet's nest, and she might even feel indebted. We can use that in the future."

Jia let out a bitter laugh. "In less than one week, we've gone from kicking at that gray line with our toe to doing a grand jeté over it."

"If I have to help a few gangsters to take down people like Talos, I'm not going to lose any sleep at night," Erik replied. "The kinds of bastards killing entire platoons are way worse than the local losers who the cops and the CID are containing. And as we've already seen, groups like Talos are making things worse. Kill the head of the dragon and the body dies."

"Yesterday's enemy is tomorrow's friend." Jia rubbed her temples. "I get it, but it doesn't make it any less annoying." She didn't want to say the next part, but sacrifices were necessary for the assignment. "I think you should go visit Tellvane alone." She sucked in a deep breath through her nose and spat it out through gritted teeth, "She obviously is into you. You might as well take advantage of that, and you won't be able to with me around."

Erik smirked. "Are you telling me to seduce her?"

Jia stood there staring at him, her stomach knotting. The whole thing was absurd. She'd gone from a cop to a pseudo-secret agent within a couple of weeks and now was planning to throw her blunt boyfriend at some oversexed mob boss for a few scraps of intelligence.

She burst out laughing, releasing the built-up tension. "Yes, go seduce her. Tell her the score from the match, and I'm sure she'll drop her dress right away."

"Hey, I can be seductive," Erik insisted. "Very seductive, and it doesn't have to mean anything."

"And I can be relaxed after six drinks." Jia snickered. "I trust you, Erik. Just get it done."

"You trust me, or you think I can't seduce her?" he asked, looking mildly insulted.

"I'll leave that for you to decide."

Erik was blunt, but he wasn't stupid. He would be around this woman for a long time, and she both carried weapons and was a weapon. Plus, he knew her mother.

You don't trifle with Lins.

CHAPTER FORTY-NINE

"I'll wait out here," Jia announced as Erik opened the door to the MX 60 and eyed the open front gate of Radira's mansion. The leader of Prism Associates was, unsurprisingly, eager to meet Erik when he'd contacted her, suggesting he come over within an hour.

"She's likely to cut me off from the inside," Erik explained. "But I don't think it's a big deal."

"Emma can still probably do a good job of detecting if a fight is happening," Jia suggested. "But I'll come knocking if you're in there for more than an hour."

Erik smirked. "Only an hour? I can do a lot of things for more than an hour."

Jia glared at him. "And make sure you do those with the right people. Not that I'm worried." She folded her arms and looked away with a harrumph.

"You aren't?" Erik shot her an impish grin. Perhaps he did have a suicide wish.

"Tellvane wouldn't know what to do with you even if she could have you." Jia motioned for him to go. "Remember, we're not here for fun. We need to find Sukorn while he's still breathing or track down his killers before they hop a transport to the HTP."

"Good luck, Erik," Emma offered. "Don't do anything that will encourage Jia to use a grenade on you."

"She strikes me as more of a shears kind of a woman." Erik nodded and closed the door, then headed toward the gate. Mr. Magenta walked down the path to greet him. The bruising and medpatch from the previous day were gone.

"Welcome back, sir." Mr. Magenta nodded toward the mansion. "If you'll follow me, I'll escort you to Miss Tellvane."

"What's your name?" Erik offered a feral grin. "I never got it when I was kicking your ass the other day."

"Felix," the other man muttered through gritted teeth. "We should hurry. Miss Tellvane doesn't like to be kept waiting."

"Don't you want to know my name?" Erik asked.

"Miss Tellvane told us to mind our own damned business about who you are," Felix explained, walking up the path. "She said to steer clear of you, and when Miss Tellvane tells us to do something, we do it."

Erik followed Felix. "Is she that scary?"

"She can be, but Miss Tellvane took our organization from nothing to something. She's smart, and because she sees something in you, that means we need to show proper respect." The front doors opened, and Felix passed throughout without slowing. "But that doesn't mean we'll tolerate disrespect of Miss Tellvane."

"If you want to go another round, that's fine by me, but

I'm here to pay my respects to your boss, so calm the hell down."

"Good." Felix muttered something under his breath.

The gangster didn't take Erik to the library. Instead, he led Erik on a circuitous route through the mansion, including through a connecting covered walkway leading to another building. They arrived at a steamy spa, a bubbling hot tub taking up most of the room.

Radira sat in the hot tub, naked but mostly submerged, a glass of wine dangling from her long, slender fingers. A bottle sat right outside the tub. Felix nodded once and stepped out of the room, closing the door behind him after glaring at Erik one last time.

"That was quick, Mr. Blackwell," Radira purred. "I didn't expect you to call me back so soon."

"You can call me Erik." Erik folded his arms and did his best casual lean against the wall.

"Thank you. Feel free to call me Radira." She lifted her glass. "I can get you a glass if you want some."

"Nah. I'm good. Not a huge wine guy anyway."

Radira took a sip of her drink. "So I assumed. Unfortunate. There's so much complexity in wine. Before, it was just dealing with Earth's wines, but now we have all the different colonies with fundamentally different soils and different conditions." She swirled the liquid in her glass. "A glass of wine is a snapshot of human ingenuity, a reflection of how far we've come since fearing the woods at night." She licked her lips. "As much as I would like to believe you've come here because you find something interesting in me, I sensed that Miss Lin is far more than just your partner. Her possessive glare could kill a man...or a woman."

"We're still figuring a lot of things out, but yeah, we're that kind of together." Erik shrugged. "That a problem? I didn't come here to screw you in any sense of the word."

"How disappointing, but again, not unexpected." Radira offered a lopsided smirk. "You know what I like about you, Erik?"

"My dashing good looks and quick wit?" he asked, smirking.

"Partially, but there's something more important." Radira set her glass next to the bottle. "It's hard to be straightforward while simultaneously concealing the most important parts of yourself. It's a skill I've cultivated over the years, and I can sense it in others."

"And you think I'm doing that?" Erik asked.

"I know you're doing that." Radira's seductive smile flickered into a sneer. "I know you have some sort of secret, but at the same time, the way you talk, I want to believe you're not holding anything back. That you can make me feel that way is impressive."

"Is this the thing where you're convinced I left the force because they caught me dealing Archangel or some crap like that?" Erik kept his tone light and breezy. He'd need to be careful around this woman. Just because she was attracted to him, it didn't mean she couldn't leak information to someone more dangerous. Kalei could gamble with her own life next time.

"You're an interesting man, Erik Blackwell." Radira sank deeper into the water, her mouth barely above the waterline. "I've looked into you. I think something broke in you on that frontier moon. I don't know why you chose to come back to be a cop. One theory I have is it was a way for you to kill terrorists to get revenge in your own way against the terrorists who killed your men."

Erik nodded slowly, pleased that Radira bought into the official story. If she'd mentioned something else, it would have complicated the conversation. Getting involved with a syndicate was dangerous enough without it having any clue about the conspiracy.

"I really don't have time for this shit," Erik replied. "No offense."

Radira raised a delicate eyebrow. "My, my. That was unnecessarily harsh."

Erik dropped his arms and walked over to the edge of the tub. He locked eyes with her. "I came here because I think you can help me in a way that helps you. Win-win."

Radira moved back up, the bubbling water not doing much to conceal her ample chest. "That's intriguing. Do go on. How can you help me in a win-win situation?"

"Thomas Draven of the Dome Society." Erik offered her another easy smile. "I want to know where he is, but I don't want the cops involved. I'm hoping you can give me a lead."

"I thought you weren't here to interfere with syndicate business?" Radira recovered her wine glass to take a sip. "And now you're moving on the Dome Society?"

"We didn't come here for that." Erik frowned. "But this is just like with your boy Felix. Draven messed with something he shouldn't have, so I need to find him. There are two ways this can go down. You can help me find him, and I can go have a nice, pleasant conversation and maybe solve the problem in a nice, calm way, or I can do things the way I'm used to, loud and messy. I know there's a bunch of shit going on right now between the syndicates, and if I do what I normally do, it might make things worse."

"You're well-informed for a new arrival."

"Sure," Erik replied. "But I also want to make it clear, I don't care. It's not my problem, but Draven *is* my problem."

"You're not a cop anymore, Erik," Radira replied. "And this isn't Earth. You can't just shoot people, say they're criminals, and get away with it. We're more civilized here in our own way. Non-Reds don't always appreciate the unique balance here."

Erik knelt by the edge of the pool, a huge grin on his face. "I might have been born on Earth, but I've traveled the entire UTC. I've dealt with more whacked-out terrorists and syndicates than you can imagine. One thing I have learned is, even the most corrupt local cops don't care if a few enforcers here and there end up dead, especially when they're afraid of the guy doing the killing."

Radira's fingers tightened around her glass. "Are you threatening my people?"

"Not at all. I don't know all the ins and outs of crap here. Is this Dome Society an ally of yours?"

"No," Radira replied, her expression softening. "Nor are they enemies. You're correct that there is currently a mild disagreement going on among several different organizations, but I'm not actively feuding with the Society. Their primary sources of income and influence are different from my organization's. If I make a move against them, I risk multiplying my enemies at a critical time."

"You wouldn't be making a move against them." Erik

pointed this thumb at this chest. "I would be, and you might not be messing with them right now, but you syndicate types always end up fighting in the end. Best-case scenario, I end up taking them down for you, and you can go take over all those rackets they control."

Radira laughed. "Take them down? You and Miss Lin by yourselves?"

"We've got other people helping us, but I think our record speaks for itself. What did you say the other day? Oh, right. Death and destruction. You help me here, and I'll remember you did me a favor."

"But you're not going to let me call on repayment whenever I want." Radira shook her head. "I can see it in your eyes. What good is a favor that won't be reciprocated?"

"It's all about how you ask." Erik stood. "I'm not going to beg, and I'm not going to offer anything more than I have. All I want is Draven, and after that, I'll handle everything. No matter what else happens between us, this ends with the Dome Society either gone or at least keeping a low profile."

"Cultivating useful allies is the path to long-term success." Radira threw back her glass and gulped down the rest of the wine. "I'll have my people look into it, but I can't guarantee anything."

"I didn't ask for a guarantee." Erik stood. "I'll show myself out." He headed toward the door.

"Wait," Radira called.

"What?"

"You sure you don't want to take a few minutes to relax?" she asked, her voice husky.

"Nah. That few minutes would cost me too much, and I can't be sure there aren't shears on my ship."

Radira blinked. "'Shears?'"

"Don't worry about it. Thanks for your help." Erik tapped the access panel. Felix was waiting on the other side. "Let's go."

Erik side-eyed Jia.

She'd been smirking since he returned from talking with Radira. He'd relayed the conversation, and they were now on their way back to the hotel. The lingering expression forced words out of his mouth.

"What?" he asked.

"I was just thinking that didn't take long." Jia snickered.

Erik scoffed. "When you know what you're doing, you don't need to take a long time."

"Some women might disagree." Jia's smirk softened into a normal smile, and she looked out the window.

Erik let it drop. If she could make jokes like that, she was fine.

CHAPTER FIFTY

Jia rubbed her bleary eyes and settled on the edge of Erik's bed. She'd been thinking before about not being alone on the ship, but they'd ended up in separate hotel rooms, and she'd not even thought about it until their second day there.

Spending so much time training and hunting down syndicates was having a negative effect on their burgeoning relationship. The memory of their last kiss warmed her body. She needed to push more, but that Martian morning wasn't the time for it, especially given her cloudy head.

"This planet is messing with me," she declared. "It hates me."

Erik looked up from the data window he was examining. "How does a planet mess with someone?"

"If Mars is going to have a different day, it should have the decency to have a day much different than Earth," Jia complained. "Not close to forty minutes. I've felt off since yesterday, and it's only getting worse."

"Yeah, that can be annoying." Erik dismissed the window. "A lot of dome colonies just fake an Earth-like day/night cycle, but all this terraforming and the few half-decent ones we can find that don't need domes are going to mess with people. You can always take something to reset your rhythms if you need to. That's what we did a lot in the Army."

"I'll live." Jia rubbed her eyes again. "It's amazing how many little things you don't think about when it comes to traveling to different planets."

They both looked over when there was a light knock on the door.

"It's an unidentified teenager," Emma explained. "He doesn't look nervous, but I can't tell if he's armed with the camera I've borrowed."

"Open the door." Erik stood. He had his holster on, but not his jacket. It'd work for intimidation. He doubted the kid was so hardened, he could quick-draw on someone like Erik.

The door slid open, and the teenager nodded politely. "I've got a message to deliver. May I come in?"

Erik nodded to the boy. The teen stepped inside and closed the door. He looked at Erik and Jia, no nervousness on his face.

"What's this about?" Erik asked.

"I was paid to come here and tell you an address," the boy explained. He rattled off the information.

"And what's at that address?" Jia asked.

"I don't know, ma'am. I was paid to give you that

address and tell you to hurry up." He turned around and opened the door, leaving without further comment.

Erik chuckled after the door closed. "That was rather complicated. Why didn't Radira just send it directly?"

"The kind of woman who jams communications in her mansion is the kind of woman who appreciates how easily information can get intercepted," Jia suggested with an approving look. "Emma, what's at the address?"

"According to public records, it appears to be a small deli," Emma explained. "I'll route some drones there. It's relatively close to here."

Erik grabbed his duster from the closet. "I'm assuming Draven's there. Let's go say hello."

"Are you sure we should trust info provided by a horny criminal?" Jia asked.

Erik shrugged. "In this case, *yes*."

Jia tapped the data window, changing drone feeds to a short man with a vulpine face eating a sandwich.

Emma's facial recognition had matched the man at the deli with Thomas Draven at over ninety-nine percent accuracy, which was good enough for Erik and Jia. They sat in the MX 60 about a half-kilometer away, in a parking lot.

"We can't go after him in there." Jia pointed at the data feed.

"Yeah." Erik frowned. "This isn't a good sign."

Jia thought a moment about her reasons but wasn't sure Erik's were the same. "Why do you say that?"

"I figured he'd be hiding somewhere after gabbing Sukorn, but he's sitting here stuffing his face with a damned ham sandwich." Erik grunted in frustration. "Radira helped us find him quicker than we could by having Emma scouring the city, but this ups the chance that Sukorn's already dead."

"We should follow him," Jia suggested.

"Yeah. He might end up somewhere we can ask him questions and not disturb the neighbors." Erik leaned back in his seat. "I feel more of what you were bitching about. Not being a cop has its drawbacks. It would have been nice to stroll on in there and drag him to a police station, but nothing we can do about that now." He checked the camera feeds. "Looks like no one is nearby. Emma, change the color to something boring.

"Like the blue of Jia's old flitter?" Emma asked.

"Hey!" Jia complained.

"Tell me she's wrong." Erik grinned. "And adjust the transponder. It'd help if this guy didn't see us coming."

Thomas Draven's sandwich-eating process was surprisingly and agonizingly slow, but twenty minutes later, he finally emerged from the deli and strolled to a tacky yellow sports flitter. Erik was in the air before Draven's vehicle left the ground. Emma's drones circled the yellow flitter, occasionally changing course so as not to be too obvious.

Draven's flitter finished rising and sped away from the deli. Erik kept a fair distance between them as he trailed him. It would have been easier in Neo SoCal to blend in with heavy traffic, but there were a sparse number of vehicles separating the MX 60 and Draven.

"The drones are having a hard time keeping up," Emma reported. "But I already spread several throughout the city, anticipating this issue."

Erik accelerated, his hands tightening around the yoke. "We should have planted a tracker on his flitter."

"That would require us to have something like that." Jia opened the storage compartment beneath her feet and started pulling out magazines for her gun. "That's the other thing. It's not just about not being cops. We also lack the entire NSCPD surveillance system to rely on."

The MX 60 closed the gap, passing other vehicles on its way to the yellow flitter. Draven slowed down, forcing Erik to slow.

"What's he up to?" Erik asked.

"He might have made us." Jia grimaced.

Erik twisted the yoke and headed in a different direction. "Emma, can you keep a drone on him for a couple of minutes?"

"Yes. His straightforward course should allow for intercept," Emma replied.

Erik descended until he was skimming the ground. He decelerated further and maneuvered beside a huge atmosphere-processing pyramid. "Emma, change to a random color and adjust the transponder again."

"Done," she replied.

Erik checked an external camera and groaned. "Hot pink? Are you kidding me?"

"It was selected randomly, per your request," Emma noted.

"It kind of stands out," Erik grumbled.

"It is distinct from your other colors, and you didn't say anything about a *subtle* random color."

"*Great.*" Erik brought the MX 60 back into the air. "Give me an intercept course with an arc."

A red nav marker appeared in his smart lenses, along with a marked course on a map on the console. Emma highlighted the target vehicle on the edge of a map expanded beyond the limits of the lidar, along with marking the position of each of her drones. Draven was moving toward the edge of the city.

"Let's see where this guy leads us," Erik murmured. "If we're lucky, it'll be somewhere we can blow him up."

"We don't *need* to blow him up," Jia observed.

"Sure, but we're following a syndicate enforcer who killed or kidnapped our missing ID agent," Erik commented. He gestured toward the map. "This isn't going to end with us sitting down to discuss our thoughts on the Dragons' goalie."

Jia stuffed another magazine into her pocket before reaching into the back. "Okay, grenades, it is."

CHAPTER FIFTY-ONE

Erik narrowed his eyes at Emma's drone feed as two other flitters fell in behind Draven's vehicle. "They aren't trying to force him down. They must be friends."

"That's not a good sign." Jia opened the hidden panel beneath her seat to draw out the TR-7. "If he realized he was being followed earlier, he might have called for reinforcements. There goes our chance for a quiet conversation."

"We're approaching from a different angle with a different color and a different transponder," Erik replied. "Even if he realized he was being followed, he might not realize it's the same flitter, but this won't end as cleanly as we wanted."

"You don't think this is too easy?" Jia asked, setting the TR-7 between the seats. "It might be a trap. We have this ridiculously customized flitter that makes us *less* vulnerable, but it doesn't make us *invulnerable*."

"Nah." Erik shook his head. "Easy is relative. Most people messing with these syndicates don't have experimental AIs and half the equipment and access we have." His gaze flicked between the lidar, drone, and camera feeds. Emma's navigational area was keeping him on the intercept course. "They don't even have friendly syndicate bosses willing to trade information."

"I just keep thinking Alina could have done this," Jia commented. "That makes me worried."

"Sure, but you saw what happened with Kalei." Erik snickered. "The conspiracy isn't the only one who can throw pawns at people. Wheels within wheels. The ID might be on our side, but that doesn't mean they're always our friends. We just all want the same thing—a dead conspiracy."

"You are not upset that we're being used?" Jia gave him a questioning look.

"No." Erik shook his head. "It's a mutual thing. I'm not going to care unless some ID ghost tries to kill us, and if Alina is half as smart as she seems, she'll know that trying to kill us would be a bad idea."

"The gun goblins appear to be heading into an industrial zone built around an old habitation dome," Emma reported. "My interrogation of local records suggests many of the properties in that area are not in active use. There are articles discussing reclamation, but the projects seem to be at a standstill, concerning planning and resource allocation."

"A dome?" Erik asked. "I'm beginning to see where they got their name. Do any of the local records mention the Dome Society?"

"There's surprisingly little mention of specific syndicates in what is publicly available. There is a press release from the CID dated several months ago that mentions the Dome Society and your friends at Prism Associates as 'organizations of interest.' The Dome Society is of greater concern to the CID because of their involvement in human trafficking. Prism Associates seems far more interested in gambling and related areas, but compared to what was publicly available about such groups on Earth, it's as if this whole planet wants to pretend there are no gun goblins here. There are even many articles claiming that organized syndicates are more an urban myth than reality and that the government has hyped up the threat to allow more Earth influence over Mars. The articles claim that what some people are calling syndicates are simply unusually colorful mutual aid societies."

Jia shook her head, the disbelief on her face clear. "The level of endemic corruption here makes Neo SoCal seem like heaven. Do people actually believe that tripe?"

"They must on some level if they're talking about human trafficking," Erik replied with a deep scowl. "But it helps a lot of people if they just look the other way." His scowl lessened. "Radira mentioned they all stayed out of each other's way by specializing in their flavor of corruption. They might have thought Chetta was law enforcement or even a journalist."

"Do we really think he's alive at this point?"

"If they think he's a cop or a journalist, that might have bought us some time," Erik suggested, doubt on his face. "Killing a gangster is expected. Killing too many others gets the wrong kind of attention. But I wouldn't mind knocking a few heads around until they give us something, and if I were going to kidnap some random guy and hold him somewhere, a nearly abandoned area on the edge of the city sounds like the perfect place." He descended.

"Make sure he's not tagging your drones, Emma."

"I'm keeping a good distance and utilizing flight patterns typical of local drones," she replied. "I've sent a few to that area, keeping them very low to avoid detection."

Jia stuffed AP magazines into her pockets. "If someone spots the drones on a camera, they might get spooked and tell Draven to run."

"If he makes a run for it, we'll know he has something to hide."

Jia's answer was succinct. "He's a gangster. Of *course*, he has something to hide."

Erik's smile turned hungry. "But my gut tells me they have Sukorn here."

"And if your gut is wrong?" Jia asked.

"It's not. We're going to follow them there, and we're going to ask for him. Even if they don't have him, they know where he is, or where his body is located. We're not leaving Mars without Sukorn one way or another."

"And if they tell us to go away?"

Erik chuckled darkly. "Then we ask not so nicely, and we have Emma hack everything in sight."

Jia's expression turned incredulous. "You seriously want to just go up and ask for Sukorn? We could try to infiltrate, take time to gather evidence."

Erik shook his head. "We're not cops anymore. This isn't about evidence. This is about getting the job done. The Dome Society can continue to exist if they give us Sukorn."

"I was worried more about staying low profile." Jia's

forehead wrinkled in deep thought. "But now that I think of it, this is a situation where punching them in the nose might get our point across quicker."

Erik touched his nose. "That's right. Think like Lanara. Efficient. I don't give a crap about their syndicate wars. Radira proves that not all syndicates are filled with idiots. Now it's the Dome Society's chance to prove they aren't. If they are, that's not our problem, but we can still be a solution."

"The three flitters are descending," Emma reported. She magnified the feed. The vehicles continued down, closing in on a cluster of tightly packed buildings surrounding a taller one in the center. The fence surrounding the entire area enclosed what appeared to be a smaller, solid fence, but after looking at it, Erik realized it was the remnants of a dome base. Low-flying drones circled the area, along with suited men with rifles. There were no sniper towers, but there were a conspicuous number of blocky towers that Erik suspected held hidden anti-aircraft turrets.

"That's pretty blatant," Jia commented. "You'd think they wouldn't walk around like that."

"It's not like it's illegal to have security," Erik replied. "They're on the verge of a syndicate war, and the local syndicates know everyone's territories anyway." He blew out a breath. "It doesn't matter to us. We just needed to know where this guy was going." He dropped lower, now flying between the buildings with the road not far below them, hover vehicles rushing over it, along with sparse flitter traffic above. There'd been a noticeable decrease in traffic in the last few minutes.

"Weird names, weird outfits," Jia commented. "These

Martian syndicates are all about theatricality. I think you're right. If we're the same way, we might be able to end this without trouble, and if not..."

She left it unsaid, but the silence was bugging Erik.

"Blowing stuff up and shooting people *is* theatrical."

Erik slowed the flitter as they approached the fenced-in buildings. He stopped near the front gate. Emma's drone feeds showed a half-dozen armed men with rifles clustered near the gate. The pair's arrival had not gone unnoticed.

"While the building's composition is blocking thermals and my other sensors in some areas, there are dozens of confirmed gun goblins inside," Emma reported. "I'm bringing in more of the drones, but even at high altitudes and angles, I've spotted ten fleshbags actively patrolling the perimeter in addition to the men guarding the gate."

"We could really use an exoskeleton or two about now," Jia murmured. "Thanks, Alina."

"I thought you were all about grenades?" Erik asked.

"It'd be nice if I could use one with a grenade launcher." Jia shrugged. "That's what I've been doing in all those simulations, remember?"

Erik chuckled and opened his door. He stepped outside. "Adapt and overcome."

Jia remained inside the MX 60, her hand on the TR-7 as he advanced toward the front gate. Drones circled above them, but no alarms rang out. No men shouted in worry. The gate slid open with a quiet hiss. A guard advanced toward the MX 60, rifle in hand and a smirk on his face.

"Who the hell are you?" the guard asked.

"Someone interested in finding someone else," Erik explained.

"And who the hell is that?"

"Chetta Sukorn," Erik announced, keeping his hands at his side. There was no reason to escalate the situation yet. "Your man Draven took him. We want him back. Give him back, and we're gone."

The guard glared at him. "Like I said, who the fuck are you?"

"I'm the guy asking for Chetta Sukorn."

The guard chuckled and shook his head. "You've got balls, whoever you are. Wait here, or you'll get shot."

"I've got all day." Erik leaned against his flitter. "Take all the time you need. I'll just check my team's scores while I'm waiting."

The guard disappeared behind the fence.

Emma had him tagged from afar with one of her drones, and he was clearly talking to someone. If the syndicate had realized that Sukorn wasn't spying on them and he was still alive, they might give him up without too much trouble.

It was like Radira had said: earning new enemies in a time where you were already dealing with trouble wasn't a good strategy. The question remained if the average syndicate head on Mars possessed Radira's restraint and foresight.

"It's difficult to achieve total accuracy at this distance," Emma declared, "but I can generally understand what he's saying by reading his lips."

"And?" Erik murmured under his breath.

"He's informing his superior that someone has come looking for 'that snoop Draven brought here,' and that they don't recognize you. They're not sure if you're syndicate or a Confed."

Erik chuckled. "They didn't use his name?"

"I'm almost certain that he said 'that snoop.' There's a slight margin for error, but the actual words can't be significantly different from those. The guard seems irritated they haven't moved said snoop, but he then was obviously chastened by his superior for speaking out of turn."

"Good enough for me. Sounds like they have him here. I'll give the Lady a shot, and we'll wait to see if they'll be reasonable before I give her any more."

A couple of minutes passed before the guard jogged back out to the flitter. "Nobody knows anything about anyone named Chetta Sukorn. Get lost."

"You sure? I can show you a picture if it'll help."

The guard sneered. "I don't know who you are, and you haven't tried anything, so we're going to let you go. Get the hell out of here. We're being nice and assuming you don't understand who you're screwing with."

"The Dome Society?" Erik offered.

"If you know that much, then you should know not to mess with us." The man ran a finger across his throat. "I noticed you brought a chick with you. You shouldn't have brought your girlfriend if you don't want her to see you get your ass kicked."

"Yeah, she wouldn't like that." Erik smiled. "But I'll take

your word that Sukorn isn't here." He slid back into the flitter. "We'll get out of here." He closed the door and lifted off. "Keep as many drones around as you can without getting spotted, Emma. Also, watch our ass to make sure nobody's following us."

Jia sighed as the MX 60 sped away. "So much for them being reasonable. I suppose we have no choice but to make a scene."

Erik chuckled. "That's one way to put it."

"How do we do this without the locals showing up?" Jia asked.

Erik shook his head. "This isn't Neo SoCal. This isn't even Earth. You said it yourself. This is blatant. This is a syndicate base in the middle of nowhere with roving armed guards. If we don't drop a plasma torpedo on them, I bet the cops won't show up until the dust settles. It'd be more trouble than it's worth."

"I wonder if Alina could get us a plasma torpedo?" Jia mused.

Erik stared at her. "*What?*"

"Not for everyday use," Jia insisted. "Just special circumstances. You never know when we might need something like that."

Erik swallowed. "Let's stick to grenades and missiles for now."

CHAPTER FIFTY-TWO

"Arrogance gets people killed," Jia declared as she strapped on her tactical vest.

They had flown away from the syndicate base and parked in an empty underground garage where they could get their magazines, grenades, and heavier weapons ready.

Emma was blocking the local cameras since they needed to pull out the carryaids and strap the laser rifle and rocket launcher to them.

"Are you talking about us?" Erik grabbed a tactical EMP and put it in a duster pocket. "We're about to storm a syndicate base by ourselves. Some people might say that's arrogant."

"I meant *them*," Jia suggested, looking insulted. "They didn't even bother to tail us or figure out who we are. Even if we're just scouts for another syndicate, the current situation is one in which they might get hit."

"It's unstable, but not open warfare." Erik patted his TR-7, an eager look on his face. "They probably figure no one is going to make the first move by going up against a major place. Take out some enforcers here and there and then make a big move."

"I'm still hoping that once they realize we're willing to use force, they'll give us Sukorn." Jia set an assault rifle between her feet. "But I'm full of doubt about that."

"Is this going to be a problem?" Erik asked. "You seemed eager before, but now I'm wondering. This isn't a police raid. We don't have a warrant. Making jokes about grenades isn't the same thing as going in there ready to shoot a bunch of guys to rescue someone we don't even know."

Jia shook her head. "These are trafficking scum. If they fire on us, I have no problem paying them back in kind. There might be shades of gray in our new job, but I don't think this is one of them. Even if we're not here to destroy the syndicates, it doesn't mean we can't bloody them a little."

"As long as we're on the same page." Erik took a deep breath. "Okay, here's the plan. Emma, you're going to fly us in low to avoid any assumed anti-aircraft turrets. We'll hit the front gate and show up armed, offering them one last chance to give us Chetta. If they say no, we fight our way in. Emma, you can hack their systems while we're doing our thing."

"And if the police show up?" Jia asked.

"Then we'll try to get back to the flitter and lose them," Erik suggested. "We don't know how easy it would be for Alina to get us out of trouble, so we might as well not test it. However, if we can't find Sukorn, or at least find where they dumped his body, we're not going to cut it going forward against tougher organizations."

Jia blew out a breath. "It always ends in a big fight for us."

Erik grinned. "It keeps things exciting."

The MX 60 descended toward the gate. The guard was waiting in front this time, his gun at the ready. Emma highlighted the targets behind the gate, and her entire squadron of drones circled the area, ready to close in for additional recon.

"Give me an exterior loudspeaker, Emma," Erik requested. "It's time to see if these guys can be reasonable."

"My analysis suggests a high probability of idiocy," Emma commented. "Gun goblins are often stupider than the average fleshbag."

Jia cradled her rifle in her arms. "I don't need to be a super-AI to figure that out."

"Hey," Erik announced. "It's me, the guy looking for Chetta Sukorn. I've come into some information that he's here. I'm not looking for trouble. I'm just looking for him. You bring him here right now, and I'll take off, and you'll never have to see my ugly face again. Otherwise, there will be trouble, and trust me, you don't want trouble from my friend and me."

The guard glared at the MX 60 from the front of the gate. It opened, and a surge of other men stepped through, all holding their rifles at the ready.

Erik killed the loudspeaker and grabbed his TR-7 with his right hand while preparing to open the door with his left. "They don't even know who we are. If I announced the

Obsidian Detective and Lady Justice were here to knock down their gate, you think they'd surrender?"

"Honestly? I doubt it." Jia shook her head. "Some people have committed their life's work to poor choices."

"Think of it more as bad luck. They just happened to grab the wrong man. I almost feel bad for them."

"I don't. No one forces someone to become a criminal, let alone a trafficker."

The gangsters lined up, all aiming their guns at the MX 60. The guard from before swaggered forward, the cocky sneer on his face not doing anything for his looks.

"Get out *now!*" he bellowed. "If you leave in the next ten seconds, you don't die. If you try to fly away, we'll blow you out of the sky. That's what you get for coming here and spitting in our faces, you arrogant bastard."

Erik threw open his door. "You don't want to do this. You have no idea what you're getting into."

"The odds are against you." Jia opened her door. "Very much so."

The guard gestured to the MX 60. "Get a load of these assholes. They come up to our base, and they start making demands of us." He made an obscene gesture. "By the time we're done with you, there's going to be so little left, they'll need to identify your body with DNA."

"This guy likes to talk." Erik flipped the TR-7's safety off but didn't pull it out of the vehicle. He edged out, staying behind the door. "Last chance before the pain comes."

"Kill that asshole!" the guard shouted and fired.

The gangsters opened fire. The first volley was simultaneous, producing a roar like a great beast. The bullets bounced off the windows, body, and doors of the MX 60 in a rain of crushed metal. Jia and Erik stayed low, protected by the flitter's armor.

"I think negotiations have broken down," Jia shouted over the gunfire and loud alarm.

"Yeah, seems that way." Erik grinned. "You can't say we didn't give them a chance." He pulled a frag grenade out of his pocket and primed it. "Emma, the quicker you can hack their systems and find Sukorn, the better it'll be for us."

"Duly noted," Emma replied. "Or you could just kill them all and take your time searching."

"It's a viable alternative." Erik tossed the grenade. "Let's get started."

The men shouted and scattered, but it was too late. The explosion parted the men like freshly cut grass. Shrapnel shredded them, leaving a pile of mangled bodies on the ground. The scream of an alarm ripped through the air, accompanied by shouts and closing footfalls. The outline of Emma-tagged targets closed on the gates, brave but foolish reinforcements.

Jia primed a plasma grenade and hurled it toward the front gate before throwing open the back door of the MX 60 and grabbing the carryaid with the laser rifle. Erik pulled out the carryaid with the rocket launcher and slipped it over his shoulders.

The white-blue explosion of the plasma grenade consumed the newly arriving thugs before they even had a chance to scream in terror. The pair charged the open gate, bringing up their rifles. They arrived at the gate and took up position on either side. Their initial assault had annihilated the bulk of the forces near the gate, but

Emma had admitted she couldn't see inside all the buildings.

"Highlight all enemy drones in red for us," Jia ordered. The sky lit up with red, so she ejected her magazine and put in AP rounds. Her burst downed one syndicate drone. Erik joined in, switching his TR-7 to four-barrel mode. It vomited bullets to obliterate a second drone. After a few seconds, whoever was controlling the drones figured out what was going on and started pulling them back, but not before the two invaders had destroyed the bulk of the syndicate drone fleet.

The remaining identified enemy forces clustered behind buildings near the back of the area, waiting, Jia presumed, for reinforcements. The gangsters had underestimated what two determined people could do when sufficiently motivated.

"Emma, bring your drones down low and have them broadcast something for me," Erik ordered.

Her squadron descended. Jia waited for a turret to reveal itself and open fire, but nothing happened. They might not have been the only ones concerned about the authorities intervening. Grenades might be pushing it, as would the rocket launcher. The alarm continued to shriek.

"I've got good coverage of most of the grounds," Emma announced. "You can use your PNIU to begin and end transmission. My system intrusion is proceeding well. I currently have control of the outer gates. I'm working on gaining interior camera access in all buildings."

"Watch their movements after my announcement," Erik suggested. He tapped his PNIU. "By now, you get that you're under attack. I want to make this clear. We're not with a syndicate. We don't give two shits about what you people do to each other. We're only here for Chetta Sukorn. Your guy Thomas Draven took him from his apartment. We don't even want Draven. You bring Sukorn, we take him, and we leave. If we're all lucky, you'll never see us again. Otherwise, we're going to go through every building until we find him, and anyone who shoots at us dies, one or every person in this place. You do the math."

Erik and Jia darted toward the building directly behind the gate. Emma's tactical feed didn't indicate any enemies near their position, but there could be an army inside the buildings.

"A number of gun goblins are pulling away from near the front and heading toward a smaller building in the back," Emma announced. "I'm sending drones closer."

She supplied blinking arrows to point them in that direction. Erik and Jia ignored their building and sprinted, their breaths quick and ragged as they ran between the structures to get to their destination. Men emerged from the back of the main building and swept around for an ambush, but Emma's highlights resulted in the opposite. A spray of bullets from Erik's and Jia's weapons cut down the men as they emerged.

"Those guys are stubborn," Jia huffed. "You'd think they'd get that they are outmatched."

"They see two people, and they think they can win." Erik grinned. "Maybe we're the crazy ones for thinking we can."

"No. Once is a fluke. Twice is luck. After three times, it's *skill*." Jia nailed a thug between the eyes as he spun around the corner. She jerked her gun up to destroy a surviving syndicate drone that had wandered too close.

"I've been able to disrupt primary camera feeds for most of the buildings," Emma reported. "But I'm accomplishing that through a trick of power. It'll take me more time to gain camera access, and the systems in the building they are reinforcing are different."

Erik reloaded. "Just concentrate on that building and watch our backs with the drones. If we could find Sukorn on a camera, it'd help."

"It might not be Sukorn in there," Jia suggested. "It could just be they're guarding their boss."

"Works either way. I bet their boss knows where Sukorn is." Erik jogged forward. "If I shove the barrel of the TR-7 next to his head and ask him politely, I believe he'll tell us."

"Warning," Emma announced. "They're deploying an armored hovercar from a back garage." She highlighted the vehicle in green. "It is equipped with a heavy machine gun."

Jia shouldered her rifle and dropped to one knee, then yanked the laser rifle off her carryaid. She activated the tripod and let the legs thud to the ground. Taking a deep breath, she lined up the rifle in the general direction of the approaching hovercar. There wasn't a huge amount of space between the buildings and it wasn't a flitter, meaning it was easy to pick out its approach angle.

"Eager, aren't we?" Erik announced. No syndicate gunmen remained near their position, but he kept this TR-7 ready, sweeping the area in case someone popped out of a building and took a shot.

The roar of a loud machine gun split the air and tracer

rounds lit up the sky, followed by two explosions in the distance. A shower of small dark pieces followed. More gunfire sounded, some of the rounds from rifles.

"I lost two drones to their new toy," Emma reported. "I'm having to make more aggressive defensive maneuvers and fly lower to avoid losing more. I'm also taking my main body off the ground to avoid potential missile, rocket, or directed energy attacks."

"They figured it out, huh?" Erik chuckled. "See if you can keep low and get any decent sensor scans of the building they're reinforcing, but if you can't, just pull back. We'll handle the car."

The green outline of the car grew closer, and its heavy machine gun fell silent. They'd gotten tired of taking down drones.

"We could try EMPing it," Erik commented.

"And take the chance it's hardened?" Jia flexed her trigger finger and licked her lips. "I'd rather just take it out with our toys." She pressed a button on the side of the laser rifle to interface with her smart lenses

Erik reached into his pocket and pulled out an AP magazine, then ejected his current magazine and inserted the new one before flipping his gun to four-barrel mode. "I guess we'll see how far we can go before the locals show up."

"Wait for it," Jia murmured. "*Wait...for...it.*"

The hum of the hovercar preceded its arrival. The rest of the facility was eerily silent, with no further alarms, no yelling, no stray gunshots.

Jia zoomed in on the approaching vehicle. To her surprise, they were coasting along slowly rather than charging, but the heavy machine gun at the top wasn't pointed in the air anymore. She aimed the laser rifle at the machine gun.

"Taking my first shot in three, two, *one*," Jia announced and pulled the trigger. The invisible beam did its work, melting half the barrel of the enemy's gun. Erik held down this trigger, the TR-7 screaming in Jia's left ear. She took another shot that severed what was left of the machine gun from its base and it skittered off the vehicle.

The hovercar accelerated, the driver now understanding the true threat. Jia held her breath and aimed at the darkened windshield on the driver's side, then pulled the trigger again and blasted a hole through the window and the chest of the driver. The car swung to the side and smashed into the side of a building, the front crumpling. Jia lined up another shot and blasted through the engine. No reason to risk an unpleasant surprise. She fired again, draining the cell to blow a hole through the back.

Jia blew out a breath and grunted as she picked up the laser rifle and slotted it back onto her carryaid. "That was fu—"

A harsh buzz echoed around them. Jia's heart rate sped up. She recognized the sound, even if it'd been a while since she'd last heard it.

"Is that a containment field, Emma?" Erik asked with a frown.

"Yes. They've expanded it around the building they reinforced," she reported.

"How is your hacking going?"

"The containment field has disrupted my immediate

access to that building, so I'm going back to the general facility," Emma replied.

Jia gritted her teeth. They were close now, but the longer they took, the more chance the syndicate would send reinforcements. For all they knew, they could be taking Sukorn away through an underground tunnel.

"They have to power that thing." Jia turned her head, catching a hint of blue past one of the buildings. "If you kill the power to the entire facility, they won't be able to put the containment field back up with emergency power immediately."

"There could be a very narrow window, Jia," Emma noted.

"That's fine. We'll head there, and you get ready to bring it down. If they throw it back up when we're inside, we'll just convince them to bring it down, or cranial ventilation will commence."

Erik eyed her. *Cranial ventilation will commence?*

Emma broke into his thoughts. "Much greater numbers of enemies are now emerging from the buildings and setting up on the way. They seem to understand where you're going."

"Any Tin Men that you can detect?" Erik asked.

"No, they all seem to be standard gun goblins with rifles," she reported.

"Yeah, definitely not Talos hiding something." Erik looked at Jia. "I say we just push our way through."

Jia pulled her assault rifle off her shoulder and flipped off the safety. "They should have just given us Sukorn."

CHAPTER FIFTY-THREE

Two thugs screamed as Erik and Jia charged around a corner and gunned them down. Survivors hiding by a corner returned fire.

Erik grunted as bullets struck his vest. They stung. He'd survive his bruises, but the syndicate enforcers couldn't survive his headshots. Jia laid down suppressive fire, her face a mask of calm and focus.

He took the opportunity to toss another grenade. The enemy sprang out, making them easy victims of Jia's bursts. The exploding grenade took out the last man. Emma's tactical feed confirmed the immediate area was clear, but a small army awaited them around the corner past the next building.

Erik glanced at Jia, who grimaced. There were now small dents in her vest. If they hadn't brought protection, they both might be on the ground bleeding out. He hoped his next major raid involved his requested exoskeletons.

Jia pulled out a plasma grenade. "You have any left?"

Erik retrieved a frag grenade. "This is my last one."

"Sweep around from both sides, toss, and shoot," Jia suggested.

"It'd take too long, and they might get the same idea while we're doing it." Erik tossed his grenade into his left hand. "I'll show you how I can cheat at sports if I want. Emma, give me a view of the space between the buildings."

She sent a small feed to the corner of his smart lenses, and he nodded.

"Yeah, I can bank this thing." Erik let out a dark chuckle. "It won't hit a lot of them, but it'll get their attention. Then you toss yours, and we'll waste whoever's left."

"Sounds like a plan." Jia took a deep breath. "How are you doing on their power?"

"I'm almost there," Emma reported.

The pair jogged forward, slowing as they approached the corner of the building. Red highlights filled their smart lenses, representing all the men around the corner lined up in the narrow space between the buildings, ready and willing to kill them.

Erik was impressed. He'd fought insurrectionists with less discipline than these syndicate gangsters.

He understood now how they'd managed to last on Mars.

They arrived at the corner. He tapped a few commands into his PNIU for an assist, and Erik brought back his left arm. He sidestepped and brought his arm forward, experiencing the strange disconnect where he was both moving his arm and it was moving on its own. He released the grenade, and it hurtled toward the exposed walls. The grenade struck and bounced off at a perfect angle, sending it deeper into the narrow space. Gunshots rang out, along with shouts. The men tried to scatter, some tripping over the others as the grenade exploded.

Erik swung around the corner and loosed a burst with the TR-7, nailing a flailing gangster. Jia tossed her grenade and then yanked down her rifle to fire. The bright explosion blasted a smoking hole in the side of one of the buildings, which proved to be enough for the syndicate men. They dropped their weapons and ran away. He couldn't blame them. It wasn't cowardice to run from certain death.

Jia and Erik held fire. They weren't there to wipe out the syndicate. They were there to rescue Sukorn. Any gangster who understood he was outmatched was smart enough to be rewarded with another day alive.

The thick smoke partially obscured the blue dome of energy surrounding a short, extremely narrow building in the distance. The fleeing gangsters turned away from the building once they cleared the narrow kill zone.

Whoever was running the syndicate was less frightening to them than the two deadly invaders. Erik looked back and forth. Every red highlight he could see overlaid on a wall moved steadily away, the men pumping their arms and legs.

"Some of the gun goblins are escaping toward a parking lot toward the back of the garage," Emma reported. "None of the other vehicles appear to be armed. The remaining men are heading toward the front. I've made a few passes near the target building. Despite the interference of the containment field, I can detect density differences that suggest a subterranean level. I'm almost ready to kill power. In addition, I've gained camera access to the rest of the compound, and I can't find Agent Sukorn in any of those other buildings. There are a few other gun goblins, and I believe their superiors, but they appear to be engaged in a furious attempt to delete data or transfer it to rods."

"Do you see anyone who looks like a prisoner?" Jia asked. "Other than Sukorn. If these people are traffickers, I don't want to leave innocent people behind."

"I don't see anyone who appears to be a prisoner," Emma reported.

Erik and Jia advanced on the containment field, the buzz growing louder with each step. If they tried to charge through it without protection, they'd end up stunned and easy pickings for whatever brave men remained to defend the Dome Society base.

"Any cops coming?" Erik asked.

"There are no drones or vehicles heading this way," Emma replied. "You have plenty of time to kill more gun goblins."

"That's handy." Erik squinted, trying to examine the building behind the field more closely. A thick, reinforced door covered the front entrance. "Is that the only way in?"

"At least from the surface," Emma replied. "I'll attempt to open it once I bring down the field. You'll lose contact with me once it goes back up. I might not have time to hack open the door."

"Take that time to figure out how to permanently cut the power to the field." Erik slung his TR-7 over his shoulder, pulled the rocket launcher off his carryaid, and grabbed one of the two rounds he'd slotted onto it. He inserted it into the tube and set the launcher on his shoulder. "I brought my own key."

Jia nodded slowly. "I'm ready."

"Very well," Emma replied. "Good luck. I'd prefer it if you didn't die."

Erik grinned. "So would we."

The containment field wavered, the buzz modulating. The field vanished. Erik and Jia rushed forward. The dome reappeared.

"That was close," Jia commented.

"She did warn us." Erik looked back at the field. "Emma, can you hear us?"

There was no response.

"It's just us fleshbags now," Jia joked.

"All that matters is that we're inside." Erik lined up his shot. "Backblast area clear?"

"Clear!"

The missile hissed away from the launcher, leaving a trail of smoke as it made its short flight. It collided with the door, exploding in a resounding boom that shot chunks of metal and a cloud of smoke backward. He notched the launcher back onto the carryaid before pulling down his TR-7.

"What a loud key," Jia joked.

"A bit, but it got the job done, didn't it?"

Smoke billowed from the gaping hole in the front of the building. There was nothing like a nice, low-key missile battle with gangsters to get the blood pumping.

Jia inclined her head toward the hole. "I think we've officially left low-key behind."

CHAPTER FIFTY-FOUR

Erik and Jia walked through the smoking hole, covering each other and then the opposite directions, ready to fire. They'd expected heavy resistance but found an empty hallway with open doorways lining it. The only sound was their footsteps echoing down the empty space. They slowed to a stop and listened.

Nothing.

"They were guarding this building for a reason," Jia whispered.

Erik nodded slowly. "Not disagreeing. Keep your guard up."

Jia edged up to the first doorway and nodded to Erik. She readied her rifle and rushed in, sweeping the room for targets, but no gangsters or captured agents awaited her. Two long tables and their accompanying chairs were inside. Plates with half-eaten meals lay on one of the tables. A pungent scent wafted from bowls of thick orange soup. She didn't recognize the smell or the soup—some Martian dish perhaps.

Erik poked his head into the room and grinned. "Good thing we messed with them on an empty stomach. No wonder we keep winning."

"This building isn't big enough to hold all the men we fought," Jia observed. She swept the room one last time before jogging across the hallway at an angle toward the next open room. Weapons lockers and racks lined the walls. Most were empty, but some held rifles or stun pistols. Crates of ammo were stacked in one corner. One lay on its side, mostly empty, but a single belt of huge rounds was halfway out.

"I wonder if this was the ammo for the car." Jia nudged the belt with her foot. "Look at the size of those rounds."

"It could be." Erik frowned. "Or there's someone waiting for us somewhere with a very big weapon."

She looked around. "That's not a comforting thought."

The next room was empty except for a small mat. There were several bloodstains on it and the wall. A lingering stench of body odor managed to beat out the acrid smell of smoke that had infiltrated the room.

Erik pointed toward a thin line in the wall and an access panel. "That's a folding toilet."

"A cell, and they kept someone here until recently," Jia observed. "I stopped believing in coincidences last year."

Erik frowned. "A lot of blood. They must have beat or tortured him. I wonder if they found out he was a ghost."

Jia crouched by the mat. "If they knew that, I suspect they would have given him up. It wouldn't make sense for a syndicate to go up against the Directorate." She wrinkled her nose. "And judging from the smell, he was alive enough to stink."

They continued down the hallway, checking the other open rooms. There were several additional empty cells, but unlike the first, they appeared to be long out of use. Another room was an office, and one was a restroom. One storage room was filled with jewelry. Jia didn't need sophisticated scanners to know it was all fake.

She was a Lin, after all. She might not follow in her mother's footsteps, but the woman had taught her daughters everything she could.

Their trip ended at an elevator. Erik hit the access panel, but the doors didn't open.

"Smart enough to lock it down," he muttered. "I wonder why the other doors were open."

"They were in a hurry." Jia motioned toward the elevator. "I'm betting this one is always specially locked."

Erik nodded. "We might have to wait for Emma to kill the containment field."

"She might not be able to from the outside." Jia gestured toward the hole in front of the building. "When the power switched over earlier, that was probably a generator. We have no idea how long they can keep the field up. We're going to have to take the power out from the inside to get her help."

Erik grinned and slowly lowered his gaze to the floor. "We already know there's something underneath here." He reached for the rocket launcher. "It might be the generator."

Jia stared at her partner like he'd gone crazy. There was adapting and overcoming, and then there was being *insanely* reckless.

"Are you planning to do what I think you're planning to do?" she asked.

"We're not going to be able to hack these systems by ourselves, and you just got done telling me that they might be able to keep that field up for as long as they need to." Erik stood the launcher up, yanked the other missile off his carryaid, and shoved it in. "We don't have any decent explosives left other than this, and the laser rifle's empty.

"But still…"

"Think of it this way. I didn't just bring my own key, I brought my own shovel."

Jia backed away from the hole. "I don't believe this is the smartest thing you've ever done."

"Nope." Erik set the launcher on his shoulder and backed up, angling the weapon toward the ground. "But it's far from the stupidest."

Jia made a face. "I don't even want to know what qualifies as the stupidest."

"No, you don't," Erik admitted. "Hey, I just thought of something."

"What? You have a better idea about how to get downstairs?" Jia asked. "One that doesn't involve firing a missile at the floor?"

Erik shook his head. "No. I was thinking about how this whole thing ended without anything crazy. No *yaoguai*. No nanozombies. No full-conversion Tin Men. Just some thugs who don't know when to quit."

"It *is* a nice change of pace," Jia admitted. "Sometimes it feels like we're caught up in the center of everything insane in the UTC."

"Well, we kind of are." Erik adjusted his aim closer to

the elevator. "I can't just fire anywhere. Don't want to cave the roof in on Sukorn if he's down there. Be kind of pointless to go through all this and kill the guy ourselves."

"You think?" Jia rolled her eyes. This was either a brilliant improvisation or a horrible mistake. She regretted not keeping some breach disks.

Apparently, there were dangers in overly relying on Emma to open every lock for them.

"Backblast area clear!" Erik shouted. She replied, and he launched. The smoke from the missile filled the hall, and the projectile didn't travel far before finding the floor. A deafening explosion blasted debris toward Erik and Jia, pelting them despite the distance and leaving a jagged smoldering hole in front of the elevator. Pieces continued to smolder, but no fire broke out.

Jia coughed and waved her hand to clear the air. "Every time I think I might be getting a little too comfortable with blowing things up, you remind me how I got that way. You're a bad influence."

"It's not me being a bad influence. It's called training." Erik dropped his carryaid to the ground and inclined his head toward the hole. "I don't think it's big enough for us to get through with all our gear."

Jia pulled the extra magazines from the carryaid and shoved them into her pocket before dropping the device to the ground. "I hope some gangster doesn't grab our stuff."

"If he's brave enough to come in here through a smoking hole to get it, he deserves it." Erik readied his TR-7 and jogged to the hole, pointing his weapon down. "We're in luck. Another corridor, and it's not that far a drop." He waited for Jia to catch up before jumping down and sweeping both ways.

After Erik moved out of the way, Jia dropped through the hole, knocking some of the smoking rubble of the way. At one end of the hall was the elevator, but it then turned and widened. A rhythmic hum sounded from the bay.

They walked that way, stopping at the corner. She nodded to Erik and counted to three with her hand. He rushed across to take up a position on the opposite side.

Both pointed their weapons inward.

The hall opened to a large underground parking garage. Stacked rectangular cargo containers occupied the space closest to them. The other end of the garage angled up to what appeared to be a rock wall, but the thin edges revealed it was a disguised door. More armored hovercars with machine guns were parked on one side of the garage, while conventional luxury cars and sports flitters lined the other.

There was a smattering of mini-flitters in one corner. A decent-sized hover-APC with twin machine guns on either side was parked near the door. A large generator was installed in the wall across from the APC, cables spreading from it like the arms of an octopus. Chetta Sukorn lay against a wall near the generator, unconscious, his hands and feet bound and his face bloodied and battered. His chest rose and fell, however.

Jia spun toward a movement she saw out of the corner of her eye. Someone crouched behind the APC. She slid behind a cargo container. Erik spun to conceal himself behind another.

"Give it up," Jia shouted. "Almost everyone upstairs is

dead or has run away. You should have just given us Sukorn when we asked."

"Who are you people?" the man demanded. "What syndicate are you from? You don't understand what you've done. We'll get our revenge."

"Just call us freelance troublemakers," Erik offered, a merry smile on his face. "And you can't bitch. It's like she said: we tried to give you your chance. We didn't even care about Thomas Draven. We only wanted our guy back. Since you didn't kill him, you can still walk out of this breathing."

The man let out a harsh laugh. "I'm Thomas Draven, you bastards. You think I'm letting you walk away from this? I'm going to have to explain to my boss what the hell happened here. I'll admit your guy's tough and he wouldn't talk, but we can make one of you do so."

"Don't be an idiot," Jia shouted. "You're outnumbered and outgunned."

She ejected her magazine and put in an AP clip. Erik did the same. There were too many places to hide in the parking garage.

Thomas laughed. "You don't get it. I'm going to tear you to shreds." He threw open the door of the APC and jumped into the driver's seat. Jia popped up and fired a burst. The bullets pelted the transparent metal of the windshield, but even AP rounds had their limits.

One of the machine guns swung her way, and Jia ducked as the gun roared to life. The bullets ripped into the cargo container, some coming out the other side. She crawled toward the other end. Erik pulled out the EMP and threw it toward the APC.

The machine guns blasted the device into bits before it'd gotten close.

"I didn't think it'd work, but I figured it'd at least get there," Erik complained. When the machine guns fell silent, he risked a burst from his TR-7. The machine gun pointed toward him and fired, and the rounds ventilated the container. Erik crawled to the edge before hurrying around to duck behind a flitter. Jia moved toward an armored car. They both risked another burst, earning return fire. Thomas swept the machine gun across the garage. The bullets didn't penetrate the car, but they shredded the unarmored flitter. Erik grunted in pain and fell backward, blood pooling beneath him.

Jia's eyes widened, and her heart galloped. "Erik!"

Her jaw tightened, and she licked her lips. If Thomas Draven had killed Erik, she didn't care if she had to charge directly at the APC to finish him off.

"It's fine," Erik called back. He rolled to the other side of the vehicle and managed to lift his left leg. There was a huge hole in his pants and a gaping wound in his upper leg. "The bastard didn't even get me directly. I think it was shrapnel from the car. We just need to keep hitting the windshield and we'll get him."

Jia let out a sigh of relief. They needed to finish this. Sukorn was alive, and that meant all they needed to do was kill Thomas Draven.

"I'll draw his fire." Jia took a few more breaths to steady herself.

Erik frowned. "What the hell? That vest can't stand up to that kind of gun."

"Use all four barrels and make the shots count," Jia

recommended. "You're always saying size matters." She waggled her eyebrows. "Prove it!"

If they weren't in such a desperate situation, she would have loved to stay and enjoy his slack-jawed look before he realized he needed to close his mouth.

Jia slung her rifle over her shoulder. "I've got the cars to hide behind, and they can take at least a few rounds. The quicker you kill this guy, the less I have to risk."

"What's the matter?" Thomas taunted from the APC's speaker. "You were so sure before. I knew we should have come out with this baby to begin with. If you want to surrender, I'll only kill one of you. The other one can tell me what syndicate you work for."

"Do you ever shut up?" Erik yelled.

Another volley from the machine gun riddled several of the flitters. He swung it back toward Jia. Her barrier car jerked under the onslaught but didn't let any bullets through.

"My plan isn't a recommendation, Erik," Jia declared. "And it's not like you're going to be moving like that. Get ready to take him out."

Erik narrowed his eyes and reloaded. "Damn it, Jia. Why do you always have to surprise me? Just when I think I have you figured out."

"Because you make me better than I was, but we can talk about that later." Jia took a deep breath. "On three, two, one." She rushed toward the back of the next car. Thomas opened up again, a bullet zooming so close her hair fluttered. Her stomach lurched.

Erik opened fire, the four barrels of the TR-7 screaming. On full four-barrel automatic, the gluttonous weapon consumed the entire magazine in seconds, but the stream of AP rounds did its work. The windshield weakened under the first hits. Thomas swung the machine gun back toward Erik, but the TR-7's final bullets ripped through and into the driver. He jerked as the rounds tore through him. Blood sprayed all over the windshield, and the gangster slumped forward.

"Some assholes never learn," Erik muttered.

Jia sprang up and rushed over to Erik. She yanked a medpatch from her pocket and applied it to Erik's wound. She grimaced. "Next time, we strip down and wear the full tac suits if we're going to do something stupid like this."

"I don't know about that, but I like the stripping part." Erik set the TR-7 down. "That was a good plan."

"It was the only plan that made sense."

"Still a good plan."

"I..." Jia shook her head and slapped her cheeks. If she could distract a heavy machine gunner, she could express how she felt.

Heart pounding, Jia leaned forward and pressed her mouth to his. He opened his own and accepted her deep kiss. They stayed that way, Jia leaning over the wounded man, kissing him deeply before she pulled back to take a breath and lick her lips.

Erik grinned. "Not that I'm complaining, but what was that about?"

"Just trying to remind you that you have something more to live for than vengeance," Jia murmured.

"I know," Erik replied, softly dragging a finger down her cheek. "I know." He forced himself to stand, then winced. "Let's go get Sukorn and carry him out that door."

He leaned over and picked up his TR-7. He slapped in a new magazine and pointed it at the generator. "All we need to do is knock out the generator." He pointed the weapon and held down the trigger.

The generator sparked and juddered as bullets penetrated it or ripped into the cables. Right before Erik emptied the clip, the main lights of the hangar shut off, replaced by red emergency lighting.

Jia produced an EMP from her pocket. "We could have just used this."

"Not as fun." Erik shouldered the TR-7. "Emma, can you hear me?"

"Yes, I can," she reported. "Whatever you did in there brought down the containment field."

Erik's gaze slid between the smoking generator and the unconscious Sukorn. "The Lady played some tricks on us today, but it looks like our guy is still alive. I'm out of keys. Please open the door."

"My pleasure, Erik."

CHAPTER FIFTY-FIVE

November 16, 2229, Unity City, Mars, Hotel Caldanza

Erik lay on the bed, his hands under his head.

His leg was sore, but the medpatch had healed more of the wound overnight, and the anesthetic was effective. He wouldn't require more extensive treatment.

They had taken Sukorn to the Rabbit for first aid and then contacted Alina. She'd arranged for them to transfer the agent to Kalei so she could get him advanced treatment from a trustworthy source. He had not regained consciousness before the transfer.

Apparently, despite what Kalei had said, her lane did extend to the missing agent. That had all happened the day before.

Erik and Jia planned to leave the following day, once his leg was in better shape. Neither was interested in sightseeing in Unity City. After everything they'd done, it made sense to leave the planet as soon as possible.

Jia sat in a chair, swiping through news articles, her brow furrowed in concentration and disapproval.

"Problem?" Erik asked.

"They're reporting it as an industrial accident," Jia explained. "I wonder if that means the local police are ignoring it on purpose, or if Alina pulled some strings."

"Hey, it's the first time we've done something in a while that didn't get our names splashed everywhere," Erik noted. "I rather like it."

"That's true. I didn't think of that. I honestly don't know how I feel about it." Jia dismissed the windows with swipes. "It'll take some time to get used to."

"Didn't it take time to get used to always being in the news?"

Jia shrugged. "Yes, but I am now used to that, not the opposite."

There was a knock on the door. Jia's hand went to her stun pistol, and she narrowed her eyes. He couldn't blame her. They'd both had some close calls during the raid.

"Another kid?" Erik asked.

"No, an unidentified dark-skinned woman," Emma reported.

"Kalei?"

"As I said, unidentified. Her facial features, hair, and dress are different." Emma made a noise of disapproval. "But it's not impossible she's disguised."

"She didn't give us a passphrase." Jia kept her hand on the gun. "But go ahead and let her in." She lifted her gun to aim for the head.

The door slid open, and the woman entered without asking. Emma was right. Other than being dark-skinned, there was little resemblance to their ID contact. The new arrival had a much rounder face, shorter hair, and different eye color, in addition to being taller than the info-broker ghost. Her carefully tailored dark suit seemed more like something Alina would wear. She tapped the access panel to close the door, and she seemed oblivious to Jia's weapons.

Jia shook the gun. "Identify yourself."

The woman sighed. "Oh, darling. You're as paranoid as Alina. I'm not fond of disguises, but after seeing how badly poor old Erik was hurt yesterday, I thought it'd be nice if I didn't make you come to me, so I came to you."

Jia holstered her pistol, satisfied it was Kalei. "Is Sukorn okay?"

"He's receiving treatment, and he's awake now. He'll make a full recovery. Those Dome Society bastards worked him over pretty badly." Kalei pursed her lips. "But you gave them enough of a whupping that he's been paid back and then some for what they did to him."

Erik sat up. "Did you ever figure out what they wanted with him?"

"Mistaken identity." Kalei shook her head and clucked her tongue. "Simple as that. Mistaken identity from bad timing. He asked a few too many questions they didn't particularly care for. He was trying to sniff out if Talos was around because of some unusual weapons shipments going through Unity City, including those armored cars and APCs. Alina thought it might have been related to some of that nonsense on the moon, but it turned out it wasn't."

She shrugged with an amused smile. "It was just a syndicate doing what it does: crime. They were trying to get contraband out to the frontier and to paying customers who specialize in the rebellion business. It takes a special kind of criminal to ship weapons to rebels when they're only three days away from Earth, but where there's money, people will take risks, even stupid ones."

"No conspiracy links?" Jia asked.

"While everything is a conspiracy of some sort, not everything is the kind of conspiracy you're talking about."

Jia snorted. "You could have fooled me."

Erik swung his legs over the edge of the bed. "We might have been disguised, but we showed up in an MX 60. It was a different color and used a fake transponder signal, but eventually, the Dome Society's going to figure who took them out, and that wasn't their entire organization. They're going to want revenge. I don't regret what we did, but it'll make some things more complicated."

Kalei shook her finger at him with a disapproving look on her face. "And that is why you should have kept things quieter, not started a war."

"We asked *nicely*." Erik shrugged. "They refused."

"So then you showed up with missiles and laser rifles?"

"It got the job done, didn't it? They tortured and beat your agent."

"That they did." Kalei laughed. "No wonder Alina likes you two so much. She's fond of overkill, too. I prefer a lighter touch." She smiled and let out a quiet sigh. "Now, don't you go worrying about the Dome Society. I spread some rumors around, letting everyone know they took a big hit and suggesting it was some big, fancy out-of-town mercs hired by someone. There are a lot of hungry syndicates on Mars, and they're always looking for an advantage." She gave a toothy grin. "I also leaked information to the CID about their arms smuggling and trafficking, based on the data Emma recovered from their systems. The Dome Society won't be able to take revenge on you because it won't be around much longer. If the other syndicates don't finish them off, the CID will."

"That takes care of that." Erik laid back down and rubbed his leg. "There you go, Jia. We got to do our jobs and cleaned up some criminals. Not bad for our first trip to Mars together."

"You're right." Jia smiled. "I'm not going to lose sleep because we overachieved a little on our first job out."

Kalei tapped her PNIU. "I've also got a message for you from our mutual friend."

A hologram of a smiling Alina appeared. "I'll be contacting you on your way back, but I wanted to thank you for locating our missing agent and proving yourselves." The hologram raised her palm and shook her head. "I know what you're thinking. 'Haven't we proved ourselves already?' Yes, you did a good job on the moon, but that was only a start, and that was a job where you still were thinking like cops. This was a job where you had to think like ghosts. I knew it wasn't a mistake to recruit you, and I'm confident you'll help us follow the stench of Talos and another dark conspiracy that threatens the UTC."

She smiled. "For now, get some rest. You've earned it. I'll work more leads and get you a new assignment. And just so you know, I've got two advanced exoskeleton prototypes coming your way. That's why it took me so long to line them up. If you're going to raid syndicates bases by yourselves, I thought it might help if you had better gear. I've also got a scout bike and some mini-flitters for you, as requested. Consider them rewards and investments in your future. I'm sure this won't be the last of your big successes." She nodded, and the image disappeared.

Kalei walked to the door. "You two certainly keep things exciting." She cocked her head. "Maybe too exciting. I hope you enjoy your trip back to Earth, darlings, but no offense—I hope I don't see you for a while. I don't know if my blood pressure can handle it."

Erik grinned. "We get things done."

She looked at Erik and Jia. "I can't dispute that."

CHAPTER FIFTY-SIX

Julia smiled sweetly at the dark shadow hologram sitting at the table across from her.

She didn't understand how people could tolerate talking to others when they could only hear the voice. It'd always made her skin crawl. Something about it felt fundamentally unnatural.

The man across from her might not be real or anything more than the barest outline of a person, but that small visual presence gave a fundamental gravity to the conversation that was otherwise lacking and pushed away any of the unpleasantness that threatened to discomfit her.

The man cleared his throat. Julia, like others in the Core, referred to him as the Agent.

It was hard to keep track of all his false names, including the last he'd used. He'd been Hadrian Conners during his previous major mission for them.

"On behalf of all of the Core, I want to express my admiration for what you achieved on the prison station," she offered. "I don't know if you were adequately praised for it at the time."

"Is that so?" the Agent replied. "It is my understanding that some were displeased. The station wasn't destroyed, and the target was not killed. I was told some were angry because of the additional pressure from the Intelligence Directorate."

Julia sighed melodramatically. "The Last Soldier and the Warrior Princess are far more dangerous than some of my associates appreciate. It's my belief that measures will need to be taken if we can't convert them into more pliable tools. Unfortunately, when you've lived as long as we have, you grow risk-averse. It's unfortunate, but that's not your fault."

"What measures are you talking about?" the Agent asked, the blank shadow of his face and neutral tone revealing nothing.

"That's something I'm going to need your assistance with. Something that requires a man of your unique talents." Julia leaned forward, her lips parting in excitement. "But this will carry greater risks than you typically face. Sophia and some of the others are being too reactive rather than proactive. We can't achieve our goals without sacrifices. I'm sure you understand that. This isn't the first time I've had you do something that required more secrecy than normal."

"I live to serve."

"Good," Julia replied. "It'll soon be time for service, unless you're worried. I understand why you might be."

"Worried about the Last Soldier and the Warrior

Princess?" The Agent shook his head. "Give me a mission and I'll carry it out. They are of little concern."

"Your loyalty will be rewarded in the new order," Julia declared. "This will go beyond anything you've been asked to do before. Are you prepared for that?"

"I live to serve," he repeated.

November 17, 2229, Aboard the Rabbit-class Transport LLT9208 *Pegasus*, En Route from Mars to Earth

Erik entered the cargo bay whistling. Lanara was hunched over the open hood of the MX 60, goggles on, mumbling a string of numbers to herself. She didn't have any tools in hand, but she tapped her PNIU on occasion, accompanied by an even faster string of numbers.

"Everything okay?" he asked. "You don't have to fix anything right away if there is damage. It's not like I'm going to take it for a spin halfway to Earth."

Erik didn't think there was any damage. If there had been, Emma would have told him.

Lanara jerked upright and spun to face him. She lifted her goggles and narrowed her eyes, then her words spilled out in a rapid-fire stream. "You had a very good mechanic maintaining this vehicle. I've been evaluating performance, fuel intake, grav field alignment, and the systems interfaces. I was just examining the thruster efficiency, and I noticed how the lateral thrusters don't have to deal with the—

"That sounds like everything's okay and you're just checking it out," Erik interrupted.

"Yes. An efficient summary." Lanara pushed her goggles

down and leaned back over the exposed machinery. "There's not a tremendous amount I can do to improve this flitter without a major overhaul. I discussed it earlier with Emma, and she agrees."

"Miguel would be happy to hear that, and I'm glad too." Erik walked over to stand beside Lanara. "Though he couldn't and wouldn't do everything I wanted."

Lanara continued staring at the MX 60's innards. "What do you need, Blackwell?"

"A weapon," Erik explained.

"You have piles of weapons hidden in this thing." Lanara's face contorted into a deep scowl. "It's more efficient for you to buy weapons and have me maintain them rather than me make them. It's not my specialty."

"No. I'm talking about something bigger. I want an antivehicle weapon in the MX 60, but something that can be concealed and protected from scans. I'm tired of having to shoot out the window when I'm chasing people. A gun and an EMP would be handy."

Lanara let out a low, long noise almost like a growl. "That will take more time than we have. I don't have the parts on board."

Erik laughed. "You don't have to do it on the way back. Just something to think about and plan for the near future. The more tools I have, the better I can do my job."

"I'll think about it and let you know." Lanara flicked her wrist to dismiss him. "I can't concentrate on my diagnostics with you talking to me. Please go away. Once I've come up with a reasonable and efficient way to satisfy your requests, I'll talk to you, but I've got a long list of projects ahead of that, most focused on this ship."

"That's okay." Erik nodded and headed toward the crew quarters. "I'm a patient man."

Lanara returned to her number-intensive muttering, having forgotten that she'd been talking to another human being.

———

An hour later, Erik sat on the edge of Jia's berth, relaxed. She sat next to him, her head on his shoulder.

"I'm suddenly completely exhausted," she murmured, her voice barely above a whisper. "All the excitement of that assignment crashed into me at once. It's like my soul's more tired than my body."

"It's all over now," Erik replied, wrapping his arm around her. "We got Alina's guy back, took down a syndicate when we weren't even trying, and convinced her to cough up better gear. Not bad for a couple weeks out of our old job."

"Not bad at all." Jia half-closed her eyes. "I keep thinking about how it was the same, and yet it was different. Some things were easier." She snickered quietly. "And we don't have to write any stupid reports. But a lot of things weren't. It'll take me a few more times to get used to not being a cop."

"It came down to the same thing in the end." Erik grinned. "Someone was stupid and stubborn and violent, and they found out there are people more stubborn than them in this galaxy. People who want to protect others."

"I..." Jia lifted her head and averted her eyes. "Do you ever stop to think about how dangerous it is? I didn't say much at the time other than a quick comment, but this was different. It's been a long time since we've had to do that kind of thing by ourselves. We're used to having armed backup, but this time we took on an entire facility, just the two of us, like it was nothing." She laughed and shook her head. "It seemed reasonable then, but it sounds insane now that I think about it. I didn't even blink at the idea of an armored car charging me. I was mostly just looking forward to taking the guy out."

Erik shrugged. "You're a veteran now, not a rookie. You react. You don't overthink. It's not a big thing."

"I did overthink during that raid." Jia sighed. "Just for a minute. When you got hurt, I..." She sucked in a deep breath and slowly let it out. "It's always going to be danger-ous, and I accept that, but don't risk your life unnecessar-ily. I'm not ready for you to die." She leaned forward and placed her forehead against his. "Give me a few months, at least."

Erik tilted her head back and stared into her eyes. "I'm not going to die until those bastards who killed my soldiers go down. You don't have to worry about me, but it doesn't matter because down on Mars, I wasn't risking my life. You were, with your crazy plan."

"I wasn't risking my life." Jia's breathing slowed. "I was trusting my partner." She closed her eyes and started to kiss him.

"Wow!" shouted a man's voice from beside them.

Erik and Jia swiveled their heads. Cutter stood near the cockpit door, a huge grin on his face.

He waved his hands in front of him. "Look, not trying to get in the way, you know?" He offered an exaggerated wink. "I just got the old munchies." He patted his stomach. "How about I go get my snack and then head back to the cockpit and lock myself in there for an hour?"

Jia groaned and scrubbed a hand down her face, then stood and walked toward the cargo bay. "I think I'm going to train for a while. I need to work off some nervous energy."

"Hey, you need two or three hours? I'm good with that, too." Cutter gave Erik a thumbs-up. "Damn, you've got stamina. Me? I don't think I can last ten minutes."

Erik facepalmed.

"We're going to need a bigger ship."

AUTHOR NOTES - MICHAEL ANDERLE

APRIL 7, 2020

Thank you for reading not only this book, but through the end to these *Author Notes* in the back!

Where do we go from here?

Right now, I am a little past editing chapter 11 for Opus X Book 07. I probably have a week to finish another 100,000 words of editing and then off to the beta readers (for story), professional editors (because you and I both know I shouldn't be allowed to edit for grammar.)

My schoolteachers in high school and college can attest to that fact, trust me.

Then, it goes to the JIT post-edit group to catch any final mistakes, and we put it up for distribution to all of the lovely stores which sell this series.

Meanwhile, the next book is in production.

MORE ANIMATION ON THE WAY

Have you seen the Opus X Series original announcement video? If not, here is a link:

https://www.youtube.com/watch?v=mbyVUigUg4U

(Make sure you stick around after the "very end" for the last little bit.)

Judith and I held a meeting with Gene, Sasha, and Cody (Gene Mollica Studios) last week related to the <redacted> we need to build in 3D same as the car (Taxútnta).

And by *we*, I believe I mean Cody.

Nevertheless, *we* need to build this <redacted> for ANOTHER AWESOME VIDEO for OPUS X!

This video is going to tell a small story about Erik and Jia getting out of trouble...*fast*. Nothing like explosions going on behind you to encourage a person to put their feet up and down double-time and a little pedal-to-the-metal.

Well, if the Taxútnta had anything like pedals. Does it have pedals? I'll have to ask the guys to let me see inside the 3D model. The models are created for the covers first (meaning, we need them to use on the covers) as well as incidental artwork and video production work. They aren't cheap, but they are worth the effort to get the looks I'm going for.

ANOTHER DAY IS JUST ANOTHER DAY INSIDE

So, excluding a run to the grocery store this morning, I've been inside our condo, and it is driving me *nucking futs*. I took my first two days of vacation last Thursday and Friday, and even my stay-cation was inside this condo.

I'm so glad I never got a boat so I could try out tiny-house living. I now realize I am wholly unprepared both mentally and emotionally to handle a tiny house. I need/want/desire a bit more square footage. While I would like to claim it is the vast amount of space creativity needs, I really believe it has less to do with that and more that I'm antsy being stuck inside.

I hope you and your family are well during this time of isolation for the world.

APPARENTLY – DARK PEANUTS SHOULD NOT BE EATEN

So, I'm typing these notes, and I have a can of Planters Lightly Salted Cocktail Peanuts. First, let me tell you I bought two (2) cans of those things and really wish I hadn't. Not because the peanuts are bad (they aren't), but I now realize that some things in abundance...like salt on peanuts... should always be in abundance.

Lightly salted is just wrong. I need more salt on my peanuts.

Second, those peanuts that I have been dodging (dark-covered peanuts) actually should not be eaten. They might just have the inner lining on them, or they might be deadly. I'm not sure. To me, they taste atrocious and only through great willpower (and not wishing to mess up my monitor) did I not spit it back out.

Score (1) point for self-control—*but it was close.*

Ready for a story in your mind? If you haven't listened to these books on audio with Greg Tremblay narrating, I think you will enjoy the experience. *If you like audio, do try them out.*

See you at the end of Opus X Book 07!

Ad Aeternitatem,

Michael Anderle

CONNECT WITH MICHAEL ANDERLE

Michael Anderle Social

Website:
http://www.lmbpn.com

Email List:
http://lmbpn.com/email/

Facebook Here:
https://www.facebook.com/groups/lmbpn.opusx/